KU-495-886

Another Man's Life

Greg Williams

First published in Great Britain in 2007 by Orion Books,
an imprint of The Orion Publishing Group Ltd
Orion House, 5 Upper Saint Martin's Lane
London, WC2H 9EA

3 5 7 9 10 8 6 4

Copyright © Greg Williams 2007

The moral right of Greg Williams to be identified as the
author of this work has been asserted in accordance
with the Copyright, Designs and Patents Act of 1988.

All rights reserved. No part of this publication may be
reproduced, stored in a retrieval system, or transmitted
in any form or by any means, electronic, mechanical,
photocopying, recording, or otherwise, without the prior
permission of both the copyright owner and the above
publisher of this book.

All the characters in this book are fictitious, and
any resemblance to actual persons living or dead
is purely coincidental.

A CIP catalogue record for this book is
available from the British Library.

ISBN (hardback): 978 0 7528 7429 6
ISBN (trade paperback): 978 0 7528 8488 2

Typeset by Deltatype Ltd,
Birkenhead, Merseyside

Printed and bound in Great Britain at
Mackays of Chatham plc, Chatham, Kent

The Orion Publishing Group's policy is to use papers that
are natural, renewable and recyclable products and made
from wood grown in sustainable forests. The logging and
manufacturing processes are expected to conform to the
environmental regulations of the country of origin.

www.orionbooks.co.uk

For Celeste

Acknowledgments

I owe a huge debt to a number of people. Firstly, my agent Jonny Geller, whose energy and skill shaped this project and who proved himself a great friend and *consigliore* throughout. Secondly, my editor, Jon Wood, whose enthusiasm and vision were invaluable. Jon, thanks for giving me a shot, and sorry about the dodgy lasagna.

Others I'd also like to thank for their hard work are Doug Keane, Alice Lutyens, Carol Jackson, Steve Walsh and Tally Garner at Curtis Brown and Gaby Young, Genevieve Pegg and Claire Brett at Orion.

Most of all I'd like to thank my family for their support and for putting up with this particular man's failings, none of which bear any resemblance to what follows.

Prologue
Tom

When I eventually walk out on my wife, when I leave her to her own devices, stepping boldly into a thrilling new life of excessive booze, ample air hostesses, time-laden days, sleep-filled nights and dazzling tell-the-whole-world-about-it freedom, there is no flourish. I open the front door and slip into the cool night like I'm popping down the offie for a Crunchie and a couple of cans of Stella. There are no weeping children, no spouse tossing my shredded clothes out of the bedroom window, no bombshell half my age revving up a red sports car to whisk me away.

I close the door behind me and reflexively pat my pocket, checking for my key, which sits, I remember now, in the hallway in a glass bowl we purchased in Siena on our honeymoon. After a couple of beats I remember that I'm not going to need it. It's as useless as a cock on a rocking horse, to use one of my grandad's more palatable turns of phrase.

Outside, the rotting-leaf smell of October has given way to the sulphuric pong of November. Rogue Guy Fawkes and Diwali fireworks arc through the murky sky. Sirens call out in the distance. Bad things are happening somewhere else, up towards Kilburn High Road where the law idles, waiting for the action to begin at drinking-up time. I walk the few paces to the end of the garden path, step onto the pavement and close the gate carefully behind me, as I always do. The neighbours, Jude and Simeon, are in; the curtains are closed, the blue light of the TV glowing from within. Momentarily I wonder what they're watching.

I think to myself: so this is how it's done. We men, we simply walk away in the night. We open the door and go. It's entirely uncomplicated, absolutely unspectacular, so damn *easy*. Part of me wants more fuss, more bother, a bit of drama to give the curtain twitchers something to get excited about. Lord knows this street could do with some livening up, a little more to tittle-tattle about than parking restrictions and the potential extension of the congestion zone.

This said, they will not see me man-cry.

There's a brief moment when something doesn't feel right, an unfamiliar movement out of my field of vision. I turn around and look at the home I am leaving behind with its pristine sash windows and immaculately pointed brickwork. I stare back at a part of myself, a place where I've spent the last six years of my life doing the stuff a man like me should be doing with a wife and two sons.

There it is again, upstairs. I gaze blankly at the silhouette of another man in the house where my sons are sleeping.

1
Tom

Three Weeks Earlier

You never know. That's the truth of it.

When I was a kid, I was going to be an astronaut, peering down on earth from a lunar perch. As a teen I had intrepid, rock-star dreams. At college I knew that my future was as a corporate titan, barking orders, forcing deals, turning left as I stepped onto the 747 bound for New York or Tokyo. I worked intently in my twenties, racking up the hours, doing whatever needed to be done, sure that I was going places, convinced that the grind would make redress, that there was a tangible end to it all. By thirty I was on course, secure that I was writing my own history, my future ever present in my mind.

One of the many truths that I held to be self-evident was that, by the time I hit forty – how reassuringly distant it seemed! – I would be married with a couple of sprogs, live in an enviable house that I, not a bank, owned, and that I would be able to view my life from a position of immunity from the huggermugger struggles of many of my peers. I would be a success, and people would know it by just looking at me.

Some of this has happened, although not all of it. I'd like to give you a percentage, something empirical that would give you greater purchase, but I've never really been able to figure it out myself. I suppose it's like getting four numbers on the Lottery: you win, but not big enough for you to feel like a champ, which is, surely, what winning is all about.

Now, I've still got some time until I get to forty (though not as much as I'd like) and I'm coming to realise that, contrary to what I thought in my twenties, I will not be an exception to the rule: I will be taxed, I will eventually have more hair on my ears than on my head, I will fight with people I love, I will die. Big deal, you might say, and you'd be right. But still, the gradual erosion of time and hope is a cruel thing. It starts when you notice that everyone in the England team – including the goalkeeper – is your junior *by five fucking years*. Then you start reading about company chairmen who took GCSEs, not O levels. Then, one terrible night, you notice that Prince Edward has got more hair than some of your mates. At the same time, your story gets more predictable. You're less likely to surprise people than you once were, people simply think that they *get* you without need for much explanation.

I'm beginning to get a sense of how other people see my life, what my story is. You know the sort of thing, the way that people who don't know you very well – and who does? – might sum up the parts of your life in two sentences for the enlightenment of an acquaintance at a party. Such as: 'Oh, Winston. He's a bigwig in politics, wartime PM and all that. Led the country through its darkest hours, but he's a little over-fond of the sauce.' Or: 'John's a musician, very successful. *Loaded*. They say that one of the others in the band is the real talent. He lives in New York with this odd Japanese woman.'

My story would be a little more modest. 'That's Tom. He's married. *She* brings in the money, though. He's lost two jobs in as many years. I think that he's at home looking after the kids at the moment. Two boys – *quite a handful*.' There would be nothing about my outstanding collection of Motown singles, my first place in the under-twelves fifty metres butterfly at the North West London inter-schools swimming gala, or my legendary ability to inform people – quickly and concisely – the shortest and most efficient route between any two random stops on the Underground. Wembley Central to London Bridge? No problem – take the Bakerloo southbound all the way to Elephant and Castle where you change onto a northbound Northern Line train for two stops.

No, none of that.

So, I guess on the report card of life I'd be looking at something like a C. Steady and unspectacular. What makes that grade worse, is that,

4

in terms of effort, I'd deserve a B. I always thought that that was the worst kind of person to be – someone who puts the effort in, but doesn't get the rewards. I always aspired to be either shiftless and unrewarded, which has its own kind of I-don't-give-a-damn nonchalance, or industrious and brilliant, a martial arts sensei who has dedicated his life tirelessly and absolutely to a single pursuit.

It's only in the past couple of years that I've come to realise that I'm neither of these. I'm like everyone else. I work as hard as I need to, I come home, I love my kids, I eat food I know I shouldn't, I watch bad TV shows that I don't even like, I play with myself in the shower, I occasionally have sex with my spouse who occasionally indulges me with the odd blowjob. I dream that one day I can make enough money to stop having to do all the crap that I don't want to have to do. But I know that that's not going to happen, so, when I'm employed, I struggle into work, trying to retain some shred of dignity, to remember the things that I hoped I might do some day.

I look forward to holidays even more than I should.

I have a twin named Sean. Our parents never revealed which of us popped out first, professing a desire to avoid either of us developing a superiority or inferiority complex according to the order with which we exited the womb. The main drama of our arrival on this earth concerned the actual date of our births. My mother, a lapsed Catholic, was determined that her children would not fulfil the expectations of her obstetrician who was predicting the less than auspicious birth date of 6.6.66. Despite not attending church regularly since leaving her family home in Withenshaw, Manchester, five years previously, the possibility of one or – holy smoke! – both of her children being the antichrist was something best not left to chance. Consequently, when neither of us arrived on 5 June she vowed that she would not become a mother for another twenty-four hours. My father spent the time shuttling between the kitchen and the living room plying her with the milky tea and digestive biscuits that she still consumes more or less constantly. For her part, Mum listened to the radio and hummed along with pop songs to distract her from the potentially imminent arrival of Satan's seed.

Despite the tea and the hit parade, my mother's waters broke around 7 p.m. Ignoring her protests, my father packed Mum into their grey Ford Anglia and delivered her to Queen Charlotte's hospital where she proceeded to plead with the medical staff not to let her babies be born on that day, much to the chagrin of the mothers clutching their newly delivered bundles of joy. Ever single-minded, she clung on as long as she needed to, delivering us as 12.07 a.m., to both her own relief, and that of those around her who had been swept up in her struggle. Years later she would tell us that her first act on our arrival was to check our heads for the mark of the beast. Neither of us knows whether this is true or not. Dad, who missed the *coup de grâce* on account of having nipped outside for an Embassy Number Six, was never able to verify it. Mum also told us that the fringe benefit of avoiding 6 June was that the Saint of the Day is St Norbert, who had always been one of her least favourite saints, mainly on account of his name.

So, thankfully, neither Sean nor I is named Norbert or is the antichrist, as far as we know, but we are twins and there are countless similarities between us. People often confuse the two of us physically, and there are more parallels between us in attitude and behaviour than perhaps either of us would care to acknowledge, but using the drinks party summary standard there is a chasm that separates us.

Sean, you see, is a huge success. Sean owns his own business, a business that he's built over the last decade by representing and marketing, wheeling and dealing, strategising and executing. Sean wears handmade suits from Kilgour. Sean belongs to the right clubs and has reservations at the right restaurants. Sean always has a girl on his arm. Sean is knowledgeable. Sean always knows the proper thing to say, and when to say it. Sean is the walking embodiment of a glossy men's magazine. If I didn't love Sean, I think I'd have no choice but to hate him.

The peculiar thing is that we were both a little like that once. We both did well at school, played sports to a decent standard, did OK with girls . . . I'm not entirely sure when my slide began. A dodgy answer would be that it started when I met my future wife, Sara, when we were in our mid-twenties. It was at the Fridge in Brixton at Halloween at a club called Westworld, the name of which had been changed to Witchworld for the night. This was the late eighties, before the rise of the super club, before going out and getting fucked up was one of the few things that people in the UK did really well. Mutual friends introduced us. I knew pretty much immediately that I wanted to sleep with her – she was, after all, attractive and female. She was slim, had wavy brown hair that was swept back from her angular, discerning features, and dressed just the right side of trashy, which I took to be a good sign on the sexual accessibility front. She was so concerned that the ecstasy she'd taken would fatally dehydrate her that she drank what seemed like gallons of water in between mad, energetic outbursts on the dance floor. I held her hair for her when she threw it all up, a Thames of Evian streaming down a walkway in the far reaches of the Fridge. She often cites this as the reason she decided to let me sleep with her.

So, she was sexy and smart and funny and we had a lot of fun. And then we got married and that was fun. For a while, at least. And then she became a mum. And that's what she still is and – God willing – always will be. I don't really know what happened to the crazy-dancing, water-puking girl at the Fridge, but she doesn't live in our house any more. There's a successful barrister here now. Still attractive, still funny and smart, but a mum nevertheless, and a mum who's got plenty of other things to be doing than indulge her husband's stock anecdotes and daily battle to keep his body mass/fat ratio lower than that of a pork scratching. (A battle, incidentally, that is as hopeless as any fought in Flanders in 1916.)

A couple of other people have come to live with us. Two boys, Michael and Patrick. Actually, they don't so much live in the house as dominate it. Never before have I heard or seen a space eclipsed by noise and physical exertion in such a way. If I could only harness their energy I could minimise the world's reliance on fossil fuels. My boys excel at many things, but mostly they excel at: fighting, mucking about, laughing, eating and farting. What they don't do so well is: listen to advice or instruction from anyone but Spongebob Square-pants. When they're doing none of these things, they idle in a daze from which neither of their parents can rouse them.

And we're stuck with each other, given that I'm now, what they call, a stay-at-home dad. Still, beats working, as they used to say . . . Actually, it doesn't. When all's said and done, I'm down with all those

Brillo-pad-haired, dykey feminists – it's work of a different kind, one in which the rewards are enormous (at least, this is what I'm told by parents whose stellar careers require that they rarely see their children during daylight hours), but less tangible than a monthly BACS transfer and pension contribution.

Some women get all weak-kneed at the idea of a man being so nurturing that he might want to wave goodbye to his career and devote his time to his kids. (Check the irony: I'm getting attention from women because they think I'm a good husband and father.) But my situation isn't like that. I'm at home because I can't hold on to a job. The damn things just slip through my fingers. I'm at home because forces beyond my control (Sara, The Man) dictate that we can't afford to hire a nanny while I've not got my nose to the corporate grindstone. Now, I love my boys, have always favoured them over a job, but I can't pretend that being a house husband was ever my thing. Ultimately, my griping (or if you want to be posh about it, my *ennui*) is down to the fact that I didn't choose to be in this position. I can imagine a time – a Lottery win, a dodgy insurance payout – when not working and being with the boys might be a choice. A lifestyle, even. But it isn't my choice, it's my circumstance, and some circumstances are more acceptable than others.

It's debilitating in all kinds of small ways, but I get on with it, because if I stopped lying to myself then I'd let everyone down. But, for quite some time, I've had a feeling that something isn't right, a dull ache of inadequacy creeps into my every self-assessment. Whether I'm chopping vegetables into ill-shaped batons or making a pig's ear of parking the car, the monkey on my back chatters away in its bitter, judgemental dialect: *Well, you fucked that up, didn't you?* I watch, hypnotised by the sheer imbecility of my sons hitting each other with plastic clubs and it chatters: *Pathetic, you're absolutely pathetic.* I make some cack-handed attempt at getting Sara in the mood and the creature shakes its furry head dolefully and offers one, simple, dismissive noun: *Loser.*

Sara is overworked and overstretched, her success a double-edged sword. While it means that, as a family, we remain solvent despite a crippling mortgage, it also means that she has to accept pretty much any case that she's assigned at a stage in her career when many of her contemporaries are cherry picking the juiciest and most lucrative work. She bears it with stoicism and a level head, but she feels that it might be harming the boys in ways that we won't notice until we hear from the school, another parent or the cops. (Did we learn *nothing* from Zammo in *Grange Hill?*) She's aware that her sons are rapidly changing, that they will be gone before we know it, and her acute awareness of this is one of the many reasons why I love her and also why we fight an awful lot.

So it is in the Cunningham household. Me and Sara and the boys – and the god-damn monkey on my back – all trying to make sense of each other and ourselves. A picture of familial bliss.

Sort of.

2
Sean

Before we go any further, you should know this about me: I'm persuasive. Always have been. I know how to connect. I get things done. I expedite. I *close*. Not in a crass or crude way, I'm no salesman, you understand. No, what I do is more insidious than that. I won't take your money; I have people to do that. What I will do is change the way that you think, the way that you feel, the way that you perceive. Think that you're happy with your brand of deodorant? You might have a problem that even your best friends can't talk to you about. Feel like returning to the same old Spanish resort on holiday this year? Why not try something different? How about a once-in-a-lifetime trip to family-friendly Gambia? Like soup? Then you'll love the revolutionary new *soupwich*! I can make you yearn for things you never even knew you wanted. I'd have a go at selling you a tumour if I wasn't terrified of the word.

Year zero it was me, a Mac, a telephone and a lot of blather. Since then we've had ten years of rock-steady growth, employ thirty fine-looking people, and have offices just off the Kings Road that are nice enough for the team not to want to go home. I spent ten grand on iPods – fully loaded by DJ Kasper from the Marquee Club in Berlin – at Christmas and you'd have thought I'd given them Aston Martins. People sometimes say to me, 'Sean, you're living the dream, pal.' And they're right, I've got everything that I want: the bachelor fuck pad, the stealth wealth car, and enough money discreetly stashed to give it all up tomorrow and live in a tepee in Wales, if that's ever what I want to do.

Which, of course, I won't.

So there it is. I've created a world in my own self-image and it mostly feels good. I thought that when I reached a certain point it would all be plain sailing from here. But that's not the case. If anything, it gets harder, the nagging at the back of my mind more incessant. Ever been walking down the street and, just for a moment, caught a glimpse of someone reflected in a shop window before realising that it's you? I get that all the time. And every occasion it happens it coincides with a momentary sinking feeling, just like the one I used to get on Sunday nights as a schoolboy when my schoolteacher mum asked to see my homework. It's haunting, like a stone in my stomach, like I've forgotten something *really bad* that's either happened or going to happen. A cursory glance over my mental desktop reveals that no one I care about has had an accident, I am not waiting for the results of a portentous biopsy, no kittens have been drowned, I have not got a *Big Brother* contestant pregnant.

I have a good life. I want for nothing. I haven't worried about paying a bill since the Spice Girls asked me what *I really, really want*. OK, so maybe business isn't as good as it was three or four years ago but, Jesus, *come on*, I can't complain. Oh, I could, of course. There's plenty for me to whine on about, but I don't want to go there, not when I can spend a week at the Four Seasons in Nevis instead. What I do is this – I go into the office early and I leave it late. In between, I make sure that my mind never wavers from the objectives of the workplace. PR, marketing and branding attracts those who thrive on Gallagher brothers levels of drama, so I make it a rule to train my people that cool, calm and clear-headed wins the day over panicky, flappy and confused every time.

I know that in an era of lifestyle choice one is not supposed to admit it, but work has given me far more pleasure than anything else in my life. I love a deal. I love a deal more than I like doing the work that precedes or follows the making of a deal. But I don't get to do another deal unless I do the work, so that's what I end up doing. Doing the actual work, the planning and strategising and launching and maintaining, is all a little like foreplay to me. It gets me where I want to go even if I don't necessarily get a huge amount out of it.

Look at it like this. I heard a new word the other day: 'foxymoron'.

It basically means you meet a super-hot girl, get chatting with the intention of closing the deal and discover that there is something about her that you find repellent. Maybe it's her voice, maybe it's her politics (although I'm not sure that anyone has political beliefs any longer – voting is as much a lifestyle choice as deciding between Italian and Spanish olive oil), it might even be something about the way she sucks ice cubes out of the bottom of her Red Bull-based cocktail. Who knows? People get on my wick in so many different ways that I have to make an exception for just about everyone. But the bottom line with the foxymoron is that, despite the annoying characteristic, you can't help but want to sleep with her, *even though* you're mildly repulsed. It's an asymmetrical equation – the Jessica Simpson of conundrums. I've rarely been able to resist girls like that, which, I think, is a good thing. It brings out the gent in me, the guy willing to bite his tongue and live and let live.

From what I gather, this is exactly the kind of skill that married people need to master – the ability to be able to ignore others' failings (and let's not forget the willingness to sleep with people they find repellent). Admit it, whether what gets to you is your 'life partner' making sandwiches with too much mayo, leaving the car in gear after parking it, stuffing the bin so full that the bag breaks when you're yanking it out, subjecting you to television shows featuring cretinous, halfwit presenters who apparently are favoured by 'the kids' . . . God is in the details. The small stuff becomes the big stuff, becomes the unbearable stuff, and before you know it, your partner – who you have promised to love until your last breath, whose arse you have vowed to wipe in times of appalling physical collapse – will grate on your nerves more intensely than your worst enemy. This is what I'm told by those who have hung in there long enough to have what they call a 'successful marriage'. Now, I could be wrong, but my feeling is that it might be worth the priests and vicars and rabbis and mullahs slipping in an additional question with the other guff about till death do us part, a question along the lines of: are you ready to feel hatred like you've never felt it before? More viscerally even than how you felt about Fred West or Peter Sutcliffe or Ian Huntley or some other death's-too-good-for-'em unspeakable scumbag?

Now, I'm not talking all the time, of course, but marriage-induced moments of apoplectic rage, brought about accidentally or otherwise, will test the extent of human endurance further than any subterranean Turkish torture chamber. Bamboo spikes stuck under fingernails cause less pain than damp towels discarded on the bathroom floor, walking on hot coals is a delight compared to the discovery of an empty cereal box that's been placed back in the cupboard, having your genitals attached to a car battery is a month in Tuscany stacked against spending a half-hour searching for the remote when your better half has decided to stash it down the back of the sofa. This is what I am told.

I simply don't know if I have the resilience for a full-on, grown-up, bathroom-door-open-when-you're-having-a-slash relationship, to keep going even when I know that my day will consist of a series of gut-wrenching domestic irritations. Because resilience is the quality I imagine any marriage needs more than it needs bedroom gymnastics or financial liquidity. Both of these, of course, are abundant in my own life, which is no bad thing, but sometimes I'll see an old couple in the street, the kind who have been together for decades of blitzing and downsizing and chemo and still dote on each other, and I wonder if I might trade some of my gak-driven threesomes and Herman Miller office furniture for the touch of a familiar hand as I'm walking down the high street. Not one of those old people's hands, you understand. That would be . . . *eeeeww*.

You know what, though? I would never let my married friends know this for a moment. For them, I'm a lost cause, a source of amusement as I wilfully dig my bachelor's trench ever deeper, and the distance between our lives grows wider. But, while I celebrate my role as the professional singleton who's sworn to fun and loyal to none, I can't help but wonder if I'm missing out a little. A few years back, when Bhangra was the next big thing and I was having a serious Asian girl phase (until I had an unfortunate encounter with a none too chuffed Sikh dad brandishing a ceremonial dagger), my brother, Tom, and most of my friends started pairing off and tripping down the aisle, and I began to wonder if I should give the committed relationship thing a whirl. But then I twigged that the weddings I was getting invited to were such fertile ground for netting hooched-up hotties

(Asian and otherwise) that I felt it necessary to wait until I'd explored the full gamut of emotional runaway trains before hoisting the white flag.

So here I am, living like a rich fucking teenager, and I know that if my private life is still the same as this in five years then there's every chance that I will spend my autumn years in a high-class old people's home having my food mashed and my bag emptied with nothing to look forward to but a cribbage tournament. Still, it probably beats growing old with someone who's steadily been driving you mad for forty years. I mean, is that a relationship or a condition?

3
Tom

I look at the clock. Goddammit. We're running late again. I can hear Sara's voice, like Jiminy Cricket's, chiding my tardiness: *If the boys don't have dinner by six, they're past it and nothing will get eaten.* I slam some organic fish in breadcrumbs (the liberal apologist parent's fish fingers) into the oven and set about preparing the vegetables that I will have to encourage and then threaten the boys to eat.

From the other room Mike Myers and Eddie Murphy are being drowned out as *Shrek 2* duels with the battling Cunningham brothers for aural supremacy. It's no contest, really.

'Keep it down, fellas!'

They take absolutely no notice.

'Get off me!' This is Michael, the nine-year-old. Having emerged from the barbarian stage that his brother and many of his friends are lost to, Michael looks like he's developing into a thoughtful, sensitive kid. He's even talked about becoming a vegetarian a couple of times. Revealingly, when it's explained to him that this would involve abstinence from bacon sandwiches, his fledgling ethical principles melt away.

His brother, Patrick, is two years younger. Paddy, as we call him, is in a near constant state of readiness for imminent attack. He treats the house and his family with suspicion, favouring pre-emptive strikes as his preferred weapon. Think John Rambo in NW6. Various trips to the A&E attest to the dedication and skill Paddy brings to his survival, although there is now a strict zero-tolerance enforcement of various regulatory measures, including a ban on toy guns, crossbows and bows and arrows. As a consolation he is allowed swords, two of which he carries with him at all times. As a fail-safe he tucks a plastic knife into his left sock – his weapon of last resort in case an assailant disarms him. Dishearteningly, when asked what he wanted for his birthday, he requested an air rifle.

Can you imagine how proud that made me feel?

This was a week after the bow-and-arrow ban that was prompted by an incident in which Sara opened his bedroom door to find herself on the receiving end of an arrow – which, fortunately, had nothing more deadly than a suction cup at its tip – to the middle of her forehead. Once removed, the suction cup left a mark that resembled a smudged bindi. Sara was concerned that clients might perceive it to be an ill-conceived love bite.

I can but dream.

'Keep it down in there!' I yell from the kitchen. *Damn!* I slice my finger instead of a carrot, and rinse it under the tap, the blood pink against the white porcelain sink. Time isn't on my side. I turn the oven up, noting to turn the fish over in a couple of minutes.

'AAAAaaaaaaaagggghhhhh!' The scream rises high above *Shrek*. I leave the vegetables bubbling on the hob.

In the living room, Michael is doubled over on the floor. In the last couple of years he's swapped screaming and writhing on the ground for lying still, sprawled awkwardly, as if he might actually be seriously hurt. The family description for this is 'doing an Argentina'. So there he is, doing an Argentina, with Paddy standing over him holding, appropriately, a football.

'He's putting it on,' says Paddy bluntly.

'Michael, get up.'

Michael doesn't move.

'Come on, Mickster,' I say in as sympathetic a tone as I can muster. 'I've got to get on with dinner. You OK or not?'

No movement. Paddy bounces the ball hard next to Michael's head.

'Stop that, Patrick,' I order. I look around the living room. It's a disaster zone. It looks like a big wooden spoon has stirred everything up into a big jumble – cushions are off the sofa, pieces of plastic that will never be reunited with their source litter the floor. There's a cup of juice spilled next to the armchair, its stain slowly spreading into a pattern that resembles a map of Ireland. The videos and DVDs have all been pulled off the shelves and, apparently, trodden on. It's hard to imagine that the petrochemical industry can keep pace with the sheer volume of plastic consumed by the Cunningham household.

This will not be acceptable to Sara.

I bend down and start tickling Michael just above his hips. He starts wriggling and laughing. Paddy bounces the ball uncomfortably close to his head again.

'Butt hole,' says Michael.

'That's enough of that,' I warn him.

'What about him?' asks Michael, levering himself onto the sofa and redirecting his attention to *Shrek*.

'As for you, young man, you can give me that,' I say, prising the ball away from Padddy, surprised – as ever – by his strength and persistence. 'You know that we don't play with balls in the house.'

They both crack up laughing.

'What's so funny?' I ask. I'm half annoyed, half want to be in on the joke.

'You said "play with balls",' laughs Michael.

This Oscar Wilde moment is interrupted by a loud shrieking noise from the kitchen.

'Shit!' I say. The moment I utter the word I know that it will come back to haunt me. 'The smoke alarm.'

I pick my way through the kid debris back to the kitchen. Pulling open the oven door I'm hit by a zeppelin-sized cloud of smoke. I grab a tea towel and yank the tray of 'delicately seasoned' plaice from the oven. The heat from the tray passes through the flimsy cotton straight to my fingers.

'Shit! Shit! Shit!'

I stagger towards the sink and drop the scalding tray, which falls with a clatter, and run cold water over my throbbing fingertips. I examine the charred fish chunks scattered at the bottom of the sink. Maybe there's a way to . . . There's a loud hiss as steam and scummy green water force the lid off the vegetable pot.

The vegetables. God-dammit.

I drain them and set about repairing the fish.

Five minutes later, as promised, I call the boys to the kitchen table. I stand and watch as they take their places. I wonder if I've got away with it. They examine the posh fish fingers that have had the burnt part of their coating removed, and witness what I'm offering them: grey fish flecked with scabrous orange patches. The vegetables have lost all form, marooned at the bottom of the pan in a sludgy mess.

'Tuck in, fellas!' I suggest enthusiastically.

The boys look at their plates and back to me. If children have the range of emotion to exhibit contempt then this is what I see. I'm bang to rights. I say the only two words that will repair the damage.

'Pizza Hut?'

The bath is running dangerously full when they finally manage to bring me down. I'm in Michael's room, trying to piece together something plastic to do with space and warfare, when Paddy locks himself around my ankles, arms grasped tight. Both of them now realise that they have an unfair advantage: they are physically strong enough to take me on unless I use force inappropriate for a dad wrestling his sons. Obviously, trying too hard is unacceptable, although I do know dads who find it impossible to let their kids beat them at anything. There's one, for instance, who lets his ten-year-old daughter win one table tennis game in three 'so that she doesn't get discouraged'.

Michael leaps from his bed. He has recently mastered a technique, learned from a disgraceful but thrillingly violent video game, whereby he is able to knock me over if he hits me at just the right angle once his brother has locked my legs together.

I topple over. A moment later, both of them are on top of me, and pin me down.

'Surrender!'

'OK, I surrender. Now get off.'

Neither of them moves.

'Come on, guys. The bath is nearly full. It's going to flood the bathroom.'

'Cool,' says Paddy.

'No, not cool,' I say. As much as I try to control myself, I am now annoyed. I lever my shoulders off the floor. The exertion required is more than I would like, seeing as my opponents have a combined age of sixteen.

'Hi, everyone! I'm home!'

Sara stands in the doorway. Her cheeks are flushed from the cold. I can smell her wool coat from where I'm lying a couple of feet away. It's the smell of Tube and damp English winter evenings. I remember how I used to smell like that, back when I had a job.

'Mum!'

The boys leap off me to give her a hug.

The relief at the boys having dismounted is tempered by my realisation that Sara has witnessed the devastation downstairs.

'Hi, boys. How are you? Good day at school?'

'Michael stole half my pizza,' says Paddy. This is a lie, but I admire his eagerness to get in the first strike.

'Did not,' counters Michael.

Sara kneels down to hug them both. I get a flash of thigh. I'm momentarily aroused until my gaze returns to the perplexed expression on her face.

'You gave them *pizza*? Tom, I thought we'd decided that they only got junk food as a treat at the weekend.'

I stand up, buying myself time. Do I tell the truth? ('The kids were fighting, I got distracted and I forgot the food.') Or do I lie? ('Richard Branson called about a job. He was going on and on and on about his planes and that and then asked me to test the new Pizza Hut menu in order to research a possible move into the food services industry.')

'Yeah, I know. I was making them fish and vegetables. It went wrong. I lost track of time . . . '

I look in the mirror. I am wearing an Indian chief's headdress.

'You've got to keep your eye on the clock, Tom,' says Sara sharply. 'They haven't even had a bath yet. And was that ice cream I saw on the dishes down there?'

'Cherry Garcia!' shouts Michael.

'Phish Food!' chimes Paddy.

The little sods sailed me down the river before I even have a chance to think about constructing a denial.

'Come on, boys, in the bathroom,' Sara orders, herding them out of the room. 'Let's brush our teeth, wash our faces and get straight to bed.'

'I got their pyjamas ready,' I say, overeagerly.

The boys head down the hallway, suddenly compliant. What does she do that I don't? Does she whisper pacifying threats while I'm not listening? Is there some magic dust that I need to sprinkle?

'I thought we said no ice cream,' Sara says to me, her arms folded.

I look at myself in the mirror again. I'm unshaven, my clothes are dishevelled and covered in sticky marks. I look like I've been working on a pig farm all day. Chance would be a fine thing.

'Tom, you need to get a grip,' says Sara.

'What's that supposed to mean?'

'Exactly that.'

'Well, I'm glad we cleared that up then.'

The light sparring, an overture to worse things perhaps, is interrupted by shouting from the bathroom.

Before the evidence is even presented to me I head downstairs to fetch a mop. Case closed. No further evidence needed. The prosecution has its smoking gun.

Once I finish mopping the bathroom floor and vainly attempt to convince Sara that the crescent of dampness fanning outwards on the carpet outside the bathroom will not leave a stain, I clear up the kitchen and living room. I have a perfunctory look in the fridge to figure out if I can conjure up something edible by combining tomato paste, pickled onions, wrinkled baby beetroot and Sapporo. Amazingly, I draw a blank.

Sara comes into the kitchen.

'You hungry?' I ask deferentially.

'I had a client lunch. I'm just going to have a tin of soup,' she says, reaching for a bottle of red.

'I think I'll order a curry.'

'Oh.'

The 'oh' isn't a good 'oh'. It's not a 'you know what, I think I'll change my mind and join you' kind of 'oh'. No, it's something different, a 'there you go wasting money again when you could have gone to Tesco and bought fresh food and whipped up something wholesome for both of us' kind of 'oh'.

I ignore it. I'm too tired to do anything other than duck and cover. I pick up the phone and order a chicken jalfrezi and pilau rice. I'm feeling a bit militant, so I push the boat out and add a peshawari nan to the order. Talk about bonkers! I shall feast like a raja.

Sara dumps a can of lentil gloop into a pan and puts it on the hob.

'I hope the doorbell won't wake the kids,' she says wearily.

'I'll keep an eye open for the guy,' I offer. 'I'll get there before he rings the bell. Want to watch a film?'

'I can't,' she replies. 'I want to get these briefs read tonight, otherwise they'll be hanging over me all weekend.'

Friday night and the feeling's . . . well, sort of tolerable, really. I leave her sitting at the kitchen table with her soup and paperwork, grab a Red Stripe and watch TV with the sound low so I'll hear the delivery guy pull up. Judging by the thuds on the ceiling the boys are far from asleep. I relish the luxury of being able to ignore them. As long as the bastards don't come downstairs and bother us then I'm golden. Quarter of an hour later I hear the rasping splutter of a two-stroke engine and race to the front door. Heading down the hallway I can see the form of the guy on the other side of the opaque glass. I whip the door open, just as he reaches for the bell.

'You must be hungry,' he says, pushing his helmet back on his head. 'Fifteen sixty, please.'

He hands me a brown paper bag with handles. The bottom of it is soaked in food grease. I've forgotten a minor part of the transaction – cash.

'Hang on one minute, will you?' I tell him.

In the kitchen Sara looks over her soup bowl at me.

'Love, can I borrow a score?'

I'm trying to sound nonchalant, like it's no big deal, but the words come out sheepish and apologetic. Strange, that. Sara offers me a long-suffering nod, and pushes her purse across the table towards me without looking up from her paperwork.

I locate a twenty, go outside and give it to the guy. He looks at me inquisitively.

'Three back, please,' I say.

He reaches in his jeans pocket.

'I don't think I've got it, mate,' he says. 'I've just started out.'

It must be a coincidence that he has a fist-thick wad of notes poking out of his jacket pocket.

'No, sorry, mate. Can't do it. Take this.'

He holds out a fiver, daring me to take it. It's the first break I've had all day. Finally, things are going my way! I take it from him.

He doesn't have to say anything. He just stands there on the doorstep giving me a look that communicates the word 'tosser'.

'What?' I say.

'Nothing.'

He walks down the garden path, conspicuously leaving the gate open.

I close the door, wishing that he'd started an argument. My victory feels a little hollow, the fiver overused and brittle between my thumb and fingers.

I forego crockery and eat out of the take-away containers, which is one of Sara's pet hates. I wolf the mediocre food and fall asleep, tranquillised by a TV show I have no desire to watch.

When we first started seeing each other Sara told me that she liked to watch me sleep. 'There's no pretence,' she explained. 'I spend all day having people lie to me. When I watch you sleep I feel like I'm getting a little bit of honesty.'

Whether twelve years on she looks at her bedraggled, rough-around-the-edges husband snoring on the sofa with jalfrezi stains on his threadbare 'James Brown's Funky People' T-shirt and feels the same way, you'd have to ask her. Anyone looking less like one of James Brown's Funky People it's hard to imagine, so I have to say that I've got my doubts. Sometimes, though, with the right lighting in the bathroom, if I suck my belly in a little, I convince myself that I remain a fine specimen of a man, albeit an exhausted and poorly groomed one.

Maybe she watches me, maybe she doesn't. Either way, she wakes me after an hour.

'Tom, if you're tired you should go to bed,' she says while clearing up the take-away. This is a concession. I try to make one too. I stand up and put my arms around her waist. She's holding a tray, her back to me. I pull her close.

'You coming up too?' I ask.

'I'm tired,' she says. 'And I'm only halfway through. I really want to get it taken care of.'

I let go. I don't want to get into another debate on the well-worn topic of who's the more tired.

'I understand,' I say.

She pauses before returning to the kitchen.

'Tom, I know that this is hard for you, but until you find another job it just doesn't make sense for us to hire another au pair. We'd be pouring money down the drain.'

I'm trying to get her into bed, and she's reminding me of the money pit.

'Sara, it's my career that's down the drain.'

'You know that's not true,' she replies, all business, like she doesn't actually believe that I might see it this way. 'Anyone can get hit by redundancy. It's happens every day.'

'What, twice in as many years?'

'Tom, it happens. You go to bed and tomorrow I'll take us all for brunch in the park. It'll be fun.'

Oh, yes, brunch – that will solve all our problems. I kiss her on the forehead and receive a chaste peck in return.

'Night, honey.'

'Is your brother still coming over for Sunday lunch?'

'Who, Sean?'

'No, your other brother . . . Of course I meant Sean, you've only got the one.'

'I'll check with him right now.'

'Pin him down to a time, I don't want him messing us around again.'

I start heading up the stairs.

'Sometimes I forget that you two are twins,' she adds. 'It's strange, but I don't think he respects your family.'

I choose to ignore this. There's no point in arguing about it. I know Sean loves us all, and that's all I care about at eleven o'clock on a Friday night with a belly full of curry and a head full of sleep. I'm pretty sure that Sara loves him too, she just cannot fathom why he chooses to live his life the way that he does, and she's not the kind of person who can let it go.

Me, I'm happy for him whatever choices he makes, although sometimes it's jarring how distant our lives are. The other week we were having a drink and he was talking about a girl that he likes, before adding, 'There's no hope for our relationship – there's not an ounce of slut in her.' I nodded, trying to think of something clever or funny to say, but all I could think was that I needed to replace Michael's goggles before swimming club on Monday.

4
Sean

It's Friday night and I'm waiting at the Wolseley restaurant in Piccadilly for my friend Leon. As usual, I'm at a respectable among-the-action table. There's a smattering of British B-listers, the odd politician, BBC pundits, media execs, even a couple of trussed and botoxed Hollywood stars. Not one of the customers in here is worried about their next mortgage payment. I relax. Rubbing up against money always feels good. An actress stops by to say hi. We worked together on a shampoo campaign a couple of years back (I sold her to the client; she remembers, which is rare, I have to say). She asks me how I am, and I tell her: 'I'm awesome.'

My BlackBerry rattles. She takes the cue and leaves, but not before asking me over to her table for a drink, which I politely decline. She's married and she's not funny, so why would I bother? I have a message from Leon. I read it and I begin to breathe a little heavier. Something has come up, it says. He's sorry. The 'something' is not specific, which infuriates me. If you're going to blow me out when I'm sitting in a restaurant waiting for you then I want a fucking explanation. It doesn't need to be plausible or even acceptable. Just apologise right, play the game with a degree of deference.

I am not feeling love from Leon. I try calling him, but I get only voicemail. The toerag is probably looking at his phone right now, waiting for the voicemail icon to appear, so that he can check in and determine the degree of damage that has been done. I decide not to take his calls for a couple of months in return. He's got a production company and had high opes of landing a financial services account

I've been working on. I'll phone the client tomorrow and make sure that he's kicked out of the frame. That'll teach him. Those who live by 3G, die by 3G.

So I have a decision to make. Do I abandon the table? Swallow the solo walk of shame and slink out of the place? Or do I tough it out? Go ahead and order, have a lone dinner, treat one of the hottest restaurants in town like it was no more than a canteen? I mull it over for a moment before beckoning to the waiter.

'I'm going to go ahead and order,' I say. Like any decent waiter he takes this absolutely in his stride. I barely notice what I ask for. No matter, it's all good, comfort food exquisitely done for the public school boys and self-made wide boys who populate the joint.

'Got a *Standard*?' I ask.

Of course he has. He has whatever sir wants when sir drops upwards of 15K a year (tax deductible, of course). I snatch a glance at the other punters who are eating, laughing, flirting. No one has noticed. My *Standard* arrives; I turn to the back for the football news and take a sip of my gin and tonic. I flick through to see if any of my clients are in there and check out the party photos to see if there's anything I missed. My job is intrinsically social, meaning that work often involves people I might describe as friends; this is both more and less fun than it would be otherwise. We're the breed who don't stay home much, roving the city restlessly looking for diversion. We're not easily pleased, and when we are, it's not for long.

I remember the first time we ever went to a 'proper' restaurant as a family (by 'proper' restaurant I mean a place where there wasn't a plastic tomato sauce dispenser set next to a laminated menu on every table). The occasion was the celebration of Tom's and my tenth birthdays. We'd had a party the weekend before when Dad had taken us and a few of our friends skating at the Michael Sobell Centre in Holloway. Even though no one enjoyed the skating a great deal – the uncomfortable boots, unforgiving ice and tough local kids all conspiring to provide little in the way of either entertainment or exercise – Dad salvaged the afternoon by taking us all to a Wimpy where we ate soggy burgers and oily chips served by a Greek waiter who performed impromptu magic tricks for the now rowdy audience who were dazzled to discover fifty-pence pieces behind our ears.

The 'proper' restaurant was Chinese, and named The Golden Palace, one of the three approved names for Chinese restaurants in our neighbourhood, the others being The Cherry Garden and The Royal Mandarin. My parents preferred The Golden Palace by virtue of its reputation of having the cleanest kitchen of the three, although this was all relative.

As the three proprietors of The Golden Palace had all bred prodigiously, there were more waiters, male and female, than customers. Tom and I ordered Cresta, Mum had a Campari and lemonade and Dad sipped on a pint of Strongbow cider while making lame jokes about drinking the contents of the finger bowls (Tom and I may have actually fallen for this had he not revealed their real purpose) and quietly pronouncing his 'r's as 'l's, much to Mum's consternation. The finger bowls were only the first elements in our exposure to this exotic new world: the food was all served at once and placed on something called a dumb waiter (cue a joke from Dad), which we delighted in spinning as aggressively as we could without the dishes ending up in our laps. But we were less prepared for the challenge of chopsticks, which were employed more for drumming than eating as, thankfully, cutlery was an option.

It's fair to say that this modest, suburban experience changed my life: the spare ribs with their sticky, salty, fatty pork; the sweet grease of the sesame prawn toast; the so-hot-you-have-to-suck-air-into-your-mouth pork balls; the waiters attending to our requests; the fact that we could just get up and leave without any tidying or cleaning . . . It was delicious way beyond the thrill of the deep-fried, formerly frozen fodder that had been smothered liberally in glutinous MSG. It spoke to me of something else, of something I couldn't grasp, or even envision, but The Golden Palace had let me know it was out there.

Riding home in the Cortina – Dad contentedly working his way through another B&H (he had switched from Embassy around the time that B&H went with their 'Pure gold from Benson & Hedges, the length you go to for pleasure' campaign) and Mum singing along with Abba's 'Fernando', which was on the tinny radio that was almost drowned out by Dad's clunky gear changing – I felt satisfied and happy in a way that I rarely have since. Like a baby turtle that's hatched miles from the sea, I knew that there was somewhere else I eventually had to get to, but at that moment I'd have been thrilled if we'd just kept driving, the four of us together.

I finish my meal and the *Standard* and head to the opening of a new hotel bar that we're representing. It's not a big money account, but it's prestige. I'm hoping that Leon might show his face so that I can give him a mouthful, but I doubt he's got the balls to tough this one out. A clutch of too-skinny girls with very straight hair and clipboards whisk me through a phalanx of pumped-up steroid abusers wearing greatcoats, headphones and moody expressions. The girls fuss over me, telling me in detail who's shown and who hasn't. We will settle scores with absentees later. On an evening like this I can forgive my girls their workday tardiness, boyfriend disarray and furtive hours on eBay. And they don't half scrub up nice.

I am shown to a table where the client and his boyfriend are sitting with a well-known fashion designer who's basking in the attention her thicko chinless-wonder financier husband is lavishing upon her. We all act excited to see each other – *ohmygod! mmmmmmmmmwaaaah!* – and I'm handed a glass of champagne. I spend a few minutes gauging the client's mood. He's happy, thank God. He's had enough celebs through the door tonight to get the press hits he needs. The place is officially *on fire* and he appears to think that I'm the architect of this. I will not disabuse him of the fact.

A waiter tries to hand me another glass of champagne. I show him that I've already got one on the go.

'Double fist it!' he shouts over the music in an Irish accent. 'You know, Irish handcuffs!' I smile and take it from him.

The music is cranking, and the body heat is building. I take in the scenery, smell the perfume and wander out to a courtyard area that's been designed like a Japanese ornamental garden. And there I am strategising how I'm going to get laid tonight when lo and behold, I bump into an ex-sort-of-girlfriend, Ellie, a scorching half-Chinese, half-Jamaican girl dreamed up, it seems, in a laboratory of magnificence. She's an art director at an ad agency I work with. We went out for a couple of months about four years ago, and we've been occasional fuck buddies ever since, booty calling each other at well-mannered intervals. We've become a mutual source of reliable, no-strings sex because both of us grasp and respect the fundamental rule of the booty call, which is never to increase frequency. Every fuck-buddy relationship has its own rules and etiquette within that; this one has the unspoken understanding that, after every encounter, there is a three-month moratorium before we text each other. We're fuck-buddy users, not abusers.

'What a surprise,' she says.

'Bit early for you, isn't it?' I joke. 'I thought you might still be chained to your desk at this time.'

'Just thought I'd come up for a little air and a couple of martinis,' she says. 'You know, all work and no play makes Ellie a dull girl.'

'And we wouldn't want that.'

'Perish the thought,' she says, taking a sip of her drink. 'So, are you responsible for all this?' she asks, gesturing at the garden, which is lit by hundreds of flickering candles.

'Yup,' I confirm. 'I lit every one of them myself, plus I made the canapés and personally interviewed every one of the koi carp in that tank over there.'

'Is there no end to your talent?'

'You know what?' I say. 'I'm not sure there is. On that note, you know what you were saying about all work and no play?'

'Yeah . . . '

'I've got a suggestion for you . . . '

Well, that was easy.

We head back to my place and close the deal. After we're finished it's too early to go to sleep, so Ellie pads off to get a bottle of white from the fridge and I grab my chess set. Playing chess in bed is our thing. I've never done it with anyone else. She claims the same, though I'm not sure I believe her. She destroys me every time.

I'm happy to admit that the past month has been a bit of a dry spell for me. It's not that there haven't been opportunities, I've been fortunate to have never had a problem meeting women, but I've got to the stage in life where I can't always activate the buttons that need to be pressed in order to fully pursue a girl. Sometimes I just can't be arsed. Sure, I'd love to sleep with them, but it's all the *effort*, both before and after the act, that I can't be bothered with. Going home with Ellie means that all the tricky stuff has already been negotiated.

Tomorrow morning we'll pull on our drawers and carry on with our lives with smiles on our faces. That's the theory, anyhow. With Ellie, I wish that there were more. I just don't know how much.

She brings the wine back, pours a couple of glasses, and I'm lying on my back. She's wearing a sweater of mine that looks so much better on her, and I'm wondering whether I've got it in me for round two, when the phone rings.

I rarely pick up the home phone because I have an aversion to speaking to people unless I'm initiating the conversation. However, it's my brother's number on the display.

'All right?'

'Yeah, fine. You?'

'Pretty good.'

Ellie starts kissing my chest. Normally this is a good thing, but when you're on the phone to your brother it's not right. I roll over. Annoyed, she gets off and disappears into the en suite.

'How are my nephews?'

'Oh, pure evil,' says Tom with feeling.

'Just like we used to be, then.'

'Something like that. How was your day?'

'Oh, the usual. Work, went for a drink, home. You?'

'Oh, the usual. Frenzy, conflict, failure. Being in Big Trouble with Sara.'

'Glad to hear that nothing changes, pal.'

'I can't remember the last time I wasn't in Big Trouble.' Tom sounds tired, but he wants to talk.

'BT is the condition of the married man, mate. Come on, you should be used to it by now,' I joke.

'I don't think that I'll ever get used to it,' he answers. 'I just don't care that I'm in it any more. Anyway, enough of this uplifting conversation, are you coming over for a spot of roast beef at the weekend?'

'Well, I think that—'

'Oh, come on,' says Tom, sounding mildly annoyed. 'I'll put in a special request to the boys that they only give you a modest kicking.'

'And Sara?'

'Just be on time, OK? And don't even think about bringing some skank you picked up the night before.'

I hear the toilet flush. For a moment I imagine taking Ellie chez Tom and Sara.

'But the boys loved Chantel,' I whisper.

'And so did I, believe me,' says Tom enthusiastically. 'But The Management won't allow it. Get it?'

'As a special favour to my absolute favourite brother I'll be there at twelve on the dot.'

'Promise?'

'On my Whimsy Ornament collection.'

'Well, I can't ask for more than that. See ya.'

'See ya.'

I put the phone down and make a note in my CrackBerry to remind me about Sunday, then roll over and start setting up the chess pieces. The bathroom door opens and Ellie comes and stands behind me. I roll over to see that she's fully clothed.

'What are you doing?' I ask, surprised.

'Going home,' she says with a smile.

'Don't be silly,' I say. 'Come on, stay over. Anyway, I've got to kick your arse at chess.'

She raises an eyebrow.

'I'll make you a martini,' I offer.

'Sean, I had two at the party,' she counters. 'Let me leave you with something my dad told me: martinis are like tits – one is too few, three is too many.'

I laugh, thinking that she's changed her mind. She shifts her bag up onto her shoulder and I realise that she hasn't.

'Come on,' I say.

She shakes her head and says, 'Let's just quit while we're ahead, shall we?'

I gently grab her arm and coax her towards me. She twists loose.

'It's for your own protection,' she adds. 'It's the etiquette of the booty call.'

She holds her hand up and wiggles her fingers as a goodbye.

'No need to see me out,' she says brightly.

'You want me to call a cab? We can have a glass of wine while you wait.'

I'm standing naked and pleading in the middle of the bedroom. I catch her eye and realise that she's staring at my shrivelled, post-coital cock.

'I'll be fine, Sean.'

She steps forward, kisses me full on the lips and trips down the stairs. I hear the front door close heavily behind her, her heels on the pavement outside. Moments later comes the ticking of a Hackney cab engine. I peek through the side of the blinds and see her in the taxi laughing on her mobile. I wonder who she's talking to as the tail lights of the cab disappear towards Bayswater.

I pour another glass of wine, flip on the TV and watch *Hip Hop's Greatest Feuds* on VH-1. Twelve o'clock on Sunday, it's in the Berry. Mustn't forget.

5
Tom

Fuck Sean.

That's all I can think, as I check the clock for the fiftieth time in the same number of minutes. Sara is quietly furious. Sean's belated arrival is, of course, my fault. My attitude towards Sean is too passive, you see. I allow him to walk all over me and, by extension, my family. For Sara, matters are compounded by the fact that we are twins. She won't articulate it, but I'm convinced that she believes that I should have unusual influence over my sibling in some creepy *X Files* way. This is a common supposition. Now, I've never known anything else other than being a twin, but I've not noticed anything dramatically different in my relationship with Sean compared to other people. Although, once, I must admit, we were in a pub and I had a premonition that he would buy a drink – and he did. Spooky.

I pace the living room surveying the street. Paddy joins me. For all Sara's difficulty with Sean, she has never made the boys privy to her opinions. Part of me thinks that they wouldn't care anyway. To them, Sean is the coolest person they have ever met, and they're probably not wrong. While their dad has worn his 501s for the past twenty years, Sean purchases denim so rare that his jeans have to be sent to Tokyo for turn-ups.

'Is he here yet?' asks Paddy.

'Any minute,' I say encouragingly. 'I expect that he's just caught in traffic.'

Sara enters the room wearing a starched, white apron. She has her hands on her hips. This is never a good sign. I have seen her do the same thing in court when she goes in for the kill – the message is this: come on then, let's see what you've got.

'The boys are absolutely starving, Tom,' she says.

'I tried his phone. It's off. I'm sure he'll be here in just a minute.'

'Well, I'm glad you're sure.'

'Look, I tell you what,' I say, 'if the boys are starving, let's feed them now and the adults can eat when Sean arrives.'

'What do you think this is,' says Sara, 'a Harvester? The point is that we're all supposed to sit down together, to eat as a family.'

She looks past me before saying, 'At flipping last.' Sara will not use language stronger than 'flipping' in front of the kids. She returns to the kitchen. The boys and I step outside onto the pavement while Sean squeezes his Range Rover into a tiny space right outside our gate. Wet leaves lie in congealed banks at the kerb.

'My peeps!' he says to the boys, getting out of the car, his breath steaming in the damp air. 'What's happening, little people?'

'Hello, mate,' I say, tight-lipped. The boys are admiring the car. Damn him – he's probably even had sex in it. 'You could have called.'

'I'm so sorry, Tom,' he says, putting his arm around me. 'I really am. The traffic was murder and my phone is dead.'

'It's OK,' I say. Actually, it isn't. But I, along with pretty much everyone he comes into contact with, excepting Sara, melt when given the full wattage of Sean's charm. I can prepare myself for a row with him, have the dialogue all worked out, but when I'm subject to his charisma I simply dry up. It's just nice to have him around.

'You're looking well, bro,' he says.

'Living large and in charge . . . ' I say. 'Or something like that.'

'Help me out, will you? I've got a couple of pressies for the household.'

He chucks me the car keys before chasing the boys back into the house.

'I'd better go and pay my respects to the chef,' he says, once we're inside.

Michael rides on Sean's back into the kitchen where Sara is in the midst of steaming food and dirty pots. I watch as she walks straight past him, carrying a stack of plates to the table. Ouch.

'Sara, I am so sorry,' he starts. He's going to need to do better than that. 'I really am. I lost track of time. I feel awful. Here, I brought you these.'

He hands her an enormous bunch of exotic flowers, a bottle of champagne and a box of chocolate truffles which he's had me fetch from the car.

'They're the real thing,' he adds. 'I thought of you when I was at this fantastic chocolatier in Paris last week. I know you'll love them.'

The boys, sensing the tension, disappear.

'Thank you, Sean,' says Sara. Her tone is artfully distracted, as if she might actually be really thankful if she wasn't so busy. 'Very considerate.'

Then she switches her gaze to me.

'Tom, can you drain the vegetables, please? And then sit the boys down. We need to eat before it's spoiled.'

She turns to the oven. Sean and I exchange looks. I nod at him and draw my index finger across my throat. He doesn't need any further persuasion – we're both in BT. It's good to share the burden.

'Is there anything I can do?' asks Sean.

'Go and sit down, and keep an eye on the boys. Make sure that they don't kill each other. Or you.'

Sean looks relieved to be exiting the room.

'Look, I'm sorry, but you know what he's like,' I say to Sara, hoping that some family solidarity can save the day.

'Just don't blame me if the broccoli's limp, that's all I have to say,' she replies curtly.

'Jesus, it's not my fault he's late,' I say. 'He's my brother. We're not the same person, you know.'

'Really,' says Sara sarcastically while pulling a sizzling joint of beef from the oven.

'Meaning?' I abandon hope of lunch being a civil occasion. Bring it on, barrister.

'You know, sometimes the similarities between you two aren't just physical. You're both lost in your own little worlds. You miss the bigger picture.'

She cuts the beef fiendishly, and places the slices on pristine warmed plates.

'I'm missing something here,' I reply.

'My point exactly,' she says, casting off her apron and carrying three plates into the dining room. 'Take the boys' food in, will you?'

After lunch Sean and I clear up, before he disappears into the garden and plays football against the boys for an hour while Sara and I watch proceedings through the French windows, snooze and dip in and out of the papers. Surfacing for a moment I notice a photo of Sean and I on the mantelpiece. It was taken almost exactly twenty years ago, at our grandmother's seventieth birthday party. Mum and Dad had announced the year before that they were separating. The news was presented to Sean and I at an awkward Sunday lunch, and came as no surprise to either of us. Our parents had lived separate lives for some time. Mum rediscovered church and the social opportunities that it provided, while Dad was wrapped up in his crosswords, TV and B&H. There appeared to be absolutely no animosity between them, it was just that their orbits had become disconnected.

Nothing much changed for a while. Mum moved into the box room, Dad went off every day to do the accounts at the small bookmaking company where he'd worked for the past decade. Then, a month before Grandma's birthday, Mum told Sean and I that she had met someone else and that she was moving with him to Cyprus. Our surprise was heightened by the fact that the man she had met was our primary school caretaker, Dean Meke. Meke was nicknamed 'The Freak' by pupils at the school, despite his being a mild-mannered man who always wore navy overalls and was rarely seen not carrying a plunger, although this may have been a little freaky. Dean's wife had passed away a few years before in a boating accident in Wales. He and his former wife had purchased a small piece of land near Polis in Cyprus where they had spent every summer slowly constructing the retirement home where Dean lives, to this day, with Mum.

Nan hadn't taken the news of her daughter's migration to sunnier climes very well. The giveaway was her almost constant repetition of a new mantra: 'Don't you worry about me, dear, I'll be fine.' The grand seventieth bash was meant to be a way of Mum alleviating at least some of the guilt she felt for chasing the sun with her 'fancy man', as my nan described Dean. A less accurate description was simply not possible.

The party was organised for a Saturday when, predictably, Sean was 'busy'. Fleeing school after O levels to go to Chelsea College of Art, Sean had, to all intents and purposes, left home to live in a squat in Brixton. Having visited his hovel, my own take was that Sean's oversupply of drugs and girls was balanced by the absence of hot water and heating. Still, my visits helped to punctuate the tedium of my A-level studies and my ambition to be accepted at any university that would consider me.

'So why can't you make the party?' I asked him, exhaling cigarette smoke in the direction of the Aswad poster in his bedroom.

'I didn't say that I can't make it,' he replied, shifting on a filthy beanbag that had partially consumed him. 'I'll just be late.'

'How late?'

'What time does it start?'

'It's old people, so it's early, isn't it? Four o'clock or something.'

'I'll be there by six. Seven tops.'

'What are you doing then?'

'I promised someone that I'd go down to Bristol for the day.'

'Bristol?'

'Yeah, it's this girl I've been going out with. She's thinking of doing some theatre course down there, and I said that I'd drive her.'

'One problem, Sean – you can't drive.'

'Yes I can.'

'You haven't passed your test.'

'Well, maybe not legally.'

'And you don't have a car.'

'No,' he says, nodding sagely, 'but her dad does – a bloody great Jag as well. Her mum and dad are in Barbados.'

I shake my head.

'You're mental.'

I happen to mention to Mum that Sean will be late for the party, which sends her into a tailspin of anxiety that Nan will blame her for Sean's casual approach to the occasion, prompting Mum to call Sean and instruct him, in no uncertain terms, to be at the party on the dot. Despite Sean having cast himself in a sort of dilettante Mick Jagger role he was still sensitive enough to know which lines were simply not worth crossing; although this didn't stop him hatching a plan, which he would probably now describe as 'expectation management'. And I, as his loving brother, was expected to execute it.

It was a variation on something we'd done before as identicals, namely switching our identities. As guests arrived at the party, which was at our house, I put myself around a bit, collecting coats, fetching drinks, keeping the grannies happy with my glowing youth.

'Where's Sean?' Mum asked me a couple of times from the side of her mouth while dolloping out trifle to the old folk.

'I dunno,' I shrug.

'The little bastard,' she muttered.

This seemed to be as good a time as any to put the plan into action. Checking to make sure no one was watching, I sneaked out the back of the house to the garden shed where I'd secreted Sean's clothes – at the time his distinctive look was a suit jacket with a solar system of badges on the lapels. I pulled them on, bunked over the back fence and walked around the block to our front door, where I was greeted by Mum who, through her smiles of relief, opted to give me a minor bollocking before parading me conspicuously in front of an indifferent Nan, who had already been at the sherry long enough that I could have been Lord Lucan for all she cared. An hour later Sean appeared wearing my clothes and carrying a tray of drinks. Working his way through the throng, he offered me one.

'Hello, Tom,' I said theatrically, although more for his amusement than anything else.

'Cheers, pal,' he replied. 'I owe you one.'

'A piece of piss,' I replied. 'How was the Jag?'

'The mustard,' he says, with a satisfied smile.

'Fast?'

'Not as fast as the girl . . . '

I look up when Sean shouts: 'Thirty-seven – fifty-two! All right, I'll beat you fifty-three – fifty-two!'

Sara has been watching. Without looking at me, she says, 'You've got to do something, Tom.'

I start getting up. 'I'll tell them to keep away from the flowerbeds,' I say.

'I mean your brother. Your *twin*, Sean.' She puts down the

Observer and curls her feet underneath herself. 'He's lost. Can't you see that?'

'He seems fine to me,' I say. My brother's well-being is not something that I give a lot of thought to. He's the last person I worry about. Worrying about Sean is like worrying about the character of an A-list star in a Hollywood action movie – you know that nothing really bad is going to happen to them. A few cuts and scrapes perhaps, but no real damage.

'Maybe he's whooping it up a little too much,' I concede. 'He loves a party.'

The boys have scored another goal and have commenced a victory lap around the lawn while Sean lies on the grass, spread-eagled.

'Whatever you say, Tom,' says Sara. 'I think that it's clear he needs help. He's closing in on forty and can't hold down a relationship.'

'Maybe he doesn't want one,' I say. 'Maybe not everyone is cut out for it.'

'Maybe,' she says. 'Look, I'm not trying to suggest that everyone who's not in a relationship is a sad case who's going to die lonely in a house full of cats, or that he's a total heartless bastard who's incapable of ever putting anyone before himself. I dunno, I watch him with the boys, and I see him with the occasional girlfriend and I think that he wants to throw himself into something more than the stuff that he's wrapped up in. I know that we can rub each other up the wrong way, but I also know that he's a good guy. He's got a big heart. He's your brother, for Christ's sake.'

'Sara, I hear you, but at the moment I've got my own situation to deal with,' I argue. 'I'm unemployed and stressed out. I've got enough on my plate. Sean will find his own way.' I snap the newspaper open and take cover behind it.

'Tom, it's really up to you.' She sighs. 'But, if you ask me, I think that, in his own way, Sean's asking for help. Look at him playing with the boys. He wants to be more like you than you realise. He just needs a nudge over the edge. Let's face it, everyone does at some point.'

I don't answer her. Behind the paper I'm trying to get purchase on what's in front of my eyes – the words and pictures are an unfathomable blur. Maybe Sara is right, maybe both Sean and I need a nudge into the unknown.

The following week I have three job interviews on consecutive days. Getting suited and booted and riding the Tube is enough to make me feel like I've rejoined the ranks of the working stiffs. Walking into the newsagent and buying a newspaper rather than a Mars Bar and a Lottery ticket, I'm aware of how even small changes to my routine can have deep significance: just tucking a paper under my arm is enough to lift my spirits.

The first is at a blue-chip company. I walk into a conference room and am confronted by three interchangeable middle managers, each of whom is competing to see who can be the dourest. Each has clearly attended enough training courses to have mastered the empty vocabulary of business speak. It's a play-it-by-the-book situation; they stick to set questions that are being asked of all the candidates, with few follow-ups. After a jittery start I settle down and feel like I give a reasonable account of myself, although with fuckers like that, you can never really tell. As we're winding down one of them, David, enquires about my family.

'How many kids have you got?' he asks.

'Two boys. And a wife.'

No! Why did I say that?

'Can't forget the wife, although she's not a kid. Most of the time.' I hate myself for the jokey answer and I try to laugh it off. I want to tell them that Sara is far from being a kid; she's close to being a QC, for Chrissakes. No one else even smiles.

'The culture here is pretty intense,' says Ameena who, so far, has revealed little more than an aptitude for taking notes. 'We work hard, we play hard. Are you sure that you're going to be able to put in the hours?'

'I'm a team player,' I say, embracing the vocabulary of cliché. 'I get work done on schedule by planning ahead and staying focused.'

'But which team do you play for, Tom?' asks David, as if the tag-team interview style had suddenly revealed chinks in my armour. 'Work team or family team?'

'Are they mutually exclusive?' I ask, faintly amused by the fatuity of the questioning. This provokes Ameena, who comes back for more.

'Tom, my partner and I adopted a child from China last year.' She says this as if she's the kind of person who takes enormous ventures in her stride. 'Just because we now have the responsibility of another human being – albeit one we rescued from a life of poverty – doesn't mean that I don't have to achieve my own career goals.'

'I hear that, Ameena.' I smile, trying to play nice. 'But I don't believe in being a work martyr.'

They look at each other.

'Have you got any questions for us?' asks Ameena, snapping shut a file with my name on it.

'Yes,' I reply. 'I'd love to hear about the company pension plan.'

There is a short pause before David outlines the employee benefits in the tone of someone who is going through the motions in case he gets hauled up in front of some busybody employment tribunal who accuse him of failing to provide applicants with full disclosure about the company.

'That's great,' I say lamely once he's finished. There's an uneasy silence as each of them scribbles some notes into my file. I wonder what they're writing. 'Imbecile', 'loser' and 'tosser' top my list of possibilities.

'Oh, before I forget,' I say, 'I want to leave you with my references.' It's a total waste of time, but I might as well play my part in the farce. I reach into my briefcase and rummage round. Clearly there are no references to be found. My fingers settle on something else.

'The paperwork seems to have been removed,' I explain. 'But I can offer you the action figure for Overlord, esteemed leader of the galactic resistance to evil Zwork.'

I pull one of Paddy's grotesquely malformed action figures from the case in a dramatic fashion. This is greeted unenthusiastically.

However, this fiasco is nothing compared to what follows. The door opens and an older, smartly dressed man walks in adjusting his shirt cuffs.

'Tom, this is our team leader, Keith Bradshaw,' says Ameena with false enthusiasm.

'I'm sorry I couldn't be here earlier,' starts Keith, reaching to shake my hand, 'but I . . . '

His enthusiasm melts almost immediately when he gets a good look at me. Both of us stand clumsily in the middle of the grim meeting room sizing each other up.

'I know you,' he says eventually.

'Really?' I reply, surprised.

'We met before, at the tennis club last summer.' He's almost spitting his words now. He face flushes scarlet. Oh dear.

'I really—'

'Come on, don't bullshit a bullshitter. We played doubles at the club. My daughter brought you.'

'Oh, no,' I say, realising the mistake he's making. 'I think that I understand, you see I have a twin—'

'She was besotted by you.'

'You've got someone else in mind, really—'

'You bastard, you broke her heart.'

At this point, he makes a move towards me, forcing me to hold my briefcase up in front of me for protection while I back out of the room. I get a momentary glimpse of my startled interviewers as I keep my distance from Keith.

'Piss off!' he bellows. 'And never come back. You hear me? Never come back!'

Standing near the exit I can't resist a parting shot.

'You've got my CV if you need to get in touch, yeah?'

With that, I turn and run back down the stairs. Outside there is a faint drizzle in the air, but not enough for an umbrella. A scrunched-up ball of paper lands on the pavement next to me. My CV. I look upwards and see Keith slamming a window closed. It's dark but, up the road, warm and inviting light shines through a pub window. I dial Sean's number.

6
Sean

Thursday. One of my favourites. People get shit done on Thursdays in the hope of keeping their heads down on the final day of the week; Friday is all about cruising a little while the clock runs down. In this spirit, there's been trouble brewing all day with a shop opening we're producing for a Milanese shoe company: we've guaranteed the tabs that some *EastEnders* trollop is going to show up, but – in tiresomely predictable fashion – her manager is holding out for more cash and ten free pairs of stilettos. I've been mildly irritable all day, the consequence of an unreturned, boundary-shattering, unbooty-related call to Ellie ('Can we just go out for a drink?'). The Berry chirps and I check the caller ID hoping that it's her. To my surprise, I see my brother's name.

'What are you doing right now?' he asks.

'I'm at work, knob skin. Where do you think I'd be?'

'Wouldn't you rather be getting fucked up with me?'

'He's off the leash!' I laugh. 'Well, if you've got a pass we'd better abuse it.'

I find him propping up the bar in a gastropub in Maida Vale, near the canal. From the shape of his body, which appears to be fused to the bar, he's had a couple of stiff ones already.

'What are you doing?' I ask, acknowledging the cigarette he's holding.

'It's not lit,' he says. 'I'm just thinking about it.'

'Why? Because it will make you look hard and cool?' I say.

'It's a way of impressing the ladies,' he replies.

'Put it down,' I say. 'When was the last time you smoked?'

He considers this for a moment. 'About four years ago now.'

'Then don't be an idiot.'

'You're right,' he says. 'Watch for the signs: when I start to smoke again you'll know that I've really lost it.'

He places the cigarette on the bar between us. The barman, a young Aussie, wanders over. He looks at me, then at Tom, and then back to me again.

'Cousins by any chance?' he asks, pleased with the wisecrack.

'There's a reason you're working in a pub and not appearing on TV,' I say. 'You might want to consider why that is. Now, can I please have one of those hard lemonades?'

'A *hard lemonade*?' questions Tom, theatrically outraged. 'What's going on?'

'I enjoy the occasional fruit-based alcoholic beverage,' I answer. 'And I can't order one in front of anyone I want to sleep with.'

'I'll take that as a compliment,' says Tom, tipping his empty glass towards me. 'Mine's a Stella.'

'Tom, here's the thing: you can be confident that I'm not going to slip any Rohypnol into your drink tonight,' I promise.

'Listen, man, right now I'd be happy to get some action.'

The drinks arrive and the Aussie makes another joke we've both heard once or twice before. We bang our glasses together.

'So, what are you doing hanging out with the cool kids after school?' I ask.

He waits a few moments before answering. 'Do you know how many job interviews I've had since I got fired?'

I shrug.

'Seven,' he says finally. 'Seven fucking job interviews. And of those, how many left me with an iota of self-esteem?'

'I dunno, the one where you discovered that you were over-qualified for French fry chef?'

'You're too good to me,' says Tom with a smirk. He polishes off his pint, which has barely had time to settle.

'Easy, tiger,' I say. There's something a little wild about him this evening, an uncharacteristic dangerousness that doesn't sit well. 'How about I finish off this Liberace of drinks and we grab a curry?'

'Goddamit,' says Tom. 'You're not taking on the role of responsible twin, are you?'

I shake my head. 'God forbid.'

We head to an Indian near the Tube station. On account of it barely being seven o'clock the place is empty when we arrive. They look pleased to see us. We order loosely and plentifully and while Tom carries on and on about how crap his life is, we drink fizzy pints and mop up the rich, creamy sauces with fist-sized pieces of nan bread.

'You know, this whole fiasco has made me wonder whether *anyone* actually has a shred of fucking decency left,' he rails.

'More rice, Alf?' I ask.

A middle-aged woman walks past our table. She double-takes before stopping.

'Ohmygod!' she exclaims nasally. '*Brilliant!* You two are *soooooo* twins!'

Tom and I exchange a weary look. The woman continues: 'It's like one of you is looking into a mirror.'

'Please,' says Tom, 'I'm not being funny, but we're eating.'

'There's no need to be rude,' says the woman shirtily.

'I'm not trying to be rude,' says Tom, coolly. 'When I'm trying to be rude you'll know about it, fatso.'

The woman storms off to her table and shares the experience with two companions, who shoot us evils.

'Wow,' I say. 'That was a bit strong, mate.' It's not Tom's style to be like that.

'She was in the wrong place at the wrong time,' he explains. 'Collateral damage. Anyway, if she comes back,' he chuckles, 'I'll say it was you.'

I put on my husky movie-trailer voice: 'His name is Tom Cunningham, and tonight he's kicking evil's arse.'

Tom takes a deep breath. He knows he was out of order. The encounter has momentarily sobered him.

'So, what the hell am I going to do?' he asks.

'I don't know, mate,' I say. 'Move to Texas and audition to become a rodeo clown?'

'Well, thanks a fucking lot. At the moment I reckon I'd even fuck that up, despite my obvious natural talent for the job.' Now he's getting a little maudlin. Time I offered some real advice. But what? What the hell do I know? I've worked for myself for the last decade. I've no idea what it's like out there.

'You know what?' I say, sounding confident. 'You've got to get back in the saddle. It's like anything, like being a striker, or picking up girls, it's a confidence thing. People can smell it on you.'

'All they smell on me right now is the stink of desperation,' he says, gesturing the waiter for another round. 'I'm sick of worrying about money, Sean. We can barely keep our heads above water as it is. And, I dunno ... The boys, I love 'em to bits, but they're, you know, a handful. And Sara, I mean, I love her too, but we've got into that married couple thing where we're too busy to actually do anything but fight.'

I'm not having this.

'Tom, let's get some stuff straight here, OK,' I say. I clear a space in front of me so that I can lean in to him, to show that I mean business. 'You're a perfectly healthy male in the country with the fourth largest gross domestic product on the planet. You have a home that's rising in value to the tune of ten million quid a week, two great kids, a successful marriage, dodgy taste in shirts maybe ... And *you're* disappointed by your lot. Do me a favour.'

'Well, if you put it like that ... '

'That's how you've got to think of it, pal. Always. Big picture, big picture, big picture.'

'I know, I know ... ' he says, nodding forlornly. 'But, it's just that ... '

'Tom, most blokes want to be like you,' I say, pressing my advantage. 'To have the wife, the kids, the house. Only wankers don't aspire to that. So what if you're not working? Working's overrated.'

'Let's put the shoe on the other foot,' says Tom combatively. 'Most blokes I know would give their right nut to be like you – you've got the shag pad, the flash car, the fuck-off lifestyle jetting around the world, the girls ... '

'You think that a revolving door of bimbos, gold-diggers, and broken-wingers constitutes healthy relationships?'

'All I know is that you live the dream, Sean,' says Tom, sounding both admiring and exasperated. Jesus, that bloody phrase again: *living the dream*. 'You're unattached, you don't have to get up at the weekend . . . '

'To do what?' I blurt out, almost choking on my pint. 'To eat brunch with a load of yuppies checking out who screwed who the night before?'

'Sean, you don't seem to understand that, from where I'm sitting, that seems like a very attractive proposition.'

'Tom, you've been out of it so long you can't remember what it's like.' I point outside at the grim, November evening. Commuters scurry home, collars turned up to protect them from the damp. 'It's hell out there. Every girl I meet is catch and release.' This is not entirely true, I think, remembering Ellie.

'You expect me to believe that?'

We bumped into Ellie in a bar once when we were having a drink. Usually I'm the soul of discretion but, for some reason, I'd let it slip that we'd spent a couple of nights together. Tom has never forgotten the encounter. As hard as I try to disabuse him, Tom's perception of the unmarried and childless is largely gleaned from building society ads in which we're portrayed as rolling around in white Egyptian cotton sheets on Sunday mornings feeding each other freshly baked croissants to a Delfonics soundtrack. This is often a prelude to a pillow fight in a gauzy room drenched in sunlight.

'Why do you think there are so many psychos and prescription freaks around?' I ask.

'I dunno,' he shrugs.

'It might sound cheesy, Tom, but everyone wants to find that "special someone",' I say, exasperated. 'Everyone. Drug dealers, that old alkie who lives outside the 7–11 on Harrow Road, even taxi drivers. Tom, you're way ahead, you've met the person you're going to grow old with. Those of us on our own are going to collapse onto the lino and get found by a caretaker when the neighbours complain about the smell three days after an Alsatian has eaten our faces.'

There's a pause. I wonder whether I've managed to get through. His mood is switching between maudlin and exasperated by the minute.

'Look, I know I'm lucky,' he says. 'But having what other people perceive to be "it all"' – annoyingly he uses his index finger to draw quotation marks when he says this – 'doesn't mean much if being a husband, a dad, an employee doesn't leave time for a life, does it?'

Jesus. Now I know what Sara has to go through. I look over at my moping brother feeling sorry for himself and it's almost enough to, well, make *me* feel sorry for myself. My business is facing some, um, challenges – I might have to lay at least half a dozen decent, hard-working people off – and I'm supposed to spend my evening helping my brother relocate his ball sack?

'What the hell are you talking about?' I say. 'That *is* life. All that small stuff. The going to the paper shop in the morning, your commute to work, the bits of crap you put in your office to make it inhabitable, pizza in the park with the kids . . . All that stuff. It's not just the marriages, the births, the deaths, the stuff you need to get certificates from the council for. Nor is it the fucking yoga retreats, oboe lessons or Cantonese classes you're pining after.'

'Well, what's wrong with that?' he says, irritated. 'Wanting a bit of time for me? You know, work on my tennis game, get some sleep and . . . ' He pauses for a moment. 'Don't take this the wrong way but, if there were no consequences, I'd love to sleep with someone who wasn't my wife.'

'OK, now we're getting to the good stuff,' I say.

'Come on, Sean,' he explains. 'You know I love Sara. But we're both so tired at the end of the day, and she's so obsessed with the kids and not being around for them because she works crazy hours . . . I dunno, sometimes I feel like I'm at the back of the queue.'

This is beginning to make me feel really weary.

'Let me tell you something: it's called having a family, tosser,' I explain. 'And I shouldn't be the one telling you that. You think that every other married bloke with a family doesn't feel the same way? Do me a favour. That's all I ever hear you dads talking about. In a couple of years the boys won't want anything to do with you anyway.'

'Yeah, they'll be round your place trying to get off with your girlfriends' skanky younger sisters.'

'We'll see about that,' I say. I know that he's being self-deprecating, but Tom's characterisation of my future as an endless stag party isn't what I want to hear. The incident the other night with Ellie has made me wonder if everybody sees me as a feckless, hopeless squanderer of life.

'Tom, I hear you,' I say. 'The redundancy, the nagging wife, the draining kids. I feel your pain. But, listen: look at it from where I'm sitting. I might get to play the field, but the horrible truth is that I'm a single fella with no serious prospects on the horizon who, in order to meet girls, is one step away from trying a jazzercise class.'

Tom laughs and leans back in his chair.

'I always knew that your yoga phase had an ulterior motive.' He finishes another pint and signals the waiter. I check my watch. We've been sitting here for nearly three hours. I've heard enough piped sitar music to last me a lifetime.

'You sure?' I ask. 'You really want another?'

'Sean, you go out every night,' he explains. 'This is a big occasion for me, so forgive me for lapsing into cliché: just one more – then I'll go home.'

'Promise?'

'I promise,' he says, waving at the waiter.

It's midnight and we're at a strip club in the West End. Up to our necks in grossly marked-up booze and potent perfume, we're just another couple of drunken mug punters pretending to be big-time charlies. I watch the gyrating girls working the shiny-faced customers like gypsy pickpockets at a fairground. God, they're good. I should employ them.

Tom is eight sheets to the wind, and close to crumbling. I brought him here to try and sober him up. I thought that seeing all the other fools, witnessing such an exaggerated circus of what men want when drunk and mildly reckless, might make him realise that what he has is good and solid and worthwhile.

I was wrong. All he can see is the tits and the arse, all he can hear are the whispers and fake giggles, all he can feel is his numb libido rousing itself like a woozy bear in springtime stumbling from its cave. Of course, the hunters are waiting.

'Hello, sweetheart,' coos one of the girls to Tom. She has a quite spectacular body that's spoiled by two really bad tattoos, one on her left breast, the other midway up her right calf. Given that we're in a lap-dancing club, Tom is tragically flattered by the attention. He's like the man who goes to a boxing match and is thrilled when a fight breaks out. She gives him a dance.

'Watch the body glitter!' I shout at him as she begins to grind. Body glitter and cheap perfume: the ruin of many a married man. The stuff clings to the poor sods, even when they have that middle-of-the-night guilt-ridden shower, hoping that their wives will miss it. It's like the stuff in swimming pools they told you about when you were a kid: *if you have a slash in the water it'll turn red and everyone will know!*

'Is Sara going to be pissed off with you?' I ask. I'm talking more about the lateness of the hour than the fact that a twenty-year-old is rubbing her breasts on the top of his head.

'Don't worry,' he says from underneath the cleavage. 'I've got it all under control. You know I can hold my shit down.' I assume that the last sentence is meant for the dancer, an attempt to demonstrate Tom's familiarity with the street, rather than a literal statement.

'Sure,' I say, playing along. No point in picking an argument with a drunk. If I had a pound for every time some booze hound in a bar has told me, in a vaguely threatening way, 'I used to do karate!' then, well, I could afford a round of drinks at a strip club.

Jesus. What the hell are we doing here? More's the point, what the hell is Tom doing here? Tom, who has a reason to leave, a home and family to go home to.

'You don't know what you've got,' I say to him.

'What?' he says, cupping his ear with his palm.

'Your family, your home,' I shout. 'You don't know what you've got. I'd swap with you in an instant.'

'No you wouldn't,' he says.

'Yes, I would.'

'You wouldn't.'

He's too drunk to hold a decent conversation.

'We'll finish this another time,' I say.

He gives me a bemused once-over before bursting out laughing. Then he looks round at the club and the girl, who has soldiered on with her routine, as if he's just woken up and doesn't know how he got here.

'There's a petrol station at the end of the street,' he suddenly says. 'I'll stop and get Sara some flowers. Women love that shit.'

Oh dear.

'Wow, you're a right silver-tongued Casanova, aren't you?' I say. 'I didn't realise I was out with Mr Loverman.'

His eyes are glazed. I'm ready to go. I'm trying to avoid seeing myself in any of the mirrors that line the walls. Jesus, I've had enough as well.

'Tom, just so you know,' I say, 'taking Sara home a bunch of faded chrysanthemums from an Esso garage is the equivalent of marking your anniversary by taking her to the Welcome Break at the Watford Gap.'

This apparently clears his head. He stands up abruptly. The girl steps back and folds her arms, as if suddenly embarrassed by her nudity. Tom pulls his wallet out and stuffs some notes in her garter belt.

'Thanks, but I have to go,' he says, before turning to leave. I smile at the girl and mouth, 'I think it's best if we get off.'

Then he's back. He moves towards the girl.

'Can I have some change?' he asks. 'I'm in a lot of trouble. I really need to get my wife some flowers.'

The girl is already gone. I put my arm around him and lead him out onto Tottenham Court Road. I tell him to stand up straight and try to appear sober. Cab drivers can spot a chunderer a mile away. Finally, one pulls over. I open the door, press a twenty into Tom's hand and tell the driver where to go.

'So, tell me again,' I say to him, 'what are you going to tell Sara?'

'Sorry, I missed the curfew, Mum?'

'No.'

'I drink because you make me hate myself?'

'No.'

'I'm sorry I stayed out so late,' he says, almost soberly. 'And I really appreciate your letting me have a few drinks once in a while.'

'Correct answer,' I say. 'Driver, get this idiot home to his wife and kids.'

'I warn you, if he fucking pukes in my cab he's clearing it up,' says the driver gruffly. 'Understood?'

I nod.

'He'll be as good as gold,' I lie.

The cab careers off across Tottenham Court Road. It could have dropped me in Notting Hill, I suppose. But I need some time to clear my head. I was only half joking when I suggested swapping lives with him. Actually, I wasn't joking at all. Bringing it up late at night in a strip club allowed me to claim I was drunk even if he freaked out. But he didn't.

I'm still thinking about it when I get home, so I flick through the channels to wind down. For no apparent reason I settle on a programme about Jehovah's Witnesses in America. Then it hits me: maybe believing deeply and strongly in something to the exclusion of everything else, being convinced that during the Second Coming non-believers will be cast into unimaginable agony as punishment for their sins, is easier than not believing anything at all? Maybe the JWs are not that far different from the UFO obsessives and Al Qaeda and the nutters in the Philippines who crucify themselves at Easter. Maybe they're just trying to achieve that most basic human impulse: to create order, to find meaning.

Which is what, although drunk and blundering, I think that my brother was trying to say tonight in his my-life-is-shit-and-no-one-understands-me way.

And that's where I can help him.

You think that you see your own life with clarity, understand why you've got to where you are, got dumped by whoever dumped you, made plans for whatever future you're imagining, know what people see when you walk in the room. But what do you really know? If Tom thinks he's been short-changed then he should join the fucking queue, and while he's waiting, learn to be happy and get his game face on.

What he needs is the help of an outsider, someone who can be objective. Two weeks living apart from his family, taking on the role of the unmarried, financially solvent entrepreneur might be the only opportunity he's going to get to bring some clarity to his precarious state of mind.

Tom, you might not even know it, but it's time for a change – for you and for me.

7
Tom

Making breakfast for the boys on Saturday I discover the shoes that I was wearing the night before are in the oven. Search and rescue activity for the briefcase I took to the interview, however, is fruitless. A quick inventory of the events of the previous night leads me to conclude that its most likely location is the cloakroom at the strip club. I pour myself another cup of Barry's Tea, which, in my experience, is a cure-all for all ills. Bring on the fucking Ebola, Barry's will beat it down and make it wish it had never reared its feeble viral head.

The briefcase hardly matters anyway; there is absolutely nothing of value inside it. It looks good, looks like I might be one of those workplace warriors who are going places, one of the new army of people I see wearing stupid headsets while typing furiously into something electronic. The truth is a little more prosaic. The contents, if my memory serves, consist of the following: two packets of Walkers crisps (empty), three of my favourite brand of pens, one of which leaks on my fingers, an old padlock that I used to take to the gym and somehow ended up in my briefcase rather than my sports bag, a copy of *Observer Money* (unread) bought on a whim at the newsagent's when buying a Lottery ticket, some old bits of post that I can't be arsed to deal with (something to do with the council and a parking scheme) and – commence drum roll – a copy of my CV, which is, I have begun to conclude, either cursed or worthless. Probably both. I bet the strippers are having a good laugh at it now. The way things are going I'm about as likely to get a job dancing there as I am the ones I've applied for.

Sara jumped out of bed early to go to the gym. It's beyond me how she finds the energy to punish those dignity-shredding elliptical machines so early on a Saturday morning. Sara's answer, of course, is the one that the health sections in women's magazines bang on about, namely that the gym gives her *more* energy. Her technique, she says, is simple: she gets out of bed and looks at her bottom in the mirror. This offers her all the motivation she needs. I can see absolutely nothing defective with Sara's bottom, and this is speaking as a man who has seen a few excellent examples the night before. The only thing wrong is that I don't get enough opportunities to get my hands on it.

I tranquillise the boys with TV, and slump with them, hoping that my throbbing head will cease laying siege to the day. As the bubbly presenters prattle on, I gaze at the boys and am somehow reminded of my biggest fear before they were born: *what if I didn't like them?* This was something that preoccupied me in the months leading up to Michael's arrival.

That didn't happen. Like any love affair, it was one over which I had no emotional governance. I look over at my pampered, adorable boys, who have never heard much other than applause, and feel a fraud. How am I meant to prepare these two for life in a world that I can barely digest myself? I feel like one of those seabirds that goes off fishing and then regurgitates the contents of its stomach so that its young can eat: I can offer them enough to keep them alive, but beyond that only a basic degree of nurture that seems unpalatable even to myself. I mean, you do your best, but who knows if they'll even remember that you tried.

The boys loll, arms splayed on the sofa, their eyes hooded and glazed. They might as well have hangovers themselves. I could leave now and return late this afternoon and neither would have moved. We should, of course, be playing board games, visiting museums, listening to the Dreem Team on Radio 1. But we're not, we're watching telly. We're together, but we're not really. We're watching telly because I'm not making other things happen like I see other dads doing. It's not like I've given up, like I don't care. I'll do anything possible to give these kids the best opportunities, the richest or fullest life they might live. And we'll start next weekend.

I pour myself another cuppa.

For God's sake, man! Pull yourself together!

'Let's go swimming!' I blurt out.

The boys turn and look at me before their attention returns back to *UK:TV*.

'Why?' asks Paddy, not unfairly. We haven't all been swimming on a Saturday morning, um, ever.

'Cos it'll be fun,' I say.

'But I need new goggles,' says Michael. 'Mine are leaking.'

'We'll get some at the pool.'

'The ones at the pool are crap. Sorry, not very good.'

'It doesn't matter,' I say. 'We're going to have a laugh, not compete at a gala.'

'It'll be too busy,' says Michael. 'It always is at the weekend.'

'I'll go and get your stuff ready,' I say breezily, trying to take charge.

'Can we wait until after we find out who's number one?' asks Paddy.

'It's gonna be Nelly,' says Michael. 'It's obvious, you plum.'

Paddy punches him on the arm. It's the reaction of a younger brother who's incapable of coming up with a fleet-footed and suitably world-weary reply.

'That didn't even hurt,' says Michael, not turning from the screen.

'Can I do it again then?' asks Paddy, his fist cocked.

I give Paddy the Dad Stare. He lowers his fist. I suspect that he's glad he doesn't have to punch Michael again. A second punch would have ensured retaliation.

'Right then,' I say. 'I want you two changed and ready to go as soon as this is finished.'

Half an hour later we are little closer to leaving. I am dressed and ready. The boys' sports bags are packed. I've even remembered snacks for afterwards. The boys, however, are stalled. Michael can't find clean pants, and Paddy is just distracted. And I'm anxious – part of the plan is to get out of the house before Sara gets back, in order to snag myself some Super Dad brownie points. Going out and getting fucked up and losing your briefcase is one thing, getting up the next morning and doing something constructive *unprompted* with your sons is something else entirely. My strategy was not, on a scale of minus to plus ten, just to get myself back from, say, minus five to zero, but to claw my way into positive territory.

I've got a plan, I say to myself while packing three Granny Smiths into my gym bag with my towel and trunks, and it's so crazy, it might just work.

I finally coax, cajole and convince both boys into the hallway. I have my wallet in my hand, when I hear Sara's keys rattling in the front door. I take a deep breath, feeling like I've been cheated out of a great victory by a dubious refereeing decision.

She's still glowing from the gym, the crispness of the late-autumn day stinging her cheeks. Very briefly I think that it would be nice to pick her up and carry her to the bedroom. Then I come to my senses: I can't remember the last time we had sex in the daytime. Sara looks at us all.

'Where are you lot off to then?' she says, directing her question more to the boys than to me.

'Swimming,' says Michael glumly, much the same way as he says 'dentist'.

'Thought we'd go over to Swiss Cottage,' I say, taking charge, making her aware that it was my idea. I wait for her to pass judgement.

'That sounds like fun,' she says. 'Room for one more?'

To the swimming pool through the London snarl. I sit behind the wheel of my sensible but sexy silver Volvo estate (paid for by my wife) safely transporting the loves of my life to their Saturday recreation. It more or less feels like we're the type of family that does the kinds of things that families are supposed to do on Saturdays: supermarket shopping, a spot of Homebase, football for the kids, going to the multiplex. Although I don't like music in the car, I turn the radio on, hoping that we might have one of those moments I've seen in films where we all sing along to the same song, joyfully sharing the moment by acknowledging each other's smiles.

But that doesn't happen. Instead, the road begins to narrow, turning from two lanes to one. I indicate that I'm pulling over, glance in the rear-view mirror, and notice that the BMW behind me, which has ample time to slow down and let me slip seamlessly into his lane, is trying to cut me up. It occurs to me to slow down, to diffuse the situation and let the dickhead have his way. But I do what most Londoners would do: I continue my manoeuvre despite that fact that it will force him to pump his brakes.

He hits his horn hard, and continues to hold his hand down.

'Tom,' said Sara. 'What on earth . . . ?'

'Sorry,' I apologise. 'The idiot tried to cut me up.'

'Tom, stop driving like a maniac,' scolds Sara.

Maniac! I was just going about my business before this arsewipe comes out of nowhere and harasses me. I throw my hand up in exasperation for the BMW driver's benefit. His horn is still blaring.

The boys turn around to get a look at the driver who stops beeping his horn and is now making wild gesticulations in my direction.

'Boys, sit back down immediately,' I say. 'There's nothing to see.'

We continue down the Finchley Road with the twat leaning on his horn. Pedestrians turn and watch him waving his arms and honking.

'Sean, you've got your family in the car,' says Sara. 'For goodness sake, there's absolutely no need—'

'It's not me hitting the horn,' I say.

'You should have just let him go,' she continues. 'You always have to get into it, don't you? Well, it's just plain stupid. You don't know who he is. He could have a gun.'

'Don't be ridiculous,' I say. 'He's just some chav.' The truth of the matter, however, is that I'm becoming more alarmed by the moment, most of all because we're about to hit traffic, which will bring both vehicles to a halt in uncomfortably close proximity.

I take another glance in the mirror. He's young: probably no more than eighteen (irresponsible!), driving a 7 Series (he can't afford that! He must be a drug dealer!) and continues to honk his horn while pursuing my car with inches to spare (reckless and out of control!). What really bothers me is that he won't let it lie. There are more of them around these days, the type who'll come after you for cutting them up, scuffing a new trainer, spilling a pint. They don't care if you're with your wife and kids on the way to the swimming pool, they just want to get into it.

We come to a halt as we hit the traffic jam. The horn-beeping has stopped. I look in the mirror again and see that he's got out of his car.

Jesus. I undo my seatbelt and reach for the door handle. Sara has seen what's going on and takes control.

'Stay in the car!' she orders. I take another look at the kid, he's only a few years older than Michael.

'Stay in the damn car, Tom!'

I lock the doors as the kid appears alongside my window, which he slaps with the palm of his hand. He's wearing a Nickelson sweatshirt with the collar of a different colour polo shirt turned up towards his pale, irate face. His eyes are sunken and pink, but there's a wiry strength about his physique.

'Come on then!' he shouts at me. 'You want some, you wanker? You fucking want some?'

I grimace at him. Put my forefinger to my temple, show him that I think he's off his rocker. He slaps the window again.

Sara leans over to my side, brandishing her mobile. 'I'm calling the police!' she shouts at him.

I am not scared any more. Who the fuck is this little shit? He thinks that it's OK to intimidate my family? We're on our way to the *swimming pool*, for Chrissakes. I size him up. If he's not armed I know that I've a chance if I can summon the right level of aggression; he's a couple of inches shorter, weighs less . . . I stop myself right there. The very fact that he's standing in the middle of the Finchley Road on a Saturday morning swearing at some family man in a Volvo estate means that he's more up for it that I am. I've not been in many fights, but the few I've had have made it clear to me that the person who wants the fight more, is less self-conscious about the idiocy of what they're doing and can throw themselves into the moment with total belief will always win.

Now, I am fucking livid. I would love to give this little prick a beat-down, grind his nose into the tarmac, make him apologise to Sara, Michael and Patrick for what he's done and promise never to behave in this way again. I want revenge . . . Actually, what I'd prefer to do is to be in the overly chlorinated waters of the swimming pool. I'd like to drive away.

While I'm thinking this I hear a screech of tyres that lasts for what feels like several minutes. There's a thud, and the crunch of glass and plastic shattering. I look up at the maniac. He's staring back down the street. He appears momentarily startled, before he – predictably – starts shouting.

'You wanker!'

He runs back to examine the damage.

'Someone's run into the back of him,' I laugh.

'Good,' says Michael.

I know I shouldn't, but I can't help myself. I open the car door and step out.

'Tom,' says Sara, but it's already too late.

I step onto the pavement to see that back down the road the maniac is inspecting his rear bumper. He turns, fists clenched tightly at his side and delivers a torrent of profanity at the white van that sits hissing behind his own vehicle. So much steam is coming from the van that the driver's compartment is obscured. I wonder if the occupants are injured – or are about to be – as the maniac continues his verbal assault. His use of profanity is quite spectacular.

The door of the van opens and a middle-aged Indian man steps out.

'I'm sorry,' he immediately says to the maniac. 'My fault.'

The maniac is momentarily taken aback, before continuing his rant.

'You fucking wanker,' he replies.

The van driver holds his hands up – I notice a mobile in his right hand – to try and calm the maniac down.

'Seven hundred quid,' snaps the maniac.

'What?'

'Seven hundred quid, that's what I want,' he continues. 'You said you did it – I want my money.'

'Let's call the police, shall we?' the van driver says firmly.

'Are you a grass?' replies the maniac.

'We need to fill out a form for the insurance,' says the van driver. He begins to punch the keys of his mobile. 'I'll need your details so we can get this sorted.'

'Don't call the police,' says the maniac. 'Just give me my money and we're finished.'

'I'm sorry,' says the driver. 'I think that it's best this way.'

'You Paki bastard,' says the maniac.

The predictability of this abuse means that the van driver barely acknowledges it.

'Actually, I'm not a Paki,' he says matter-of-factly while holding his phone to his ear.

'Whatever you are then . . . ' says the maniac, struggling with his abuse for the first time. 'You . . . Al Qaeda bastard.'

'Police, please,' says the van driver, ignoring him entirely.

It's then that the maniac reaches over and snatches the phone from the van driver. It looks like he's going to hit him.

'Give me my fucking money,' he shouts.

That's it. I've had enough of this. I can't stand by and watch any longer. I start moving towards the pair of them, unsure exactly what I'm going to do, when I see that another two men have climbed out of the van. They're much younger than the driver, sons or nephews maybe, and – thank you, Lord – are built like they might actually be able to pick the van up.

'Give him his phone back,' one of them says to the maniac who, not fancying this any longer, hands the phone over.

'I'm going to need your contact details,' says the van driver. The maniac mulls this over for a moment. While he's doing this, an unmarked police car pulls up. Two officers jump out, one of them walks over to the group of men, the other reads the vehicle licence plates into his radio. Deciding that it's now time to leave, I start to walk back towards the car. I turn to see that Sara and the boys are also on the pavement watching the show. I smile at them and say, 'Let's get out of here.'

No sooner have I spoken than I hear a shout go up. I turn to see the maniac sprinting along the pavement towards me, with the police in hot pursuit. I am in an episode of *The Bill*. What I do next, I would like to report, was a considered and thoughtful act of public service. Actually, I just wanted to see the bastard suffer. I stick my leg out just as he scurries past me, knocking him so that he stumbles before eventually falling. Within moments the police are on top of him, locking his hands behind his back. A little cheer goes up and I look towards my family and see my boys jumping up and down and pumping their fists. Sara has a wry smile on her face, perplexed as well as amused by the situation.

It turns out that the BMW is stolen. We have to hang around to give police statements, which thrills the boys, who are delighted to be part of the process of apprehending a criminal. Once we get on our way they spend the rest of the journey recounting the incident in exhausting detail. And although there is no sing-along this Saturday morning I can't help feeling that the trip to the pool is already a resounding success.

The water feels good, cleansing. I swim a few lengths and then bask. The road-rage incident has reminded me of something. I only ever had one fight at school. Sean and I were, generally, popular kids. It wasn't like we were particularly hard, or sporty, or funny, or mucked about enough to impress our peers. But we did enough of those things to be well liked by the rougher kids, and our distaste for bullying meant that we'd sometimes hang with the nerdier kids most people wouldn't be seen dead with. Sean, in particular, was very popular with the spazs and spackers, as they were known. He would regale them with his presence, a visiting dignitary from the land of cool and popular.

When we were about fourteen and the school was in the grip of a sportswear craze, Sean went up to the West End with a couple of his mates. He came back with a few new purchases, which he spent most of the rest of the day modelling in front of a mirror in his room. One of the items was a tracksuit top by Fila, which were all the rage. He wore it out to a crappy disco at the youth club that night and turned heads. I've got to admit that I was mildly jealous of the aforementioned item, principally because I had told him that I was saving up to buy the very same top. Sean was always a little better than me at making money and had worked out ways of raising extra cash: one scheme involved canvassing the neighbourhood for dads too lazy to wash their own cars, taking orders for a Sunday carwashing service and then hiring teams of local kids to do the work while he counted the cash.

The following Monday Sean came downstairs to breakfast wearing his tracksuit top. Mum told him to go and put on his blazer. He was only allowed to wear it after school. Sean complied, but tucked the top away in his bag, changing into it as soon as we were round the corner. We were heading up the street when we saw a bus coming. We missed it, and as it sailed past a kid in the year above us, Robbie Nicholls shouts out the window, 'Nice tracksuit, wanker.'

Now, insults are the primary currency of communication when you're in your mid-teens, so neither of us paid much attention to it. We got to school and Sean was getting compliments on his new top from a lot of the kids, including one of the prettier girls in our year, whom he was scheming on. Things changed later on though. I didn't see the incident as Sean and I weren't in the same class, but the way I heard it was that an older kid, who was big and hairy and should have known better, started picking on Sean in the corridor, asking him who he thought he was wearing Fila, telling him that no one was wearing Fila any more. Sean tried to shrug it off, but the kid came up to him and yanked at the top. Sean pushed him away. The big kid was coming back at Sean when a teacher happened by and broke it up. Sean knew that he was in trouble. Word got to him that, in typically dramatic schoolboy fashion, he was 'dead'.

Sean didn't mention all this to me, but word travelled around the third year pretty quickly, and I wondered what I would do if I saw the kid first. Sean and I had never really been ones for fighting, but there was an inevitability to the confrontation that I could tell was bothering Sean, who was quiet and withdrawn that night. The next day I was coming out of biology, and there, hanging around at a crossroads in the corridor, is the big fucker. I slung my Adidas bag over my shoulder and tried to get by without being noticed, but one of his pals tapped him on the shoulder and pointed me out.

'Oi, freak!' he shouted. 'Freaky twin.'

I kept walking but, for some unknown reason, the corridor suddenly became quiet and empty.

'Cunningham,' he shouted.

I stopped and looked over at him.

'Don't worry,' he said. 'You ain't gonna be a freaky twin for long; not when I've finished with your brother.'

I put my bag down and started walking towards him. I heard him start speaking: 'Tell your brother that he's . . . ' but I didn't hear the rest, I just felt myself going a little cold, a rage rising inside me, and watched as my right fist landed very slowly on his nose, shifting it into a grotesque mish-mash of cartilage and blood. He looked at me, his nose haemorrhaging blood, before putting his hand to his face, as if to confirm what had happened to him. His eyes widened momentarily, before he fell on me, and we rolled around the corridor which was now packed with kids chanting, 'Fight, fight, fight.' As scared and uncomfortable as I was with the situation, I was more self-conscious than anything else, aware that rolling around on the floor fighting someone significantly taller and stronger than you makes no sense whatsoever unless you've sent off for one of those martial arts training courses advertised in the back of comics.

The noise attracted the attention of the Deputy Head who hauled us off to her office and read us the riot act. The kid's white shirt was covered in blood and he was pinching the top of his nose and sniffing, trying to stop the flow. I didn't tell the teacher about Sean. She wasn't interested anyway. I got off with a Saturday-morning detention, which was fair enough. I was happy to do it.

Sean and I rode the bus after school, chuckling all the way home. I was feeling rough, as the other kid had given me quite a seeing-to. God knows what he'd have done to me if the fight had gone on longer. I saw the kid around after that and we just ignored each other. Mum wanted to know why my shirt was ripped. I made something up about a bit of rough and tumble in the playground. She wasn't impressed.

That night Sean and I sat and watched telly after we'd done our homework. I decided to go to bed and listen to the radio. I went into my room and there, lying on a chair, was the tracksuit top. A gift from my brother.

I see the boys and swim over to them underwater, grabbing their legs like a monster from the deep. They swim off towards the diving board. Sara powers through the water gracefully, I put my arm around her waist and try to pull her closer. She resists.

'You feel any better?' she asks. We haven't discussed the night before or my hangover.

'I did before I got jumped by Giant Haystacks and Big Daddy,' I say. The boys, bless their hearts, had bombed me as soon as I got in the pool.

'Oh, they mean well,' says Sara, proceeding to dive underwater and perform a handstand.

Yeah, I know, I say to myself. Still makes you understand why some species eat their young, though.

'How's Sean?' she asks, having resurfaced.

'Oh, you know. Same old, same old.'

She splashes some water at me. 'Come on, Tom. Help him out a little. He's got to grow up sometime.'

'I think he's trying, I really do,' I say. 'It's not easy for him, you know.'

'Sweetheart, there are so many girls out there who'd love to meet someone like him.'

'I dunno,' I say, watching a group of little kids messing about in the shallow end. I wonder how many of them have added to the level of liquid in the pool. 'He says different, that there's nothing he wants more than to have what we've got. You know, debt, rogue kids . . . '

Sara smiles.

'Keep talking to him,' she says. 'He needs you. More than you know.'

She swims off and I run a little diagnostic. The post piss-up self-loathing isn't too bad and the earlier nausea has cleared up. Other than tiredness, I'm right as rain. But there's something at the back of my mind that I can't quite shed. I think about Sean. Maybe I whined a little too much, last night. Maybe I wasn't listening. Maybe I need to be asking him more questions. But somehow that seems wrong. It's just not the dynamic of our relationship. It's *Sean*, for God's sake. Sean can take it all in his stride. Nothing bothers him; he just gets on with it. Sara keeps going on about him needing help, reaching out. She seems to think that we never talk about anything much other than football and movies and maybe politics if we're a bit pissed. It's a common misconception. Ask most women and they'll tell you straight: *men don't talk*. To my mind, it's a false impression that us men should hang on to for dear life; if women get wind that we're different from what they thought then they'll want to talk about every god-damn thing under the sun.

Here's a topic of discussion for them: there are only two reasons married men don't cheat: 1) They can't find anyone to cheat with, 2) They're scared of getting caught. You might have heard other reasons but, believe me, they're all bullshit. The urge to roam exists from day one until the day you fade out on a nasty set of NHS sheets. It might diminish over time but it's like silt in a bottle, shake it up and it's still there.

I push out from the side of the pool towards where Michael and Patrick are searching the bottom for something. The only thing they'll find down there is stray plasters. I think about Sara. I have never cheated on her. I can't say that it's never crossed my mind, that I've never been out with friends or work colleagues and, a few drinks in, played out a prospective scenario in my mind. But I've never followed through. Not once. This gives me infinite pleasure. I love my wife, couldn't bear to hurt her. But it also makes me ask questions of myself. Is this it? Can they, effectively, write my obituary now that I've made my bed, settled into a life in which my substantial achievements are all behind me?

I'm comfortable with these thoughts most of the time. But sometimes I wonder whether I'm just lazy, weak and unadventurous. Or whether I'm just plain scared. Sean made some comment last night about our switching lives. It's a pretty funny idea, and I suppose it would offer me the chance to go 'extracurricular', but it's rooted in lunacy. He must have been as drunk as I was. I can't believe that he was actually serious.

8
Sean

An unexpected call from a client late in the day is rarely good news.

'It's Margaret Spitzer from Red Channel,' announces Aileen, my assistant, crisply. Aileen is the best kind of assistant: a chubby suburbanite with little interest in anything other than my schedule and well-being. I'd be lost without her, which is an unlikely scenario, as I grossly overpay her and shower her with attention that she's unable to procure elsewhere. Fortunately, loyalty *can* be bought.

What's put me on red alert is that Margaret *never* calls directly. Red Channel has so many layers of management that she's got plenty of shiftless lackeys available to call me to find out how I'm earning my corn. Margaret is the *grand fromage*, she who must be obeyed; she won't be wasting ten minutes of her highly compensated time just to gossip. I stand up. I always do for the important calls. I like to pace and gesture. I feel stronger that way, my voice more rounded, my bearing more accomplished. I slip on my headset, the one that dictates that I am, beyond all argument, yuppie scum.

'Margaret, hi,' I say breezily, trying to convey genuine enthusiasm for a call that, at the very least, spells trouble.

'Sean, how are you?' she says. It's not really a question. Margaret Spitzer doesn't waste time on either protocol or custom – courtesy is just a way of accomplishing commerce. I wait for what I know will be a faultlessly prepared monologue. She's good, this one.

'Sean, first of all I need to say that I'm sorry to have to have this conversation on the phone, but I'm stuck in Amsterdam.'

'I appreciate that,' I say. I now know what's coming – my biggest client is bailing on me. As she talks I can barely hear her, I focus solely on what I'm going to say after she's slipped the knife in. You've got to go down sounding like a winner – go big or go home, baby.

'We're reassessing a lot of our objectives for next year, and I'm afraid to say that I've had to make the decision that SC Communications will not be part of our plans beyond the extent of the current agreement,' she announces.

'Are you saying that we're not even going to be able to repitch for the contract?' I ask as aggressively as I can get away with. I know that it's over, but I want to make her work for it.

'I'm afraid not, Sean,' she says, not missing a beat. 'Look, what I can say to you is that this decision has, to a large extent, been made due to the internal workings of the company. Five years is long enough with the same agency. We need a change, Sean. It's not personal. We really appreciate the work that SC Communications has done for us and we are certainly not averse to considering a further relationship with you down the road. For the moment, however, I feel that it's only right and proper that there should be some breathing space.'

I drift off. She's being decent, doing the right thing. At least she put a blindfold on me before she took me out and shot me.

Losing a client isn't unusual. It's the norm. It's like musical chairs; everyone moves around, settles for a while, and then moves on. Some of them keep you around for a while, even when you know that neither of you is really excited by the relationship. Others pipe you onboard with a big fanfare, and are gone before you've had a chance to learn all the names round the table. But losing three long-term accounts in the last month, nearly twenty per cent of my business, is more than a coincidence. It's a fucking calamity.

Spitzer finishes the boardroom beat-down. I take the headset off. The numbers start spinning round my head. In this business, make that any business, the numbers are the only things that don't lie. I need to find Theano, my financial director. Even without her explanation, the implications of the conversation are clear – within the space of a few weeks we've gone from being a company with a fifteen per cent margin to a company that's barely breaking even; that is, unless I hustle up some business, PDQ.

I open the bottom drawer of my desk and pull out a bottle of Johnny Walker Blue that a client sent over at Christmas. I pour a finger and throw it back. I pour another and start thinking about who I need to call internally to break the news.

Fuck it. It can wait until tomorrow. Tellingly, rather than act to shore up the crisis, I turn my attention elsewhere and start to wonder how I avoid the mental illness, depression, excessive drinking and premature death that are the statistical destinies of single men. Other than Ellie, I've not met a woman in the past couple of years who has pressed all the right buttons. Maybe I've got it wrong. Maybe I need to approach it from the other side and think about the kinds of girls who *don't* float my boat. That way I can be more focused. I grab a writing pad and pen and go at it.

1. *Rock chicks. Girls who heave around to Guns 'N' Roses when it comes on the pub jukebox, or is dropped in an ironic fashion in a nightclub.*

2. *Specifically: girls who play the bass. Or drums. (It's just not natural.)*

3. *Girls who are actually pretty good at pool, who consequently deny me the opportunity to lean in close to 'teach' them how to play.*

4. *If there are any soft toys in evidence at the domicile, particularly in the bedroom, it's enough to take the curl out of my moustache, if I had one.*

5. *Wearing big floppy hats if you're not Annie Hall, or Amish.*

6. *Wackiness. (See floppy hats, above.)*

7. *Girls who use their fingers to denote parentheses. ('Technically we're not [index and middle fingers raised] "going out" [fingers lowered], we're just having a [fingers raised] "good time" [fingers lowered].')*

8. *Girls who put on a little-girl voice when they're trying to get round you.*

9. *Girls who wear cow prints on clothing. You eat cattle; you don't take fashion hints from them.*

10. *Girls with pushy, posh mums. You say, 'Pass the peas, please,'*

what she hears is, 'I'm going to turn your little princess into a ten-pound-a-poke coke whore.'

11. *Listing shopping as a 'hobby'. As alluring as castrating a wild boar and all the virtue of collecting the royalties for* Mein Kampf.
12. *Self-obsessed crazies who always manage to turn the conversation back to themselves. ('I took 9/11 very personally . . . ')*
13. *Girls who refer to football as 'footie'.*
14. *Girls who have elaborate, health-related dietary requirements, but are quite happy to vacuum up gak of questionable provenance from a pub toilet seat.*

After half an hour of this utterly futile exercise I realise that I have narrowed the female population of the UK down to Ellie and a rare species of gorgeous, highly compensated, smart-arse sommeliers who can't wait to laugh at my jokes while serving me expensive Barolo. Frankly, I'm as likely to encounter one of them as I am to see a unicorn trotting up Fulham Road. I wander out of the office, past the smiling receptionists who seem to change every day or two, to get some air. Upliftingly, there's a couple breaking up in the street. I watch, transfixed. She's crying, but *she's* the one doing the dumping. She clearly chose a public place in the hope that her boyfriend wouldn't put up a struggle.

Better luck next time, sweetheart.

I try calling Tom on his mobile to see if he can get out for a beer. I get the answerphone. I leave a long, rambling message, which I then delete. I start walking towards Hyde Park. The walking feels good, even as the sun fades and the crabby, frenetic rush home begins.

By the time I eventually get through to Tom I've passed through Kensington, treating myself to a delicious kofta kebab on the way, and am nearing the stuccoed Victoriana of Notting Hill and home. It is the first time that I've gone directly from my office to my house for as long as I can remember. Opening the door and wrangling the alarm without the impairment of champagne or vodka is to be recommended. My phone rings and Tom rambles on about something he's heard on the news about London being one of Al Qaeda's top-five targets.

'What are you doing tomorrow?' I ask.

There's a pause. I can hear the boys in the background. I wonder whether he's pausing because of them, or whether he senses something is up.

'Um, nothing,' he replies.

'How about a little pitch and putt?' I say.

'Sean, it's Wednesday.'

'Precisely, we'll have the place to ourselves,' I point out.

'Aren't you going to work?'

'I'm taking some time off tomorrow. Going to the dentist, running errands, that kind of thing. Thought that we could give it a bit of Tiger Woods in the morning.'

'Yeah,' says Tom. 'Look, sorry about the other night. Jesus. Going on about my job and how my wife doesn't understand me and all that shit . . . Talk about a cliché.'

'No problem,' I say. 'We're brothers.' I can sense how odd he thinks this is. I just don't say this kind of thing. 'Catch you tomorrow,' I say and switch off my phone for the night.

When we were growing up, the worst thing I ever did to my brother wasn't something that humiliated him or caused him pain. In fact, it was so insignificant that he might not even remember it at all. We were sitting watching Saturday-morning TV one weekend when an advert came on for a *Six Million Dollar Man* action figure. We fell silent, mouths agape. By way of toy-making genius, Colonel Steve Austin had a bionic eye, skin on his arm that could be rolled back to reveal the electronics that he'd had implanted, and a bionic arm, which was operated by pushing a button on his back. He came with a hunk of grey plastic that had been painted to look like an iron girder. Even in toy form the Bionic Man could lift this above his head – *that's how strong he was.*

Tom wanted one, but I *really* wanted one. Wanted it more than anything I'd ever seen. I burnt with excitement at the prospect of the hours of distraction that could be had with such a prize. There was only one problem. I had no money. Tom, however, did. At that age Tom always seemed to have money squirrelled away somewhere and, as it had been our birthdays recently, I knew that he was flush.

'We need to get it,' I told him.

'Do you think Mum and Dad would buy it for us?' he asked.

'I doubt it,' I said. The recent birthday meant a moratorium on gifts

and, more dispiritingly, there had been complaints from the neighbours after our football smashed a pane of glass in their greenhouse.
We were not in anyone's good books.

'How much did they say it was?' I asked Tom, fully aware of the
price and the fact that my brother had a fiver plus change in his safe,
which he thought no one knew about. It was hidden at the back of his
cupboard, behind his school uniform. I'd never nicked any of his
money, but I'd check occasionally to see how much was in there.

'It's 4.99,' replied my brother. This was serious money. Ten weeks
pocket money. It would take us until the summer to find that kind of
dough. And the summer was simply too far away for this to be an
option.

'Did you see that bionic eye?' I said, amazed.

'Yeah,' said my brother, chewing on a slice of toast. We continued
watching the ads. I was wondering what my next move should be
when my brother said, 'I've got 4.99.'

'Yeah?'

'In my safe.'

'You've got a safe?'

'It's hidden in case we get burgled.'

'Yeah?'

'Yeah.'

'So you think we should get it?'

He pauses for a moment.

'We could go halves,' I say. 'I'll give you my pocket money until I've
paid you back.'

'OK,' he says. And I'm thrilled and deeply guilty at the same time.
Somehow I feel that I'm ripping him off.

That afternoon we climb on a creaking old Routemaster – result!
We got the back seat on the top deck – and headed down towards
Swiss Cottage. We stared out of the window, breathing in the smell of
hot oil and listened to the rattle of the conductor's ticket machine.
Standing outside the toy shop on Finchley Road I felt like we were just
about to do something bad. It was the same feeling I had had when we
nicked one of Dad's cigarettes and lit it up under the bridge in the
park. We pulled open the wooden door that had a metal bell attached
to it, walked inside and went round to where we knew the Action

Man stuff was located. And there it was – Steve Austin, 'a man barely alive', as they said on the show. Actually, there were dozens of Steve Austins, dozens of men barely alive. The Colonel was stacked from floor to ceiling. My initial reaction was that the box didn't impress me; it was pink for a start and the illustration on the cover made him look old, not bionic.

'We can rebuild him,' said Tom in an American accent. He picked one of the boxes and examined a series of illustrations demonstrating Steve's multiple capabilities. There was a hole in the back of the box that allowed us to check out the bionic eye. I picked up another box and did the same thing. I put the box down. Same thing. The bionic eye was shit. I could just about make out a box of Monopoly that was barely six feet away. I didn't want to tell my brother that I thought that it was shit. I don't want to spoil the moment, to be the naysayer. So I watched as my brother went up to the till, retrieved a pristine fiver from his pocket and slipped it across the counter to the toyshop owner who would always say the same thing to us once we'd completed a transaction: 'Grassy arse,' he'd chuckle. 'That's what they say in Spain, you know: grassy arse.'

We returned home in silence, Tom holding the brown paper package that contained the doll until we got home. Once there, we took it to his room and pulled the Bionic Man out. And as much as I wanted it to be great, and talked it up to Tom as the most exciting thing I'd played with in a long while, I wasn't surprised to see it discarded the following day, the rubber skin on his arm ripped, the plastic implants lost and the crappy eye scratched and foggy. It was a bad buy. My brother was a fiver down. Actually, we were both a fiver down, but Tom was the one who'd laid out the cash. We were suckered by an advert and our own imaginings. We had wanted it to be a miracle, but it wasn't. If I hadn't pushed Tom into going all the way to Swiss Cottage with his fiver we wouldn't be in this predicament. The disaster was all down to me.

I arrive at his house before ten and we head across to the park, where the pitch and putt isn't even open yet. We find a parkie, who gives us a funny look before leading us over to a dusty shed from which he pulls clubs and balls. He refuses money, telling us not to worry about it.

This is the kind of attitude that has made municipal London the freewheeling success that it is. We start to play, battling through thick dew, which holds the balls up and soaks the bottoms of our trousers.

Then I let him have it.

'So, have you thought about what we talked about the other night?' I ask.

'I'm trying to concentrate,' he says, lining up a putt.

'What I said at the strip club,' I say, 'have you thought about it?'

He ignores me. I know that Tom holds to a well-established version of my life that he considers unequivocally to be true (riches beyond the dreams of avarice, not a care in the world, womaniser), and in some ways he's right. I have more fun than perhaps I should. I imagine that I go to more parties and know more hot girls than all but a tiny percentage of the population; maybe the tiny percentage that is Peter Stringfellow. What he doesn't appear to understand is that it's just the life that I happen to have. I don't necessarily desire this version any more. I'm more interested in developing Sean 2.0, and I want Tom to know this.

Tom is focusing hard, hunched over the ball, eyeing up what passes for the green. I forgot how competitive he is, how beating him at tennis or cards can change the complexion of our relationship for days. I keep talking and he keeps listening, saying very little until he screws up a simple putt, which puts me three strokes ahead. Not actually caring about the game has relaxed me to the point where I'm playing pretty well. I can tell that he's not listening properly by the way that he's fussing with his shots.

'To be honest, you say you want the wife and kids and family and all that,' he says, 'but I just don't buy it.'

A pair of crows land near us, and proceed to make a racket.

'I'll prove it to you,' I say, sinking my putt. Tom's look is thunderous. I should have made sure that I missed.

'What are you going to do?' he asks. 'Send off for a mail-order bride?'

'Nope,' I say, 'I'm going to take yours.'

He laughs. 'You're welcome to her, pal.'

I walk towards him, kicking up dew as I go, my club slung over my shoulder.

'I'm serious,' I say.

'Yeah, right.'

'You know what? I'll say it again – I'm serious.'

He gives me a quizzical look.

'What are you talking about?'

'We swap lives,' I say. I've come close for this bit. I put my hand on his shoulder, so he has to pay attention. Those fucking crows won't give it a rest.

'You get my life for a fortnight, I get yours. I've got holiday due. Why disappear to Thailand to hit on Swedish students, when I can become a whole new man?'

He swivels his shoulders, walks off and putts wildly.

'You're not serious,' he says. It's a prompt. He wants to know more.

'I'm serious,' I say, picking my ball out of the hole.

'I mean it's insane, there's no way ... '

'You get my life of nymphomaniac party girls, CIA-grade marijuana and non-stop glamour, and I get your life of sexual abstinence and soul-crushing drudgery. Deal?'

He laughs. 'Well, if you put it like that ... '

'Tom, I *am* serious,' I say. 'We both need a change, to take a walk on the other side to see if it's all that it's cracked up to be. I'm offering you something here, bro, that most men in your situation would jump at. I've got a pass for you – a pass to doing whatever the fuck you want for two weeks.'

He puffs out his cheeks.

'Come on, man. Where's your spirit of adventure? Don't tell me the idea doesn't appeal to you. We swap clothes, you get a haircut, tell me what to sing in the shower, whether I put on my pants before my socks ... We're twins, for Chrissakes. Identical in every way except for my weakness for alcopops and belief that the only talent a barmaid needs it to be able to knot a T-shirt underneath her breasts.'

Tom sighs. 'This is fucking insane,' he says.

'I'll pay off all your credit cards,' I offer. He gives me a look of pity.

'You think that I'd take part in your bizarre experiment for money?'

'Maybe.'

He gives me another filthy look before bursting out laughing.

'Full English?' he asks before tossing his club back towards the parkie's shed.

We sit in the café amongst the mums and Eastern European nannies and work our way through plates of delicious, hot cholesterol. We chat about being kids, which we haven't done for ages, flick through the sports section of a discarded super, soaraway *Sun*, scope a couple of the nannies. And then I notice something: we've both built bacon sarnies. The bacon and bread has come separately, but we've put them together, squirted on a bit of brown sauce. Maybe my life swap idea isn't so totally far-fetched. I decide to go for broke.

Tom gives me a confused look. 'I thought you were pissed when you brought it up at the strip club,' he says suspiciously.

'I've never been more serious,' I say. 'We're in an amazing . . . a *unique* position to figure out a lot of stuff. Don't you see that? Do you know how many people would, would . . . *kill* to be able to do this? You get two weeks' holiday, get your head together and realise how fucking good you actually have it. I get time out from the lunacy. A chance to step off the merry-go-round, and get my hands dirty, instead of all the bullshit I'm surrounded by.'

'So you want me to leave my wife and kids, move into your place and . . . what?'

'Do whatever the fuck you want. You're always complaining that you've got no time to do anything. I'm giving you two weeks to do whatever the hell it is that you're not able to do.'

'And you? What revelations are you expecting?'

It was a good question. I have no idea what I'm expecting, it just seems that the experience will make me somehow . . . better. I want to know whether being part of a family will inject meaning into my life in the way that working in paediatrics at Calcutta General would, or whether I'm clinging onto the idea of the wife and two point four kids mistakenly, a deluded Japanese soldier living on a remote Pacific island, still fighting a war that everyone else has given up on.

The bottom line is this: I have absolutely no idea what it means to have any concerns other than my own needs or agenda. Somehow this situation is no longer desirable. I've seen the exhausted dads, sleep-walking pushchairs around town, the cracked mums rhapsodising at dinner parties about how Calpol has changed their lives, and I know that I can't trust any of them. Their pitch is too self-aware and affected to be about anyone or anything else other than themselves. They're conditioned to tell everyone and anyone that having kids is the ultimate life experience, the sole thing that has brought meaning to their lives. Which would explain why they underpay a Czech teenager whose surname they can't even spell to watch over their little darling while they spend the evening evangelising about parenthood over several bottles of Pinot Grigio and other A-class refreshment. You know the kind, the parents who have photos of their adorable kids all over their desk, but linger at work later than they need so that Sneja or Ana or Tanja or whatever au pair is currently occupying their back room can deal with the bedtime meltdown. They aren't to be trusted.

Then there's the other type: the Toms of this world, who clearly love their kids but are now so hopelessly off track and overloaded by responsibility that they can no longer look upon their lives with anything like enthusiasm. Bewildered, they've lost all sight of themselves participating in their own lives, hoping just to muddle through, that answers lie somewhere as long as they can hang in there long enough to uncover them.

What I'm offering Tom is an opportunity to do just that. If he agrees, he might save me as well. Let's face it, it's either that or we desperately need the help of an élite reality TV multitasking strike force.

'Just think about it,' I ask him.

He nods, eyeing someone else's bacon sandwich.

9

Tom

I never thought that I would be the kind of man who enjoyed a morning's golf, and I was right: given the choice between demolishing a full English or pitch and putt I'll take the double sausage and a slice every time. An hour later the delicious pork, egg, beans and fried bread squat heavily in my stomach while my mind turns over Sean's regurgitation of his life-swap bombshell. Opening the front door of the house I'm relieved to get back to the drudgery that's come to fill my day. When he remade his case, or – as this is Sean – I should say, his pitch, about our swapping lives, I could feel the itch that he needed to scratch: a single on the brink of forty jammed in a soulless yuppie rut wants to sample family life in order to jolt himself from an existence of frivolous selfishness and find deeper purpose in life.

His motivation I understand, but the broader context is trickier to grasp. For instance, if Sara and I were the kind of couple who might go away for a dirty weekend to some posh country hotel, we would leave the kids in the care of family or friends. Chances are, we'd leave them with Jessica, Sara's oldest friend, and her husband Kamran. The kids have stayed with them before, messing about with their mildly unhinged tomboy daughters, and viewing their parents' absence as a treat rather than abandonment. Second on the list would be Sara's brother, Jay, and his wife. They don't have kids, nor do they appear to have any interest in having their own, but they're great with ours, even though their over-indulgence of the boys always precedes a mild impatience to hand them back. Then there are several school parents and Sara's parents, and our cousin Geoff and his kids who have moved out to Norfolk to open a gastro pub . . .

So Sean might not make the top-ten list, or even the top-twenty . . . But if there was some kind of a bio attack on London and Sara and I couldn't get home to the boys and Sean happened to be in the neighbourhood I might just – *just* – contemplate his being in sole charge of them until the hot zone has been cooled down, or whatever it is happens to hot zones.

It's not that I necessarily think of Sean negatively in this context – the boys adore him and I have no doubt about his ability to protect and nurture them in every way, although I'm keen for them to avoid meeting women who work as 'dancers' for a few years yet. It just wouldn't *occur* to me, in the way that I wouldn't think to use salad tongs to paint the kitchen ceiling. I remember what Sara talked about at the weekend, how she was worried about Sean and how she thought that he was 'reaching out'. Maybe it was female intuition, maybe it was *Trisha*-style psychobabble, but somehow she put her finger on it, predicting Sean's need to get back on the straight and narrow, reading his internalised cirri and cumuli like a weatherman evaluating foreboding storm clouds. But gaining perspective by playing the role of a burdened brother for a couple of weeks . . . that's extreme. There's no denying it. It's like joining the army just to see what wearing boots is like.

Yet when I consider it from an entirely selfish point of view (which Sean has urged me to do) I can't think of many negatives. I get time off to do as much or as little as I want (I prefer the little option), recharge my batteries, while Sean cares for my family. I can monitor the situation closely and intervene at any moment to ensure that Sean isn't going to screw the whole thing up. He's asked for a cast-iron, no-backing-out two weeks in our new roles, but I reckon I can terminate if there is the slightest hint of danger or discovery (and it wouldn't surprise me if he bails after a few days anyway). I can be an observer of my own life, able to correct the mistakes that only detachment and distance can offer. I think of the number of parents I know who skip off for work trips and long weekends leaving their precious little darlings in the hands of an Aussie twenty-something wearing an 'I

Couldn't Give A XXX' T-shirt. Why shouldn't I briefly entrust my wife and kids to my own brother?

Sara is another matter. There is no way that Sean and I can pull the wool over her eyes for even a short period of time. Sara is too observant and sharp to be deceived, and the dire consequences of detection are not even worth considering. I will have to stand firm with Sean on this one – he can have his fortnight as a burdened father of two, but the spousal beat-downs that serve as our relationship will have to happen at a distance. Sean and I might be physically identical to the extent that Sara has, on occasion, confused the two of us, but married life is (sometimes) as intimate as it gets, and I'm not convinced that Sean's domestic endeavours will bear close scrutiny. Such is the level of assistance to which Sean has grown accustomed, that we're talking about a man who last cleaned a bathroom to raise money for Live Aid.

We need to be strategic. Sara is due to go to Liverpool for a trial in a couple of weeks. It's a two-week deal – she's using the weekend in the middle to go and visit an old college pal who's moved up to the Lake District to practise as a GP. If Sean and I swap over on the Saturday it means that Sean and Sara will only be together in the house for a single night. The rest of the fortnight it'll be just Sean and the boys, with yours truly in the background. Sara will be in phone contact, which, as long as I coach him, I'm sure Sean can handle. I will be reinstalled as master of my own domain before Sara returns.

My idea is to let Sean have one night with Sara as what marketers call a 'sampling exercise'. In the same way that you can't really claim to have experienced Paris unless you've seen the Eiffel Tower, Sara's total absence would render the whole thing imperfect. Even at my most paranoid I have to admit that Sean blundering his way through a single night with Sara in the house has an appeal. If he screws up or annoys her she'll just put it down to a hangover or some distraction. On the average weekend I am no stranger to either. Conversely, there's no question that I'd like to dip my toe in Sean's work life, discover whether it's all I imagine it, to decipher the strange alchemy that channels money and success to him in impressive measures.

And the boys. Well, they probably wouldn't notice if I decided to swap lives with Saddam Hussein. As long as Sean can keep them fed and ensures that nothing calamitous happens to the electronics in the living room, then I am one hundred per cent sure that they will be oblivious to the whole thing, which is a bit sad, but wholly fortuitous. Two divisions of Republican Guard could march through the living room and the boys wouldn't comment unless the Pop Tarts ran out.

The next day the boys head off to school and I get the Tube over to Sean's office. He meets me in a Starbucks round the corner where he orders a coffee that costs more than some people earn in a week. I can tell that he's itching to hear my answer. I look glum, string him along a bit.

'Well?' he asks, unable to wait any longer.

'I'll do it,' I say.

He smiles, stirring his coffee. He doesn't say anything, savouring the moment.

'But no Sara.'

He stops stirring. 'No Sara?'

'It's too risky,' I say. 'There's no way she'll buy it. She's going away in a couple of weeks. We'll do it then.'

'Tom, I think that you're underestimating me . . . '

'Maybe I am, but I can't do it any other way. There's too much at stake for me. If Sara suspects anything, even for a moment, then I'm dead meat. Remember, she's smarter than both of us.'

'Well, if it's a deal breaker . . . '

'It is.'

Sean takes a sip of his drink.

'OK,' he says. 'We're on.'

'She's going away on a Sunday. We swap on the Saturday. You get one night with her, just so you get the full flavour, but you have to make an excuse not to sleep in the same room. Claim that you've got a cold and you don't want to pass it on to her. Say you've got the shits and you're going to be up and down in the night and you don't want to disturb her as she needs her sleep for the trial. Stay up late and claim that you fell asleep on the sofa. Actually, I don't care what you say. You've just got to agree to do it.'

'All right, all right . . . ' says Sean. 'I am a gentleman, after all.'

I can see that he's excited. He wipes the palms of his hands on his pinstripe-covered thighs.

'But how will you know if I don't?' he asks mischievously.

I raise my eyebrows. *That's not right.*

He puts his hands up.

'Out of order. I know,' he says. 'Relax, I get it. I'll kip on the sofa, no problem. This is going to be fucking great.'

I smile and wonder if it's possible to sleep for three hundred and thirty-six hours consecutively.

So the coaching begins. We meet in the evenings, have a couple of beers, and Sean tries to commit the family routine to memory. I have secured further assurances to the effect that, if the exchange is to have any meaning whatsoever, he has to fully commit to the humdrum, the exhausting and the pointless. Crucially, he has to develop an instinctive knowledge of the Family Schedule. After all, he will have no CrackBerry to make notes on; he will be armed solely with my five-year-old mobile with its archaic Nokia ring. This is just one of many humiliations he will face in his temporary life as Tom Cunningham.

'One more time,' I insist.

Sean rolls his eyes and mock slumps against the counter.

'OK,' he says, 'Seven o'clock, get up. Wake up the kids. Make sure they get dressed and then bully them downstairs for breakfast. I feed Patrick Shreddies and Michael Rice Krispies. Michael doesn't like much milk. They both have apple juice to drink and might ask for a cuppa as well. Then they have toast: they both have jam, but Michael has no butter.'

I exhale sharply with exasperation.

'Come on, man – focus. Patrick has no butter.'

'OK, OK . . . I then make coffee for Sara and myself. Sara takes soy milk. She'll come down around seven thirty and will then oversee the kids while I have a shower.'

'You missed something,' I prompt him.

'She'll turn the radio from Radio 1 to 4?'

'Not that. I want to hear that you'll put the rubbish in the bins out front.'

'Damn.'

I can see that Sean is frustrated. This is an entirely new world to him.

'OK, keep going.'

'Michael's rucksack is Chelsea and Patrick's is Spider Man . . . '

'Good, good . . . '

'And they need lunch prepared every day except Fridays.'

'I don't expect you to remember the lunch menu. I can't myself. So either go for a classic cheese and tomato or tuna salad thing, or do what I do and say to Sara, "What do you think I should get the boys for lunch?" She'll be annoyed, but she'll give you an answer. It'll be consistent with my behaviour.'

'But she won't be here,' says Sean.

'You're right, but I want to get you in the zone, all right? Stick with tuna, ham or cheese. But not together. OK, so what's the best route for collecting the boys from swimming club?'

'Avoid Kilburn High Road at all costs.'

'Get in!' I say.

'Getting back to the morning . . . ' Sean continues. 'The boys get on the bus. I tidy the breakfast stuff, clear up the house, get the shopping . . . Jesus, this is going to be tedious . . . '

'Hey, this is my life you're talking about.'

'Correction: masturbate furiously for several hours while pretending to look for work.'

'Now you're getting it . . . ' I laugh. 'All right, listen. I know that a lot of this is irrelevant if Sara's going to be away, but you've got to have all the details in your head if you're going to sample the full delights of family life. OK, rapid-fire round: what's Sara's beverage of choice in the evenings?'

'Green tea,' says Sean confidently. 'She'll drink two or three in an evening.'

'Who's got control of the remote?'

'She has, although mostly she potters around while you watch Sky Sport.'

'Name three recent films that she has yet to see that she's asked you to pick up from the video shop.'

'Shit,' says Sean, exasperated. 'I know this . . . Sorry, man. I'm blanking.'

'All right, all right, we'll come back to it. Who, generally, goes to bed first?'

'She does. Around ten thirty, eleven. You get major brownie points if you nip upstairs and run her a bath beforehand.'

'I'd also like you to note that a hot bath makes her sleepy, and this limits the likelihood of her being in the mood,' I say firmly.

'Got it,' says Sean, nodding.

'It's the unspoken rule that you "drop a deuce", as they say, in which bathroom?'

'Downstairs, and light the scented candle afterwards.'

'Correct,' I say, pleased by his attention to detail.

'The dishwasher. Generally speaking, who does what?'

'You pack. She unpacks.'

'Good. And for a bonus point, what is Sara's preferred bedtime snack?'

Sean thinks for a moment, tilting his head to the side and scratching it. I'm feeling pretty proud of Sean, who appears to be taking the preparation seriously. This bodes well.

'Got it,' he beams. 'My penis!'

This sort of ruins it, to be honest.

10
Sean

When Tom comes out of the bathroom with a towel wrapped around his waist and offers me a pile of his just-worn clothes, I'm not happy to see that, on the very top, are his still-warm underpants.

I look at him quizzically.

'Go on then,' he says, pushing the clothes towards me.

'You expect me to put *those* on?' I say, nodding at the pants.

'Well, what kind of pants are *you* wearing?' he demands. Silly question. Calvin Klein are my intimates of choice. I show him the waistband.

'We can't let Sara see those,' he continues. 'I'm strictly an M&S man.'

'Please tell me that Sara doesn't buy your underwear for you,' I prod.

He ignores the question, walks back to the bedroom and returns with a clean but off-white pair, and throws them at me.

'Y-fronts!' I burst out laughing. 'They from the Boer War?'

'Sssssh! You'll wake the boys!' he says, putting his index finger to his lips. 'Sean, you're going to have to take the rough with the smooth this week – first lesson in being Tom: learn to love the Y-front.'

'All right,' I concede. 'As long as I don't have to put my boys where your boys have been.'

I pick up Tom's warm pants at the waistband, fling them in his face and leg it to the bathroom. I pull on his outfit, which consists of an old Carrhart T-shirt and a beaten-up pair of 501s. I ruffle my hair a little before examining myself in the mirror for a moment and Tom stares

84

back at me. I take a deep breath. There's still time to back out, to tell Tom – who has far more to lose than I do – that what we're doing is deluded.

But I don't. I just breathe deeply, stare in the mirror, and tell myself that this was my idea, what I wanted all along. I've heard stories about actors who 'find' their character once they put on their costume, and now I understand the luvvie mumbo-jumbo. I feel like Tom, with his worries and responsibilities and disappointment. I even smell like him. The boys' toothbrushes are propped up in a glass on the sink. Seeing them gives me pause: the fact that he's entrusted me with his family is daunting. Be careful what you wish for, they say. Well, I got it, and I've got two weeks to make it work. I open the bathroom door and hand my clothes to my brother in order for him to make his own leap of faith.

We stand there, the two of us, and I wonder whether he might be having second thoughts too.

Tom blows his cheeks out nervously.

'I dunno,' he says.

'It'll be OK.' I put my hand on his shoulder. 'You don't have to do anything you don't want to.'

'Is that what you say to all the girls?' he says. He picks up a framed photo of Sara and the boys and smiles.

'That trip to LegoLand was a bloody disaster,' he says, lost in thought. Then he fixes his gaze on me, concentrating hard. 'I can't lose them. That's my worst fear, you know that.'

'I know,' I say.

'I just don't know,' he says. 'I just don't know . . .'

I wait for him to get it out of his system. It's natural that he's having last-minute jitters.

'The boys,' he says finally. 'You will take care of them, won't you?' Again, there's a nuts-and-bolts edge to his voice.

'Of course,' I reply. 'I promise.'

'Right then,' he says.

I follow him downstairs. We've swapped wallets and mobiles. I'm literally standing in another man's shoes, in another man's house. We shake hands and he turns to leave.

'One other thing,' I say. 'The Range Rover – you will take care of it, won't you?'

'Let's roll,' he says with a wink, and it feels like we're fourteen again and up to no good. I'm momentarily hit by a wave of sentimentality, like I need to protect Tom from something. I've always assumed he's my little brother, although neither of us knows for sure. Except, of course, he isn't a kid brother any more; he's a thirty-nine-year-old man about to perpetrate a bizarre fraud on his wife and kids.

He walks out of the house, closing the door quietly behind him. I saunter into the living room and sit down on the sofa, not quite sure what to do. It's a total reflex action, like I've come round for a visit and I'm waiting for Tom or Sara to bring me a cuppa. I hear him start the engine of the Range Rover. There's a pause before he guns it hard. He keeps gunning it, before peeling up the road, tyres screeching. *Bastard.*

I mooch around the house, examining things I've looked at dozens of times: framed photos of Tom and Sara at various times in their relationship, photos of the boys as grotesque but adored babies, group shots at family occasions and on holiday with friends. To the outsider it doesn't get any better than that. I think about my house, there's not a single photo of anyone that I know. Every photograph on my walls has been bought from a gallery, not captured, processed, selected and lovingly placed in a frame from Habitat.

I wander into the kitchen. Tom reckons that Sara will be back around elevenish. She's gone all the way down to the Ritzy in Brixton with a friend to see some French art-house movie. Sounds like a fun night out. I stack the dishwasher and clear the kitchen table, try to keep myself busy, to get into some kind of groove so that I don't feel like an interloper.

Then it occurs to me that I don't think that I've ever been in Tom and Sara's bedroom. This is my first moment of panic. How the hell am I supposed to pull this off if I don't even know which side of the bed Tom sleeps on? I go upstairs and push the door open, and there it is, the marital bed. The room is cool. There's a window open, which I decide to leave, in case it's something that Sara prefers. I reach under one of the pillows and pull out a pair of pyjama bottoms. That's that then. Sean sleeps on the right side of the bed. I have a moment where I

86

want to reach under Sara's pillow and check out her nightwear, but decide that this is just too creepy.

I walk over to the chest of drawers and slide open a couple. The first one contains Sara's underwear. I close it quickly, as if someone is watching me. I work my way down and eventually find Tom's stuff, a chamber of horrors consisting of clothes he used to wear that were trendy once, clothes that are still trendy but he's now too old to wear, and clothes that have never been trendy, the only possible use for which is cleaning the car. This is not encouraging. His underwear and sock drawer bears out my apprehension. Has Tom just not got round to replacing the old stuff? Does he not realise that every dosser on Charing Cross Road would reject his smalls? Has he just given up? It's absolutely baffling.

I pause for a moment. I'm sure that there was a noise . . . There it is again. One of the boys is coughing. I realise now that it's been going on for some time; it's just that my hearing isn't accustomed to scanning for such eventualities. It's Patrick. The cough sounds quite nasty, the kind that'll keep him up. I need to do something about this. In the bathroom I rummage through the medicine cupboard and find a bottle of kids' cough syrup. I check that it's age appropriate (how diligent am I?) and sneak into his bedroom. He stirs, but just rolls over and coughs again. Amazing – kids cough in their sleep. I sit him up. He's in a strange half-awake/half-asleep state in which he can hear what I'm saying, and do what I ask, without actually being conscious, like me on a Monday morning.

Patrick swallows the medicine and I tiptoe out of his room, close the door and punch the air. I feel like doing a victory lap of the house. It's my first real test and I *kill* it. I take the teaspoon back downstairs, stack the dishwasher, wipe up around the kitchen and begin to feel more settled. Maybe I can handle this after all. I mean, how hard was that? OK, so the house and boys feel controllable, but what about Sara? I look at my watch. It's ten-thirty. She'll be back in a half-hour. I decide that it's a good idea to get ready for bed before she gets back so there's no awkward nudity.

I return to the bathroom and take a quick shower. Then I encounter another obstacle: I investigate Tom's side of the cabinet and discover that there's no moisturiser. I decide to steal some from Sara, and hope that she won't notice. I feel pretty sure that this is the kind of thing that women detect instantly, so I remind myself to buy some for the rest of the week while she's not around. I go to brush my teeth. Tom's toothbrush is dog-eared and he has no floss. I'm rummaging through Sara's side of the cabinet hoping that she's got some of the mint-flavoured stuff when I sense a presence behind me. I look in the mirror to discover that Sara is standing in the doorway. She's leaning on the doorframe, arms folded, smirking at me. I wonder how long she's been there.

'Lost something?' she asks.

Could I feel any guiltier?

'Um, just looking for some floss,' I say.

'Floss?'

'Yes, floss. I must have run out.'

Sara laughs. I've been exposed. Jesus.

'Maybe the reason that you've run out is that you've never bought any.'

'Um, probably.'

'Well, don't let me discourage you,' she says, stepping forward and pulling some out of the cupboard and handing it to me. Mint flavour! Sara moves towards the mirror and examines herself.

'You see, that's the difference between men and women,' she says offhandedly. 'Men would rather forage for something than actually ensure that it's there.'

'Yeah,' I say, spitting post-floss blood in the sink. 'How was the film?'

'Depressing,' she says.

'Good times!' I say.

'It's not a joke, Tom,' she sighs. 'We're so lucky to be born in this country. In Thailand kids the boys' ages are being pimped out to fat, middle-aged Austrians. It's just awful.'

'Yeah, Austrians. It doesn't get worse than that.'

'Tom, can you just give it a rest, please?'

She's annoyed. Great. Good work, Sean. Tom would have probably behaved in exactly the same way. I reckon consistency is the key to avoiding detection, so there's an upside to Sara's irritation.

I leave her to it, wanting to get into the bedroom and change before she gets out of the bathroom. I'm looking for a pair of Tom's pyjamas, when I hear her calling.

'Noodles!'

Noodles?

'Noodles!'

It's a harsh whisper. She wants to get my attention, but doesn't want to wake the boys. 'Noodles' must be some kind of pet name she has for Tom. Fantastic! Valuable information for future mockery on my first night. I go back to the bathroom and push the door open and – Jesus – she's standing there naked. I recoil and step back into the hallway so that I can't see her.

'Can you be a love and get me a towel out of the airing cupboard, please?' she asks.

I trot along the landing and fish one out for her. When I return I stick my hand round the door to give it to her, so that I don't have to get an eyeful again. I leg it back to the bedroom determined to get out of there. I jump into Tom's pyjamas and a T-shirt, and head downstairs with a blanket. Bugger. I need to explain this to Sara. I come back up. When I return she's already in bed reading. She looks up from her book and pats the spot where I should be.

'I need to go downstairs for a while,' I explain.

'What's the matter?' she asks in what, to me, appears to be a suspicious tone.

'It's a weird one,' I explain. 'Earlier on I sat down awkwardly and, um, well I sat on my right nut, and it's still hurting. I need to walk it off.'

Sara looks at me like I'm completely insane. And maybe I am. Of all the excuses not to get into bed, I choose this one.

'Sounds odd, doesn't it?' I say in the most self-deprecating way I can.

I try to laugh it off. She doesn't appear to be having it.

'You see, no matter how little men know about women's bodies,' I continue, 'women know less about the, um, rope and tackle than we know about, say, the uterus and, um, the womb.'

'They're the same thing, Tom.'

'Which sort of proves my point.'

'Actually, it doesn't, but have it your way. You go and "walk it off."'

I feel like I need to offer her more. 'Anyway, it's for a good reason,' I explain. 'Why would you want to know about them if you didn't possess either?'

Sara turns the light off.

'Goodnight, strange husband,' she says.

'Night,' I say, relieved to be going downstairs.

I'm thinking that I really should check my Berry when I realise that I'm not carrying one any longer. I put on the TV and watch most of *Deliverance*. The deformed hillbilly makes me think about incest, which, disturbingly, makes me think about sleeping with Sara. It's hardly the same thing, is it? There are all kinds of biological reasons that make a bit of how's your father with your sister taboo. But a quick bunk up with your brother's wife? Clearly it's wrong, but it's hardly the end of the world. Not that I'd ever really consider it.

Honestly.

With this kind of highbrow thinking occupying my mind I drift off to sleep, content that there are other human beings sleeping in the same house.

I'm woken by Sara shaking me and thrusting a cup of tea into my hands.

'Morning, handsome,' she says.

'Morning.'

'So, what happened to you last night? Plums still in one piece? Sorry, two pieces.'

'What?' I have no idea what she's talking about.

'The family jewels. Intact, are they?'

'Oh, yeah. Fine. Thanks. Suppose I must have fallen asleep. I watched *Deliverance*.'

Sara sits down on the sofa next to me, blowing on her tea to cool it.

'I love that film,' she says. 'When Burt Reynolds starts getting those hillbillies back it's fantastic.'

'Squeal like a pig,' I screech.

Patrick and Michael come walking past without acknowledging me.

'What kind of a way is that to greet your dad?' I ask. They look unimpressed. I get up from the sofa and walk into the kitchen behind them.

'Right then, who wants a full English?' I ask.

The boys look at me like I'm speaking Swahili. Sara pads into the kitchen.

'You're going to do a fry-up, are you?' she asks sceptically.

'Not for you,' I say. 'I thought that you might like to go to the gym this morning while the boys and I spend some man-time together.'

'I'll take you up on that,' says Sara approvingly and disappears upstairs.

'All right, fellas, what do you want to do today?' I ask. In unison they stare at me blankly and shrug, before grabbing some juice and leaving the room. I can see what Tom's up against. This is not going to be easy. I go upstairs to get dressed. Sara is in the bathroom, which gives me time to get dressed before she reappears. However, knowing that the boys are downstairs, she's left the door open, meaning that I can hear her having a pee. *Eeeeew.* I hum to myself to mask the sound and search for a clean pair of pants. Given that our bodies are the exact same proportions but very slightly different (Tom's gym regime being more, um, relaxed that mine) we thought it best that I should keep on a T-shirt at all times. I pull on one of Tom's sandpaper T-shirts, a jumper and a pair of pants, and I'm just putting my right foot into the leg of a pair of trousers, when Sara walks into the room. Shocked, I try and hurry myself. Disastrously, my big toe catches on the edge of the waistband and my bodyweight topples me over.

I'm lying there trouserless on Tom's bedroom floor with Sara standing over me hooting.

'Are your balls all right?' she asks.

I scramble up and whip the pants on, before retreating downstairs, relieved that she's going to Liverpool this afternoon.

Sara has laid out the boys' clothes, so I don't have any decisions to make on the outfit front. Michael is in the bathroom brushing his teeth and doing something he claims is 'washing'. Paddy is having trouble getting his socks on, however, as he's distracted by a drawing he's been doing.

'I need to finish it,' he insists.

'You can finish it later.'

'But I want to finish it now.'

'We're going out now,' I say, being as upbeat as possible, distracting him from the deadly important Incredibles portrait he's working on.

'Where are we going?' asks Michael, entering the room. There is toothpaste smeared on the side of his mouth.

'I'll tell you when we're in the car,' I say. When the company started taking off a few years ago I bought myself a management book to try and work out how the hell I was going to run things. Its central hypothesis was that all human relationships are founded on incentives. To get people to act in ways that you want them to act – whether personally, or in business – you must 'incentivise' them. I decide that this is the way that I will tackle the boys.

'No, tell me now,' says Michael.

'When we're in the car,' I say, pulling the now-dressed Paddy to his feet. 'Right, I've got something to say to you two . . . ' I pull a serious face before blurting: 'Last one downstairs is a chump!' I'm first out of Paddy's bedroom, but both boys squeeze past me in the corridor and, by the time I arrive downstairs, I have the dubious status of being a chump.

We get in the car.

'Come on, chump, tell us where we're going,' presses Michael.

'What do you want to listen to?' I ask, switching the radio from channel to channel.

'You never let us listen to the radio,' says Paddy.

'Yeah,' says Michael. *'It's dangerous while I'm driving,'* he continues, doing a rather poor imitation of Tom that sounds suspiciously like Cartman from *South Park*. *'I can't concentrate.'*

'Well, I thought that you might like to listen to something, that's all,' I say. The boys exchange a look, clearly baffled by this new development.

'Do you want a CD or the radio?'

'Radio,' they agree.

I fiddle around and find Radio 1. The Foo Fighters burst through the speakers to the cheers of the boys, and we're off down Harrow Road, with our heads nodding.

The boys forget about asking me where we're going, until I pull up next to the Westway.

'Where are we?' asks Michael.

'The Westway,' I reply.

'Duh,' he says, rolling his eyes.

'We're going climbing,' says Paddy suspiciously, pointing to a grey wall about a hundred yards away that has been made to look like a cliff face in Snowdonia, other than it having brightly coloured grips for hands and feet. I've driven past the place hundreds of times and never visited. I'm banking that it's the perfect place for some father–son bonding.

'That's right,' I say. 'It's you versus gravity.'

'Look,' says Michael, standing still as Paddy and I walk towards the sports centre, 'I'm not sure that I want to do this.'

Paddy immediately starts squawking like a chicken and strutting around with his hands tucked into his armpits. I walk back to Michael and put my arm around him.

'What's the matter?' I ask.

'I don't think that I'm going to like it,' he says.

'Well, how will you know until you try?' I ask.

'I just know.'

'Look, I know that it might not seem like your kind of thing, but just give it a go, OK?' I say. 'If you don't like it you can stop.'

'I dunno, I really—'

'Michael, I'm going to come up with you,' I say, putting my arm over his shoulder. 'The second you want to stop I'll get you down, OK?'

'OK,' he says reluctantly, and slouches into the sports centre.

We meet the instructor, a young bloke from Derbyshire with the weathered face of a wino who's fallen asleep in the park on an August afternoon, and long, blond dreads. He hands the three of us helmets and helps us into safety harnesses. Michael's lack of enthusiasm has made me wonder whether bringing them here really was a good idea – maybe they're going to loathe the experience. But, as Michael slips on his helmet, he turns and smiles as me.

'Wicked,' he says. I should have known it: any activity involving red-blooded equipment and crash helmets is bound to stir their interest. Within minutes they're out on the wall, hauling themselves up ever more challenging climbs and mocking me for my own inability to keep up. I join Michael at the top of one of the faces.

'You like it?' I ask him, catching my breath. He doesn't answer. He just says, 'Watch this!' and abseils back down. I watch him land safely and wave to me. On the other side Paddy the fearless has just mastered a climb that involves him negotiating a semi-horizontal piece of fake mountain. He ignores his brother and me, concentrating hard on the task in hand.

Before I know it, the lesson is over, we've returned our gear and I'm sitting in the sports centre café doling out pound coins so that the boys can get some snacks from the vending machines.

'So, what did you think?' I ask.

'Wicked!' comes the reply between mouthfuls of Walkers crisps and Sprite.

'Yeah, I'm not bothered about the climbing,' says Michael, 'but the abseiling is dope.'

'I like the climbing,' says Paddy, emptying the crumbs from a crisp packet into his mouth. 'Did you see me do that difficult bit at the end?'

'Yeah,' I said. 'That looks hard.'

'It is,' says Paddy nonchalantly.

'So, what's your prediction for today then, Mr Chump?' demands Michael.

'Two–nil Chelsea,' says Paddy, folding his crisp packet into halves until it's an immovable lump.

Of course. Chelsea are playing Liverpool today.

'When are you going to take us, Dad?' asks Paddy. 'It's not fair. Just because you hate Chelsea.' I'd forgotten about this. Tom, a lifelong QPR supporter, refuses to take the boys to Stamford Bridge.

'"Hate" is too strong a word,' I say, taking the opportunity to dole out a parenting lesson. 'Let's just say that I'm disinclined towards Chelsea, and with good reason, may I add. Now, wait here, I'm just going to the toilet.'

I walk up the corridor until I'm out of earshot and make a couple of calls. A business associate, Kyriakos, has access to a corporate box. He ums and ahs theatrically for a few moments before promising me

94

three seats. He lets me know that this is going to cost me dear further down the line, but I'm not worried about that. I'm just thrilled to be able to take the boys. I herd them back in the car and we go to pick up a ready-roasted chicken and some salad.

'I think that one looks good,' says Paddy, looking at the rack of roasted poultry.

'How about that one?' I ask, pointing to the one next to it.

'No,' says Paddy, 'I think it looks sad.'

'It's a roasted chicken – how can it look sad?' I ask.

'Well, you'd be pretty bloody sad if it was you,' says Michael. I'm not sure how the word bloody scores on the acceptable/unacceptable profanity scale, but I let it go.

'Right, what else do we need?' I say to myself.

'Salad, chump,' says Paddy helpfully. 'Can we have a beetroot salad as well as a green one?'

'Yeah,' I say, surprised that he likes beetroot. Paddy drifts off to look at the lobster tank.

'Why does he like beetroot so much?' I ask Michael, mystified.

'Because it turns his poo red,' replies Michael matter-of-factly. I turn to see if Michael is serious but he's straying elsewhere too. From the cast of his face I think that he's not joking.

Lunch is on the table at twelve thirty on the dot.

'Very impressive,' says Sara. She uncorks a bottle of wine and pours a couple of glasses.

'Thanks,' I say, as she passes one to me.

'No – thank *you*,' she says. 'I've had a really relaxing morning. Just what I needed.'

'So, are you going to win?' I ask.

'Of course we're going to win,' she says with a smile. 'I wouldn't be going up there otherwise.'

'Good for you.'

'Good for me, bad for them,' she laughs. 'Look, we'd better eat. I've got a taxi coming in a bit.'

We all sit and eat and it's exactly how I imagine family life might be: there's banter and laughter and jokes and I can't help wondering if I might have somehow got myself mixed up in an episode of *The*

Waltons, albeit one with parents who use birth control and offer less faith-based moral guidance.

'So, what do you want to do this afternoon?' I ask the boys.

'I dunno,' says Michael. 'Go the park?'

'What about a film?' asks Paddy enthusiastically. 'It is the weekend, after all.'

I suck on a chicken leg nonchalantly. 'Because I was just wondering if you might want to go to the Chelsea game.'

The boys look at me.

'Very funny,' says Michael drily.

'We'd go if you'd take us,' says Paddy. 'But you won't, so we're waiting for Uncle Sean to get some tickets.'

'I've got tickets,' I say.

'No you haven't,' says Michael. His eyes are narrow with disbelief.

'Yes, I have.'

'Where are they then?' asks Paddy.

'We've got to pick them up at the ground.'

Sara gives me a look.

'Have you really got tickets?' she asks. I can tell that, should this be a joke, I would be in Big Trouble. I nod my head.

'Wicked!' says Michael.

'Thanks, Dad!' shouts Paddy, punching the air.

And Sara, a woman who's just about to prosecute a gang of Nigerian drug dealers, squeals with delight and stamps her feet. I didn't even know that she liked football. The phone rings, her cab is outside. The boys and I escort her to the taxi, carrying her bags. The boys hug her and we embrace and I feel a sadness come over me. It's like I'm actually saying goodbye to my wife.

'Be good, boys,' she shouts to the boys, before leaning in close to me and whispering in my ear, 'I might have time to do some underwear shopping while I'm away . . . '

I smile a big, foolish, spoiled husband grin and hope that Tom will get the full benefit of this promise. And then she's gone, and it's just me and the boys and Chelsea FC. And, frankly, I don't think they could be happier. I wish that they'd stop calling me 'chump' though.

*

96

It's nearly dark when we get back, but the boys are still fired up from the game, so I take them to blow off some steam in the playground. I'm chasing Patrick across the monkey bars when I notice that there's a kid in trouble. He's hanging by his legs, but can't work out how to get back up. He's not making a fuss, but I can tell that he's in distress. I grab him and help him down and he runs off. Moments later, a woman approaches me. She's probably mid-thirties with straight, jet-black hair tied back loosely, high cheekbones and dark eyes.

Hello.

I'm hanging on the monkey bars like an orang-utan. I should just drop off so that we can talk like adults, but I'm up here now and letting go would draw even more attention to my clinging on to a children's play apparatus with the determination of an asylum seeker hidden beneath the Eurostar. I decide to tough it out, *as if nothing unusual is happening.*

'Hi,' I say, with an expression that I hope conveys affability. This doesn't appear to register with her. She glares back at me.

'You do realise that this equipment is meant for kids, don't you?' she says firmly. Her English is perfect, but she has an accent I can't place. I remain frozen by the sheer presence of this life force. For the first time in as long as I can remember I can't find the requisite words to fill the moment.

'I suppose I shouldn't be throwing my weight around like some heavyweight clown,' I announce, chuckling at my own wit.

Tumbleweed.

A heavyweight clown? Where the hell did I get that? I suppose it's better than a lightweight clown, or an arse clown . . . Or is it? I slowly let my legs extend downwards until my feet are touching the rubberised surface – so gentle on children's skulls! – below.

We both hesitate, as if the conversation has become too loaded. It's like the lull after a wave has crashed on the shore and the sand fizzes with hissing water. We wait for the next thing to happen.

'I just wanted to thank you,' she says, revealing a manner that I take to be the version without artifice.

'What for?' I ask.

'Just now,' she says, gesturing to the boy who had been struggling. 'You helped Matthew off the bars.'

'Oh, no problem,' I reply.

'He could have banged his head,' she observes.

I nod.

'You're a bit of a wind-up merchant then.' I say this as if I'm paying her a compliment, which I am.

'You could say that,' she replies, straightforwardly. 'I thought that you looked like you could take it.'

'Or that I deserved it?'

She doesn't answer. Shit. Shit. Shit. She's pulling back . . . *She's pulling back* . . .

I can hear Paddy and Michael shouting for me elsewhere in the playground. I scramble to think of something else to say that might make her stay a while.

This is what I come up with: 'Nice to meet you then.'

Pitiful.

She replies in kind and walks away with an enigmatic look that best translates as 'what a sap'. I'm left standing in the playground, wondering how on earth I managed to screw that up so badly. That kind of chance encounter is my bread and butter, for God's sake. A simple tap-in. When I conjure up a few bons mots women are drawn to me in the way that men are hypnotically drawn to building sites. As I chase Michael and Paddy I notice her gather her son and leave. I resolve to bring the boys to the park at the same time tomorrow. You never know who you might bump into.

11
Tom

What a bloody loser. I'm driving *another* car that somebody else has paid for. The Range Rover is a bit different from the Volvo: while the Volvo is like marrying the sensible girl from school, the solid, insurable bet, the Range Rover is a little more dangerous, the hottest girl in class, the one who's going out with the lad two years older and harder than you. The one who is out of your league. As I nudge the silver goliath along Kilburn Lane I glance over and notice that people in the queue for the 316 to Neasden are looking at me curiously. What they're observing is clear: a tragic figure desperate to advertise his wealth and masculinity by purchasing a chunk of muscular metal. The inference is that it was either this or I'd spend the money on pec implants. At least Sean just looks like yuppie scum.

I eventually get used to the extra horses beneath my right foot and become accustomed to my ability to nip in and out of traffic. I cross over the Harrow Road onto Ladbroke Grove with its all-terrain amalgam of public housing and million-pound trust-fund palaces. I pass the Tube station and proceed up the hill, taking a right into a street of pastel-coloured stucco-fronted houses, one of which, I still marvel, is my brother's.

I close the door to Sean's place and stand in the hallway.

It's a little unsettling. Something tells me that I shouldn't be here; all this space and expensive furniture combined with the absence of children's stickiness doesn't seem right. I shift about uneasily before responding to the situation, as any decent Briton would, and go to put the kettle on. A nice cuppa tea – that'll do me. As the element begins to warm up, the kettle makes a ticking sound. The sound of a kettle boiling? Already there's novelty in my new life. I haven't heard a kettle boil for about as long as I can remember. Not with the shouting, the fighting, the rapping, the TV and the general white noise of boys. I remember learning about the Russian T-60 tank drivers in the Second World War – the German Panzers couldn't pierce their armour with shells, so they'd gang up on them and shell them until the Russian tank crews would emerge battered and deafened onto the battlefield with their hands up. I know the bloody feeling.

I walk into the living room, grab the remote, and attempt to turn on the TV. Sean has got one of those integrated remotes that allows the household electronics to run off the same device. At our place we have four of the damn things – TV, satellite, DVD and VCR. I sat up one night attempting to programme them into a single device, but decided that it would be easier to clone a chimp butler to switch channels and platforms at my command. Having considered it carefully I think that what Microsoft should be doing, rather than worrying about seamless computing and virtual communities, is to train a chimp army that can ease our lives by mastering technology, mowing the lawn and taking out the rubbish. Some women might argue that this would make men redundant, but clearly they haven't thought through the issue of who would do the barbecuing.

The quiet in the house is getting to me. Music. That's what I need. I start looking for the stereo, opening cleverly disguised and recessed storage units that contain painfully hip books, vases, gifts deemed too appalling to re-gift (I notice a piece of the Berlin Wall that I'd bought for Sean when on holiday back in 1991 stuffed at the back), thousands of CDs (sorted by genre and alphabeticised) and a chess set.

The landing is lined with contemporary art, most of it abstract and Crayola influenced. There is a huge photograph of a naked woman pulling her red knickers aside at the top of the stairs. As it's blurred and you can't see her face properly, it's clearly art. A theme is emerging, namely the house as display cabinet, for art, music, furniture, appliances and hardware. This is confirmed on visiting Sean's study, which is an excuse to have lots of up-to-the-minute Apple products show-cased with more expensive furniture. I half expect to see price tags and sales assistants. An entire wall contains books, most of them lavish coffee-table editions. I stare at them blankly, recognising some of the names, but mostly they serve to remind me that, since leaving college, I've rarely stepped inside a museum or gallery unless under duress from Sara. We once got halfway to the Tate Modern, but then Michael threw up all over the car, stranding us on Waterloo Bridge.

I can't help but wonder how often the study gets used. It's as if Sean has felt the need to fill the room, to justify the existence of the space, rather than it being a vital home from home for his communications empire, his own Cape Canaveral.

I run my hand along that rail of Sean's suits. I can tell from the cut that most are Savile Row. As is the way with much of Sean's life, he's not really a ready-to-wear bloke. I try on a couple of the jackets and am enveloped in featherweight wool and silk engineered in a way that I'm not aware even existed. My own suits, by comparison, are a rare blend of sandpaper and cardboard. Sean's version not only feels good and moves in tandem with my body, it also furnishes my body with contours that I recognise as the province of Sean and not myself. Why bother with a 700-pound-a-year gym membership when I can get a gentleman's outfitters to take up the slack?

As with the rest of the house, the en suite looks like it's never actually been used. The bathroom, almost more than any other space in a family house, takes a real kicking. What with all that water, and soaps, shampoos, conditioners, lotions and the other fruit-based gunk that we should be slapping on pitta bread rather than massaging into our scalps. Even a pristine space can be decimated without a great deal of effort. And let's not even get into the horrors of the lavatory with two young boys, distracted by whatever Power Rangers moves they're planning, practising their aim with all the precision of Donald Rumsfeld planning a bombing raid near an Iraqi orphanage. (Although we should skirt the issue of dads deciding to have a slash 'hands free' after a few too many at the pub.) Shame on the person who desecrates Sean's limestone-and-glass retreat.

I have an overwhelming urge to run myself a bath. Rock'n'roll! Talk about letting yourself run wild – my first night off the leash and I'm thinking about jojoba bubble bath, but my thoughts of Keith Moon-style excess are arrested by the doorbell ringing. Momentarily,

I think about hiding – Sean's walk-in closet seems like a good idea. The house is too alien for me to be comfortable opening the door and interacting with a stranger in my new role as Sean. The buzzer goes again. I notice that there's a handset in the hallway. I pick it up and an image of a woman comes into focus on a small screen. It's actually inaccurate to describe her as a woman – she's more like a goddess, and a goddess that I recognise as a girl named Ellie who Sean and I bumped into a couple of years ago when we were out for a drink. This settles it – there is no way that I'm opening the door to such a creature. I would barely be capable of opening my mouth, let alone making intelligent conversation in the role of my brother. Then the buzzer goes again, more insistently this time, and I think to myself: What would Sean do? (Or, WWSD? as I begin to think of it.) Sean would, of course, open the door. Not just because there's a supreme being standing on his doorstep, but also because it's his house – the lights are on, she knows someone's here, and that person is me, or 'Sean'.

I run down the stairs and open the door. The girl smiles.

'Interrupting something, am I?'

'Sorry, I was upstairs,' I explain.

She walks in with the confidence of someone used to being in the house. She puts her bag down and turns to speak. One thing is going through my mind: this is Sean's girlfriend and she's expecting to stay the night. *Why the hell didn't he warn me?*

'You didn't get my messages, then?' she asks.

'What messages?' I say dumbly, more Tom than Sean.

She laughs.

'I'm joking, doofus. We're still in the two-month zone, remember? At least I have the courtesy to call. Can't say that I like getting those little randy texts from you, though.'

'You love it,' I say, in a Sid James growl. I have no idea where it comes from. Concerned that I've made a total arse of myself, I wait for her response. She arches an eyebrow disapprovingly, but I can tell that she does, indeed, love it, and that instinctively I've figured out the dynamic of her relationship with Sean, which appears to be a horizontal one.

'Cuppa?' I say, lamely. It's a weak safety shot after the blinding drive of my previous comment.

'Love one,' she says. 'But I can't be long, I've got to finish off this presentation.'

This is music to my ears – she's intending to leave. Thank the lord. Then it occurs to me: maybe it's a ruse. Maybe she's not intending to leave; maybe she's intending to stay until I jump her bones. Maybe this is how it works. I go through to the kitchen to make the tea. It takes me three or four attempts to locate the mugs and teabags, but I get there in the end. As I pour hot water into the mugs I notice that Ellie is dressed down in a tight T-shirt, jeans and flip-flops.

'Why are you wearing those?' I ask her, nodding at her footwear. It can't be much more than five or six degrees outside.

'Pedicure,' she explains. She extends her leg and examines her toes, tilting her foot from side to side.

'You like the colour?'

'Yeah,' I say, feigning enthusiasm. She's not buying.

'Like you give a shit!' she laughs. 'By the way, if we're on the subject of personal grooming, I like your hair a little longer. It makes you seem less, I dunno, severe I suppose. It softens you up a little.'

'Come on, you know I'm a fragile being,' I say. 'If you cut me, do I not bleed?'

'Well, now you're quoting Shakespeare, I can see that you're all heart.'

I'm beginning to relax a little. I'd even venture to say that I'm enjoying it. Amazing, really, that I can take pleasure in sitting alone in a luxury house with a goddess. She takes a slurp of tea and her tone changes a little. I get the feeling – and I'd be the first person to admit that my radar for these things is not as finely tuned as it once was – that I'm getting something of a mixed message from her. It seems that she's vaguely annoyed at me for not making a pass at her, and yet . . . I suspect that if I did make a pass at her it would not be welcomed. Fuck me, I'm out of practice.

Ellie puts down her mug on the glass coffee table. Reflexly I lean over and place a coaster underneath it, as if she's one of the boys.

'Look, it's very pleasant sitting here and drinking your Jesus Juice, or whatever you've given me,' she says, 'but I need to get that book for my presentation.'

Before I can ask her what she's talking about, she adds, 'Nice tea, by the way – usually your tea is awful, total piss.'

Result! I'm a superior tea-maker to Sean. Next stop a badge with gold stars on it and – who knows? – employee of the month. I've got dreams, you know.

'The John Lautner, remember?'

'Sorry, I'm blanking,' I say, hoping that I can busk it. Clearly not . . .

'Bloody hell, Sean, you must have been more pissed than I thought. I was telling you about that car commercial we're pitching and how they want it in a modern house in LA . . . you don't remember any of this, do you?'

I consider whether I have enough information to busk it. I can remember the name Lautner. The books are upstairs, and I dare say that they're alphabetised. WWSD? He'd take a risk . . .

'Of course I do,' I lie. 'I'll just nip upstairs and get it.'

Upstairs in the study the book is exactly where it should be. I take a quick flick through, ogling the precise lines and glass blurring the margins between inside and out. So very different to the houses that I've grown up in – those buttresses against the gloom and damp, with their thick walls and London grime stained deep in the brickwork.

Every winter Dad would climb up the ladder to clean out the gutters. Sean and I would stand at the bottom holding the creaking aluminium steady for him. Every summer we'd do it again – him up the ladder with us holding it so that he could touch up the paintwork with the runny gloss that sometimes fell in strings onto the crazy paving below. The week before he died, sucked hollow by cancer and deranged by drugs, he insisted on doing the same thing. Only this time, Sean wasn't there – it was just me holding the ladder.

Sean drifted away after Dad was diagnosed. His role before that had been central to Dad's well-being. At family functions we'd be in the middle of something and I'd look over to see Dad glancing at his watch, or staring out of the window, hopeful and hopeless as a dog missing its owner. Sara and I would do our best to jolly things along, encouraging the boys to stick around, but he never really began to enjoy himself, never saw the occasion as special until Sean showed up. Once Dad was diagnosed, Sean's bonhomie, charm and gifts seemed only to remind him of what he was going to miss and Sean withdrew, unsure as to why the jokes and stories and back-slapping weren't working any more.

When I get back, Ellie is lying on her side on Sean's sofa, her head dangling in mid-air. I put the book down on the coffee table.

'I'm knackered,' she says.

I need to steer the conversation carefully.

'Do anything interesting last night?' Jesus, I sound like a hair-dresser.

'No, not really. Just went for dinner. Ended up at Kabaret. I hate that place, but it was all right, I suppose.' She moves her hand behind her head.

I sit back down. I'm now worried again that she's thinking of staying. I don't really care what Sean would do at this point (that is entirely obvious); I just want Ellie to leave. I've done OK, I've held my own, Sean would be proud; it's time to wrap it up. She's lying on his sofa with her eyes closed and I really have no idea how to shift her and stay in character. I mean, there is absolutely no way that Sean would be trying to turf her out so that he could get his pyjamas on, warm a nice mug of Horlicks and curl up with a bit of Harry Potter. (Not, may I add, that this is my intention – I'm merely hypothesising.) How would I get the kids motivated? Well, there's, um, pleading, then there's bribery, then there's shouting. I wonder how Ellie would respond to my telling her that she can't watch *Star Wars* tomorrow unless she gets the hell out of here.

But there's still a part of me that wants to know whether I could get a result; turn up the Marvin Gaye, open a bottle of vodka, light a few scented candles, and let nature take its course. (By the way, why are women such suckers for scented candles, and where the hell did they come from? It seems that they popped up out of nowhere in the late nineties; there was no creep, no occasional sightings reaching a level of critical mass, suddenly *everybody* had them. We all woke up and the things had sprouted in our homes, like mushrooms. Sara now spends half her annual income on objects that she sets fire to.)

I look over at Ellie and a crushing sadness comes over me, knowing that, let's be honest here, I've never slept with anyone as good-looking as her.

Where in my regular life would I meet a girl like Ellie? I have no idea where women like her are even kept. In some glass case that mustn't be opened unless it's an extreme emergency? A romantic version of a heart defibrillator? And who's to say, even if I did manage to close the deal with her, that I could even consider it a victory? Ellie would simply think that she's having sex with Sean (although, obviously it will be the best sex with Sean that she's ever had), which is not the case so, technically, I'm actually considering something unsavoury that might even be illegal, let alone unethical . . . Jesus.

'I need to go,' she says. She doesn't move, her eyes are still closed.

It's a huge relief that my ability to seduce this woman is absolutely zero.

'Got much to do?'

'Quite a bit. Probably another couple of hours.'

'You like it?'

'What do you mean?' She rolls back onto her side and props her head on her hand.

'You know. Your job, working late, responsibility . . . '

'That's a strange question coming from you.'

'Well, you know, I've never asked before.'

'Yeah, I do. Don't get me wrong. I'd walk away tomorrow if I won the Lottery, but I like it. I mean it's something that I'd be interested in anyway, so making a living out of it is nice.' She stretches along the entire length of her body, pointing her toes at me so I can see the sinews in her feet. 'It's funny how you end up somewhere and it's not really by intention, it just sort of happens. After art school I could have ended up doing loads of different things but I got offered a job and I took it because it was a job, not because it was graphic design. And now look at me – I'm a graphic designer. That's what I tell people: "I'm a graphic designer." And I don't even really know what that means any more. I just think of it as an answer to a question. The rest of it, the getting out of bed, dealing with clients, finding solutions to whatever it is that I'm working on, the thought that goes into it. I suppose it's just what happens when it's light.'

'There's no grand plan?' I say. I'm enjoying guiding the conversation. The intimacy is – and this might seem a little sad – titillating.

'C'mon, Sean, you know me.' She laughs. 'There's no grand plan, never was, never will be. I just don't think like that.'

She appears to have settled in. I glance at my watch. It's eleven thirty. The darkest recess of the night for me, but surely just cocktail hour for Sean. I've no idea what kind of hours Ellie keeps, but I assume that, given it's a Saturday night, she'll be up for quite some time yet. I wonder if I need to take drastic action to scare her off. Maybe I should ask for a lock of her hair, tell that that I need it for my collection.

'I saw that,' she says.

'What?'

'You glancing at your watch. You tired?'

Oh shit. Does that mean 'are you tired because, if so, I'll leave'? Or 'are you tired because, if so, we can go up to bed and I'll help you to reach a truly comatose state'?

'I was out late last night,' I explain.

'Oh yeah . . . ' she says. 'With who? Come on, I want details.'

'Oh, my brother,' I say. 'Just a few drinks.'

'I remember meeting him a couple of years ago,' she says. I'm not sure if I want to hear what's coming next. 'Seems like a nice guy. Didn't look like you much, though. I mean, for a twin.'

'Well, we're not identical,' I lie.

'Is he still married?' she asks.

'Why, are you interested?'

I'm sorry – I just can't help myself.

'Oh yeah, I love wrecking marriages,' she snorts. I've touched on something that I'd best leave alone. 'Look, I should be going.'

She unfolds herself from the sofa and perches on the edge of it, leans forward, and sips the last of her tea.

'You going out later?' she asks. I forgot that's what people without kids do. They leave the house any time that want to, day or night. I could leave now if I wanted to. I could get in the car and just go. A bar, a club, late-night bagels in Brick Lane . . .

'Nah,' I say. 'I'm knackered.'

'Me too.' She gets up with a yawn. 'Anyway, Saturday night is a mug's night. You don't want to be out in all that.'

'Yeah, you're right,' I agree. 'A mug's night.'

She stretches before walking towards the front door. She holds out her arms and we hug and peck each other on both cheeks.

'I'll see you later,' I say, hoping that it's true.

'Yeah,' she says non-commitally. I imagine that this is how Sean's relationships work, but I can't pretend to understand them in the least. She leaves, and I close the door, left to my own devices in Sean's big, empty house.

BEEP-BEEP, BEEP-BEEP, BEEP-BEEP

I roll over and slam my hand on the alarm clock, trying to swat the life out of the damn thing. I lie there for a minute before I can summon the energy to crack my eyes open and take a look at the time. It's . . . SEVEN FUCKING THIRTY!

I leap from the bed like I've been tasered, trying to collect my thoughts. I need to rouse the kids . . .

'Boys!' I shout, trying to hide the panic in my voice. There is *no way* I'm going to be able to get them to school on time. 'Boys. Get dressed, quick . . . '

As my senses come into focus it's clear that I'm acting in an even more deluded manner than normal. Underneath my feet is beautifully fitted parquet flooring, not the gappy, stripped Bodgit and Scarper version we have at home, which generates dust in much the same manner as a candy floss machine spins the pink crap that's a surefire child lunacy inducer. I am in my brother's bedroom, warm from sheets with a thread count high enough for a spoiled diva. It's Sunday. There are no children. There is no panic.

I am in heaven.

The stillness is intoxicating. The longer I lie staring up at Sean's expensive big-ticket glass chandelier, the more I want to be here. After a while, I wonder if I'm actually ever going to be able to get up. But then I get a waft of something coming through the gap I've left at the bottom of the window. Something primeval in me stirs, my body shifting immediately from rest into action.

Bacon.

No smell can motivate a man on quite such a primitive level as a frying pan full of delicious, sizzling back bacon. I untangle myself from the sheets, slouch into the en suite and embark on a series of procedures that go part-way to explaining why Sara appears to spend half of each day in the bathroom, things that I would never even consider doing in my normal life. I exfoliate. I moisturise. I use something called eye balm, and I find an array of stainless-steel instruments that look like they might have belonged to the dungeon master of Cologne castle during the Middle Ages and spend – and I am not exaggerating here – a good ten minutes removing nasal hair and plucking my eyebrows.

My eyes stream with the exquisite pain of nasal hair removal; the area between my eyebrows is redder then a female baboon's backside, but I feel like I've done myself some good. At the very least, I've entered into a ritual that Sean perceives to be habitual rather than extraordinary, the sicko. I wonder if I am now categorised as a metrosexual.

Having availed myself of Sean's extraordinary wardrobe, I head outside on my hunt for pork. Heading down Sean's immoderately wealthy street I survey the grand, sedate homes set back aloofly from the street. People always say that money doesn't buy you happiness, but I don't see why a positive outlook on life can't be purchased along with a Mercedes, a plasma-screen TV or depleted tropical hardwood garden furniture. I look up and see a huge stucco-fronted palace protected from the non-privileged by ivy-covered brick walls and iron gates. The house has been painted French blue, which is not the sort of colour you usually select for a house but, on this one, feels right. It's impossible to imagine what other colour it might be. When we were growing up, only three miles away in Willesden Green, we rarely came here. We used to go to Portobello Road occasionally where our parents indulged in fruitless searches for valuable relics while both Sean and I gradually lost our will to live.

Walking around the neighbourhood I realise that, despite the fact that I regularly drive through the place and even, when I'm not feeling too financially castrated, shop here, I barely know it because I'm always in a rush going elsewhere on a crazed, self-imposed deadline. My ability to stop and grab a coffee, or peruse the over-priced retail has withered in tandem with my bank balance. Consequently, I've treated it like it's an unknowable oasis on the way to somewhere else – the supermarket, a meeting or, God forgive me, baby yoga. (And, before you ask, it's as ludicrous as it sounds; bursting with people who have the time and resources to have their heads as firmly planted up their own arses as is humanly possible.)

So today, with time on my hands and money in my pocket, I check the cynical, chippy Tom at the door and revel in the fact that I am now a local resident (albeit a temporary one) and I too have the resources to compare Japanese selvedge jeans that retail at over three hundred quid a pair, fritter away time at the organic supermarket concocting elaborate juicing options and arguing with poorly paid baristas regarding the exact temperature of my espresso.

In this spirit I wander into what seems to be a clothes store to discover that the negligible items in there appear to be on display rather than on sale. Aware that the eyes of shop assistants are on me, and not having the balls just to walk out, I approach a shirt and examine it closely, although, such is the reverence with which the clothes are displayed, I resist actually touching it. I feel like I'm in the presence of Tutankhamun.

'It's beautiful, isn't it?' A well-spoken, suspiciously thin blonde girl is at my shoulder. I turn and see that she's gazing at the shirt as if in a state of rapture.

'Yes,' I say, lost for something else to say. 'Nice colour,' is the best I eventually come up with. Seeing as we're both looking at a black shirt, this isn't perhaps the most perceptive of comments.

'Yes,' the girl agrees. 'Black is never just black, is it?'

Clearly I have stumbled into some kind of day-release halfway house. *Yes*, I want to say, *and do you foresee a time in the future when we'll all be wearing trousers made of anchovies?*

'Would you like to try it on?' the girl asks.

Feeling that it's now appropriate for me to handle the goods, I reach forward, lift the shirt from the rail and examine it more closely. *Behold – the Ark of the Covenant!*

'Nice, isn't it?' I say.

'I think that you'd look great in it,' says the girl, turning her gaze from the shirt to me. Clearly, she's working on commission. Mind you, this is someone who sees different shades of black, so there's a chance that she might really mean what she's saying.

Who am I trying to kid?

'Um, what's it made of?' I ask, knowingly.

'Cotton,' she replies.

I nod sagely. *Cotton*. Yeah.

'And how much is it?'

'It's on sale today,' says the girl brightly. 'It's available for 399.'

'That's pounds?' I say, aghast.

'Yes,' says the girl, without any hint of humour.

I place it back on the rail. The girl steps forward and removes it again, holding it against me, her hand brushing against my moisturised chin.

'Why don't you try it?' she asks.

I pull a face and shake my head very slowly while nodding at the same time. It's the movement of someone who is having a tough time making a decision. Of course, there is absolutely no decision to make; I will not be buying a shirt for nearly four hundred quid, even with Sean's credit card. I'm simply not physically capable of doing it. Should I attempt to reach into my pocket to retrieve Sean's wallet, my arm will freeze into a rigid, incapacitated memento to retail overreach.

'You know,' I say, 'maybe I don't need another black shirt.'

Quick as a flash the girl replaces the black shirt on the rail, whizzes over to another and picks out an identical garment.

'How about a white one, then?' she asks brightly.

I extricate myself from the situation politely and find my way out onto Westbourne Grove, which has settled into an easy Sunday groove. I keep reading that shopping has become an obsession for many urbanites, how retail is now a way in which Londoners can express themselves and find solace in otherwise burdened lives, and I just don't get it. Shopping, unless it is taking place at an off-licence, simply makes me feel *more* stressed, *more* burdened.

Slipping into a café, I spot a seat free at the zinc counter and head towards it. The guy behind the bar, who's in his mid-thirties with messy, short, blond hair and redness to his skin that suggests either marine-based recreational activities or excessive boozing, catches my eye as he stacks glasses. I look away momentarily, and then back at him. He's still staring at me. I grab the spare seat, hang my jacket over the back of it, and lean on the counter. The barman is over in a shot.

'All right, Sean?' he asks, extending what looks like a mildly damp hand. I reach over and, on seeing the way in which his hand is cocked, realise to my horror that he wants me to participate in a multi-part handshake, the type that ends in us snapping each other's fingers. It's something that the boys do, while addressing each other as 'blood'. I reach my hand towards him, wondering how on earth I'm going to avoid making a total tit of myself, when I remember that the boys will sometimes do a thing where they just sort of bump knuckles. I shape my hand into a fist as I extend my arm and – thank Christ – the barman reads it and reciprocates. Disaster averted, gangsta cred confirmed.

'Usual?' he says.

'Yeah,' I answer, kicking myself, knowing that I will now be served a foul beverage containing milk.

'So, what you been up to?' asks the barman as he persuades the hissing, steaming coffee machine to life.

'Oh, you know, the usual,' I say evasively. 'Trying to make a living.'

'Saw you on TV the other night at that première.' He smiles. 'You were with that girl, what's her name, the one in the band . . . Oh, yeah, Kelly Vermeer.'

'Oh, yeah.' Who on earth is Kelly Vermeer? I should know this, I watch enough *UK:TV* with the boys.

'What's she like then?'

'Oh, she's nice,' I say blandly, wishing that I'd never set foot in the door of this place. 'Hot.'

That sounded awful. Just plain wrong. Perverse even. For all I know, Kelly Vermeer could be some kind of teeny-bop sensation.

'What?'

'I said, make my coffee nice and hot. Please.'

'It's steam, Sean,' he says with a chuckle. 'Evaporated water. It's well fucking hot.'

He slides a coffee that I don't want to drink over to me with a wink.

'There you go.'

'Thanks.'

I expect him to leave me alone now. There are, after all, other customers to tend to. Instead, he hunkers down opposite me, his elbows on top of the bar. I can see that his eyes are slightly bloodshot, the lines in his face deeper than his apparent age should warrant.

'So, Sean, look, I was wondering . . . ' he starts, a wolfish smile on his face. 'I was up for this Eastern Airways job last week, and the audition went really well. It's great money, I was wondering if . . . The director is Mick DiPaolo, and I know that you fellas have worked on a lot of stuff together, and I thought that, if it were possible . . . '

'You want me to have a word?' I ask, putting him out of his misery.

'Yeah, that would be great.'

I take a small sip of the coffee. The milk makes it totally undrinkable. The barman notices that something isn't right.

'Everything OK?' he asks, worried that the favour he's asked might be adversely affected by my dissatisfaction with his coffee-making skills.

'Yeah,' I say, quickly. 'Fine. Look, I'll see what I can do on the other thing, OK?'

'Wicked, mate,' says the barman, standing up and biting his lip. 'Thanks, I owe you one.'

'No promises though.'

More like *no fucking chance though*. Will bad things happen to me because of this deceit?

'No, no . . . I understand,' he says, showing me the palms of his hands. 'Miracles not expected.'

Or delivered, for that matter.

He attends to another customer while I kill a little time flicking through a much-thumbed copy of the sports section of the *Sunday Telegraph*. I'm thinking about leaving when I notice that he's standing near me again but is working on something below the bar level. Without explanation he briskly slides an overturned cup that's been set on a saucer towards me and disappears to the other side of the bar, setting a couple of Bloody Marys in front of an attractive couple who have a pile of estate agents' listings in front of them. He looks over at me and, sensing my bewilderment, nods towards the cup. I lift it off the saucer to discover a plastic bag with something . . .

Hang on, I remember what that is . . .

Jesus.

I slam the cup down quickly in case anyone has noticed that I've just been staring at an eighth of grass, and return my attention to the sports section. After a while I look up to see if anyone is staring. The coast is clear. I am still a free man. I will not be doing a stretch with my cellmate 'Mr Big' demanding the privileges of the top bunk. I'm not entirely sure what to do. I know that Sean likes the odd spliff, so maybe I've inadvertently stumbled on his dealer. If that's not the case, then maybe I'm risking acting out of character by not scooping up the drugs provided by a thankful friend. The barman comes close and offers me a wink.

'Just a little something,' he says.

I smile, trying to look cool, but worried that I might be the victim of a sting operation and that 'the pigs' will swoop the moment I touch 'the merchandise'. I lift the edge of the cup, snatch the packet from under it and stuff it in my jacket pocket. Following this I carefully fold a paper napkin over it to prevent prying eyes from even getting a glance of the contraband. I wait for the cold hand of the law to descend upon me ... But there's nothing. Just Sunday-afternoon laughter, and the hissing of the cappuccino machine. I suddenly feel like I've been given a second chance, like my kids won't grow up with a bottom-bunk dad they see at weekends on visits to Wormwood Scrubs. I leave some money on the counter for Sean's friend/dealer and step out into the November afternoon.

Dillydallying on the pavement outside, I consider my first day as Sean, my achievements have been: a conversation with a rapturous twenty-something shop assistant, devouring a ham baguette that was shorter than its fucking price tag, and drinking enough coffee to enable me to fly without assistance from London to Marrakesh. Sounds like an average Sunday for a grotesque self-satisfied yuppie such as myself.

Hopped up on caffeine, I glance at Sean's monstrous chronograph and discover that I've only got twenty minutes before the Sunday game on Sky, the very Sunday game that I'm normally prevented from watching because I'm out doing something familial, or because I need to use the TV to cosh the kids. This is exactly the kind of opportunity I need to capitalise on while I'm free of the shackles of family.

Excitedly, I head back towards Sean's place, picking up all the Sunday papers on the way (yes, that's the Sundays I normally never get the time to read) and a six-pack of Heineken. I pass a pizzeria and decide – what the hell, in for a penny in for a pound – to pick up a sixteen-inch 'meat lover's delight'. (This isn't really a product that I'm comfortable requesting, but the teenage sales assistant doesn't seem even remotely bothered by it.)

Holding the hot pizza box horizontal I step from the shop savouring the imminent delights of football, lager, pizza and the *News of the World*. I'm not far from Sean's, but only have five minutes to spare, so I pick up the pace a little. Coming down Ladbroke Grove I turn the corner into Sean's street when – wham! – I bump right into something. The pizza box slips from my hand, lands on its side and its contents flop face down on the pavement. I'm still looking at this symbol of my crushed dreams when I hear a word that sends a shiver down my spine.

'Tom?'

I look up and, dear lord, it's Jessica. Jessica with whom my kids have sleepovers, Jessica whose Andalucian villa I've stayed at, Jessica who is Sara's best friend.

Guilty as charged, m'lord.

'No, it's Sean,' I say, filled for a foolhardy moment, with bravado. *Why the hell did I say that?*

She looks at me suspiciously. I manage to resist the urge to simply run off down the street.

'I'm sorry about your pizza,' she says. Her pale face, which is close to translucent at the best of times, looks a strange shade of green, pistachio perhaps, in the twilight.

'It's OK,' I say. 'Actually, it's probably for the best.' I pat my stomach. 'Could do with trimming off a few pounds.'

'Couldn't we all?' says Jessica, who could actually do with eating a couple of meat lover's delights to get her above skeletal. She smiles self-consciously, as if reading what I'm thinking.

'I think we've met at one of Tom and Sara's parties,' I say, trying to act normal.

'Yes,' she says. 'Last summer, wasn't it?'

'Yeah.'

She eyes the six-pack of lager I'm holding and the plastic bag of Sunday newspapers before looking back at the pizza. Tiny smears of grease from the pepperoni have appeared on the pavement. I stoop down and lever the pizza back into its carton and close the lid.

'Good as new,' I say, wiping my hand on the lid.

'Do you need a tissue?' she asks.

'Actually, I think that I've got one in here,' I say, reaching into my jacket pocket. I grab the tissue and snatch it out . . . depositing the little bag of grass at Jessica's expensively shod feet. I wipe my hand with the tissue and acknowledge the package lying inches from her Adidas Y-3 trainers.

'Er . . . Catnip,' I offer, half-heartedly.

'Looks like hydroponic skunk to me.' She smiles.

I nod. Busted. She bends down and retrieves the bag, hiding it in the palm of her hand with practised skill. She then extends it towards me.

'Nice to see you,' she says.

I reach out and she palms me the bag.

'You too,' I reply.

We say our farewells and 'see you at Tom and Sara's' and head into what has become a gloomy evening. All the way back I wonder if she suspected anything rotten, or whether the fiasco with the pizza and the skunk was enough to put her off the scent.

As reckless as it seemed at the time, I'm glad that my instinct was to claim to be Sean. If we're going to get through the next two weeks both Sean and I need to be on top of our respective games. I dump the pizza in the bin outside Sean's house after a moment's deliberation as to whether, with a little scraping here and there, it might still be edible. Even though I'm in time for kick-off it takes me five minutes to figure out how to work Sean's TV. Suddenly a picture springs to life and excitedly I stare up at Sean's state-of-the-art plasma screen to see that I'm going to spend the next ninety minutes watching . . . Blackburn Rovers and Middlesbrough kick lumps out of each other.

Oh joy!

Still, after a couple of bottles of Heineken I'm so lost in the *News of the World* that it doesn't really matter. Against my better judgement I order another pizza – the meat lover's special with extra pepperoni, of course – as a reward for a flawless first day's performance. Giving

Sean's address is a pleasure, especially the moment when the guy asks, 'Is it a flat or a house?' and I can say 'a house', which, of course, means, 'one of those bloody great houses, so get over here pronto and you might get a decent tip'.

I put the phone down and, momentarily, speculate what Sean and the boys are up to and how Sara's getting on in Liverpool. But, as I lie back on Sean's mammoth sofa, my thoughts are dominated by just one notion: that, after all this time, I might finally have found a life that fits me.

12
Sean

So, what with Sara having time at the gym, the boys' conquest of the climbing wall, the full-on Chelsea prawn sandwich experience and the unforgettable – all right, competent – roast chicken lunch, I *killed* it on Sunday. (Not to mention meeting the *muy caliente* mum at the playground.) Seriously; I did some damage. But I'm aware that Monday is a totally different challenge. Getting the boys up, dressed, cleansed, fed and to school on a strict schedule is going to be like trying to drive a Formula 1 car after mild success on the dodgems.

With that in mind, I'm out of the blocks like a sprinter, rousing the boys, generating noise and movement to give us some momentum.

Paddy stands at the top of the stairs wearing nothing but Shrek underpants.

'I can't find any socks . . . ' he says, stifling a yawn. I start rifling through his drawers. He's right, there's nothing clean in there. Shit. We're losing time.

'Michael,' I call, 'do you know where Mum put the clean washing?'

He wanders into Paddy's bedroom wearing the clothes he had on yesterday, his hair a tangled rat's nest.

'What are you doing?' I ask him.

He looks at me blankly.

'Why are you dressed like that?'

Another blank look is punctuated by his scratching his head before examining his fingernail. I dread to know what he found there.

'Michael, it's Monday. You've got to be at school in just over an hour. Go and get dressed.'

'Oh, sorry,' he says, before returning to his room.

Paddy is now on the floor arranging a set of medieval knights into a complicated attack formation.

'I'll find you some socks,' I say. I search the upstairs of the house, with no luck, before heading downstairs to the kitchen. I glance at the washing machine and notice that I neglected to turn it on – there's a load of dirty washing still waiting to be cleaned. I turn the machine on and return upstairs. I check the laundry basket in the bathroom and discover it to be brim full with dirty clothes. Clearly this is a chore that needs doing today.

'What's going on?' asks Paddy, standing behind me.

'I'm looking for some socks for you,' I say, examining the pair that he wore yesterday to see if we can get away with him 'recycling' them. He comes and leans against me, before rummaging through the basket himself.

'How about these?' he asks, brightly. I take a look at them.

'OK, they'll do,' I say.

'But they're a bit stinky,' says Paddy, flapping his hand as if to generate some air.

'I know, but they'll have to do just for today,' I say, trying to persuade him. The clock is running away from us. 'Think of it like a lucky dip.'

This appears to convince him. He disappears back to his room. I peek in and see that he has his school uniform laid out and seems to be aware that he needs to put it on. Michael emerges on the landing dressed, this time in the right clothes. Since when did school uniform feature sweatshirts? What next? Hoodies?

'Michael, go and have a wash and brush your teeth and your hair.'

'Shall I use toothpaste?' he asks.

'Of course.' I'm flabbergasted. 'What do you mean, shall I use toothpaste?'

'With my teeth *and* my hair.'

'What?!'

'Just checking, Homer,' says Michael.

Clearly I have been the victim of some cutting pre-adolescent repartee. He walks into the bathroom and I hustle downstairs to get the next part of the operation under way. The kitchen is where my forward-planning skills come into full effect: the breakfast things are all laid out and the boys' lunches (tuna salad sandwiches, crisps, celery sticks, apples and Penguins) are waiting in the fridge. I put the milk on the table, pour them each an apple juice and go through to the hallway to organise their shoes. I mentally run through the list that Tom has equipped me with and put a tick next to each completed task. I check the clock – we've got half an hour before we need to leave the house.

We're cruising, baby. That's right: *cruising*.

A couple of minutes later both boys drift downstairs, apparently oblivious to the time constraints upon them. Paddy goes and switches the radio on, mutters 'wicked' to himself in approval once he hears which song is being broadcast, before pouring a very generous helping of cereal into his bowl. Michael does the same thing before drinking his apple juice in one gulp and emitting a deafening burp.

Nice. I would have been proud of that one. Oh, hang on, I'm a parent now . . .

'Michael!' I scold him.

'Sorry,' he says with no emotion.

'Dad, can we call Mum?' asks Paddy between mouthfuls of Shreddies.

'Yes, later on,' I say, trying to undo a knot in Paddy's shoelaces that it must have taken him at least an hour to construct with knitting needles.

'What about now?'

'Later on.'

'Why not now?' whines Paddy.

'Because we're late,' I say.

'No, we're not,' he disagrees. 'I can read the clock, you know.'

'Paddy, we'll call her later, OK.'

'Thanks a *lot*,' he says sarcastically. I try not to laugh.

'Why do you need to call her now?' I ask.

'To tell her that you're making me wear dirty socks to school.'

'Grass,' says Michael.

Paddy glowers at his brother over the breakfast table. Thankfully Michael just ignores him.

'No name-calling please,' I intervene. 'Five minutes now, boys, and we're leaving.' I want to get them out of the house as I'm not sure how long the car journey will take, although knowing London traffic, a fair guess will be vastly longer than it should. Once breakfast is over I hurry them into their coats and shoes and out of the house. We stand in the street and I realise that I can't remember where I parked the car.

'Anyone remember where the car is?' I ask hopefully.

Both of them shrug their shoulders. I have a strong suspicion that it's towards Chevening Road. We head up there, the boys lagging behind, before I remember that it's actually at the other end of the street, on Harvist Road. I check my watch, we're still OK for time, but it's getting a little tighter. As at least half the cars in London are silver we're virtually on top of the Volvo before I spot it. The boys pile in the back. OK, we're in business. There's a light frost on the windscreen, which the wipers quickly remove, leaving a white frame round the edges of the glass.

I head up our road and am indicating right when Michael pipes up.

'Dad, did you put my homework in my bag?' I put my foot on the brake.

'No,' I say. 'Was I supposed to?'

'I don't know,' says Michael. 'Usually you remind me, or put it in my bag or something.'

'OK,' I say. 'Let's go and get it.'

I swing the car back round and return to the house, hurrying the boys back inside, and sending Michael upstairs for his homework, while monitoring Paddy to make sure that he doesn't get distracted and disappear in the direction of the PlayStation. Michael comes back downstairs.

'I can't find it,' he says.

Jesus Christ. We are going to be late. Before I can say anything, however, he pulls an exercise book from beneath his coat, smiles and says: 'Wind up.'

The little sod. I get them back in the car and put my foot down. We're cutting it fine. I can't use the major roads at this time and, even though I know that all the rat runs will be chocker, I still think that I might get a break . . . Which I don't. We crawl to school, every road nose to tail, and every junction a sod's opera. I get us there with a couple of minutes to spare. The boys pile out, seemingly oblivious to the logistical feat I've accomplished. I drive home listening to the radio, astonished that so much time can be eaten up by the morning dash.

I need to pick up some bread and milk, commodities the boys appear to consume in quantities that are vastly disproportionate to their physical size. I walk over a couple of streets to a corner shop, where I also pick up a paper from a bored Indian shopkeeper who is watching an obscure Test match from Sri Lanka. As I'm paying I look down at the array of confectionary that's been ideally positioned at kid height. I pay for a KitKat, and make to leave. I'm exiting the shop when I hear a voice behind me.

'Excuse me, sir, but did you pay for all those items?'

Startled, I turn to face my accuser.

'Well?'

Babe alert! The woman from the playground stands with her arms folded and her head tilted to the side, with an inquisitor's glint in her eye. Behind her, the shopkeeper chuckles.

'Don't worry about her,' he says. 'She's crazy.'

'Crazy enough to pay your prices, Mr Adiseshah,' she says over her shoulder before returning her gaze to me.

I put my hands up in mock surrender.

'You've got me bang to rights,' I admit.

'We have CCTV,' interrupts the shopkeeper, getting into the swing of things. 'You're in big trouble.'

Shut up, mate. I'm trying to get something going here.

She moves towards the doorway. The pair of us exit the shop.

'Where are you off to?' I ask.

'I have some really tedious chores to take care of,' she replies.

'Me too.'

'Any chance you can do mine at the same time?' she asks.

'None whatsoever,' I reply.

'You can't hold it against me for trying, though.'

'It would be silly not to.'

We both start walking up the street, past the estate agents and coffee shops that have gradually replaced the TV repair shops and hardware stores. A car drives past blasting out Marvin Gaye's 'Sexual

Healing'. I want to bung the driver a fiver for exhibiting such perfect timing.

'You know,' she says, 'sometimes when I hear a really great song I feel like it's been written just for me.'

'Great art is like that,' I say, immediately aware that I have already crossed the line into twattery. Can I take it further? Oh, yes. 'It touches the personal and the universal simultaneously.'

She stops walking and looks at me with surprise.

'What?' I say, expecting a beat-down.

'I don't know,' she replies cagily. 'It was funny, what you just said.'

'Well, it's true,' I say, sticking to my guns.

'No,' she says, shaking her head. 'I'm not talking about the sentiment, more the way you said it. You sounded like that guy in that movie, *Manhattan*. You know . . . '

'Woody Allen?'

'Yes.'

'I suppose I'll take that as a compliment,' I say.

'Good.' She nods. 'You should. Take them where you can, you know.'

'Oh, I do.'

We arrive at a junction.

'I'm going to the station,' she says.

I think for a moment if I can come up with an excuse to accompany her, but the house is in the other direction.

'Nice to see you again,' I say, reprising my famous line in shitty farewells. She smiles and turns to cross the road.

'Hey,' I say. *I'm going to ask her out, I'm going to ask her out . . .*

'What?'

God, she's gorgeous.

'Um, want some KitKat?'

'I never accept stolen goods,' she says, before dodging between speeding vehicles. She doesn't look back, but I sense that she knows that I'm watching her walk away. I wait until she's gone before I remember that I don't even know her name.

I get home around quarter to ten. Normally I'll have been in the office for an hour, dealt with any business we might have in the Far East, drunk a couple of cappuccinos and be gearing up for a senior staff meeting on the hour. Back at Tom and Sara's house I'm wondering what on earth I should do to fill the five hours until I meet the boys for swimming. Then it dawns on me: only five hours! How am I supposed to get all the domestics sorted in that time? You see, in my normal life a daytime congregation of cleaners, gardeners and maids ghosts in and out of my house removing obstacles that might distract me from the twin poles of making money and love. (I cancelled them while I was away.) Wouldn't want to spoil Tom. I arrive home to find that the place has altered since I left it, as if it were some kind of self-regulating organism. My new role, however, demands that chores, far from being massaged from my presence, are the actual content of my day.

Let me tell you something, I've met people who claim to *like* housework. Many reasons are given for this: it's cathartic, it's rewarding, it's physical, it's a distraction, it frees the mind allowing one to think clearly. Well, call me crazy, but I don't do my best thinking while cleaning children's skid marks off the bottom of a toilet bowl.

Nor am I particularly fond of vacuum cleaning. Tom and Sara's Hoover looks like a Martian assault craft, not an electrical cleaning device. Once I've actually figured out which of the bloody lozenge-shaped yellow buttons turns the thing on I spend the following hour taking the damn thing apart in order to retrieve the various – no doubt highly valuable and utterly irreplaceable – plastic figurines that have become lodged in the bowels of the beast. Of course, once I've taken the thing apart I can't get it back together again. I sit on the living-room floor cursing my own stupidity. I imagine that cleaning the entire place from top to bottom would have taken Tom around an hour, while I'm slumped in the living room surrounded by the contents of the Hoover, picking through hair and God knows what in search of an inch-tall figurine of Chewbacca.

And don't get me started on laundry. The boys informed me yesterday that I had forgotten to dab 'stain remover' on the mud, paint, food and dog shit they manage to plaster their clothes with. Isn't that what a washing machine is *for*? Do you clean your dishes before putting them in the dishwasher? Shower before you get in the bath? Go to Burger King before dinner at The Ivy? Sheer. Bloody. Madness.

Aside from that, what's thrown me most about the Cunningham household is the sheer amount of *stuff* going on. To try to get the hang of the family unit thing I started by just observing. Once I felt I'd got the gist of it, my response was to be super efficient, discovering that, as long as I don't think too hard about tending the boys, I slide through my days like I'm in my socks on a freshly polished floor. To make a success of my situation I must avoid looking downwards – self-consciousness is my enemy.

So that's the way I do it. The boys get the bus home, and I take them to swimming club, I help them take a bath and do their homework and then I feed them a nutritious meal that I've prepared myself. All done without looking down. Mission accomplished, I'm settling into Tom and Sara's rather over-plush sofa that evening when the phone rings. Without thinking, I declare out loud, 'Who the *hell* can that be?' with a degree of outrage that even a retired colonel in the Home Counties would admire.

I see from the number on the phone that it's Sara. My first thought is that Tom and I are busted, and that Sara is calling to berate me while her divorce lawyer is working Tom over with a cosh made from an old sock stuffed with pound coins. (Not that I'm paranoid or anything.) I decide to let it ring out; Sara can leave a voicemail. Then it occurs to me that not answering will be *exactly* the kind of thing that will raise suspicions and, perhaps, surveillance. Where else will Tom be at night with his kids fast asleep than sitting at home semi-comatose on Stella Artois waiting for his wife to call?

I pick up the phone.

'Hi, Sara.'

'Hiya. How are you?'

'Fine.'

'The boys OK?'

'Fast asleep.' This isn't actually true. I've heard the odd set of elephantine footsteps overhead, which I'm choosing to ignore. 'They're knackered. We went to swimming club after school. They were wiped out after that.'

'They weren't too tired for their homework, were they?' She sounds disapproving.

'No, no . . . we got it done after dinner . . . ' For a moment I wonder if I've slipped up on procedure, but Sara doesn't follow up. 'So, how's it going up there?'

'Not bad, I suppose. We laid our stall out. Jury seems pretty attentive and the bad guys look like bad guys. So, you know, we'll see. I'm optimistic that we'll get them. God knows, they're guilty as sin.'

'You sound tired.'

'I'm fine. I miss you all though.'

'We miss you too . . . ' We're straying into territory seething with unspecified threats. I swerve the conversation in another direction. 'So, how's the hotel?'

'It's great. It's on a street called Hope Street, so that bodes well. Look, I've got a bath running. I better go. I'll call tomorrow. Oh, and if some big blokes calling themselves "The Lagos Connection" come knocking make sure you don't let them in.'

I stand up, suddenly feeling a little queasy. I forgot about this. Sara does important work, work that can make you enemies.

'Um . . . '

'Their bite is worse than their bark, if you get my drift,' continues Sara. I walk over to the window and peek out to see if there are any assassins idling outside.

'You're always reminding me about how you used to do karate,' she adds. 'I'm sure that you must know top-secret death chops or something – you'll be fine.'

'But that was only for a couple of months when we were ten,' I explain, remembering Tom's and my short-lived career in martial arts. After deciding that we didn't like getting dressed up in white pyjamas and getting beaten by our former PE teacher we'd take the money Mum had given us and spend it on saveloys and chips, which we'd eat in the bus shelter before heading to the arcade and indulging in electronic combat on the Space Invaders and Asteroids machines.

'Oh, come on, Bruce Lee – where's your fighting spirit?' chides Sara, who is now clearly taking the piss, although I'm not sure how seriously to take her earlier warning.

'Look, got to go,' she says. 'The ice is melting in my gin and tonic.'

She's gone.

Bloody hell – I did it. Not only have I got away with impersonating my brother, but I'm inclined to believe that I performed with the right degree of marital familiarity, the zone of informal intimacy tinged with a vigilant edge that appears to define the conversations I've heard between married couples who have managed to keep their shit together not to be just sparring partners.

I hit the remote and the news pops on. It's the usual litany of Bush and his cronies' fuck-ups, and my mind snaps back to the current situation. A single word comes to mind: lies. In fact, more than that, an idiomatic expression: a tissue of lies. We're two days in now and I've got to say that this child-rearing thing isn't exactly what Tom has been selling me all these years. I'm familiar with Tom's appetite for drama and self-pity, but the element that's surprised me I can only describe as the 'parenthood conspiracy'. Now, fair enough, I dare say that sleep-deprived parents of a newborn might be deserving of sympathy but, after that point, is it much worse than having a Dobermann? The phone rings again.

'Sorry about that,' says Sara.

'What?'

'Just thought I was a little brusque – I suppose that's what happens after a day in court.'

'So, what are you doing?' I say.

There's a pause.

'Sorry, Tom . . . Are we having phone sex?' asks Sara. 'Hang on a minute . . . um, I'm just wearing underwear and I've got my hands down my pants. How's that?'

Good Lord.

'Um, no, I, um . . . That's not what I meant,' I splutter.

'That's a shame,' says Sara.

I had better crush this before it gets out of hand.

'So, the boys had a great time at swimming.'

'Tom,' says Sara, 'don't take this the wrong way, but we don't always have to talk about the boys.'

'I know,' I say. 'I was just making conversation.'

'I know,' she replies. 'Just conversation.'

Now I know what it is to be Tom, to have little conversational material other than whether new Bold automatic washes whiter than Ariel, or the fact that Sainsbury's is having a special on Dutch cherry tomatoes. I hear the washing machine, which is in the kitchen, spinning a load. I'll need to put that in the dryer once it finishes, if I can figure out how it works. Just call me the king of the colourwash, the sultan of the spin dryer.

'Let's catch up tomorrow, shall we?' says Sara. 'I'll try and think of something to talk about other than work and you brush up on something topical. You know that Kennedy was shot, right?'

I hear her yawn.

'I'm knackered,' she says. 'Not sure whether it's the trial or all this wanking.'

'The wanking, I expect,' I say.

'Probably,' she says.

'Night then.'

'Sleep well.'

'And you – good luck tomorrow.'

'Night.'

I put the handset down. The washing machine has stopped spinning. This is the first time today that there hasn't been some kind of noise – either electronic or human – in the house. Since becoming a 'dad', quiet is the sole commodity that I'm aware that I'm missing. It appears that the boys are capable of this only when sedated by DVDs. Back in the day everyone watched the same stuff: *Swap Shop*, *Magpie*, *Top of the Pops* ... These days absentee parents ease their consciences by purchasing premium channels that offer 'educational' programming. They champion videos with conscience-easing titles like *Baby Mozart* and *Baby Einstein* so that they don't feel too guilty leaving the kid in front of the box while they disappear off to check whether the suede boots they're tracking on eBay are still the bargain they thought they were.

Now, I don't want to be too hard on Tom. I am, it's fair to say, still new to the whole child-rearing racket, and I have been fortunate enough to come to it without the scars from years of dead-of-night trauma. I've managed to avoid arse-wiping, sleep depravation and buggy-hauling, which, in my book, is pretty much right up there with dodging testicular cancer. But I'm still not convinced it's *that* hard.

Beginner's luck? Maybe. It's early days yet. But if I can keep this momentum, generate enough energy to keep the boys distracted, I get the feeling that I can add 'natural dad' to my list of accomplishments. The Lagos Connection can stick that in their pipe and smoke it.

And the bonus? I can't get that mysterious, brassy woman in the park out of my head. Maybe Tom's and my experiment might have even more to recommend it that I first thought. Let's just call it the 'dad dividend'.

13
Tom

Despite Ellie's compliment about my hair I need to get my barnet to look more like Sean's, a messy, hinting-at-ironic statement that could only have been created by a highly skilled and expensive 'artist'. Given that, over the last fifteen years, my hair has only been touched by a middle-aged Cypriot who never stops talking about Arsenal and whose shop boasts black-and-white photos of potential haircuts modelled by men who, by now, must all be dead, I'm dreading the inevitable 'so who cut your hair last?' interrogation. Nevertheless, it's a good test.

Sean has given me the name of his barber, so mid-morning I head over to his 'salon' in Soho. I'm slightly the worse for wear, having consumed the six-pack during the dire broadcast from Ewood Park, while single-handedly working my way through the sixteen-inch 'meat-lovers' pizza. Not all at once, you understand – three slices were consumed late at night as an accompaniment to an impromptu whisky tasting following my discovery of Sean's impressive collection of single malts.

The 'salon' is just the kind of ponce parlour that I fear it will be, featuring fish tanks bursting with unnaturally colourful tropical fish, painfully white walls and lots and lots of clear plastic furniture in which it's almost impossible to get comfortable. The look of horror on the receptionist's face when I walk in immediately puts me on edge, although when she addresses me as 'Sean' I realise that her alarmed expression (which is something close to the initial stages of registering a really, really bad smell) is simply the face that she has been born with. Before she can call him, an implausibly hip Japanese man approaches me.

'Oh, here's Takamichi!' says the girl, perking up a bit, as if amazed by the coincidence of his happening to be in his workplace.

'Takamichi, Takamichi, Takamichi,' I repeat to myself, searing the name into my brain.

'Hey, Sean!' he says, smiling broadly.

'What's up, man?' I say, silently hating myself for not having the balls to use his name. He gives me a full-on hug, smelling good and citrusy. I'm glad that I've made generous use of Sean's grooming products. There's not a lot of hugging going on in my world. I mean, I hug the boys and I hug Sara, but I don't really hug anyone else. I imagine that if I tried to hug Tony the barber he'd chase me down Kentish High Road with a cut-throat razor and some choice epithets that question the authenticity of my parentage. Thankfully, it lasts for no longer than a couple of seconds, the brevity of the interaction meaning that I avoid deploying my genetically installed rigid-upper-body anti-hugging device.

Takamichi ushers me onto one of the uncomfortable plastic chairs and examines my hair with both his eyes and hands in the way that someone who's arrived late to a buffet takes stock of the picked-over food.

'So, what are we doing?' he asks.

'Um, same as last time,' I answer.

'It worked for you then?'

'Yeah, absolutely.'

'It's grown quickly,' he says suspiciously.

'Um, yeah,' I agree.

'I don't think you're going to go bald soon.'

'Good. I never agreed with all that "bald is beautiful crap",' I say. 'That's like celebrating because you got picked out in a police line-up.'

'You want a little colour in there, like last time?'

Sean has his hair coloured?

'No, no,' I say. 'Let's keep it natural.'

'OK, let's get you shampooed.'

A severe-looking girl whisks me over to a basin and bends my neck back into a position that could easily require me to wear a brace for several months afterwards. I get shampooed and conditioned and, just when I think that the misery is over, she starts to massage my head with her knuckles. Now I don't doubt that this is the kind of thing that people like Sean pay highly for at luxury resort hotels, but on a Monday morning in Soho when the vomit stains are still fresh on the pavement, and the pizza I had the night before has only just sunk below my sternum, it's about as welcome as Michael Jackson at the Tyneside Boys Brigade annual sausage cookout. But I grin and bear it, all in the name of living like Sean Cunningham, businessman, swordsman and, it appears, sadomasochist.

I sit back down in the chair and Takamichi returns bearing a coffee.

'There you go,' he says, putting the mug down next to me. I take a look at it and, before I can catch myself, tell him, 'Can I have one without milk?'

'No milk?'

I realise my mistake.

'I stopped drinking milk,' I explain. 'I'm trying to get off dairy. Eczema, you know.' I scratch my arm as if to prove a point. Takamichi looks sceptical.

'Me too!' he says, giving me a thumbs-up.

'Soy rules, right!' I add, feeling a total tool. *Soy rules*. What a twat. With talk like that I deserve to be living in a peace encampment somewhere near a ley line in Gloucestershire. Nevertheless, it's a good lesson: I need to pay attention to the details of Sean's life. I wonder whether I need to start talking about media platforms and generating buzz, but the conversation flows nicely after that. I even start throwing in a couple of Sean's conversational gambits like 'let me tell you something' at the beginning of sentences and 'you're on crack, man' when I disagree with him. But the best part? Paying with Sean's credit card, a sleek piece of black plastic that makes my own worthless Nat West Visa card look like it was given away with a McDonald's Happy Meal.

Out on the street, with the day stretching ahead of me, I see a record store in what used to be an pub. Vinyl. I used to love vinyl. Once vinyl was the most important substance in my life. But I can't remember the last time I laid a 'fresh crisp biscuit' on a turntable. In our teens Sean and I would swing by Bluebird Records on Edgware

Road every Friday afternoon to see what had arrived in the latest shipment from the US. I duck in, the only customer in the place, nod to the stoner sales assistant and head to a random rack. Finding myself perusing the German techno section I wait a reasonable amount of time before shuffling along the racks looking knowledgeably at their contents before moving on. I find a section with artists organised alphabetically and work my way through a large part of it, pulling out records now and again to check for track listing and production credits.

It dawns on me by the time I get to the letter 'F' that so far I have yet to recognise the name of a single artist. Granted I'm in a dance music specialist shop but, Jesus, it hasn't been that long since I was at the Hacienda, or Dingwalls, or the Lyceum for the Radio London Soul Night Out. I do a quick calculation. I'm right; it isn't so long if you consider ten years not so long. I decide that there is no way that I'm going to leave the shop until I recognise a record in the racks. It takes me half an hour until I find a remix of George Benson's 'The Ghetto' by a Dutch DJ. I ask to listen to it on one of the Technics decks they have set up at the edge of the shop. If ever a great record has been butchered in a more accomplished manner I have yet to hear it. I take the disc back to the counter.

'You looking for anything in particular?' the assistant enquires, a little too late, if you ask me.

I look around the shop.

'You don't have any Phil Collins, do you, mate?' I say, straight-faced.

'No, no, we don't,' he replies, quickly busying himself behind the counter, and refusing to acknowledge me any further. I warm to my task.

'You know,' I say, brandishing an invisible pair of drumsticks, 'da-da, da-da, da-da, da-da, da-da-da-da . . . I can feel it coming in the air tonight . . . '

'No,' he says firmly, now clearly keen that I leave the shop. Frankly, I'm a little surprised that even someone as uptight as this guy can't get into the Phil Collins drum break from 'In the Air Tonight'. It's one of the great levellers that eradicate class, age, taste and sexual preference. Every bloke, given the opportunity, will grab a pair of invisible drumsticks and rock that drum break in a suitably dramatic fashion. But not the angst-ridden hipster music snob in the record shop, he's got his Brazilian imports to worry about, his Norwegian funk samplers to rack.

I head back to Sean's but feel too restless to settle, so I stroll over to the gym round the corner. I've never seen a gym so full during the day – clearly, there is no relationship between owning a multi-million-pound home and having a nine-to-five job. As I lumber away on a treadmill, instructors offer chilled towels (chilled towels!). I suppose normal towels are just not, um, chilled enough. Pretty soon it dawns on me that the purpose of Sean's gym with its effortless, gliding machines, frigid towels, absence of odour, and gleaming cleanliness, is to make punters forget that they're here to exert themselves doing something that's fundamentally boring.

By the time I get home it's past three o'clock. Having still not had lunch, I fire up the juggernaut-size industrial stove that sits at one side of the kitchen looking like a plutonium enrichment plant. As the smell of the cooking food that I picked up from M&S wafts out of the oven I search for a plate. The first cupboard I investigate reveals a cocktail shaker . . . Well, it's nearly cocktail hour so, given that Sean is sure to have all the necessaries, I get the thing out and decide to mix up a drink. I keep it simple, making myself a whisky sour. It slips down nicely, maybe a little too sweet though, so I make another with less sugar.

I walk through to the living room and switch on the TV to Sky Sports News. It's the same old shit, so I flick through the channels, but nothing holds my attention until I get to the pay-per-view. At home I would never think of watching a movie during the day – so that's what I decide to do. I look for a film that Sara would object to watching, namely anything that a man might like, and settle on *Walking Tall* with The Rock. I click on the £7.99 fee (thanks, Sean). While the credits are rolling it's a good opportunity to freshen up my glass a little. I walk back into the kitchen to discover smoke pouring out of the oven. I open the oven door and am hit full force by a mushroom cloud of murk before seeing that the two plastic food packages containing my meatballs with rice have melted through the bars of the oven rack and deposited a glutinous mess at the bottom of the gleaming Swedish-engineered monster. I dump the packages in the bin, their magma-hot contents splattering on the slate floor, and return to the cocktail shaker.

I'm not exactly sure how many whisky sours I rustle up. I only have a vague memory of The Rock straightening out a few unsavoury characters who were, frankly, asking for a damn good hiding. I definitely don't remember nipping down to the kebab shop for a large doner and chips (unless I got it delivered), but I do remember waking up on Sean's sofa and it being nine o'clock at night and not knowing where I left my trousers. I must have taken them off at some point, probably to relieve the pressure of my doner.

I stumble around not feeling right. I need to know how my boys are. It's the end of my second day and I haven't checked in. I must speak to Sean. He picks up the phone on the second ring.

'Sean, it's me.'

'Hello, "Noodles",' Sean whispers. Bloody hell. He's already gathered dangerous information.

'OK, my secret's out,' I confess. 'Why are you whispering?'

'I've just put the boys down, Noodles. I was worried the phone would wake them up. By the way, why Noodles?'

'It's a long story.' I don't want to get into this.

'Oh, I've got time,' says Sean gleefully.

'How are the boys?'

'It's not because you remind her of something limp and bland, is it?'

'Give it a rest, testicle breath.'

I realise that I might be slurring my words.

'You, OK?' asks Sean. Clearly, I'm slurring.

'Yeah, yeah, fine, you know, just missing the boys.' Actually, I'm pissed.

'Don't worry, mate, they're fine. Been following the routine without any hiccups. Sara went off yesterday. She called to speak to the boys on the phone. She was a little abrupt.'

'That's how she is when she's on a trip – stressed and busy.'

'We had a great time yesterday,' Sean continues. 'I took the boys climbing on that wall near the Westway. They were both really good at it, you know. They loved abseiling. I was surprised how quickly they started getting up those walls.'

'They're ballsy little bastards when they want to be.'

'Yeah, we had a laugh. Look, I've got a confession to make.'

'What?' I'm mildly alarmed. The booze and guilt are making me paranoid.

'I took them to Chelsea.'

This is both much better and much worse than I thought it might be.

'You did what?'

'Look, they hadn't been, and I thought that it would be a good way for me to get my confidence as a "dad". I know you won't be happy—'

'Too right I'm not happy. I hate those fucking show ponies.'

'But the boys really wanted to go, and I know how you feel about going to Stamford Bridge, so, you know . . . How are you getting on?'

'Excellent,' I say. 'Having a great time. Met your friend Ellie on Saturday night.'

'How?'

'She came over to the house, fool.'

'I, yeah, I forgot to mention that she might come by. How did it go?'

'Great – I fucked her.'

'No, you didn't,' he says, without missing a beat.

'No, I didn't,' I confirm. 'Have to admit that I was a bit freaked out at first, but she definitely bought it. Said that she liked my hair.'

'You mean, she liked *my* hair.'

'Technically speaking, it's lit-er-ally mine.'

'So, we're getting away with it then,' he says.

'Yeah, I suppose we are,' I agree.

'Amazing, really.'

'Now, remember . . . '

'I know,' he buts in. 'Michael needs to remember his guitar for music tomorrow.'

'Your Spidey senses are tingling.'

'You should come and meet us in the park tomorrow. I've signed the boys up for a football training programme.'

'That's a bit keen, isn't it?'

'Look, I better go.'

'Rushed off your feet, are you?' he says sarcastically.

I look around the house at the empty take-away cartons, half-drunk mugs of tea, beer bottles, CDs scattered around the place and think about the unctuous gloop smeared on the kitchen floor.

'Yeah, there's just a little tidying up to do. And I'm thinking of doing a bit of redecoration – freshen things up a little, you know.'

'We'll make a yuppie of you yet, Tom Cunningham.' He yawns. 'I'm knackered. I'm going to hit the sack. We'll catch up tomorrow.'

I slump back for a minute before noticing that there's a huge grease mark in the middle of one of the cushions. I leap up – Sean is going to go metrosexual mental.

14
Sean

On Tuesday, unconvinced that London Transport is up to the task of getting them to football practice on time, especially with its current crop of drivers, who appear to be more schooled in *Gran Turismo* than customer service, I decide to pick the boys up from school. Heading over to West Hampstead in the Volvo I notice a faint odour in the car, nothing too powerful, just some vague fusion of boys' bodies and confectionary. I'm waiting outside school when a car pulls up to the kerb and a familiar kid gets in. I'm wondering where I know him from when I recognise the driver: it's the KitKat thieving woman from the park. She looks up at me, before offering a wave a woman might describe as 'cute', which happens to be the kind of wave that women are good at – more of a wiggling of the fingers than a full-on arm or wrist movement. She drifts off into traffic and I watch her go. Her son, whose name I can't recall, is strapped in the back stuffing his face with something. I like the look of this one, and clearly I've got purchase. I can't imagine that she'd wave at just any bloke she'd bumped into in the park whose kids happen to go to the same school. Not that I'm deluded or anything . . .

I ferry the boys to the park and, while they're getting changed, grab myself a coffee from the café, where I see a familiar face.

'Nice jacket,' I say to Tom.

'Thanks,' he replies. 'It's one of yours.'

'That's why I said it, you plum,' I explain.

'Shit, sorry, you know, bit preoccupied.'

He's looking round, as if this is a Cold War era meeting in a neutral zone and he's just about to hand over state secrets that could get him executed.

'What's up with you?' I ask.

'It's just so fucking weird being here and not being me. I'm nervous that I'm going to put a foot wrong if I bump into someone I know . . . It happened on Sunday. Some bloke who worked at that café near your place thought I was you and . . . '

Oops. He met Brent.

'Made a little offering, maybe?'

'It's not funny, Sean. I bumped into a friend of Sara's near your place and I was sure she knew I was lying to her.'

'So you pretended you were me?'

'Yeah. It was a bit hairy, but I got through it.'

He looks around furtively before reaching out and stuffing something in my hand. I can tell just from the feel that it's an eighth of grass. I quickly stuff it in my trouser pocket.

'What am I supposed to do with that?'

'I dunno. Smoke it?' says Tom.

'I'm going to give it back to you – just stash it somewhere in the house. I can't be holding this,' I whisper. 'I've got kids to look after.'

I'm reaching out to give it to him when a mum with a couple of kids barges through the door of the café. Another couple of kids follow her and suddenly the moment has passed. I'll give it to him later on. I slip the package in my jeans pocket.

'So, what's all this then?' Tom asks with a wink that acknowledges that we've got to exchange later on.

'How do you mean?'

'This. The football.'

'You mean to say that you come here all the time and you've no idea that there's an after-school football programme?'

'Yeah, yeah . . . I just, you know, never knew how to get involved, that's all.'

I lead him to a noticeboard next to the ice-cream freezer.

'How many times have you queued up here?'

Tom examines the rudimentary green pamphlet tacked up on the wall. In a way that I'm sure is meant to appeal to 'the kids', it advertises 'Football Skillz'.

'It's just a phone call,' I explain. 'Think you can handle it?'

'Well, that's great,' Tom concedes. 'I know the boys will love it.'

We grab a couple of coffees and wander across to where a trainer has rigged up a small pitch and has the kids shuttling between plastic cones.

'So, how are you doing, "Uncle Sean"?' I ask.

Tom smiles. 'Not so bad, you know. Been getting a lot of shut-eye. Got my hair cut . . . '

'I can see Takamichi hooked you up.'

'All in all, been easing into it nicely. One thing though: why did you take them to fucking Chelsea? I mean *come on*.'

'How about this: because they wanted to go,' I say sarcastically.

'They want to meet Pamela Anderson, for God's sake. That doesn't make it a good idea.' He's exasperated.

'It was going to happen one day, Tom.' I laugh. 'They're men of taste and refinement, not sad sacks like you.'

Tom is restless, pacing in small circles.

'I was up late last night,' he says, as if explaining his behaviour.

'Oh, *really*.' I raise my eyebrow.

'No, not that. Just watching telly. Had a couple of nerve-steadiers too. Before I knew it, it was three in the morning.'

'Living the life, eh?'

'But don't worry, Sean. I've got big plans for the next few days. I've just got to concentrate on not getting caught.'

'I'm looking forward to hearing about it.'

'How are you getting on?' he says, nodding towards the kids.

I pause for a moment. He watches me closely, expectantly. I get the feeling that he might want me to run my hands through my hair and express exasperation, to fall on my knees and beg for the misery to end. This is not what I do. I offer him no crumbs of absolution.

'What the hell have you been complaining about for the past ten years?' I ask, punching him playfully on the shoulder. He shoots me a sardonic, heavy-lidded look. 'You've sold me a pup, mate. It's not that bloody hard, is it?'

'Just you wait,' he says, watching Paddy commit a foul on one of his own teammates. 'You'll see.'

I laugh and shove him on the shoulder again. He doesn't smile back.

'You'll see,' he repeats.

'Come on, man,' I say. 'I'm just messing with you, just getting inside your head.' Eventually he relents. I suppose he's stressed out by the potential for getting busted. Believe me, I am too. I'm just a bit better at hiding it.

In the distance, over by the playground, I notice someone familiar. It's her! It's the dark-haired woman I've got my eye on. I wonder if I should go over but she's deep in conversation on her mobile. She's wearing a military jacket, with a thick knitted scarf wrapped around her neck several times. She's chatting animatedly, but at the same time has her spare arm wrapped around her middle, underneath her breasts. She appears oblivious to everything around her. I get the feeling that this might not be the ideal opportunity to slide over there. I'll keep an eye on her and wait for the right moment. After a couple of minutes she heads towards the café. I tell Tom that I'll be back in a minute and scoot over there. I follow her inside and take a moment to examine her before making my 'coincidental' approach. Her straight black hair is pulled back in a bunch. Her features are fine, although there's a slight heaviness around her eyes and jawline suggesting that she might be older than she actually looks.

'Hi,' I say.

'Hi,' she answers, offering me a wonky smile. 'How are you?'

So far, so good. It appears that she actually wants to converse.

'I'm great. Everything all right?'

'Oh, I'm just awesome,' she says. 'Phenomenal.'

I'm a little taken aback by her irony, when I realise that she's not being sarcastic, she's just being funny.

'Well, I'm very glad to hear that,' I say, emitting a small laugh.

'And how are *you*?' she asks intensely. This is a challenge. Be amusing, Sean.

'Well, I haven't committed a crime yet today.'

A questionable six out of ten, but not a disaster.

'I suppose it's only mid-afternoon – you've got plenty of time,' she says.

'I'm not worried – it's pension day tomorrow,' I add. 'So if I don't manage it today I can make up for it tomorrow outside the Post Office.'

That's better. Victimising old people. She'll love that. Jesus.

She glances out the window at the boys playing football. I turn round to look and see that one of the boys is her son.

'So, your boy is playing too?'

'No, I'm a talent scout,' she says.

'You're in the wrong place then,' I offer, turning to look outside as well.

'"Playing", actually might be a little generous as a description of what Matthew is up to,' she says. 'Running around desperately trying to get a touch of the ball would probably be more accurate.'

'Come on,' I mock scold her. 'You're in the discouraging zone, snap out of it.'

'Yeah, you're right,' she adds. 'Otherwise he'll end up as a cross-dressing serial killer on *Trisha* in ten years and blame it all on me.'

'Yeah, spread the blame around a bit,' I suggest.

'Oh, believe me,' she answers, 'I'm not spreading the blame, I'm *dumping* it categorically in other places.'

She delivers a you-know-what-it's-like self-deprecating laugh and I want to kiss her there and then.

She looks out at the threatening sky.

'Looks like it's going to rain,' she says.

'Goddammit,' I say. 'It'll ruin my hair.'

'I thought your hairdresser had got there first,' she comes back at me.

I examine her, wide-eyed.

'I'm sorry,' she says. 'That was a little forward of me.'

'It's fine,' I say. 'Seriously.'

Of course, the thing to really prove that it's OK is to make a funny joke, but I'm too in awe of her to offer much beyond a stare.

'Sometimes I can overdo it,' she acknowledges, as if talking to herself.

'I can take it,' I say.

She turns back to watch the game and I get the feeling that she's smothering another saucy comment.

Good Lord. I've got to pull something out of the bag quickly . . . Got it!

'Look, we're putting a team together for this tournament next week and we need another player. I was wondering if – Matthew, isn't it? – would like to join us.'

'Can I play as well?' she asks.

'Well . . . '

'That's just a joke,' she says, her eyes wide like she's talking to an idiot.

'Of course,' I say.

'I'm sure that he'd love to,' she says, nodding. 'I'll ask him.'

'We'll be here most afternoons this week – we're going to have a few practice games so the boys can get to know each other – so, just let me know,' I say brightly, hoping to close the deal.

'Sounds good,' she says. 'I'm Maja, by the way.' She extends her hand. I take it.

Just call me Mr Magic. 'And I'm actually a pretty good striker, although I'm not as quick as I used to be.' She pats her leg. 'It's the knees, you know.'

'Tom,' I say. I'm quietly pleased that I utter this without any hesitation, although it occurs to me that I might regret it later.

'All right, I better go and show an interest,' she says, sprinkling sugar into her cup. 'Don't want to miss a goal – I'll never hear the end of it.' She says this in a dry way that I like, acknowledging the power that her child has over her, but also implicitly stating that she wants to be there as a witness.

I follow Maja outside to watch her kid and mine (well, sort of mine) get muddy and out of breath. I catch Maja's eye a couple of times and we share small moments of amusement relating to our boys' rather over-serious attitude to the game. As the kids trudge off the pitch, I catch her having a word with her boy. I see him nod. Maja turns and looks at me from about fifty yards away and gives me a smile and a thumbs-up. I put my arms over Michael and Patrick's shoulders just long enough to experience a little joy and hope – yes, hope! – before the short, muddy trudge home as evening falls and the street lights flicker to life.

Tom does a fair impression of me, including my trademark messing with their hair (am I that predictable?) and joke-telling (he gets a laugh with the one about the man who walks into a pub holding a dog turd and says, 'Hey, look what I almost stepped in!'). Fair play – he's definitely thought about it.

I announce to the boys that there's a five-a-side competition the weekend after next and we're going to enter a team. The boys are thrilled. I'm beginning to understand that competition – and mud – is pretty much the key to motivating them. Tom appears less enthusiastic. Maybe he feels a little upstaged, maybe he doesn't want the weekend of our re-exchange disrupted. We all walk back towards the house. The boys are full of the session, replaying every moment, asking who we thought was man of the match (funnily enough, it was awarded to them jointly). Now, I could be living in a dream world, but it appears to me that the boys are more animated than they were only three days ago. The standard foot dragging and eye rolling is not apparent today. Both have asked to walk home in their football kits hero-style, their knees covered in mud, their hair plastered saltily to their foreheads.

'Can we come training again tomorrow, Dad?' asks Michael.

'Well, I'm not sure that we've got time . . . ' says Tom. The jackass has forgotten himself. There's a brief moment of uncertainty before both boys start laughing.

'Keep it buttoned, Uncle Sean,' says Paddy.

'Yeah, Uncle Sean,' I chime in, 'don't stick your nose where it's not wanted.'

'Easy, fellas,' says Tom, forcing a smile. 'No need for a beat-down. Just winding you up.'

Michael does an impression of Tom: '*I'm not sure we've got time,*' he says in the most pompous way that he can muster.

'That's enough, Michael,' snaps Tom. He flashes Michael a testy glance. We continue down the street in silence, the boys occasionally kicking at the thick piles of leaves heaped against the fence.

'How was school?' Tom asks the boys eventually.

'Fine,' says Paddy.

'I need to remember to take in that form for the class trip,' says Michael.

I can see Tom itching to say something, but he manages to control himself.

'I'll dig it out tonight and put it in your bag,' I say.

'Thanks, Dad.'

I look over and see Tom turn his collar up, his face flushed unusually red.

We get back to the house and the boys slump in front of the TV while I prepare some pasta and vegetables. Tom puts on a brew, which is something I wouldn't generally do. I let it go.

'So, what happened back there?' I ask, slicing a cucumber, my voice down low.

'What?'

'When you nearly screwed everything up by answering Michael's question as yourself.'

'Totally forgot. Sorry about that.'

'Yeah, well, you'll be the one who's sorry if Sara's around when you make a slip.'

'Well, she won't be,' says Tom dismissively. 'The trial's set for at least two weeks.'

'I know. I'm saying "what if", not "when". I'm just trying to make sure that we keep in character at all times. We should probably even be in character now.'

'Don't worry, the boys won't surface until Vader has told Luke that he's his father.'

'Now that's more messed up even than the stunt we're pulling.'

'So, you're into it then?' asks Tom, changing tack. 'The fatherhood thing.'

'Yeah.' I nod my head. 'Whether I'm going to feel like this in a week or not we'll see.' I take a bite of cucumber.

He takes a considered sip of his tea. 'You're not missing work, then?'

'Not really,' I say.

'But won't they miss you?'

'I'm going to tell you something: I think that it's time that they learned to manage on their own.' I drain some pasta. 'You know, I've been away on holiday before. I go every year, but I always keep my phone on. Can't stop myself from checking the Berry. I've always been available. Now I'm not. And you know what? I like it like that. Anyway, if anything calamitous happens they'll call my mobile and you can bell me, right?'

'Right.'

I put two bowls of steaming pasta on the table to cool before placing a side dish of salad next to both.

'But they shouldn't need to call you, is what you're saying?' he continues.

'They'll live without me.'

'So business is good?'

I look at him for a moment. I can't work out whether this is a leading question, or Tom trying to get a better grasp of my life. Are we having a moment where he's reaching out and trying to connect, or is he up to something?

'Business is great,' I say. 'There's ups and downs, but we're in great shape.'

'Good,' says Tom, apparently satisfied, but clearly not. 'You must have a very loyal set of clients.'

I look up from the sink.

'I do,' I say. Tom's persistence in talking about the business is like a series of internet pop-ups. As fast as you close them down, another one appears: 'Click here and you're a winner!', 'Penis enlargement!', 'You've been pre-selected . . . '

'So, who's your biggest client at the moment?' he says.

'Tom . . . ' I check myself in case one of the boys is nearby. 'Sean, I mean, can we do this later? I need to finish the boys' dinner.'

'Absolutely. What have you made?'

'Just pasta with veg in a tomato sauce.'

'You made the sauce?'

'Yeah.'

'There's a jar of Ragu in the cupboard, you muppet.'

'I know there's a jar of Ragu there, Sean.' I peek out the door to see if the boys are within earshot, before hissing at him, 'And it'll fucking well be there when you come back.'

'All right Ramsey,' says Tom, getting up and rooting through one of the cupboards. He pulls out a packet of Walkers.

'What are you doing?' I ask.

'It's just a packet of crisps.'

'You can't do that, not when the kids are about to eat. It's not right,' I tell him.

'All right, all right, keep your hair on, grandma . . . '

I walk into the living room and tell the boys that the food is on the table and that they can watch the rest of the movie afterwards. They come through without a struggle and sit eating while I clear away the kitchen things.

'When's Mum back again?' asks Michael, splatters of tomato sauce on his chin.

'A week Saturday,' I say. 'You want some more?'

'Yes, please.'

'Did you hear that we went to Chelsea, Uncle Sean?' says Paddy enthusiastically.

'Yeah, your dad told me,' Tom says.

'It was wicked,' adds Michael earnestly.

'Yeah,' adds Patrick. 'We had really good seats in the West stand and Dad got us programmes—'

'At three quid each, may I add,' I tell Tom.

'"Stand and deliver," that's what he said to the man selling them,' Michael tells Tom, laughing.

'Yeah, the seats were brilliant. We could see everything really close.' Paddy is warming to his subject. 'It looked like Liverpool were going to give us a game until we scored. The goal was amazing. The keeper didn't have a chance.'

'Sounds like a good game,' says Tom. 'So, are you giving up on QPR, Tom?' he asks mischievously.

'Oh, I'll never give up on QPR, Sean,' I answer. 'It's in my blood.'

'He likes supporting a team of losers,' scoffs Michael.

'I think that your dad would rather refer to them as plucky underdogs,' Tom says, with a little too much edge. 'We can't all be glory hunters.'

Simultaneously the boys raise their hands in the air and start chanting, 'Champions! Champions! Champions!' clapping in between each exclamation. Tom is trying to laugh, trying to get into the spirit of things as 'Uncle Sean' might, but I can see that it's getting on his nerves. And who can blame him? He's spent the last few years trying to indoctrinate his sons into following his boyhood heroes, only to have overwhelming forces of history, not to mention dodgy Russian oil money, steamroller his sons into the celebration of the triumph of money over all else.

The boys finish up their meals without the use of coercion. Not only that, they pick up their plates and deposit them next to the sink before returning to *Star Wars*. I haven't asked them to do that. I look over at Tom, who has noted the change.

'So, have you put them on drugs or something?' he asks, once they're gone. 'No fighting, finishing their food, tidying up . . . All unheard of. Where's the lithium?'

Again I check to make sure the boys aren't in earshot.

'Tom,' I say putting on an American infomercial voice, 'today I'd like to talk to you about the transforming power of love.'

'One thing though,' he says, 'you offered Michael Parmesan. He hates it. Rather poetically he describes it as smelling like "pooh that goats have eaten and then thrown up".'

'The kid's got class.' I grab a piece of paper and a pen and start writing.

'What are you doing?' he asks.

'Well, how the hell am I supposed to remember all this stuff that your faddy kids either like or don't like?'

'No pens. Nothing gets written down,' says Tom firmly.

'You're absolutely right,' I agree, putting the pen down and screwing up the piece of paper. I can't believe that I'm missing my BlackBerry. What a tart. 'No paper trail.' I look over at Tom wearing my clothes.

'Got to say, mate, you're looking good,' I tell him.

'Thought I'd make the effort to dress like a pompadoured ponce, given that I'm representing you for a couple of weeks.'

'Well, you're doing something right – I suspect that it's mainly not wearing the tat I found in your bedroom.'

'Easy now,' he says, pointing at the top I'm wearing. 'That's one of my favourite John Smedleys.'

'And it was probably one of Albert Steptoe's too. How long have you had this? There are artefacts in the British Museum younger than this.'

'I'll tell you what the difference is,' says Tom. 'It's sleep. I'm getting as much sleep as I can handle.'

'Well, you're looking good on it, you soft git,' I say. 'So you're cool with me taking them to this soccer coaching after school until we swap back?' I ask. He considers this for a moment before eventually nodding, *like it's his bloody decision* what happens over the next fortnight.

'Good,' I say. 'And I'm going to take them over to Brent Cross to get new boots. They need proper studs, the pitch is getting muddy.'

'They'll never do it,' says Tom knowingly.

'Really?'

'They hate any journey that takes longer than consuming a Happy Meal,' he says dismissively.

'You know what, Tom? They complain that you never let them listen to music when you're driving.'

'It's a distraction,' he blurts out, like he's had the argument dozens of times. 'The way I see it, it's dangerous. I need to focus when I'm on the road.'

'Well, it's a distraction for them too, knobskin. If they've got tunes going they're less likely to be annoying you.'

'It doesn't work like that,' says Tom. 'If there's music on I've got them chattering away, asking questions, and the bloody music to listen to, plus I'm surrounded by maniacs whose last experience of driving was commanding an armoured personnel carrier in the Balkans.'

'All right,' I say, holding my hands up, laughing. 'You're right. Music is a prelude to motoring disaster.'

Tom can tell that I'm unimpressed by his reasoning, and sits stewing for a minute, while I tidy up the boys' dishes. I've stumbled on a family argument that has deeper roots and is more involved than I suspected. He's like that, is Tom. Carries things on long past their sell-by date. He did it when we were kids; still does it as an adult: sits there with a brooding sense of injustice, like he's been wronged. It didn't serve him too well at school, where he was constantly engaging in wordless feuds. We were in the minority at school, middle-class kids at a London comprehensive that had little to recommend it. We didn't have any more money than anyone else in our class, in fact, the kids whose dads had jobs where it was all cash in hand – builders, plumbers, anything to do with markets – tended to be the ones who went off to Florida on Skytrain and got the flashy trainers.

I suppose the only thing that marked us out was that we had books in our house: Mum's novels and Dad's history. That was all it was really. I remember once asking my mum a question and her answering, 'I don't know, but it's all in books, you know.' They weren't too bothered about exam results or any of that strict academic stuff. They knew that we'd find our way, although they weren't happy when I decided to drop my A levels and go to art school.

Best thing I ever did, to be honest. Three years of messing about, making stuff and going to parties. But, strangely, the most remarkable thing about it was meeting posh people for the first time, particularly posh girls, whose mums and dads owned galleries, made programmes for the BBC, had houses in France. A total eye-opener. It touched something inside me, made me realise that it was all there for the taking if you just dressed the right way and made out that you deserved it. That was what I took from them and why I've always stuck up for the upper middle class against their detractors (Tom, for one, although with a wife who's a barrister I should remind him about stones and glasshouses). What they taught me was that behaving with confidence was the key to others trusting you. If you phone someone up and sound plausible, act like you've every right to be talking to them, then they're likely to buy whatever it is that you've got to sell, whether it's double glazing or yourself, which is what I've been doing for the past decade.

Paddy wanders back into the kitchen. He approaches Tom and asks him if he wants to play chess.

'Sorry, mate, I've gotta make a move.'

Paddy twists his body in frustration.

'Oh, Uncle Sean, you're the only one that will play with me. Michael won't and Dad's always too busy.'

Tom looks at Paddy with alarm, before steadying himself.

'Next time,' he says. 'I'm around this week. I promise. By the way, why did the monkey fall out of the tree?'

'I dunno,' answers Paddy.

'Because it was dead.'

Paddy smiles faintly and rolls his eyes.

'All right, try this one: Jordan and Peter Andre are walking down the street one day when Peter says, "Aw, look at that dead pigeon. Poor thing." Jordan looks up in the sky and says, "Where?"'

He did it well, I've got to say. Turned the charm on just like I might. Paddy walks away amused. But there's a difference: I would have played chess. Tom knows this as he sits on the kitchen counter eating a banana. The exchange with Paddy has altered his bearings a little.

I try and cheer him up.

'I'll play with him later,' I say. Tom nods in acknowledgement.

'So, you're getting on all right then?' He says this emphatically, with a hint of sourness in his voice. I decide to treat it as a question.

'Yeah, fine,' I say. 'You don't need to keep checking. It's good.'

Tom nods. I sense that he's hoping I might ask him for advice, or maybe reveal a problem that I need some guidance with. I know that I'm still finding my way down the nursery slopes while Tom is a black-run veteran, but I can't think of a single thing that I need to know. Maybe he'd prefer it if I was struggling a little more. Tom prises himself off the kitchen counter and deposits the banana skin in the bin.

'Right, I'll be off then,' he says, rubbing his hands together.

'Anything I need to know?' I offer.

'No,' he says, patting me on the shoulder. 'You appear to be getting along just fine.'

He walks through to the living room to hug the boys.

'You better get some chess practice in,' he says to Paddy. 'I'll be back.'

'Bring it on,' says Paddy.

Tom laughs, and I can see that part of him wishes that he could stay. Nevertheless, he's not exactly dragging his feet as he steps out of the front door.

Later that night I get into bed and fall asleep after a couple of chapters of one of Sara's highbrow novels. I sleep fitfully. Tom and Sara's bed is the place where I am most aware of the perversity of what I'm up to. I wake up several times, always fully conscious, my senses keen to the different shapes, sounds and smells of the room. Proximity to the boys is bringing back memories of my own childhood, small details about mood, fragments of conversation, moments of awkwardness.

I can't help reflecting; even by my slipshod ethical standards, what we're doing is questionable, but just how wrong is it? As far as the boys are concerned I don't think that there's a problem. But Sara is a different matter. Her presence is the ultimate doomsday scenario, one that I'd rather not contemplate as I drift off to sleep.

15
Tom

I should know better than this. Wrenching myself out of bed at a respectable nine thirty, I commence another day of bachelorhood with a mild but niggly hangover. Despite my best intentions, I'm too hungry to go to the gym (check that out as an excuse – certainly beats forgetting your jockstrap) so I search out nourishment in the kitchen, skidding on the greasy residue I dropped the night before, which almost sends me arse over tit. The absence of both cereal and bread suggests that Sean foregoes breakfast. I get dressed and go to a café. On my way I pass a bookshop and, chastened by my somewhat dismal showing in the self-improvement stakes over the past forty-eight hours, I decide to pick up some reading. A woman at the 3-for-2 fiction table gives me the once-over. I idle over towards her, thinking that I might just try and see if the old magic is still there when, before I know it, some flash Harry has swooped in. Outrageous! It's all gone rotten before I've even got out of the traps. And, more's the point, isn't a woman even allowed to browse in a bookshop without being approached by some predator? I wander over to the Classics section and pick up a copy of *Finnegans Wake*. This serious purchase will anchor my drive for the new, well-read and enlightened me. I have visions of lying on Sean's modernist sofa devouring ideas of import as if they're Maltesers.

At the café I snag a window table and crack open *Finnegans Wake*. Easing into the book I scope the room and spot a youngish, professional woman in a suit scanning some documents. She glances up at me and I smile. I'm acknowledged with a brief nod of the head before she returns to her work. It might have been momentary, but something just happened there. Would she have acknowledged any old Tom, Dick or Harry – or was it me? Now, I'm not sure if this is strictly in the rules – I am, after all, still a married man – but surely a little 'research' isn't beyond the pale here? Something harmless to demonstrate that my lady-killing skills, while maybe not as sharp as a sushi chef's knife, still have a pulse at least. I mean, this isn't like the other night with Ellie, there's no real danger here. Why am I even torturing myself? It's just a bit of a laugh, and what are the chances of anything untoward happening? We're in the middle of a bloody café, for God's sake.

Resolved, I turn my attention back to her. She looks like she's in her late twenties and her life is currently all about her career, although the prospect of marriage and kids isn't that far off. She might live with a boyfriend who she's trying to suss out, wondering whether he's the real deal, someone she wants to father her children, someone she can trust not to hear the call of the wild.

The woman, engrossed in her paperwork and BlackBerry, doesn't look up. I order a coffee and a bacon and egg sandwich and wait for the woman to sneak a peek at what I'm reading. Now, the heavyweight fiction might be a little off-putting for some, but I'm hoping that the garms carefully put together from Sean's man closet will have the appropriate effect: style and brains. Come on, girls, it doesn't get any better than that. You know it makes sense . . .

I begin to read. The words translate into sounds and meaning in my head, but absolutely nothing is penetrating beyond the façade. The majority of my brain function is devoted to keeping discreet surveillance on the woman to my right, thus rendering the rest of my brain largely inactive, like the screen of a computer that's going blank due to a lack of activity. She works away on her *very important stuff*. Her BlackBerry vibrates occasionally and she snatches it up and punches in messages with furious self-assurance. I begin to wonder whether she might not be a Joyce fan when I notice her looking over. I smile and nod knowingly, acknowledging the King Kong of fiction.

'How are you getting on with it?' she asks, a half smile playing on her lips.

'Well, I've only just started,' I explain. 'Still on the first page, actually.'

Nice bit of self-deprecation there. Women *love* that.

'You've done well to get that far,' she says. 'Are you studying it?'

'No, no.' I smile. 'Just trying to catch up on some of the classics.'

'Well, you'll have more fun eating a tin of boot polish,' she says. I notice for the first time that she's got a faint Geordie accent. 'I studied Irish literature at university, and I love Joyce, but I've never managed to finish *Finnegans Wake*. I'm sure it's brilliant but, really, it's a bloody slog. Stick to the Sidney Sheldon. Seriously.'

I nod slowly. 'Well, thanks for the encouragement.'

'Oh, don't let me put you off,' she explains. 'It's good for you, but in the way that those breakfast cereals with millet in them are good for you. You've got to wonder whether it's worth it.'

'Well, a lot of things are like that,' I say.

'Sting's solo albums, for instance,' she says.

Her phone goes and I stuff my mouth with sandwich and go back to looking at the words in *Finnegans Wake*. The woman suddenly stands up.

'Look, I've got to go,' she explains. 'Nice talking to you. If you ever fancy talking literature again this is my e-mail.' She hands me a corner torn from an A4 pad with a Yahoo address on it. She heads out of the café with her laptop case, which is undoubtedly full of *very important stuff* and out onto the street. I examine the piece of paper and, while I should be rather flattered – maybe even exultant – that I've semi-pulled, or at least managed to pull within the same species, I'm actually just staggered. This kind of thing has never, ever happened to me before. I haven't been exposed to the singles scene for nearly fourteen years, so I'm not exactly sure that I'm up to date on its finer points, but one thing I know is that a woman has never given me her phone number without me begging, paying or finding it printed on a card in a phone box. Clearly my vital signs are still a glimmer on the cardiograph.

In my fantasy bachelor life this, of course, is exactly what I have longed for: available women making themselves available to me. I put down the copy of *Finnegans Wake*, finish my coffee and examine the piece of paper again. Did she really mean, 'Get in touch and we can talk about James Joyce, Oscar Wilde and Colm Toibin'? Or was it more like, 'Get in touch and I'll let you glaze my doughnut.' I have absolutely no idea. Is this the game now? Is this how modern women behave? I can't pretend that the notion of arranging an internet date culminating in strings-free sex isn't something that I've thought about, oh, several hundred times a day since I heard of such a possibility, but it's the closest that I've been to realising it. I pay my bill and leave, but not before I've screwed up the note and left it in the ashtray.

Contact with the Geordie princess and a lurking low-grade hangover have made me long for the comfort of Sean's house. I scurry back clutching the copy of *Finnegans Wake* half wishing that I'd at least had the balls to hang on to the woman's e-mail address to prolong the fiction of the possibility of meeting for meaningless, anonymous sex. On my return I'm actually more excited by the fact that, until this point, I've forgotten that Sean owns a PlayStation and *Grand Theft Auto San Andreas*. I set the thing up, create my character and am transported from West London to East LA. Four hours later, my wrist is beginning to ache. I need to get some air. I call Sean and he's at the park with the boys. I'm not keen on the idea of showing my face over there, but I want to see the boys.

I get back and, try as I might to settle down with *Finnegans Wake*, the PlayStation kept calling me. *Okay just one game then.*

Before I know it, it's two in the morning, I'm surrounded by curry containers and empty lager bottles and I've just been shot in the back by a Cuban pimp. Now I'm not going to pretend that I don't know how this happened. I'm frighteningly aware of how it all went down and, frankly, none of it is the Cuban pimp's fault. The screen contracts to black, I conduct a rudimentary tidying of the room and shut the lights off. After nearly twelve hours of battling other criminals and the LAPD I'm slinking off to bed unfulfilled and deeply resentful, as if somehow I've haven't achieved quite what I might. It's a much deeper sense of unfulfilment than I've experienced in any other aspect of my life. True, I haven't slept with as many girls as I could. True, my career has been a stop-start affair that's just about been on the right side of ordinary. True, I could have held my place on the school ping-pong team if I'd just had a higher level of concentration. But getting gunned down when you're reaching for the drugs and your back is turned . . . that's the definition of injustice, right there. Sliding into Sean's large and comfy bed it occurs to me that I might distract myself by working on *Finnegans Wake*. I'm not sure of the exact total, but I think that I manage a mighty three paragraphs before falling asleep.

I'd like to report that I rose early and headed to the gym for the kind of cathartic workout that would set me up for a productive and wholesome day, but I can't. I rose early, grabbed a bowl of cereal and powered up the PlayStation for a 'quick' game of *San Andreas*. Entirely predictably I'm still sitting there in my underpants two hours later after getting a hiding from a group of Crips, and I'm *this* close to smashing the fucking machine up. I need to calm down, so I turn on the TV in search of something to anaesthetise myself. I remember when I first lost my job that this was the time, the lull after everyone else has gone off to do whatever it is that they have to do all day – working, schooling, thieving – that always made me feel the most marooned. It was the equivalent of grey skies in February stretching interminably towards the horizon.

Feeling guilty I get up off the sofa, do a couple of stretches and some callisthenics. Suddenly invigorated, I roam the house. In my quest for distraction I open the under-stairs cupboard. Amongst the tools and cleaning equipment (which, I suspect, if it were dusted by a crime lab would not reveal Sean's fingerprints) I find a football. It's brand new, never been used, but saggy, needing air (don't we all). Like most men, it's still an impossibility for me to see a football and not want to kick it. Occasionally I've been at barbecues with the kids' friends running around with a ball and it's as much as I can stand to sip my beer and chat politely about house prices – all I'm gagging to do is slam the ball against a fence, or drop a nicely weighted pass into the path of a marauding four-year-old. I scoop the ball up and start messing around. I'm juggling it reasonably successfully; I manage twelve consecutive keep-ups on my good foot, before I hit it against a wall. It comes back at me with some pace, so I trap it, look up, pretending to search out a teammate, and thread the ball through to them with precision and skill (something that I've never achieved in match conditions). I repeat this a few times until the ball comes back to me off the wall and bounces a couple of feet off the floor, and I just can't stop myself from volleying the thing. I catch it sweetly – there's no way anyone's stopping it. The ball arcs through the air, as if in slow motion, before thumping off a wall, narrowly missing a limited-edition Diane Arbus print, and rebounding into a glass fruit bowl that shatters, causing the, by now, over-ripened fruit to skid across the dining table and onto the floor.

My idiocy, candied in Wembley dreams, is apparent. The ball rolls idly across the room while I trudge back to the under-stairs cupboard and retrieve the dustpan and brush to sweep up the shreds of fruit bowl. Serves me right. Dickhead. I better not tell Sean – I'll find out where the thing's from and replace it. I clean up the mess and lie on the floor looking up at the ceiling.

I've been fighting it for a while, but only now will I admit it to myself – I am paralysed by boredom. It's ten thirty in the morning and I can't think of a single thing that I'd like to do. This is no fun at all. And what if I get caught? I'll lose everything, I imagine. And for what? I think about my family. What kind of a dad would do something like this? I never thought of myself as a psycho, but maybe I am. I phone Sean.

'Hi, mate,' he says. It's the kind of 'hi mate' that actually means 'I'm busy, let's talk when I'm not'.

'Yeah,' I say, unsure why I even called him. 'Just checking in.'

'Well, I've no major news to report,' says Sean. I can tell he's cradling the phone under his chin while he's doing something else. 'I seem to be winning the war on the boys' skid marks.'

'What are you up to?' I ask, rather lamely.

'Oh, you know, just stuff,' he says.

Stuff. Yeah. I know all about stuff.

'I've got to take them to football after school, then I've promised to take them to that new film, *Cyber Ninjas*, one evening. They've been going on about it for days. I thought we'd grab a burger while we're out. It'll be fun.'

'Yeah.'

'Look, got to go – the Ocado van is here. Let's catch up later, OK.'

'Right, later.'

I'm bewildered. Ocado? *Cyber Ninjas*? Is this the same family? *My* family? Are we actually speaking the same language? As I lie on the floor of the house examining the cracks in his ceiling, Sean is making his mark on my boys. *Chelsea, climbing walls, after-school football, Cyber Ninjas . . .* All this bloody *action*, it's like Sean is leaving his tyre marks on my forehead as he races off while I lie prostrate and stunned at the starting line like a hedgehog that's just met an Aston Martin. I stand up, tidy up the place, stick the dishwasher on and try and think about my next move. The copy of *Finnegans Wake* idles accusingly on the kitchen table; its weight and intellect a reminder of my own wafer-thin life achievements. Then it occurs to me . . .

I stride upstairs, taking the steps two at a time. I take a shower, shave, and open up Sean's dressing room, or man-closet, or whatever the hell it's called. I keep it simple: a crisp white shirt with a French collar and a grey flannel two-button suit. I pull on a pair of black Oxfords and gather myself in front of the mirror.

Not bad.

But there's still something missing; something's not right. I can't quite put my finger on it. I wander back into the dressing area and see what I'm looking for: a briefcase.

I pick it up and go downstairs where I stuff *Finnegans Wake* inside before leaving the house.

Sitting in Sean's mansion is doing little for me other than getting me drunk and fat. Or fat and drunk, depending on which way you look at it. I'm learning nothing. The only way to try and get a real sense of his life is to enter the place where he is at his best and (probably) his worst as well. So I walk out of Sean's house and spend some of his hard-earned cash on a taxi to his modestly named company, SC Communications. I get the driver to drop me a couple of streets away so that I can compose myself before walking slowly towards Sean's office, which is in a nondescript nineteenth-century building that has had the guts ripped out of it before being remodelled in the eighties to make way for Thatcher's service industry revolution.

What am I hoping to achieve by doing this? It's a huge risk. I know little of Sean's world of presentation and positioning. The last thing I put some spin on was a cue ball. Realistically, there's a good chance that I'll be exposed. At the very least I'll probably make a complete arse of myself. If she noticed something was awry, Ellie was more than likely to write it off as a quirk of behaviour. In a working environment I'm less likely to have that luxury. And, let's face it, working environments have not exactly been the scenes of my greatest triumphs over the last couple of years.

But I want to know exactly what Sean does, how his skills, or methods, his luck or attitude divide the two of us into neatly separated packages: the working stiff and the self-made millionaire. Secondly, I want to walk into an office and not feel like I'm going to be fired at any moment. I want to lord it a little. More than that, I want to reclaim a little ground, convince myself that I can hustle a living, demonstrate to the world that I've still got some moves left in me. I've been in there before, of course, admired my brother's corner office, had brief, uncomfortable conversations with some of his employees. But walking in as Sean himself, well it's bound to be something else.

I summon all the confidence that I can muster and walk into the lobby, where a middle-aged Afro-Caribbean security guard looks up from the *Daily Mirror* racing pages just long enough to take me for someone he recognises. He nods a curt greeting.

I take the lift up to the fourth floor where I see a young girl wearing a headset seated behind a reception desk.

'Hi, Sean!' she says brightly.

'Hi,' I say, keeping moving, heading towards a wide corridor that ends with my brother's office.

'I thought you were out for a couple of weeks,' she comments. She's not being accusatory, just trying to make conversation with the boss. I cringe at memories of doing the same thing to people who were plotting to shitcan me at the first whiff of redundancies. I turn back and approach her desk.

'Ssssssh!' I say, putting my index finger to my lips. 'You haven't seen me, OK? The last thing I want is to get dragged into some finance meeting.'

Thrilled by this intimacy with the boss she leans closer to me and whispers, 'OK, let's keep it our secret then.'

My shoes hit the polished concrete floor with the solid sound of business. I walk down the corridor exchanging the occasional nod with various employees. Fortunately, most people are too busy to notice, or pretend not to, avoiding interaction with the boss. I approach Sean's office and see that his assistant, Aileen, isn't stationed at her desk. Entering Sean's office I'm, as ever, dazzled by the size and elegance of its furnishings. There's a clutch of paintings by artists who have clearly not had their emotional needs met and bits of furniture that I've seen reproductions of in swanky department stores. Sean, of course, has got the fifties and sixties originals. There are piles of art books, magazines and catalogues like smokestacks throughout the office. A titanium iBook rests on top of a lustrous wooden desk, which I slip behind, spinning around in his pornographically comfortable office chair.

'Well, hello,' comes a voice. I complete a revolution and see Aileen, Sean's 'Executive' Assistant.

'Hello, Aileen.'

'Look, no offence, but what are you doing here?' she demands, hands on hips.

I look at her. We've met several times before. I'm concerned that she's addressing me as Tom, and not Sean. Is my act so fragile that I get busted the first time I try and pass as Sean in a working environment?

'Well . . . ' I start.

'I knew it!' she cries triumphantly, a smile breaking on her face. I rise from the desk, working on a lame excuse about having arranged to meet Sean at the office. 'I knew that you wouldn't be able to take the whole week off without checking in, but I didn't imagine that you'd last just three days before returning to the office. Just how empty is your life?'

I chuckle, relieved and amused by her chutzpah.

'I'm just here for a couple of hours,' I explain. 'There are a few things I wanted to check on.'

'Oh, well, if you're in town, do you want those U2 tickets that Vodaphone sent over?'

I try not to jump out of my chair.

'Mmmm,' I muse, drumming my fingers on my chin thoughtfully.

'And I got a call from Adidas about the Champions League game, if you're interested, that is . . . '

'Oh, I dunno . . . ' I say, clearly meaning exactly the opposite.

'Let me grab those U2 tickets then. You know that they're for tonight, don't you? You want anything? Coffee? OJ?'

'Both would be great.'

Aileen leaves the office. I pick up the phone and dial.

'Sean, guess where I am?'

'Tom, I told you earlier – I'm really busy.'

'Come on, guess where I am.'

'Behind my desk.' He sounds tired.

'How did you know?'

'Caller ID, idiot. Look, I told you to stay out of there.'

'C'mon, man, I wanted to get into the swing of things. Thought I'd see how you fritter your life away.'

'Look, don't take any calls, OK? If anyone asks you any questions, look thoughtful, tell them that you need to think about it, and that you'll get back to them. Surf the internet, eat as much free stuff as you want, just don't fuck anything up, all right?'

'All right, all right . . . '

'I'll speak to you later – I've got laundry to do.'

'How are the boys?'

'They're mentalists.'

'Send them my love. Shit! You can't. You're me. Oh, never mind.'

'Later.'

I put the phone down and touch the space bar on Sean's laptop. The screen glows to life. Let's see what we've got here. I move the cursor across the desktop and open Sean's hard drive. Entourage springs to life and I browse Sean's inbox. It's the usual dreary stuff – production schedules, procedural memos, HR guff – until I stumble across something juicy. It's a sequence of e-mails between Sean and the finance director and, although I'm only skimming the words, it's clear that their discussion is regarding the financial state of the company. This I'm interested in. I'm examining the e-mail trail when the phone rings. I look to see if it's Sean, but the number isn't listed. I pick it up anyway.

'Sean Cunningham.'

'Sean, hi, it's Mara Green.' The voice bursts out of the receiver like an explosive. 'Howareyoutodaygoood.'

'Um . . . '

'Look, here's the thing. Very unexpectedly Magenta Carlson is coming into town for the première of the new Pierce Brosnan movie. The studio is desperate to have her there. And I remembered how well you guys got on when you were working on the Virgin Atlantic thing and wanted to know whether you would be available to attend with her on Friday.'

'Well, I . . . '

'That's great. Awesome. I'm so happy. You're the best. I'll get my assistant to arrange a car. You can swing by and pick up Magenta and we're good to go.'

'Sure, I . . . '

There's no longer anyone on the other end of the line. Mara, it seems, has executed her business and migrated swiftly to the next item on her 'to do' list. I absorb what has just occurred and arrive at the inevitable conclusion that last week I was worrying about whether the kids need insoles for their shoes, whereas this week I'm accompanying a starlet to a movie première. Who said Sean and I live different lives? I return to Entourage and continue to read.

16
Sean

I wake with a start. There's a noise. Yeah, definitely a noise. I tense, straining to identify whatever it is. My ears ring from the intensity of effort.

'*Dad!*'

There it is. Unmistakable. It's Michael. I leap out of bed, my heart thumping. I hear him calling again as I head along the landing to the back bedroom. I push open the door and he's sitting on the bed, pyjama leg rolled up. I turn on the bedside lamp and see that there's a livid red patch of skin on his knee.

'It hurts,' he explains. 'It was all right earlier, but it's really stinging now.'

I take a closer look. There's no blood, but he's skinned it quite nastily.

'Don't worry,' I soothe him. 'I'll get you something for it. You relax, OK?'

I creep along the landing, trying not to wake Patrick before turning the bathroom upside down looking for a first-aid kit. I can't locate it, so I tiptoe downstairs and search through the kitchen. Michael appears at the kitchen doorway, limping like Stuart Pearce has just clumped him.

'Where does Mum keep the plasters?' I ask.

'In there,' he tells me, pointing to one of the kitchen cupboards. I open it up, but can't figure out where he means. Sensing this, he comes closer to help.

'It's not there,' he says. 'That's where she keeps the first-aid box, but it's not there.'

'I wonder where Mum's put them,' I say calmly.

I open a few more cupboards. Michael is looking a little discon-certed, and his lurching around like a bereaved orang-utan isn't helping me feel like I'm in control of the situation.

'Go back to bed,' I tell him. 'I'll find something. Go and get some cotton wool, dip it in some water and bathe your knee.'

He hobbles back upstairs. OK, stay calm. It's not that bad. I won't let Michael down. I just need to think clearly. I pick up the phone and dial Tom.

'HELLO?' he shouts. Static, and the power chords of 'In The Name of Love' largely drown his voice out.

'Tom, it's me!' I whisper back fiercely.

'HELLO!' he shouts as Bono wails in the background.

'Where are the damn plasters?'

'Hello, Sean?'

'Michael's hurt. He needs a plaster. Where are they?'

The line goes dead. I call him back, as livid as Michael's knee. The phone immediately switches to voicemail. I leave him a shitty message, which I immediately feel bad about but, for God's sake, I've got a child's welfare to think about. I wish I had Maja's number, she'd know what to do. And maybe afterwards we could . . .

Concentrate, Sean, for God's sake.

I have another scout around the kitchen and, sure enough, score the first-aid box in another cupboard that, for some bizarre reason, contains a large number of sugar bowls.

I take it upstairs, slap on some antiseptic ointment, which initially makes Michael flinch, but some egghead chemist has had the good sense to lace it with Ibuprofen, which soon kicks in and dulls the pain. I put on one of those old-fashioned plasters that you have to cut into strips. I stand up as Michael gets back in bed. As he does so he pats me on the arm and says, 'Thanks, Dad.'

It's a terribly simple act, but not a childish one. You don't expect kids to give you a reassuring pat – that's what adults are for – and I find the small transaction astonishingly moving. I turn out the light, go back to bed and sleep soundly until the phone rings. I pick it up, knowing exactly who it is.

'Tom.'

'Is he all right?' His voice is slightly slurred. Nice to know that he's managed to get a few drinks in before checking his voicemail.

'Yeah, he's fine. Look, it's two in the morning . . . '

'What happened?'

'He skinned his knee at football. I gave him a plaster. No big deal.'

'Is he OK?' I can tell Tom is upset. 'Are you *sure* he's OK?'

'He's fine.'

'Do I need to come back?'

'Tom, everything's fine. He's fast asleep.'

'Jesus, what a nightmare.'

'Tom, it's not a big deal.'

'I knew that we shouldn't have done this.'

He is currently the embodiment of the phrase 'tired and emotional'.

'Tom, how about this? If you were here you wouldn't be able to do any more than I've done.'

'Did you put on some antiseptic?'

'Yes. I'm putting the phone down now.'

'Hang on . . . Why didn't you see it earlier?'

'I don't know. He was covered in mud. It didn't start hurting him until later on.'

'OK,' says Tom, although I can tell that my explanation doesn't fully satisfy him.

'Oh, one other thing,' says Tom. 'You know that fruit bowl in the living room.'

'The crystal one.'

'Oh, it's crystal, is it?' His tone is apprehensive. It's a give-away if ever I heard one.

'You've broken it, haven't you, you twat?'

'No,' he says firmly. 'No, no, no. I just like it, that's all.'

'So maybe you'd like to know where you can buy one then?' I say.

'That might be a good idea,' agrees Tom.

I get the kids off to school the next morning with Tom's reproachful tone still fresh in my ears. Last night's incident has given me pause for thought. Could I handle a real emergency? Is it unethical for me to be around the kids if they're suffering? I run a few errands, tidy up the place, do the laundry, have some lunch and before I know it, it's time for football practice. As the boys begin the session I slope off to the café to get coffee when my mobile rings. It's Tom, sounding a bit sheepish.

'I'm a bit freaked about what happened with Michael,' he explains.

'Why?'

'Well, what if something serious was to happen?'

'It didn't, and it won't.'

'How do you know it won't?'

'It just won't.'

'It didn't feel right, Sean,' he says. 'Look, I know that you'll do your best and all that, but it's not the point, is it?'

I let his words hang there for a moment. Jitters are going to be part of this for both of us.

'Anyway, you haven't told me about last night,' I say enthusiastically.

'It was amazing,' says Tom. He sounds a little worse for wear. 'The crowd were really up for it, and the band were electric. The place was going wild.'

I snag a table by the window so I can watch the boys' session.

'They started out with "City of Blinding Lights",' continues Tom. 'And then they really mixed it up, you know. The old stuff with the new stuff. They did "Elevation", "I Will Follow", "I Still Haven't Found What I'm Looking For" . . . '

'That's what Sara chose for your first dance at your wedding, isn't it?' I say.

'Very funny. "Beautiful Day", "Sunday Bloody Sunday", "In The Name of Love", "Pride", "One" . . . It was amazing. Totally amazing. You should have seen the light show. Oh, and they did "With Or Without You" for the encore. Mindblowing.'

I gaze out of the window to see how the boys' ball-control skills are developing. Michael appears to be running without any ill effects from his knee.

'I was up in the VIP area, which was wicked, so I was on the free champagne all night. And then we went to the after party over at that new place, what's it called? Over in Victoria . . . and *everyone* was there. I mean *everyone*. And I got talking to that girl off the telly. What's her name? That girl that used to do kids' programmes, and now she does the Lottery or something. The blonde one? Anyway . . . '

And he keeps going on. To be honest, it's getting a little tedious. Tom pauses for a moment.

'So, I've been meaning to tell you – I've been in to your office.'

'I know,' I reply tersely. 'You called me from there. Why the hell did you go in?'

'To be you, of course. To get the whole picture.'

'Jesus.'

'No one suspects. Least of all Aileen.'

'Do not do anything when you're in there, OK?' I stress. 'No decisions, no conversations. Remember, if people ask you anything look thoughtful and tell them that you'll get back to them.'

'Yeah, I understand,' he says. 'No paper trail.'

'Well, no bullshit trail as well, OK? Also, never, ever sign anything that's put in front of you. We could both go to jail.'

'All right, Sean. I get it,' he says, somewhat peeved. 'You don't need to be arsey with me. It's part of the deal, Sean. I'm trusting you with my family. I've got to see what your work life is like. Not only that, it's having an effect on me. Just getting up in the morning, putting on a nice suit and having a place where I'm expected to be, it's . . . I dunno, helping me find my feet in the workplace again.'

'All right, Oprah, just don't do anything stupid, OK. I can't afford any mistakes.'

'Affirmative.'

'Good. So now you've discovered the joys of Savile Row, and got a decent haircut and a high-flying job – are you becoming super yuppie?'

Tom takes a deep breath.

'Have you tried the new iced mango chai at Starbucks? It's *delicious*,' he says theatrically.

17
Tom

On Thursday, I take the plunge and arrange a meeting with the finance director, Theano Georgiadou. Big surprise, it turns out to be a little awkward. Given that I still have an unclear picture of the financial state of the business, and whether the mini meltdown that's unfolding on the e-mails is at this moment metastasising into a fully grown crisis, I have to ask questions that will build a clearer picture, while at the same time not revealing that it has taken me a good ten minutes to find her encouragingly modest office. The way I imagine Sean-world is a happy place where pink bunnies drink from lemonade streams and children of all ethnicities frolic in wild flower meadows. It's a place where there are no stresses, concerns or worries. I have to admit to being nervous about what Theano has to tell me.

Theano is, I imagine, a few years younger than me, in her early thirties, and is still in the full bloom of optimism regarding the upwards curve of her career and economic potential. I feel like a barnacle-encrusted battleship in her presence as she skips through the spreadsheets laid out in front of us, navigating the numbers with a deft familiarity, revealing their secrets with an objective competence.

I'll spare you the details, but the numbers tell us this: without the two recently lost accounts, SC Communications now has only three months' worth of cash flow. Beyond that there is a terrifying abyss.

'Are we close to breaking any new business?' asks Theano.

'I'm working on it,' I tell her.

'But are you confident that any of the potential accounts will deliver revenue in the next month or so?'

'I don't know,' I say.

'You don't sound very confident,' she says gravely.

'I've got balls in the air,' I tell her. 'I need to work out where they're going to land.' This sounds like the kind of thing that Sean would say.

She pauses for a moment, crosses her legs and fixes me with a serious look. 'Sean, I know that you've never wanted to consider this, but you might have to look to outside finance.'

'Investors?'

'Yes.'

'That's not an acceptable proposition,' I say dismissively. Again, I'm pretty sure that I'm nailing the language.

'Acceptable proposition or not, it might be the only way to keep the lights on,' says Theano, organising the paperwork into files.

'We've got time,' I say confidently.

'Not much. I think we can only afford a couple more weeks until we need to get a wriggle on it if we're going to stay liquid.'

I leave her office feeling utterly lost. What the hell am I doing sitting here having this conversation? I shouldn't be getting into this. A business on the brink, with employees' livelihoods at stake ... I should be walking away, telling Sean that he needs to get back here to sort out his own mess. But I'm also oddly exhilarated. The situation is relatively simple. Bring in more clients or the business closes – that's the challenge, and I either rise to it or slink away and look for another path in life, maybe mink farmer or cheese maker. Something that will take me out of the troublesome arena of human interaction. I just don't know if I've got the wherewithal to make it happen.

I sit in Sean's local gastro pub that night. I'm accompanied not only by a pint and a steak sandwich, but also by printouts of Sean's recent correspondence with Theano and the company accountant. I tried working in the house, but the PlayStation kept beckoning, so I thought it best to hole up in the boozer where there's 'only' lager to turn my eye. I jot down dates and numbers and try to make some sense of it all, to form a narrative from data. I know that I must be missing significant information, but I'm confident that even if I can only establish part of the picture then I can draw broad conclusions; if not about the financial health of the company, then about Sean's business practices.

The other information that I'm trying to process is quite why Sean would decide to swap lives with me at a time when it's clear he should be bailing out his empire. Is he resigned to his fate? Doesn't he care? Or is there a master plan that I'm not aware of, the cavalry coming over the brow of the hill at any moment? Maybe he's made so much money that he's become removed from the day-to-day workings of the business. I've lived in Sean's shadow for so long now that discovering his successful, confident persona rests on thin ice is both puzzling and liberating, like discovering that Norman Tebbit is actually a bit of a laugh.

I finish up my pint and go back to Sean's.

I'm surfing around on the internet looking for some grot when I notice a new message arrive in his inbox. Mildly guilty, I open it to discover that it's an invitation from an agency for Sean to pitch for the contract for a German mobile phone company that's launching in the UK. No sooner have I replied that SC Communications would be *thrilled* to work with them then a message bounces right back. It turns out that the client, Andrea Schnell, is in London, but leaves tomorrow evening. Am I available for lunch tomorrow?

Jesus. I get up and walk around, trying to think my next move through. Here's the thing: I can pass this up and avoid the possibility of looking like a fool at a meeting, or I can take some action. Can I live with myself knowing that I had an opportunity to turn the company around? Sod that. Can I live with myself knowing that I had the opportunity to do this for myself, to get back in the game and shake off the frustrations of the past few years?

I sit down at the computer and reply in the affirmative. I would *love* to have lunch.

Five hours later I'm still staring at the computer screen, flexing intellectual muscles that atrophied months ago. I'm tired but my mind is still racing with excitement. It's a long time since I've felt this good without the numbing blanket of booze. I want to get this business not because I want to bail out SC Communications or save people's jobs; I want to prove to Sean that I can do a job of work as well as he can – and I want to do it for me. There have been all kinds of easy explanations for my employment woes – wrong place, wrong time; tosspot boss; failing business – and some of it might be true. Some of it. What's undeniable, though, is that all of this happened to me. All of it. And I'd like to think that it's all serendipity, a function of economics and vindictive managers, but the truth is that it might not be. It could just be me and the things that I've done wrong, or not done at all, or the things I've simply not done very well. And Andrea from Deutsche Mobilen might offer me some way to confirm or deny this theory. Even if most of us get no closer to accomplishment than living somewhere named the Gold Rush Caravan Park, knowing that we've been out there on the dance floor giving it all we've got might just be enough to get us out of bed in the morning.

I look at my watch. My eyes are tiring. If I can just squeeze in another half an hour then I might have something interesting to say over lunch tomorrow.

Lunch is in another of those palaces of plush eating in which Sean appears to spend most of his time. Andrea is a no-nonsense middle-aged executive with perfect English and a good sense of what she needs to do to launch her company's brand in the UK. We discuss various strategies that SC Communications has employed before (she knows a lot more about Sean's business than I do) and what kind of ideas they're looking for to break through to the coveted twenty-something consumer who is known, I learned the day before, as a 'Millennial'. She hands me a document outlining what they're after before mentioning that she's talking to several other agencies.

I want to get things moving right away and get Aileen to set up a meeting with some of the people who I've discovered produce the best work at SC Communications. When I arrive, there's only one other person in the room. This is Denton McKenzie, a broad-shouldered, rugger-bugger type with tight blond curls that he's pushed back so that his hair resembles a breaking wave. I guess that he's in his late twenties, although he's one of those upper-middle-class types who always look a bit older than they are in their teens and twenties but, miraculously, in early middle age, begin to look younger than their peers. I imagine that after a couple of drinks Denton would nudge you in the ribs and point out: 'Nice bit of totty at ten o'clock.' He's the kind that smiles all the time – wherever he is, he's *delighted* to be there. Denton is a brand manager, meaning that his primary job is to liaise with agencies and clients, interpret their needs and, mostly, go out and get blind drunk with them; something that years of drinking his age in pints will have prepared him for.

'Hi, Sean,' he says brightly. 'Want one of these?' Without waiting for my answer he tosses me one of the small bottles of water that have been laid out on the table.

'See the game last weekend?'

'Not really,' I say, when a straight, 'hell, no,' would have done.

'Bloody good game,' he continues. 'Just hope that they're all fit for the Six Nations, eh?'

'Yeah, absolutely. Can't wait for that to start.'

'I fancy our chances this year. If you want to go I can procure some *billets.*'

Not wanting to subject even Sean to an afternoon of beered-up public schoolboys and farmers bellowing 'Swing Low Sweet Chariot', I change the subject.

'You used to play, didn't you, Denton?'

'Until a couple of years ago. I was a flanker for the school old boys team. But got the wedding coming up next June, and the little lady told me she's had enough of the training and the injuries.'

'And you coming home pissed up.'

He laughs. 'I can't pass up an opportunity for a few beers with the chaps, can I? That would be just plain rude.'

'So your athletic career is over, is it?'

'Decided to try my hand at marathon running. You know, raise a bit of money for charity. Suppose I've got another year or so before the first sprog pops out. That should keep her busy, eh?'

'Well, at least until you pack it off to boarding school, I suppose.'

He looks at me for a moment, and I wonder, if I wasn't his boss, maybe he'd lamp me one.

'Been looking into that, you know,' he says, folding his arms. 'Some places take 'em as young as five. Not sure that that's right, myself. I reckon that seven is young enough.'

'Yeah,' I say. 'Five's much too young, but by seven they're ready for it.'

'Ready for what?' Another man in his mid-thirties has entered the room while distractedly punching the keys of his BlackBerry.

'Hi, Ollie,' says Denton.

So this is Ollie. From my research I've discovered that he's one of the company 'creatives'. Judging by what I've seen of SC Communications so far, the main criteria for being a 'creative' is that they have a haircut that looks like a twitchy baboon has done it with a scythe. Ollie has got the obligatory messy coiffure and is rocking the selvedge jeans and only-available-in-Japan trainers.

'Oh, you know, fags, booze,' I say to Ollie.

'What?' he asks.

'We were talking about what seven-year-olds are ready for ... '

'If only those pesky government regulators would just get off their high horses, eh?' says Ollie. I suspect his *Lahndahn tahn* vowel-strangling might be masking a Home Counties upbringing.

'So, who are we waiting for?' I ask.

'Rachel,' says Denton.

'Strange,' says Ollie, still distracted by his Berry. 'Usually Miss Goody Two Shoes is the first one here.'

I don't know Ollie yet, but I decide then that I might not grow to like him.

I've met Rachel briefly when I was with Theano. From what I understand, she appears to work every hour God sends and always seems mildly anxious. The dynamic between Denton and Ollie seems pretty well balanced – one is the hail-fellow-well-met, the other the troubled individualist who works hard at being a maverick. Rachel fits in by being the most clearly talented of the three, but also the one who appears to allow her work to weigh heaviest upon her.

'I'm so sorry I'm late,' she says, walking into the room. There's a slight hint of estuary to her accent. 'The bloody copier machine was jammed.'

'What's that?' asks Ollie, nodding towards the files she's put down on the conference table.

'A profile of Deutsche Mobilen,' she explains, handing out a binder to each of us. 'Thought we should have a clear idea about the client.'

Ollie restrains himself from rolling his eyes. Clearly his 'creative' approach is far too free flowing to be based in the real world.

'Anyone see that new Nike spot?' asks Ollie. 'Total shit. I knew the director at St Martin's and he's an idiot. It's totally shit.'

'OK,' I say, taking control of the meeting. 'I'm going to say a few words about my preliminary discussion with Andrea Schnell from Deutsche Mobilen. After that I'd like you, Denton, to talk a little about things from the account manager's perspective and then I'd like Rachel and Ollie to offer some rough ideas regarding creative.'

Ollie gives me a look, which I take to mean that he'll tell me about the creative when he's good and ready.

'Is there anything you'd like to say, Ollie?'

He shakes his head slowly before proceeding to doodle on the file that Rachel has given him. I watch as he exchanges looks with Denton. I'm messing this up, being too stiff and formal. It's the nerves. I need to loosen up, try and encourage some banter.

'So, I met Andrea for lunch and they're looking for ideas to help them launch the brand in the UK. They've already done their TV and print buying but they're looking for ideas for other forms of marketing and branding – and quick.'

Loosen up, idiot!

'Actually, before we start I wanted to ask if anyone has been to that new place that's just opened in Smithfield?'

'The Meat Market,' laughs Ollie.

'Yup,' I say. I have read about the place in one of the many fashion magazines that Sean has lying around his office. 'That's, unbelievably, what they've called it,' I say.

'That is one of the worst names ever,' says Rachel. 'Why not just call it The Knocking Shop?'

'Is it any good?' asks Denton.

'What? The Meat Market or The Knocking Shop?' laughs Rachel. 'Sounds like you're interested, Denton.'

'I've not made it over there yet,' I say.

'Me neither,' says Rachel.

'Negative,' adds Ollie.

'I don't believe it,' I say, mock outraged. 'I'm paying you lot all this money to be out there, and none of you has had the courtesy to sample the delights of The Meat Market. I'm shocked and disappointed.'

I get a laugh out of this. The mood has shifted a little. I think we've hopped over the fence into Sean bonhomie now. And the longer I talk, the more I begin to feel confident. I lose my self-consciousness a little and realise that I'm capable of sitting in a meeting room and talking to other adults about something other than the benefits of new Jif with scrubbing bubbles. I offer my ideas – a consumer-led approach where we encourage customers to talk by sharing information and stories at a series of events throughout the country. I call it 'Give us your spiel' – and while Ollie and Rachel aren't exactly standing on the table pumping their fists in the air and chanting 'Leader! Leader!', I get the sense that I have acquitted myself in a way that won't have them doubled up with laughter the moment I leave the room. After an hour or so, we agree to try and have something more tangible decided within the next couple of days to send over to Andrea. We don't have a huge amount of time.

I'm leaving the office that night when I bump into Rachel. She's coming back in the building holding a Pret a Manger bag.

'Hungry?' I ask.

'Starving,' she says. 'I missed lunch. I just ate half a sandwich walking down the road. You off then?'

'Yeah.'

'Have a nice evening.'

'And you.'

'Think I'll be stuck here.'

'Try not to stay too late.'

'All right.' She turns to go. And I don't want her to leave, I want to stay chatting to her, making small talk all evening. Swept up in the moment I say to her: 'We should go for a drink some time.'

'Yeah,' she says. 'I'd like that.'

'Yeah, me too,' I say, almost to myself, as I watch her disappear into the lift.

18

Sean

Knowing that Maja is bringing Matthew to football practice, and hoping to patch up the awkwardness of our last encounter, I rummage through Tom's disastrous cupboard trying to find something to wear that will distinguish me from a compost heap. In addition, I spend a little more time on the grooming front than Tom might. I know that this isn't strictly within the rules, but I'm sure that Tom would approve. Extenuating circumstances and all that. I find it hard to imagine that he hasn't put on a decent shirt or trimmed his nasal hair inspired by the prospect of bumping into some yummy mummy at a parents' evening or school fête.

The boys and I are a little early for practice, so we hang round the café eating our pre-match meal – ice lollies that cost the same as a small family runabout. Maja appears with Matthew – oh, happy coincidence! – and both adults watch with mutual indulgence as the boys talk nonsense for a few moments. Paddy has brought a plastic robot that is, no doubt, vitally important to the P&L of one Hollywood studio or another, and the three boys are now partaking in yet another who's-harder-than-who debate, this time featuring super-heroes rather than sharks, the SAS or wood.

After an appropriately lengthy display of interest, Maja and I break away to grab a couple of coffees to drink while we're watching what could only loosely be described as 'practice'.

'Seems like they've struck up quite a friendship,' comments Maja, wiping cappuccino froth from her mouth.

'It's the universal language of robots,' I agree. 'Men are programmed to be able to hunt, gather, watch sport and get excited about shiny metal things. I should start carrying one around as an icebreaker.'

'I'm sure that you'd be the toast of junior four.'

At this point, another dad passes by and greets Maja. He's rocking combats and retro trainers, and is a little bit too pleased with himself; probably a 'creative' of some kind. Wanker. I eye him up, trying to work out whether I don't like him because he might be competition or because he's too much like me. She doesn't introduce me.

'His daughter is in Matthew's class,' she comments.

'I suppose it's inevitable that all the parents end up crossing paths,' I say, fishing a little.

'Oh, I'm not Matthew's mum,' says Maja quickly, as if she's forgotten to do something urgent. 'No, no. I'm, um, just looking after him for friends. I'm staying with them for a few months.'

Bingo! In one fell swoop the pesky-kid-from-a-previous-relationship situation is dealt with.

'I suppose I did detect an accent,' I say.

'No shit, Sherlock.' She laughs at her own joke. 'Forgive me. I heard that in an American movie once and I love to use it.'

The boys have moved outside and are enthusiastically warming up for the session. Our conversation feels different today. It's missing the nervous, jokey banter of our initial conversations, like we've achieved a new level of confidence around each other.

'So, where are you from?' I ask, blowing on my coffee to cool it.

'I'm Bosnian,' she explains. 'I met Matthew's dad at a medical conference here. I'm teaching at Central Middlesex Hospital and working in the ER. I'm living with the family while I'm here, so I hang out with Matthew when I'm not working. He's a great kid.'

'He seems it,' I say. 'What do you teach?'

'Surgery. I specialise in trauma wounds.'

'You mean gunshot wounds?'

'Well, they can be. There are all kinds of trauma wounds. It depends where you are. That awful war had to be good for something. I got a lot of practice. We see the odd gunshot wound here, but I spend most of my time stitching drunks and patching up after domestics. Car accidents can be interesting.'

Oh Lord. I feel like a total fool. She does *serious stuff*. I, on the other hand, do absolutely pointless stuff. I am the anti-Maja.

'What about you?' she asks. I do what any man in the same situation would do and lie.

'Oh, I'm currently between jobs,' I explain.

'I see that you spend a lot of time with your boys. That's good.' Excellent – I'm a 'good dad'. I press my advantage.

'As much as I can. They're only this age once,' I say.

'Make the most of this time,' she says wistfully. 'It's over before you know it.'

'You're right. I'm lucky. I was part owner of a PR company. I sold up. Wanted to get out.'

'Your wife works?'

'Oh, um, yes, she does . . . ' I watch Patrick and Michael rushing about the pitch, blissfully unaware of the grand deceit that is being hatched only feet away from them. 'Actually, she's an ex now. It was, you know, a mutual decision. It's for the best. We're both moving on with our lives.'

'It's never easy, is it?' she says. I look at her for a moment. There's a definite suggestion that she's been through something similar. But before I can ask what she means I see Michael skid over and twist his knee. Not again. The other kids stop the game and watch as Michael truly 'does an Argentina', writhing around on the floor. I'm wondering whether he's actually hurt and I should put my coffee down and do something when I notice that Maja is next to him. As I approach I can hear her talking to him softly but firmly, asking questions about how his knee feels. Michael stops wailing and answers before, eventually, standing up and limping around for a few moments. Maja gives the knee a final examination, pressing and prodding before turning to me.

'He's fine,' she says calmly. 'I thought that maybe he'd twisted something, but there's nothing wrong.'

True to her words, Michael hobbles away with a tortured expression before forgetting that he's hurt and breaking into a sprint.

'Great,' I say, rather pathetically. 'Thanks.'

She nods, cracks an easy smile, and we continue to watch the kids dash around. I snatch furtive looks at her when we're not chatting, just to see if she's as lovely as she is in my imagination. She is. I feel like I'm fourteen again and sitting in class dreaming about whichever unattainable teen princess it was that I'd mentally ditched irregular French verbs or geometry to fantasise about.

There have not been any incidents that I can recall in my adult life where I have been scared or intimidated to approach a woman. I grew out of this in my teens, when I realised that I didn't much care what people thought of me. It was around this time that I began to understand that the easiest way of getting what I want is simply to ask for it. Academics and social commentators like to think of peer pressure as having the determining effect on an adolescent's taste and behaviour. Largely, I think that they're right. But there are aberrations; those who do not fit the research.

I'm one of them. Not in the sense that I think I'm rare or special; don't believe the Hallmark guff about all of us being special – you only meet a handful like that in a lifetime. No, it's not like that, I just don't fit the pattern. I was never contrary, behaving in a particular way because I thought that being marginal or an outsider was a more interesting way to be. I was never interested in being tortured, precious or misunderstood. I didn't care to be squeezed out of the mainstream, I just didn't want to join it. I've never been a big joiner of clubs, I prefer that the club sees the world the way I see it, as opposed to the other way around.

So it's peculiar to find myself as a fully paid-up member of the ultimate non-exclusive club: the marriage club. It's strange how even the slightest link to a convention towards which I have never even cast a glance can change you. Though I've never shared a marital bed with my 'wife', have only a passing acquaintance with her tastes and desires, I feel a degree of guilt about my flirtation with Maja, as if I'm a philanderer breaking a vow, a bond of trust witnessed by God, or even an Elvis impersonator.

And this is my problem. Within the space of a week I have discovered the capacity to imagine possibilities within a relationship that extend further than regular visits to Agent Provocateur. Finally, I've met a woman who I want to get to know, and within minutes of our first conversation of any substance I've lied about my identity. Oh, and beyond that, let's not forget that I'm currently perpetrating a complicated fraud upon her and numerous other people.

To confuse matters further, in the past couple of days I've begun to think about what it would really be like to be married to Sara. Lying awake one night I construct a scenario whereby I tell Tom that I've decided not to return to my old life, that I'm enjoying things just as they are, thank you very much, and he's welcome to claim whatever is mine for himself: the house, the business, the train-wreck girls. Once he realises that I'm serious and plucks up the courage to confront Sara in order to rectify the situation I can roll my eyes, proclaim 'Sean' as officially insane, and live in blissful harmony with my new charges. How simple is that? Tom would eventually come to appreciate his new circumstances or, for once, have a really good reason to moan about them. This might actually make him happy. Although, probably not. So nothing changes.

I can understand my attraction to Maja, but quite why I've developed feelings for Sara when she's not even around is baffling me. Is it some inherent genetic trait that's triggered when even *pretending* to be married? A Jiminy Cricket-type conscience that's activated to prevent us (and the 'us' here refers to the three billion of us on this planet who possess a penis) from getting into too much trouble? Or is it something that's been lurking for a while, latent and unspoken, between Sara and I, like we're in some seventies sitcom called *Three's Trouble*, the plot of which hinges on the love-hate repressed sexuality between a maverick serial philanderer and his buttoned-up sister-in-law?

My daydreaming is interrupted by Michael tapping me on the arm.

'We just decided,' he says, matter-of-factly, 'Matthew is coming back to our house for tea.'

I don't like the sound of this conspiracy. It's got huge potential to backfire.

'Can I – pleeeeeease?' intervenes Matthew.

'Well, it's OK with me,' says Maja.

I've been put on the spot here. If Maja gets a look at the legions of family photos on display it's curtains. An image of Sara's disapproving face flashes into my mind. Despite the fact that we're not married,

I feel like I'm cheating on her. Clearly, I look uncomfortable with the idea.

'Well, maybe we should do it another time, sweetheart,' Maja says to Matthew.

'Oh, *Dad*,' says Paddy, identifying the villain of the piece.

'That's not fair,' says Matthew.

'Matthew!' says Maja. 'Don't be rude.'

'Killjoy,' says Michael.

Clearly my years as a spinmeister have served me well.

'No, it's just that . . . ' I begin to explain.

'Really,' says Maja, 'it's OK.'

I don't believe that I've ballsed this up as badly as I have, that I've allowed Maja to walk away with the idea that I've knocked her back.

'*Dad*,' whines Michael.

'*Dad*,' whines Patrick.

'I'm sorry,' I say pathetically.

'Another time,' she says a little too brightly, like she's trying to end the encounter on a positive note. She hauls Matthew off in the opposite direction. The boys traipse disconsolately towards home while I feverishly make plans to play catch-up.

Sara calls just as we get in the door. Thank God Maja didn't come back. I hand the phone to the boys before speaking to her myself.

'How are you?' she asks.

'I'm great.' It's true. I'm mixed up and concerned about this mess, but I'm actually very good in the confused and exhausted way one feels good after a day fighting off a raging hangover that has lifted.

'That's good to hear,' she says.

'Why's that?' I ask. It's a bit provocative, but I want to push her. And, let's face it, asking questions is less likely to get me in trouble than making bold statements.

'Because it's not very often that I hear you saying something positive or upbeat,' says Sara baldly. There are no barbs, just straight talk. 'Or, to put it another way: it's a relief not hear you fucking moaning.'

This is an opportunity to say something positive, to try and help mend the rift between my brother and his wife.

'Sorry,' I say. 'I know I can be a bit downbeat. I'm going to work on it.' Conciliatory, no? The kind of gesture women encourage men to make . . .

'Downbeat? You make Eeyore look like Jim Carrey.'

Now that's good. I like this woman.

'My God, Tom,' she continues, 'how many times do I have to tell you to focus on the positives? It's so tedious hearing you going on like some adolescent.'

'How was your day?'

'Fine, thank you.'

'So you'll still be back next Saturday?'

'Looks like it. I can get a train late Friday night, but I'll be knackered, so I might wait until Saturday morning.'

'Well, I'm looking forward to seeing you.'

'Are you?'

'Well . . . '

'Tom, I'm just answering the way you did earlier. See, that's what it feels like.'

I skew the conversation towards the kids. Sara's straightforwardness might not be the most comfortable experience but it's invigorating all right. But, then again, who looks to a relationship for invigoration? I tell her I have to go and make dinner. She signs off with a sour note in her voice.

A dispiriting look in the fridge prompts me to pack the boys in the car and head to Sainsbury's. There, in the bread aisle, we bump into Maja and Matthew. This was meant to happen, it's my chance to make amends for what happened earlier. I need a little privacy to work, so I usher her across the aisle and seek her opinion.

'What do you think?'

'Neither,' she says firmly, taking the baguette and granary loaf I'm holding and putting them back on the shelf.

'Try this instead.'

She finds some ciabatta and offers it to me, holding it with both hands, as if she's holding a communion chalice.

'But that's an inferior baking product if you want to make toast,' I object.

'Pah,' says Maja. 'You English and your obsession with toast.'

'I like toast.'

She ignores me, as if she won't lower herself to this discussion. I turn it over than check the tag.

'It's only good for a couple of days.'

'Well, eat it then,' she say, mock outraged. 'That's what it's for.'

'But there's bound to be something fresher,' I protest.

'You guys are so spoiled,' she sighs. It's not exactly clear who she means by 'you guys', although I suspect that I'm being lumped in with all the other whining Western European babies.

'Thank God for that,' I say.

She eyes me testily.

'Watch it, pansy,' she says, masking a smirk.

'So work's busy?' I say, tossing the ciabatta in the basket.

'You know,' she laughs, 'raucous but good.'

'Gang warfare broken out in Willesden, has it?'

'It's mostly the old ladies causing the trouble,' she says with a smirk. 'They're all using hollow-point bullets these days. They leave very tricky exit wounds.'

'Yeah, I heard they were doing drive-by shootings from buses.'

'They call themselves the Pensioner Posse,' she says, deadpan. 'Watch out when the number 79 goes past.'

While she's telling me this last joke I take a deep breath.

'Look, I know that your work schedule is tough, but I was wondering if you might be free one night to go out.'

It hangs there between us for a few moments. She cocks her head ever so slightly and considers the bread. Is it me again or the ciabatta?

'I'm not working evenings this week,' she says.

'So you're available,' I press.

'Yeah. I'm free tomorrow, if you like.'

Tomorrow. That's keen.

'Great, well, how about, if it's tomorrow, I've got a couple of tickets a friend gave me to a movie première.'

'That sounds like fun. I've never been to a movie première.'

'It's an early thing, so maybe we can get some dinner afterwards?'

'I love to eat.'

'Me too.'

We have so much in common.

So there it is – my first date with Maja. I can't wait. If only I wasn't a married man.

We mess around at home for a while. I disappear to the kitchen to cook dinner from where I hear the boys getting into a dispute. What's odd is that although the argument is real, they're not talking in their own London-inflected middle-class accents, but in an Ali G-like hybrid of Jamaican meets cockney at a Bengali rap event. It's the voice I hear on the street from pretty much every kid between twelve and twenty but have never heard my nephews use.

Paddy: 'You frontin' me?'
Michael: 'I ain't frontin' ya.'
P: 'Cuz if you is frontin' me you is gonna get merked.'
M: Sucks his teeth. 'Cha. Now you *is* frontin' me.'
P: 'You know I don't roll like that, innit.'
M: 'You fink you is buff, yout.'
P: 'Yo bluh, why you buggin' me?'
M: 'Bitch, you be buggin'.'
P: 'Why you callin' me bitch when we be bredrin'?'
M: 'Cuz you be frontin' me.'
P: 'You fink you is a bad bwai.'
M: 'Black heart, man.'
P: 'Blahd clot.'
M: 'You is dry, bwai.'
P: 'You vex me I'll boff you, bwai.'

'I think that's quite enough of that,' I interrupt, hustling into the room. The boys regard me nonchalantly before staring at each other disdainfully. I wonder if they're actually 'packing heat'.

'What's for dinner?' asks Michael, misplacing his Trenchtown accent.

Paddy has picked up a Batman comic and is now oblivious to his brother and me. It's like nothing happened.

After dinner (I manage to get both rude boy gangsters to eat asparagus) we read for a while before they fall fast asleep around eight thirty with no further signs of nine-millimetre handguns. The phone rings at half-time in the Champions' League game I'm dozing through. I know that it's Sara again. I steel myself. It's another opportunity to turn everyone's life to shit – mine, Tom's, Sara's, the boys' – if I screw it up. Sara's voice is slightly muffled, as if she's trying to shield the phone from other people. I can hear voices in the background; not the singsong and jabber of pub voices, but balanced, solemn ones.

'Still working?' I ask.

'Yeah,' she answers. 'We're going to be here for a while tonight. The defence pulled a fast one on us.'

'How?' I ask.

'They're trying to argue for a mistrial. It's a technicality, but I think that the police might have ballsed up some of the evidence gathering.'

I hear chatter in the background. She takes a slurp of something. Beer? Coffee? Wine? Water? And then I find myself wondering if she's ever suffered a moment's indiscretion, whether some dazzling QC has turned her head while they've been burning the midnight oil on behalf of the CPS a long way from home. I can't say that I'd blame her. She's an eminent, attractive woman involved in a complicated and significant process. Not only that, but the emotional toll is legendary. I know what it's like, I've seen all those courtroom drama movies.

'Are the boys OK?' she asks.

'Yeah, they're great. We're having a good time.'

'I miss them so much.'

'I know.'

'And I miss you too.'

'I know that too.'

'And sometimes I wonder whether all this is worth it. The being away, the missing out on the everyday stuff, the worrying about you all . . . There's a big cost, you know.'

'Look, it's good for the boys to have a mum who's so successful,' I say, meaning it. 'What do you want to do, show up at the school gates twice a day in some 4X4 that you can barely drive, like some of the other mums? Rear your kids between tanning sessions and trips to Harvey Nics? You'd go spare.'

'But it doesn't have to be that extreme, does it? There's got to be a compromise somewhere,' she says. 'And we need the money.'

'I can feel a guilt trip coming on.' *How good was that?* That's *exactly* what Tom would say. I *nailed* it.

'I'm not trying to make you feel guilty, Tom. Look, we should talk about all this when I get back, okay. It's late and I've still got a ton to do.'

'Sure. Give us a call tomorrow when you get a chance.'

'Will do.'

'I love you,' she says, which stops me in my tracks. I know that I should say 'I love you too,' but somehow, despite everything else that Tom and I are up to, it just doesn't seem right, no matter how scared I am of getting found out.

'Your husband loves you very much, as well,' I reply. This, I hope, is appropriate and forgivable, although how I think about Sara that night as I drift in and out of troubled sleep is not.

The day of the première I'm tempted to go out and buy some clothes that will prevent me from looking like Wurzel Gummidge. I restrain myself and, instead, spend an hour examining pretty much every item that belongs to Tom to see if I can put something together. Eventually, I settle on an outfit that has the right degree of casual chic. Maja asks me to pick her up outside Queens Park Tube station, which seems a little odd to me, but there you go. As I crawl over the bridge I wave to her and she jumps into the car before the road-rage merchants can get too worked up about someone halting their progress for several seconds.

We park in some rip-off NCP at the back of Leicester Square, where there's a modest crowd hanging around to see the woeful collection of *Big Brother* fifteen-minuters and retail-crazed footballers wives that the agency handling this thing have managed to corral. Large men playing out power fantasies wearing black suits and headsets use the body language appropriate for a UN summit, not the new Pierce Brosnan movie. I can see that Maja is having a good time, taking it all in. A wry smile is spread across her face, as she watches the outsize posturing and preening. The whole farrago must seem absurd to her. Eventually we get to the clipboard bitch at the front of the queue who clutches her guest list like it's the holiest of Talmuds. She eyes me suspiciously. I might as well be wearing a Burberry baseball cap with a hood over it.

'Can I help you?' she asks, although she clearly doesn't want to.

'It's Cunningham,' I say as clearly as I can, wanting to avoid the inevitable look of incredulity. 'We're on the list. SC Communications.'

The girl runs a manicured nail up and down the list while the heavy at her shoulder shifts his weight uneasily. The girl, discouragingly, starts flicking through the sheets of paper on her clipboard.

'You've already been crossed off,' she says smugly.

'Excuse me?' I employ my patented 'do you know who the fuck you're talking to?' look of incredulity.

'You've been crossed off.'

'I think that there must be some confusion . . . '

'Someone of that name has already come in.'

'I understand what you're saying to me. But what I'm telling you is that there's been a mistake. That's me.'

After feigning indifference to what's going on, the goon behind the clipboard Nazi has come alive. He begins to stare at me menacingly. The PR witch is dealing with the problem by looking past me, at the people behind. I now, officially, don't exist.

'Next!' says the PR girl.

'You mean that you're not going to let us in?' I say this as coolly as I can, just to let her know that she's making a decision that could have disastrous long-term repercussions on her career.

'Next!' says the girl, ignoring me.

'This is a joke, right?' I say to no one in particular. I'm embarrassed and annoyed and want to play this right. Maja is watching, and a scene in which a steroid-crazed bouncer puts your date in a headlock is not the best way to start an evening.

'This isn't good enough,' I say. I know that I should walk now, but I just can't help myself.

Finally the PR girl acknowledges me. 'Sir, you're going to have to leave now.' She beckons other people forward, trying to regain control of the red carpet.

'But I'm the real Sean Cunningham,' I blurt. I immediately turn to see Maja has a puzzled expression. 'It's my professional name,' I explain. 'Sean is like a nickname.'

'Yeah, and I'm the real Slim Shady,' comments the PR girl, unnecessarily. I turn back and start giving her the evils when the security goon steps forward and ushers me to the side of the queue with an anvil-sized hand.

'You're holding everyone up,' he says, with surprising, mumsy calm.

'Come on, Tom,' urges Maja. There's a balance to her voice that clears the red mist that's descended on me. 'There's just been some kind of mix-up. Let's just go and eat.'

I look at her before turning back to the clipboard girl.

'Remember,' says Maja. 'Pizza. Good. Mmmmm . . . ' She says this in one of the best Homer Simpson voices I've ever heard, while rubbing her stomach. I smile, despite myself.

'This is ridiculous,' I say, partly to myself and partly to the bouncer.

But I'm no longer talking about our being turned away. The 'ridiculous' I'm referring to refers to the fact that down the end of the red carpet, where the ranks of photographers are set up, I see Tom strolling towards the cinema with C-list starlet Magenta Carlson on his arm. He waves occasionally at the crowd, a huge shit-eating grin on his face. I watch as he steps aside to let Magenta preen herself in front of the sponsors' boards for the benefit of the gathered 'snappers'. They must have come in just before us and been working the carpet while we were getting knocked back by the clipboard bitch.

Tom Cunningham, you are taking the piss.

'Come on,' says Maja, oblivious to what I'm staring at and offering me her hand. 'I'm starving. Let's go and eat.'

'Yeah . . . right,' I say, tearing myself away from the Tom show.

Maja takes me to a nice little Italian place on a back street in Covent Garden. A glass of wine later and the whole thing seems ridiculous. Much to my relief, Maja finds the episode thoroughly amusing, although had she seen Tom she might not have been of the same opinion. We talk and work our way through antipasti and a meat course and dessert and probably far too much booze for me to drive home under the limit. And the evening goes so much more smoothly than I hoped it might, so smoothly that I don't feel the need to steer the conversation, which is usually something I can't help but do. I'm so relaxed that I forget that I'm even meant to be playing the role of Tom. Afterwards, I can barely recall what we talked about. What I do remember is an overarching feeling of satisfaction. Jesus, I'll go ahead and say it: *happiness*. Until, that is, I pull out Tom's credit card to pay and the damn thing is refused. At which point Maja giggles and graciously whips out her Mastercard. Of course, I'm totally mortified and blather on about having forgotten to transfer money from one account to another. She simply puts her hand on mine and says, 'My treat.'

There has been a brief rain shower while we were in the restaurant. The roads are slick and shiny with water, the street lights sparkling in the liquid film stretching before us. We drive west and then up Park Lane. Neither of us talks, we just listen to the music on the car stereo. The silence is a kind of contentment, I suppose; there's nothing more to say this evening. It's like we're reflecting on ... what? A fun evening out? The beginning of something?

My reverie is interrupted as we head up the Harrow Road when I remember that we're in Sara's car. I know that because Tom told me after a couple too many drinks one night, that Sara makes the car payments (as well as keeping the Abbey National at bay). I realise that if one of Tom and Sara's friends should see us now there could be nasty repercussions. I slouch down in my seat a little to avoid detection, hoping that Maja doesn't notice my odd behaviour. I take her up Salusbury Road towards Willesden before she tells me to make a left and pull the car up. The car idles for a few moments while we both sit staring forwards, as if we're still moving. I've decided a while back that I'm going to make a move – no tongues or anything, just a firm kiss, with intent, on the lips. I don't want to screw up what has undoubtedly been a successful evening.

'Well,' she says, 'here we are.'

'I had a great time,' I say.

'Me too.'

She pulls the lever on the car door. I make a move, but it's a little too sudden, and the seatbelt snaps into action and halts my progress.

'That was smooth,' says Maja. She puts her hand over her mouth to cover her laughter before, to my surprise, leaning over and kissing me.

'I'd love to do this again some time,' I say.

'What's that?' she asks.

'Going out together.'

'I thought you meant the kiss.'

'Well, that as well.'

'We will,' she says. She gets out of the car and proceeds towards an Edwardian terraced house. When she's near the front door she turns and waves. I can see that she's got her key out. The front garden appears free of skulking attackers, so I wave and set off for home.

The night, it appears, is a success. We talked. We listened. We ate and drank. And it all happened with such ease that it was less like social interaction than being in a band, picking up on each other's notes, reading the intentions, cruising along without any real thought. Just pure instinct. But underneath my satisfaction there's a nasty undertow that's dragging me down. I feel like a philanderer, like I'm letting Sara down. And this is doubly distressing because I should be on cloud nine after this evening, yet I feel *bad* about going out with Maja.

Also, I need to talk to Tom to find out what the fuck he thought he was doing at the première. There were major possibilities for ballsing the whole thing up, and he made me look like a fool. Fair play to him, though – walking down the red carpet with a hot bit of talent like Magenta is a major coup.

I get back, get a glass of water and switch on the telly to try and still my mind a little. *London Tonight*, a programme seemingly made by idiots who assume that we're all as thick as them, pops up. It's one of those shows where you actually become more stupid from having watched it. I'm just about to flip channels when they start an item on the première. They've got some footage of the minor celebs who've managed to drag themselves out of their Essex coke dens and . . . Look who it is: Tom, that's who. Looking a little bashful, stepping to the side so that the snappers can get their shots of his consort, but still tripping down the red carpet for all the world to see.

19
Tom

There's no other way to describe the movie we've just endured other than spirit-crushingly awful. Which maybe explains why the poor sods who snoozed through the ninety minutes of visual refuse are now three deep at the after-party bar, throwing as much free booze down their necks as they can manage in an attempt to obliterate the brain cells supplying the memory of what they've just been through. Vodka, beer, champagne, you name it, they're chucking it back.

There are a lot of blokes wearing excessive amounts of hair gel and rocking Donatella Versace-deep fake tans, and numerous girls with knockers of questionable provenance and an attitude that translates as something like: *you're probably not rich enough for me . . . But if you are, I'll take you in the bogs and blow you for a line of chang.* It ain't exactly Last Night of the Proms. More like soap stars and cable TV wannabes jostling at the trough, hoping that they can prolong their fifteen minutes to a full half-hour. Fame's cruellest blow is its departure.

Still, I'm in a banquet with a British starlet of limited talent and accomplishment accompanied by her entourage of over-excited friends and hangers-on. The conversation this evening has been, to put it mildly, lacking a degree of sophistication. I realise fairly early on that I'm not there to actually interact with Magenta, but simply to indulge whatever it is that's occupying her thoughts before the next thing to occupy her thoughts emerges, which is never longer than a thirty-second gap. Earlier, there was some arm touching going on and this, coupled with her eagerness to laugh at even the lamest of my jokes, caused me to speculate that she might be in the mood for some how's your father. But then the ghastly truth of bimboism hits me in the form of a confused series of questions regarding the film we've just watched.

'So, you know that film, right. How come when the geezer hit that bloke with the spade he didn't feel nothing?'

'Because he was undead,' I explain.

'But what about when they shot him as well?'

'Same thing: you can't kill someone who's already dead.'

'But how did he get into that place when they'd locked all the doors?'

'Because he was undead and could pass through walls.'

'That girl was well shocked.'

'Well, I suppose she didn't expect her dead dad to come back and warn her.' I'm being as patient as I can, but it's getting embarrassing. Thankfully, Magenta appears to have a high threshold for bewilderment.

'So she was a human, right?'

Please God put this woman out of her misery.

'Well, that's what we think. But then we find out – right at the very end, remember – that she's actually dead too.'

'You mean that she was a *ghost*?' This is big news to Magenta.

'That's why the film is called *Almost Dead*, I suppose.'

'Yeah, I suppose,' she says, taking a thoughtful drag on her cigarette.

Since we've been at the party she's mostly been preoccupied by the rabble she describes as friends. This is actually something of a relief as I was running out of bollocks to talk to her about. I watch as she greets acquaintances over-enthusiastically and keeps half an eye on her mobile, thumbing back texts like she was born with a Nokia attached to her right hand. I wonder about her relationship with Sean. Does he need her for work purposes? Is it an ego thing where he just wants to hang out with the hot new thing? Or does he just want to shag her brains out?

What the hell? I've had a few glasses of champagne and I'm feeling pretty good about life, or maybe it's just the novelty of being sat in a booth with a pretty girl who may or may not rise beyond the ITV mini-series that released her into the celebosphere. The music is loud enough that I don't have to make conversation with anyone, which is fortunate as I end up sitting next to Magenta's stylist, a young gay man with a shaved head, who appears to wish his hands had been plunged into a deep fat fryer rather than suffer the humiliation of sitting next to me. I watch as he fiercely works his way through a pack of Marlboro Lights, apparently seething with annoyance that he's stuck next to the middle-aged stiff, when all the fun is occurring with the bright young things on the other side of the table. And I can't blame him either. If I were him I'd want to be over there too.

I feel a vibration on my hip. It's Sean's Berry. It often rings late at night, and I've got used to ignoring it. I fish it out of my pocket and see my home number on the screen.

'Sean!'

'All right, dickhead,' he says flatly.

'*Aaaaaah*! Big daddy! How's fatherhood treating you? It's nearly midnight. They still giving you the runaround?'

'Actually, I've been out on a date.'

This catches me unaware. He's been on a date?

'What?'

'Don't sweat it,' he says. 'I got a sitter off the list up on the wall. There was one drawback, however: things were not enhanced by my getting knocked back from the première tonight.'

My initial concern that he put the moves on one of our sixteen-year-old babysitters is dwarfed by this latest piece of information.

'You came to the première?' I say incredulously. I stand up, getting a dirty look from the stylist.

'Yup.'

'Seriously?'

'Why would I joke about it?'

'Hang on a minute, Sean. The way I see it, that's not in the rules. We're swapping lives for two weeks. I would never go to one of those things.'

'Even if you were on the guest list?'

'Well, you weren't on the guest list, were you?'

'Actually, I was.' He says this in a manner that can best be described as cold. Annoyed even. Is he really getting pissed off about this, or is he just winding me up? It's hard to tell. It's harder to hear him. I need to find a quieter spot.

'Sean,' I say as patiently as I can muster, which means that I assume a voice similar to the one I use when I'm explaining something to Paddy, 'hold on a minute. In case you haven't noticed, we've swapped lives. You don't get to go to parties. I do. I'd also like you to know that I'm with your close personal friend Magenta, who appears to have a little bit of a thing for you. This is maybe explained by the fact that she's dumb as a rock.'

'So, are you going to make a move, Romeo?'

'No, I am not.'

'I would,' says Sean.

'Well, I'm not you.' By now I'm standing in the toilets, which is about the only place that I can hear his exact tone of voice.

'What happened to our having traded lives for two weeks?' he says. This sounds like a wind-up. 'I thought that you wanted to do this for real. That was your motivation.'

'It still is,' I answer.

'OK, now we're getting somewhere. So, what I'm telling you is that if I got the chance to go home with Magenta then I would.'

'Sean, do me a favour, will you? I am not going to shtup Magenta.'

'But she'd go home with *me*, and to all intents and purposes that gives you a free pass to happy-happy night!' The tone of his voice tells me that he doesn't really believe this.

'Well, that will do my marriage a ton of good.'

'Well, if you're not going to cheat on Sara,' he says with a playground singsing, 'I'm going to turn up to movie premières.'

'Sean, you're missing the whole fucking point! I don't think that you should be taking girls out. You shouldn't be trying to get into movie premières either. It bears no relation to my life.'

'Tom, I had to. I've met a girl—'

'Right. You've met a girl—'

'Hear me out. She's totally different.'

'Right. Until the next girl you meet who's even better. Sean, please, spare me. How many times am I going to hear this? Can't you hold back on the sharking for just two weeks?'

'Tom, you don't understand. This is different. It's not sharking. I don't know how to describe it really, but it's different. Grown up, I suppose.' His tone has changed – he's now sincere.

'Sean, this is getting sad, mate ... '

'I'm serious. She's smart, she's funny, she's sexy as hell. She's a doctor. From Croatia or Bosnia. Or something ... I haven't quite worked it all out.'

'And you want to fuck her brains out.'

'Of course, but it's not just about that. This is different, Tom ... '

'I cannot believe this. I'm sitting at an after party with Magenta Carlson who might just want to take me home with her, and you're calling me up to moon about some girl you met at ... ?'

'The playground.'

'The playground! Well, that's just fucking perfect, isn't it? Do you know the amount of times I've been to that god-dam playground? Thousands, and I've never even seen a great-looking girl there, let alone picked one up. Sean, you're a piece of work, you really are.' I raise my glass. 'Sean, I salute you.' The champagne has gone flat. 'Now, if you've quite finished, I need another glass of champagne, and to pretend to be the fabulous Sean Cunningham. And may I add that your success with my kids is being mirrored by my own mastery of SC Communications.'

'What are you talking about?'

'I had lunch with Andrea from Deutsche Mobilen ... '

'You what?'

' ... and she loved the ideas I mentioned to her.'

'Now hang on a minute ... '

'Sean, I've got people waiting for me. You know how it is with after parties, they take a while to warm up. Anyway, I need to get another glass of champagne ... Because that's how I roll. I'm turning my phone off now.'

I hear him beginning to say something, but I cut him off, the phone chiming its message of farewell. He was seriously pissed off about my dabbling in SC Communications, but if he can't save his own skin then maybe he's better off letting me have a go. He knows that the Deutsche Mobilen deal could be huge, might even turn things around for the company. He just needs to get his head around the idea, that's all.

I plunge back into the throng at the bar and return double fisted. It's all getting a little messy, there are dishevelled, drunk girls everywhere, which is a source of both pleasure and bemusement. As someone who's largely expended his sexual energy over the past few years in the ball pit at the Wacky Warehouse, the complexity of closing a deal like this and its inevitable train-wreck aftermath is ruled by the laws of diminishing returns. I wouldn't know where to start.

The DJ drops a couple of tunes that I've heard on the radio, so I find my way onto the dance floor and cut a woeful parents-at-a-wedding figure. Fortunately, everyone is so mullered they don't notice me. After about ten minutes, I get into a groove and fall into the fatal trap of kidding myself, that *yes, I can actually dance*. I pull a couple of moves remembered from teenage discos back in the, um, eighties, but, thankfully, call it a day before realising an ill-conceived notion about a moonwalk. I'm sweaty and hot, and there are too many people close to me. I look around the place, see the shiny faces, the 'party hands' beginning to come alive, and realise that it's time to get the hell out of here. The showbiz phoniness, the sheer bogusness of the bollocks that's being talked within these four walls, the pretensions and illusions of those I'm surrounded by makes me see how much I'm missing my boys. What the fuck am I doing here when they're fast asleep across London? I can't deny that over the years I've allowed myself to get overwhelmed by the business of fatherhood but, right there and then, it's all I can do not to jump in a cab and head back to them.

We're up against it time-wise with Deutsche Mobilen so, mildly hungover the following morning I'm on my way into the office for a Saturday meeting with the creative team when I stop to grab a quick take-away coffee at an upmarket patisserie on Kensington Church Street. I'm just about to leave when I notice Theano huddled at the back of the place deeply engaged with a middle-aged man wearing a camel coat that screams 'I'm a successful businessman'. He's looking at documents laid out in front of him while Theano talks animatedly. She doesn't see me, and I decide it's best not to interrupt. As I head to the office I wonder why she's meeting someone off-site first thing on a Saturday. Surely if the meeting is important enough for her to be producing financials it makes sense to have it in her office or, at the very least, a decent restaurant during the week? Even more suspiciously, I notice later in the morning that she's in her office.

'Hi,' I say.

'Hi,' she says, smiling brightly.

'Everything OK?'

'Everything's fine,' she says, not missing a beat.

I close her office door and sit down.

'Theano, look, I saw you this morning at the café.' She looks me in the eye with no trace of emotion. No confirmation or denial.

'Who was it you met?' I press her.

She sighs and looks out of the window for a few moments before turning back and speaking.

'Sean, it's hard for me to tell you this, and you might want to fire me after you've heard.'

I remain silent, waiting.

'I don't see how we can continue on our own. I've been talking to venture capitalists.'

'I see,' I say.

'I'm sorry,' she says. 'I know that I should have told you, but I felt that it was incumbent on me to see what our options are. I know that you're strongly against the idea. This is your business, after all. But I felt that I needed to see what was out there. I thought that it was the right thing to do.'

'And how did the meetings go?'

'Well, you know the score with VCs, you can get the cash, but they want equity.'

'And how much would I have to give up?'

'Well, that all depends on how much cash you want.'

'Theano, I'm going to get new business in. We'll be OK.'

'Sean, we're nowhere near OK. Once we pay this month's salaries we're down to two months' cash flow. I can't stress enough how close we are to the edge. You've got to acknowledge the situation. You can't keep sticking your head in the sand.'

'We'll be OK,' I say calmly, feeling nothing of the kind. 'The new business is coming.'

'How?' she asks, frustrated.

'Because I'm going to go out and get it.'

20
Sean

Waking on Saturday, a week on from the swap, my first thought is this: I survived. My second thought is that it's all gone too quickly. My satisfaction at having got through a week with neither Sara nor the boys identifying me as an unsatisfactory substitute parent leads me to award myself a thumping seven out of ten. Then I think about it for a moment, and maybe it's not so good. I might be a satisfactory substitute, but I'm a satisfactory substitute for a supposedly unsatisfactory husband/father. This makes me both satisfactory and unsatisfactory. The vagaries of my performance as Tom aside, my rapidly developing relationship with Maja is offering me more than I could have hoped for at the start of this shenanigans.

I can hear the boys downstairs foraging for cereal and I get a rush of excitement at the prospect of seeing them. I pull on Tom's threadbare dressing gown and go down to see that the kitchen is carpeted with Rice Krispies. My feet crush them to powder as I walk to the coffee machine.

'Dad, why do you drink coffee?' asks Paddy.

'Because I find it physically impossible to function without the aid of stimulants,' I explain, scratching my chin.

'What?'

'It's not "what", it's "pardon", young man.'

'What's a stimulant?' asks Paddy.

'It's something that gives you energy,' says Michael, not taking his eyes from the packet of cereal he's reading.

'It's not really something that applies to you,' I say to Paddy. 'You don't need stimulants. But, talking of stimulants . . . anyone for some *Halo*?'

The boys look at each other, warily.

'Dad, what do you want?' asks Michael.

I turn from the fridge where I'm fishing out the organic milk that I bought along with our supplies for the weekend.

'Oh, you know, world peace. An Aston Martin DB7. The usual.'

'I mean, why do you want to play *Halo*?' adds Michael.

Paddy is sitting chewing his cereal, watching us both closely.

'Well, why not?' I say.

'Because you hate video games,' says Paddy with a poker face. 'You're always telling us how bad they are for us, how they kill our imagination, turn us into zombies.'

'Well, maybe I want to be a zombie too,' I joke. Their faces reveal that they're not buying. This isn't like their dad.

'Because I think that it'll be fun,' I say eventually. 'It's not about the video game. It's about you. I thought it would be fun for us to do something together.' I can tell that, although unimpressed by the sappiness of the answer, they find it a little more plausible. Whether it's from school or Hollywood or genetics they understand that *this is what parents are supposed to say to their offspring.* That we love them unconditionally and that when all the family bickering and time pressure evaporates, all we want is a little time spent with those we love most.

Michael scrapes his bowl clean before placing it in the dishwasher. There are still red marks on his face from where he's been sleeping.

'I'll go and set it up then,' he says, disappearing to the living room. I make a pot of coffee before joining the boys, who are busy calibrating the game to their exact requirements. Michael starts cutting through the marauding aliens with practised efficiency. For a while he is simply going through the motions in order to get to a stage of the game that's challenging for him, I sit sipping my coffee, offering the odd piece of encouragement.

As the three of us are hypnotised by the game my mind returns to my conversation with Tom the night before. It's the first time that we've had a row in years, but I'm unclear if it was the booze talking, or whether he was genuinely annoyed at my turning up to the première. I don't see that my showing up with Maja goes against the spirit of our agreement. So what if I want to leave the boys with a babysitter for the evening? Tom and Sara do. I'm taking excellent care of them the rest of the time.

And what has Tom been doing? Getting comfy over at SC Communications. I'm glad that he's finding his business legs again, but I can't believe that he'll be able to pull off anything constructive. Landing that Deutsche Mobilen account is going to take a lot more than some bullshit over lunch at Nobu (although, frankly, that would have been my approach). I try and shake work from my mind. It's the last thing I really want to think about.

Interesting that Tom's not picking up his phone the day after a bender. I tried calling him this morning and either he's sleeping it off at home or he's not speaking to me because of the whole première thing, the big girl. What's more troubling, though, is that Maja isn't picking up either. She's probably just at work but I'm feeling a little paranoid. Probably for good reason. For us to have any future, I'm going to have to come clean at some point. That means I've got to try and work out how I'm going to 'readjust' our relationship, whether I go for the full hand-wringing disclosure accompanied by a grovelling apology, or the fudged 'I-think-that-there's-been-a-miscommunication' bullshit. Either way, it's relationship hara-kiri. *I really like you Maja – fancy getting together? Oh, by the way, sorry about not being who I said I was.*

Great work, Sean.

It's bloody typical: I meet someone I can imagine developing a relationship with and within a week I've filled her head with unforgivable lies. I look over at the boys and it's the same story: I'm a dad, but I'm a fraud.

The phone rings and Paddy runs over to answer it. He wanders back and sits down next to me. I can tell just from the tone of his voice that it's Sara. The pair chit-chat for a few moments while Michael continues to blow up aliens, progressing through the levels in much the same way as Godzilla works his way through Tokyo. I can just about make out Sara's voice, warm and involved and with a little tinge of tiredness and some sadness that she's not here to share our domestic routines. But then something alarming happens. In answer to one of Sara's questions, I hear Paddy say, 'Yeah, he pimped me out.'

I hear Paddy repeat the words. There's a moment before he says, 'Take a chill pill, Mum.' Clearly Sara doesn't take a chill pill, before I hear him signing my death warrant when he says, 'Dad.' There's a short pause and he says, 'But he's playing *Halo*, Mum,' and then he offers me the phone and says, 'She wants to speak to you.' Rather sweetly he cups his hand over the mouthpiece and whispers, 'She's vexed.'

'This had better be important,' I joke to Sara. The moment I utter the words I regret them. It's almost as stupid as telling her the truth when she says, 'Just tell me the truth, I won't be angry.'

'Just kidding,' I say. 'How are you? Not too tired, I hope.'

'Tom, can you explain to me why your seven-year-old son just used the term "pimped me out"?'

'Erm, no. I suppose he must have heard it at school.'

'Apparently, he got it from you.'

'Hmmmm . . . I doubt it.' Pathetic. Truly pathetic. Clearly my balls have disappeared somewhere inside my body. Or maybe Sara took them with her when she went up to Liverpool. Maybe she's rolling them around her hands right now, like those executive stress toys some promo company sent me a while back on the premise that they were used by some ancient Peruvian tribe that had extraordinary longevity.

'Firstly, I've never heard you speak like that before, and I'm disappointed,' snaps Sara, taking control of the exchange. 'Secondly, do you really want your child talking like that?'

I can hear the boys laughing. I turn to see that the hilarity relates to my getting a beat-down from Sara. Clearly this is highly amusing to the boys who are rolling around on the floor pretending to smother their laughter while, of course, not smothering it at all. It's a moment of such pure connection between the three of us that I'm willing to take the beat-down in exchange. The boys' realisation that the shoeings that men take every now and again from our better halves are an intrinsic part of the male experience is a smart and worthwhile one. Michael puts his finger to his temple and pretends to shoot himself in the head, slumping to the carpet. Paddy draws his finger across his throat. I try not to let the smirk on my face become apparent in my voice.

'No, I don't, Sara.'

She says something else and I find myself suppressing laughter and saying, 'Sorry, Sara.'

'Tom, they're impressionable at the moment. I'm away, so it's up to you to make sure that they get the parenting they need.'

I get the feeling that, despite my best efforts, Sara is partially pissed off because she *feels* what's going on in the living room at this exact moment. It's a sixth sense. Someone spilled orange juice on the sofa? Toilet roll run out? Tom upstairs having a crafty wank? Sara already knows. She can feel it in the very core of her. It's like the household is hard-wired into her central nervous system. What chance have the rest of us got with RoboMum around?

Paddy is shaking his arse at Michael. Accordingly, Michael is doubled over with laughter, never happier than when he's encouraging his little brother to behave badly. I reach my leg over and try to kick Paddy in the backside, but he leaps out of the way.

'Yes, Sara, you're right, I'm sorry,' I say, having lost track of the conversation but knowing that this is an appropriate answer to whatever is being said. Of course, she's right. She knows that she's right, I know that she's right, and what's occurring now is that she's making this very clear to me, knowing that the rules of the shoeing prevent me from curtailing her flow. Eventually, she asks me how I am, before telling me how tired she is, yet she still can't sleep because she's got so much on her mind, and how she wishes that she'd arranged to come home for the weekend rather than go up and see her old college friend in the Lake District as she's got a new baby and lives in a tiny cottage, so there's no chance of getting any rest . . .

We end the call amicably, largely due to my instinct for self-preservation, which has led me to shut the fuck up and let her work through her annoyance. However, once I put the phone down I decide that, in my new role, I need to address the situation.

'All right, boys, enough is enough. I was just talking to Mum and she's concerned about what Paddy said. And she's right. We've got to keep an eye on our language, OK? Me included. Let's keep it clean and avoid inappropriate words that you might hear at school, or in the street, or wherever.'

There's a pause, before Paddy says, 'Fashizzle, Dad.'

I try not to laugh, but it's no good. Both boys join me, and the three of us roll around on the floor, howling. I need to do better than this.

'All right, fellas, we need to talk about Bloke Code.'

I have their attention: the carrot of learning the ways of their elders is as powerful as the stick of no TV.

'OK, here's the deal. There are things that we can say to each other that shouldn't be said anywhere else, or in front of anyone else – especially Mum.'

'Like what?' asks Michael. He knows better than this, he's just testing me.

'Well . . . ' I begin.

'Is "arsewipe" OK?' Michael offers.

'Well . . . '

'How about "knob"?' says Paddy keenly.

'Let me—'

'Or "bum bandit"?' Paddy is on a roll. This is a great opportunity for him to use all the words he's been storing up for a rainy day.

'No, none of these are OK,' I say, trying a stern voice on for size. 'Let me make it easy for you. Anything I say is OK.'

'Like "pimped me out"?'

'No, that's not OK.'

'But you said it,' questions Michael.

'Well, I made a mistake.' I was trying to get them excited about going *shopping*, for God's sake. Getting 'pimped out' is a better motivator than 'Let's stand in Dolcis for half an hour arguing about which shoes you hate the least.'

'So how do we know when it's OK to repeat something, and when you've made a mistake?'

'If you hear me say it twice.'

'How come?'

'Because your dad never makes the same mistake twice. Mistakes are the way we learn.'

The boys are unimpressed by this.

'What about when you kick the post at the top of the stairs?' asks Michael.

'How do you mean?'

'You're always doing that,' he continues, mimicking a limping Tom. 'You must do that at least once a day. That's the same mistake. And you always say "bollocks!" when you do it.'

'All right, smarty pants,' I say, secretly amused at the idea of Tom stubbing his toe in exactly the same place every day. 'I hear what you're saying. Well, my answer to you is that everybody makes mistakes.'

'Like saying "bum gravy",' chimes in Paddy.

'Well, saying "bum gravy" is not exactly a mistake, is it, Patrick? Let's be honest.'

'I suppose not, but I might say—'

'All right, Paddy, I get your point.' I cut him off before he runs the whole gamut of his bowel-related vocabulary.

'Look. There are two points I'm trying to make. The first one is that Mum is right. We shouldn't be using bad language either inside or outside this house, OK?'

The boys nod.

'And my second point is that we all make mistakes.'

'Like when you tried to carry that TV from the car and dropped it on the floor?' says Paddy. Michael laughs at the memory.

'Wha . . . ? Oh yeah,' I reply imagining Tom, too proud to ask for help, heaving a TV out the back of the car and then dropping it on his foot. Fucking fabulous.

'But not just that. Stuff like trying to do your best but not quite making it,' I explain. 'Like saying "bum gravy" – Ooops! – when you don't mean to. See what I mean?'

The boys laugh and I wonder if I've managed to communicate anything that's worth knowing. Is this how you're supposed to do it? Or do you take the kids aside and school them through tidy coaching, give them instruction like you're Akela? Or is it supposed to be subtler than that? Am I supposed to sidle up to them and use clever life examples so that they aren't even aware that they're being guided? Should they be absorbing information without even knowing it? I wish that I could pass on the snappy aphorisms that I saw on *Kung Fu* when I was a kid. 'Fear is the only darkness', 'Seeds of our destiny are nurtured by the roots of our past', 'Never assume a man who has no eyes cannot see'. That kind of thing. I could be Master Po and the boys ciphers of Caine. Having said that, knowing Paddy, this would all probably be translated into 'Man who goes to bed with itchy bum, wakes up with smelly finger'.

The boys have gone back to playing *Halo* now, and I'm pretty sure that I hear Paddy call Michael 'knobskin', although I'm not certain. I have no idea where they got that ... In the spirit of flourishing parenting I really can't be arsed provoking a fight, so I saunter back to the kitchen to fetch us a round of toast, which we devour, wolf-like, on the living-room floor. The boys grunt that they want more, so I return to the kitchen to make another batch. While I'm there I decide to start preparing the lunch and slice some veg for a couscous salad, which I've convinced the boys isn't 'gay food', although the concept is an interesting one. I'm turning up the heat on the peppers when I hear a noise in the hallway. Probably one of the boys going to the bathroom ... But this sounds different, like there's more bodyweight to the person making the sounds. I'm just about to go and investigate when I hear the refrain from Eminem's 'Without Me' ...

'Guess who's back? Guess who's back? Guess who's back?'

Holy fucking shit. It's Sara.

I hear Paddy and Michael's pounding feet as they race to give their mother a hug. I walk through to the hallway.

'Hello,' I say, my voice pitched in that tone that people use when they're demonstrating a happy surprise but that also contains a question.

'We didn't expect you back so soon ... '

'What's that smell?' she asks.

I sniff the air. 'Oh, that's peppers roasting.'

She pulls a look somewhere between disbelief and shock.

'Lunch,' I say weakly. This is not good. Tom can barely butter toast.

We all move through to the kitchen. Sara snakes an arm around my waist and pecks me on the cheek. I'm numb with fear, scared to open my mouth, to move, to be in the room with her. This wasn't part of the plan.

'But we just—'

'I was in a cab. Thought I'd surprise you.'

Well, you fucking did that all right . . .

The boys are jabbering away now, trying to catch Sara up with a week's worth of events at school.

'We've got a football tournament next weekend,' Michael tells Sara.

'Dad told me,' she says.

'I'm going to be captain,' adds Michael.

'No, you're not,' says Paddy.

'OK, both of you,' says Sara, 'go and grab my bag. I've got a little something for you.'

The boys run off, and suddenly it's just the two of us. There are a couple of slices of red pepper on the cutting board. Sara picks them up and starts crunching through them.

'So . . . ?' I ask

'Mistrial,' she says by way of explaining her presence. 'Bloody police not following procedure. I hate it when you get beaten on a technicality. It's like losing to a dodgy penalty. Anyway, two of them walked. The other is still banged up on some kind of immigration charge. He'll probably be deported before we get another court date.'

'What a pain in the arse,' I sympathise, mostly with myself.

'That's show business, Tom,' says Sara, shrugging her shoulders. She sits down on a kitchen chair, unzips her boots and pulls them off. She casts her eyes around the room. Standing before her in Tom's pyjamas and dressing gown, I'm scared of what she's going to say next. Have I committed a terrible error?

'Has the window cleaner been?' she finally asks, massaging her feet.

'Um, no,' I say.

'Then . . . ?'

'I gave them a quick once over,' I explain.

She turns her head slowly to look at me for a moment, but appears to take this in her stride.

'I tried to get on a train last night, but there was no room. Got the first one out of Lime Street.' She yawns and leans her head back, her hair falling on the kitchen table behind her.

'I'm knackered.'

'Why don't you go upstairs and have a bath and I'll do you some breakfast?' I ask.

'That would be lovely.' She smiles. The boys walk back into the kitchen. Both are wearing brand-new Chelsea shirts. Paddy's says 'Lampard', Michael's 'Makalele'.

'You went to *Liverpool* and bought them Chelsea shirts?' I ask.

'I know we said that we'd get them for Christmas, but . . . I dunno, I wanted to get them something nice,' she explains.

'Um, Sara . . . ' I start.

'Dad, already bought us Chelsea shirts,' explains Michael. 'When we went to the game last week.'

Sara swivels towards me in her chair.

'You what?'

'How did I know that you were going to buy them the same thing?' I explain.

'Jesus, Tom, you know how much they cost?'

'Of course, I do . . . '

'That was a rhetorical question.'

'We still like them, Mum,' says Paddy.

'And they've got different players names on the back,' explains Michael.

'There you go,' I say, trying to lighten proceedings. Helpfully, both boys now give Sara a hug and thank her, which lessens her annoyance.

'You should have told me,' she says. I want to add that she should have told me that that she was coming home from the trial because I'm an imposter and it would have given me a night to consider what the hell I was going to do rather than stand around in M&S pyjamas keeping an eye on my roasted vegetables and debating the price-gouging activities of football kit manufacturers. I feel toxic, like I've just found out some really bad news and it's become such a part of me that I'll never be able to shake it off. How can I possibly get away with this? Her mission on earth is to use her wit and guile to outsmart others with similar amounts of wit and guile. Now, I might have some guile, and I've definitely got some wit about me, but I'm not sure that I'm up to this, and the thought of what would happen if she were to expose us, well, it's too awful to contemplate. But contemplate it I do, as I imagine the look of betrayal on her face as she confronts me, my stuttering denial becoming a desperate apology and a pitiful explanation . . .

Sara traipses to the bathroom, tired and clearly a little disappointed by the Chelsea shirt fiasco. I lug her suitcase upstairs. Before she can start to undress I swallow hard, walk over and embrace her. We hug and she comes up for a kiss, which I duck, telling her that I need to go and check on lunch.

'Please yourself,' she says. I'm making a hash of this. As I walk downstairs I hope that she hasn't noticed that I'm sweating like I'm being interrogated by the Stasi.

I return to the living room panicked and scared, not sure what to make of this turn of events. Michael is still playing *Halo*, while Paddy is working furiously on a drawing.

And then it hits me. Everything is . . . normal. The kids are doing their thing. Sara is glad to be home, thrilled to see the boys again. She's probably a little perplexed by her husband, but when isn't she? Maybe the way to handle it is to roll with what's happening, to play the part of lovable, put-upon Tom acknowledging his shortcomings and finally getting his act together. I nip into the kitchen, dig out a Jamie Oliver recipe book, and leave it open on a plausible recipe.

Maybe Sara is simply relieved that nothing has occurred in the past few days to trouble the emergency services. There have been no severed limbs, no scaldings, no falls or impalings. There have been no executions. No one has been lost or abducted. Here we are . . . a family, intact and relieved to be together. Opening a cupboard I see a packet of KitKats. I think about Maja. I wonder where she is now, whether I dare risk taking the boys to the park on the off chance that I might bump into her. I'm going to have to be careful about calling her, will need to avoid using the home phone in case Sara checks the dialled numbers.

Paddy comes into the room. He seems a little different, his mischievous swagger discarded in the living room. He hands me the drawing he's been working on. I stare at the picture. It's a football pitch with three figures on it, holding up a cup. The two smaller figures are labelled 'Paddy' and 'Michael'. I pause when I see the larger one – it's marked 'Dad'. I look up and he's lingering in the doorway, waiting for my reaction. I look at the drawing, which isn't actually that bad a representation of the three of us. (Is it just me that cringes when parents display their offspring's crude scrawlings in the kitchen as if they had an original Matisse?) But this is not the point.

'It's for you,' he says, making the distinction clear between work that he shows me, and this particular work, which is an offering. I look back down at the drawing – the thick green grass, the meticulously detailed netting, the cup that looks suspiciously like the FA Cup borne aloft by a father with stunted arms and two sons with freakishly extended ones – and for the first time since I've come to live with the boys I talk in my own voice rather than my brother's.

'Thanks, Paddy,' I say. 'Can I keep it?' He nods, seemingly satisfied with the outcome. I smooth the picture down on the kitchen table and contemplate his work. Is the picture really for me? Recognition for my participation in the boys' lives? Or am I a terrible phony accepting a token that actually belongs to my brother? I look at the drawing and try to work out whether the hulking figure with chestnut hair and teeth that have been drawn individually and with great care is Tom or me? Of course, I'll never know, but if there's a chance that it could be me, I'll settle for that.

Sara comes down from her bath slightly pink and fragrant.

'I need to run a few errands,' she says. 'Expect you could do with a little peace and quiet. I'll take the boys with me.'

'Sounds good,' I say. 'How long are you going to be?' I'm hoping for as much time as possible to get my head straight.

'Oh, not long,' she says, rummaging through her bag. 'An hour or so.'

'OK,' I say, secretly disappointed.

She slings her bag over her shoulder and looks at me. Her hair is pulled back in a ponytail and she's put some make-up on; I can see why any bloke my age might give her a second look.

'Are you OK?' she asks.

'Who? *Me?*' I say.

She takes a deep breath. 'Yes, you.'

'Yeah, I'm fine,' I say, entirely implausibly, which, after a moment's consideration, might actually be *exactly* the way Tom would answer the same question. 'Why?'

'Oh, nothing,' she says. The words sink like a stone in my stomach. The damage is done.

The boys are distinctly unhappy about having their morning of *Halo* disrupted by a trip that, from what Tom tells me, will inevitably involve the purchase of a soy latte, *Heat* and some expensive pastries from the testy Belgian ponce on Salusbury Road who calls himself a *boulanger* so that he can jack up his prices by fifty per cent.

Once they're gone I pace around the house like a demented cartoon character trying to work out my next move. This is not what either Tom or I bargained for. Not only is it exactly what Tom sought to avoid in the first place, it infinitely increases the chances of detection. Sara is no mug, and the slightest slip-up could lead us all down a path that's simply too ugly to contemplate. Quite honestly I'm not sure that I can pull it off – playing the role of my brother with Sara around is an entirely different proposition to bossing around a couple of distracted kids the same way their dad does.

I pick up the phone and listen to the flat note of the dialling tone. I have to tell Tom that we need to call everything off. There's no way that we're going to get away with this. Besides, I owe it to Tom to let him know what's happened. It's his marriage, after all . . .

But before I can even start to punch in the numbers I press the 'end call' button. It occurs to me that maybe I'm being a little rash. Maybe I'm rejecting a golden opportunity – for isn't Sara's return the ideal way to fully experience Tom's life? I know that if I call and tell Tom he'll put an immediate end to the swap. I begin to realise that I'm not ready for that to happen. So far, we've both had some fun and proved a point to each other, but if we call it off I'd feel like we still had unfinished business. For starters, I'm having a great time. I love hanging out with the boys. If I can have another week of organising their lives and mucking about then I'll take it. Then there's Maja. I've not had enough time to really develop the relationship. I sense that there is something there, but I'm having a hard time reading her signs. Maybe the fact that she hasn't yet returned my call shouldn't be too hard to read, but I'm convinced that we've just got to get over something that she can't make herself say. A few more days and we might get to the promised land. Most importantly, I need to work out how I can return to my old life while retaining the possibility of a relationship with Maja. I might be fleet of foot in the spin stakes, but this one is still totally baffling me.

And, finally, there's Sara, one of the smartest people I know and one of the least forgiving. Not in the sense that she doesn't have compassion, which she does. No, it's more that Sara has high standards, and while she's not arrogant enough to assume that everyone else should live up to them, those who are close to her can feel a little bleed between the way that she feels you should handle a tricky situation and the way that she would handle it herself. And this is usually for a good reason: Sara is more often than not accurate in her emotional pitch. She reads people and situations well, if sometimes critically, but that criticism isn't always judgemental. I have to admit that I'm intrigued by the opportunity of living with her. I enjoy the cut and thrust with Sara and have always suspected that our adversarial relationship was driven by a mutual attraction.

As tempting as it is to fold, I decide to play my hand, to give Tom's marriage a go, hoping, with all my heart, that I'm not making the biggest mistake of my own and Tom's life.

The rest of the day I manage to keep my head above water. The boys are enough of a distraction for Sara and I not to have to indulge in any close interaction. My game is to play it safe – to take Sara's lead and just blend into the background. This seems to work, but throughout the afternoon and evening I'm dreading the moment when the boys go to bed and it's just the two of us in a situation where it's impossible to avoid potentially catastrophic intimacy.

I comfort myself with the knowledge that, during the week, Sara will be working late. But tonight and tomorrow are so loaded with latent jeopardy that I flit around the house finding things to do that keep me a safe distance from her. I spend an hour alphabeticising Tom's DVDs before finding myself at a loose end. I need an activity that will kill an hour or so, something that will fill the time between now and a reasonable time to go to bed. My musing is interrupted when I notice a powerful smell coming from the kitchen. I sniff again. I can't be right. I know what it is, but can't believe that it could be in Tom and Sara's house: the sickly sweet aroma of ganja.

I walk into the kitchen to see Sara toking on a huge, badly rolled

Camberwell carrot. The air is so thick with smoke that I close the kitchen door in case the smoke alarms are set off.

'What are you doing?' I ask, sitting down opposite her at the kitchen table.

'Um, what does it look like?' she says with a chuckle. 'Skinning up.' In front of her is the bag of grass that I meant to give back to Tom for safekeeping. I freeze. Fuck. Shit. Bollocks. She must have found it. How could I be so stupid? The first night she gets back and I've catastrophically screwed up.

The phone rings. Distraction. Excellent.

'Well, *I* don't want to talk to anybody,' says Sara.

It rings three times before clicking over to the answer machine. To my horror, a familiar voice comes through the speaker.

'Hi Tom, it's—' Maja! Oh, Lord. I rush over and pick up the receiver before she can say anything incriminating. Sara is staring directly at me, not even pretending not to be listening.

'Hi there, how are you?' I ask, feeling the heat of Sara's surveillance.

'Fine,' she replies.

'Good, good . . . '

Sara narrows her eyes as she draws deeply on the joint. Maja senses something isn't right.

'Um, if this isn't a good time maybe I should call back?'

'That might be a good idea.'

'OK.'

And with that she's gone. No niceties, no speak-to-you-laters, she just absents herself. Jesus, after this and the incident when I stopped her and Matthew coming for tea with the boys, she must think I'm something of an oddball. I put the receiver down, steeling myself for the imminent inquisition.

'So who was that?' asks Sara in a scarily non-confrontational way.

'Oh, *that*,' I start, as if I was confused by what she meant. 'Just someone from football practice.'

'I see.'

I think that maybe you do.

'We're organising a team for the competition,' I smile. 'Bloody hard work, actually. I can see why they pay football managers so much.'

'Really,' she says stiffly. 'Let's return to the matter in hand, shall we? So there I was, doing the laundry this afternoon when I check the pockets of your jeans and, lo and behold, I find, what do they call it, a "Henry", you know, from Henry VIII, of grass in your pocket. Strong stuff too, I'd say. Hydroponic.'

'Yeah, it is,' I say. I immediately regret it. Noting her successful identification of drug type and weight is hardly a tactic for digging myself out of this.

'What the fuck are you doing with this, Tom?'

'Well, it's a long story,' I splutter. There's nothing for it but to . . . Blame someone else.

'It's Sean's,' I say.

'So why the hell do you have it?' she demands. 'Do I need to remind you that you have two young sons in the house who in no way should be exposed to illegal drugs, even if it is the one classified by Her Majesty's Government as "soft"?'

'Well . . . '

'"Soft" is actually more like a description of your head,' she says. The grass doesn't appear to be working. Far from mellowing her out, she seems to be getting more aggravated.

'Look, he gave it to me in the park to hold for a few moments and I forgot to give it back to him. I'm really sorry.'

'I'm not sure that I believe you,' says Sara, taking another toke. 'Why should I?'

'Jesus, Sara, it's the truth. I don't even like the stuff.' Not strictly true, of course, but I'm engaged in so many different levels of lying now that adding another one to the pile hardly seems to be my primary concern at the moment. She offers me the joint. I shake my head. I'm not that foolish, no matter how delicious the aroma and desperate I am to chill out.

'This really is another turn for you, isn't it, Tom?'

'How do you mean?'

'Well, self-medication with a bit of Amsterdam's finest; it's hardly a step in the right direction, is it?'

'I told you, Sara, it's not mine . . . '

'I know, I know, it's Sean's. Your twin brother who gets to live a life of hedonism that you can only dream of.'

What? This an issue in Tom and Sara's marriage?

Sara coughs a little before stubbing out the blunt.

'That "shit" is too strong for me,' she says, banging her chest.

'Look, I'm sorry, OK,' I say. 'I'll get rid of it.' I walk into the toilet and show her that I'm tipping the contents of the bag into the bowl. I flush with a flourish and return to the smoky kitchen.

'Very dramatic, Tom. Very dramatic,' says Sara, her voice a little huskier than usual. 'One thing, though: you ever bring drugs in this house again, and I don't care how or why they get in here, I'll be the one who's doing something dramatic. Understood?'

I look at her and I'm more scared of the life swap going wrong than I imagined possible.

'Understood,' I say meekly while I watch the red-eyed Sara stagger out of the room.

21
Tom

I've not spoken to Sean since we talked two nights ago. Now, I'll be the first to admit that maybe I didn't acquit myself too well. I'd definitely had a little too much Dom Perignon and I probably blurted things that I might not have said had I not been as 'refreshed' as I was. However, I think that there's a principle to be observed. If the two of us are attempting to bring ourselves as close as we can manage to each other's lives, then there has to be a point at which both of us are able to call bullshit when we see it. We have to force ourselves to remain within certain boundaries, otherwise, well, otherwise we're not buying into the original spirit of our agreement, which, unless I'm mistaken, sought to wipe clear the opaque screens to each other's lives rather than deliver a mutual cock punch.

Of course, I have to wonder how much of what I formerly believed about Sean is right anyway. But Sean's clients' recent rush to the exits must surely indicate something. Maybe Sean has done exactly what he would do with any of the brands that he might be hired to represent – he's created an image and a set of beliefs about himself that don't necessarily correspond to the truth. And, as with brands, reality increasingly recedes until it's replaced by the new, upbeat message that – and this is the genius of Sean's business – becomes a new reality. The question is, how much of this does Sean believe?

A good example of this is one of the accounts that Sean is clearly not worried about – a Hong Kong-based group specialising in spas at luxury hotels. I know that he's not worried about it, because the revenue from this account is part of his forecast for next year. But a chance e-mail encounter with the client has enlightened me to the fact that SC Communications can in no way be guaranteed this account. The deeper I get with the client it appears that they are not averse to re-signing with SC Communications, they just need to be shown some love. So I show them some love. I show them several hundred pounds' worth of sushi and sake love at a swanky eatery in Mayfair. This seems to help, as we end up discussing strategy for next year. Bloated and pleasantly woozy at the end of the lunch I'm trying to focus on the little Amex slip and calculate whether our waiter was trying to pull a fast one with the tip, when I realised that, holy crap, I'm back in the game. The account is worth eighty-four grand (plus disbursements), which is revenue the company in all likelihood would not have seen, had I not intervened. The experience is made all the sweeter knowing that the charge for the fatty toro and maki rolls will appear on Sean's Amex bill next month. Delicious. *Burp.*

I'm looking forward to letting Sean know about the successful deal and dropping the sushi bill on him, when I get a text message from Theano. Can I make a meeting in twenty minutes? Apparently she needs to run through some numbers with me that need to be signed off for VAT, blah, blah, yawn. Fine, I'll do it. I know that it's not new business, but at least I've got some good news about the spa clients to tell her.

Heading towards my office I see Aileen look at me anxiously. She jumps up from her computer and comes round to the side of her desk. Her body language is different; her shoulders are hunched and tight.

'Sean . . . ' she starts. 'It wasn't scheduled, but Theano said you knew about it. I'm sorry if . . . '

Inside my office I see Theano sitting at my small conference table. Opposite her, with his back to me, is the man I saw with her in the café. I walk in and close the door.

'Theano?' I say. Both of them stand up. Theano brushes a crease out of her skirt nervously while she starts to talk.

'Sean, I know that this is highly irregular . . . ' She hasn't had a chance to give her prepared speech before the steel-haired smoothie steps forward to shake my hand. I shake it, and them immediately regret letting him take the initiative.

'Geoffrey Blake,' he says. 'Trident Investment.'

There's a venture capitalist in Sean's office.

'Following our earlier discussion, Sean,' continues Theano, 'I know that you're resistant to taking on any partners. I know that this is awkward, but I felt it was in the best interests of the company for you to meet. I think that you should hear Geoffrey out. In my opinion, he's making a generous offer.'

'An offer?' I say. 'For what?'

'Shall we sit?' asks Geoffrey. I ignore him.

'An offer for what?'

'Sean, I have a group of investors who are looking to acquire SC Communications,' says Geoffrey. 'The finance is in place. I approached Theano about three weeks ago in the hope that she would act as a bridge between the two of us. When she told me that you weren't interested I just wanted the opportunity to come and talk to you face to face.'

'Hang on,' I say to Theano. 'We talked about bringing in investors. Not a fucking takeover.'

'Tom, I think that it's in the best interests of the company,' says Theano boldly. 'To grow we need capital. We're barely bringing in enough revenue to keep the company functioning, let alone grow it.'

'Sean, according to our valuation, do you know how much your company is worth?'

'Of course,' I say, bluffing.

'Well, I'm sure that you won't be surprised to learn that our valuation was zero. Zilch. All you have is your intellectual capital. There are no assets. Unless your clients re-sign you have no projected earnings. However, we can add value – a lot of value – to your business by rolling it into another major media concern to create a larger, synergistic business with real value and potential for growth.'

This is utterly surreal. I'm standing in Sean's office talking about the future of his company while he's . . . what? Peeling potatoes. At soccer practice with the boys?

'We're offering to buy the company for ten million pounds,' says Geoffrey. 'You would become a non-executive director and have a seat on the board. You would continue to earn your current salary.'

Ten million quid? Holy fucking shit. I need to get a grip. Fudge it until I can get Sean involved. I mean, ten million quid sounds like a lot of money . . . *Sounds* like a lot of money? It's a *ton* of money. Roll around on banknotes laughing in a *Mwahahahahahahhaha!* fashion. He'd be able to retire and, well, . . . I'm not really sure. But Sean's identity is so wrapped up in this place and its daily dramas that I'm not sure that he could function anywhere else. I wonder what my brother would make of this. After a moment's thought I know what Sean would do: he'd make a decision. He'd lead from the front.

'Get out,' I say to Geoffrey Blake.

'Do you really mean that?' he says patronisingly.

'Yes,' I confirm. 'Get out.'

He closes his attaché case and picks it up from the table.

'You're making a huge mistake,' he says. 'Theano, thank you for your help in this matter. I'm sorry that we didn't manage to reach a successful conclusion.'

He walks out of the office, leaving Theano and myself.

'Sean,' she says, 'I think you might have just blown our best chance of staying in business.'

'I'll be the judge of that,' I snap.

'I suppose I'd better go and write my letter of resignation,' she says.

'There's no need for that,' I reply. Theano makes to leave the office. 'I won't accept it.'

She looks at me, surprised.

'Stick with me here, Theano,' I say. 'We're going to get out of this.'

I spend a fretful hour looking over the Deutsche Mobilen presentation barely able to concentrate. The pressure is taking me close to boiling point. I need to make this deal happen after my rejection of the takeover. Why didn't I call Sean? What the hell am I doing? I've no right to make such major decisions on his behalf. I'm thinking about him when I get a message on the Berry. He needs to see me immediately. He's at the Natural History Museum. How did he find out? He's going to kill me, I know it. He's going to rip my head off. What I've done, well, it's unforgivable. I jump in a taxi and head to Cromwell Road.

My heart leaps a little bit when I come across the boys marvelling at the dinosaur skeletons that I've brought them to see dozens of times. They both high five 'Uncle Sean' and we mess around a bit, but the entire time I can feel Sean watching me, like he's itching to talk. He looks different, somehow less polished, and without the slightly contrived upbeat can-do energy that he usually possesses. Something's up. He definitely knows – but how?

We follow the boys around the museum, moving quickly between displays as they seek new objects for their attention. At the first opportunity to talk without the boys overhearing I open my mouth, only for him to beat me to the punch.

'Sara's back,' he says, in the low, flat voice. He gives it no more weight than if he were telling me he'd put petrol in the car on the way over.

'*What?*' I say, thrown as much by the way he's delivered the news as the news itself.

'There was no warning. Nothing. Saturday morning, she just breezes through the door.' We stop by a case displaying dinosaur eggs that are too big and oddly coloured to register as natural.

'How the hell did that happen?'

'The trial finished early. The dealers walked.'

'Shit,' I say, the fear rising rapidly up my body. 'Shit. Fuck. Shit.'

'Sssssshhh,' says Sean, gesturing at the boys.

'Does she suspect anything?'

'I don't think so . . . You know, I can't read her mind. I mean . . . I dunno. Not really.'

'Look, stay cool, OK,' I say helpfully. I press the index finger and thumb of my right hand against my forehead, as if to help me think more clearly. How can I tell him about the takeover now? It's overkill, too much information. I need to deal with the Sara situation first.

'OK,' I say adamantly. 'Time's up.' I need to get home and he needs to get back to his business.

'Let's think about this clearly,' says Sean. 'Let's not rush to a decision.'

'Look, this has been great. I've got some real insight into your world, and hopefully vice versa, but we've got to pull the plug. Now.'

'But we said two weeks . . . '

'That's before Sara came back. We've got to quit while we're ahead.'

'Tom, how about we examine all options before bailing out?'

'What are you talking about?'

'Tom, you're missing the point of this whole thing,' says Sean. He's smiling like a Jehovah's Witness, hopeful that he might save you from the raging fire, and has moved so that he's standing squarely in front of me. I can see him summoning the salesman within. 'How about we see it through? Like a marriage. For better or worse, richer or poorer, in sickness and in health.'

'Sean, I think we're the last people on the planet who should be drawing a marriage analogy at the moment.'

'All right, but you take my point, right? In for a penny . . . '

'Sara coming back messes everything up,' I explain. I can't believe he's actually entertaining the idea that we continue. I feel sick, scared that Sara has already smoked us out. I glance around the museum, suddenly terrified that she's followed Sean. 'Come on, man. Her trip was the basis for the timing of this thing. The stakes are too high for me now, pal. If she finds out what we've done, well, I'll have to change my identity and look for work spinning cars on the waltzer.'

'Look, everyone loves a go-getter.'

'Sean, I'm serious.'

'Me too. You're not the only one with something to lose. I want to close the deal with that girl I told you about.'

'How can you equate my marriage with some girl you've just met?'

'She's not a girl, she's a woman,' he says, irritated. 'OK, sorry, a doctor, if you must know. And I'm not equating them. I'm trying to let you know how important this is to me.'

'You had better be fucking joking . . . '

'Don't worry about Sara. She's already deep into something else. She's working late all week.'

'For fuck's sake, Sean, I'm not one of your employees, I'm not a client. I'm your brother and we're talking about my marriage.'

'Keep your voice down,' he says, looking over at the boys. 'Let's keep this conversation "offline", shall we?'

'Sean, this is lunacy.'

'So, what are you proposing? That we do a quick switch in the bogs?' he asks. He raises his hands and offers his palms to me, like a market trader who's negotiating technique is, basically, to suggest that you're insane. Actually, swapping clothes in the bogs doesn't seem like such a bad idea to me.

'Because that's not going to happen,' he cuts in before I can say anything.

'Sean, we've got to figure out how we sort this thing.'

'No, we don't. No, we don't,' he says. 'We just have to keep our nerve, that's all. The worst thing we can do right now is to lose our bottle.'

'Sean, it's not a question of "losing bottle", for Christ's sake . . . I mean, how old are you? Are you going to start clucking and accuse me of being a chicken? This is my marriage.'

'I know, I know,' he says. 'I hear that, but we've got to follow through. We've both got business to finish.'

'Sean, I really—'

'Let me tell you something, Tom – we're not going back.'

I sense him hardening a little. His brows bunch and his jaw is a more pronounced than normal, like he's gritting his teeth. I need to take control of the situation.

'I'm taking the boys home,' I tell him. 'Today.'

'I can't allow that,' says Sean.

I want to laugh, but I can tell that he's not joking. The boys are examining something to do with the speed of a veloceraptor, oblivious to our conversation, and briefly I manage to peer over my burning rage and see something much worse: what if this is actually the best thing for the boys? I've noticed the changes – the football practice, the straighter backs, the general absence of Kentucky Fried lethargy. There's no doubt that Sean is responsible for this 'attitude adjustment'. Fake dad nor not, he's a decent bloke, and someone I'm sure would do a wholly competent job as a father . . .

But then red mist descends upon me.

'You can't allow that?' I say. My voice as emotionless as I can manage. 'You can't allow that. Have you any idea how fucking ridiculous that sounds, Sean? Have you stopped to think, just for a moment, that I'm going to allow you to speak to me like that on the subject of my kids?'

'We're in too deep . . . '

'No, no, Sean, we're not. We're not in too deep. We're in too deep when I lose my wife and kids because we continue a bizarre social experiment, *that's* when we're in too deep. No, right now, we're paddling in the shallow end.'

Sean shakes his head, and with a wry grin says to me, 'You're losing it, mate . . . '

'*I'm* losing it? *I'm* losing it? Sean, what do you think I've been doing for the past week? I've been sitting in rooms with your financial controller talking about how we save your fucking company.'

'Well, thanks, Tom,' he says condescendingly.

'It's over, Sean.'

'Tom, don't be impetuous.'

'It's over, Sean.'

'Just four days to go, bro'.'

I make a move towards the boys, and he steps in front of me.

'Do you really want to explain all of this to them?'

I look at him, wondering if he's actually serious, and see in his eyes that he is. I feel sick, knowing that we're now at a whole new level of emotional complexity. A scenario that relied on both of us playing a role but being anchored in our real lives has spun into the realm of mentalism. We have now, officially, super-sized the trouble we're in. My brother, the person I love beyond anyone other than my wife and kids, has become my nemesis. And on top of that I might just be responsible for his losing ten million pounds.

'Sean, I can't risk it. I can't jeopardise everything I care about for this.'

'I know that this isn't easy for you, but you're just going to have to trust me,' he says coldly. 'You have no other choice but to be confident that I can to pull it off. Don't worry about the boys. They're oblivious, like you said. And Sara is totally distracted by work. It's a piece of piss.'

I look over at the boys, trying to figure out how best to handle the situation. What Sean is suggesting is, of course, bonkers – even more bonkers than when we embarked upon our swap. This isn't the usual Sean. Oh no. There's something about this scenario that's changed him, given him an edge of desperation, and I have to admit that I'm enjoying seeing him struggle to resolve what should be the most simple of decisions even though it enormously compromises my own situation.

'The kids are happy, man,' he says. 'They really are. And I swear to God I can handle the bedtime arrangements with Sara.'

I decide to push him a little. 'What the fuck does that mean? "Bedtime arrangements". Are you trying to tell me that I should be thankful to you because you won't fuck my wife? Wow, Sean, that's really great of you.'

He takes a deep breath. 'I'm just trying to tell you that I'm a man of my word. We'll see this thing through, swap back on Saturday and—'

'Just like the SAS, eh? In and out. No one gets hurt. And what are you going to do, Sean, if I say no to you? Tell the boys, right here, right now? Give Sara a bell so that we can conference her in?'

He shrugs.

'Because I just want you to understand that, to my eyes, that's exactly what's happening here. You're threatening to tell my wife and kids about this so that you can get what you want.'

'I'm just asking you to stick to our agreement,' he says.

'Or . . . ?' I ask.

Nothing. I wait. Still nothing.

'Well, I'm certainly glad to hear, Sean, that, as ever, you've got my best interests at heart.'

I wait for some kind of smart-arse answer, but none is forthcoming. Instead, he looks at me and says, 'The boys are really happy, Tom.' And I don't know whether he's saying this to make me feel better, or whether he's revealing that, even in childrearing, he's a winner. I decide that, whatever his motivation, he's right. The boys are happy, and my coming home isn't going to make them any happier. As for Sara, well, if she's having one of her heavy weeks there's a chance that she might not even see Sean, let alone interact with him.

So . . . Sean gets to see the swap through. But what about me? If there's one thing that taking on my brother's life for the past few days has taught me, it's that I need to work the angles more, to hustle a little bit.

Sean wants my family? Fine, I'll take his company in exchange. I look him in the eye; it's only been just over a week but our roles appear to have realigned themselves. I feel like the assured negotiator, and he appears to have become the rattled dad. I demand a concession, something that I would never have dreamed of a week ago.

'Sean, if you want to do this, then I have some non-negotiable demands.'

He clicks back to being his usual self: 'Everything's negotiable, Tom . . . '

'Shut up, Sean. Believe me, I am more scared of this going wrong than anything in my entire life. But, if you're so certain that you want them for a few more days, then here it is. You sleep in the spare bedroom. You leave the house next Saturday night for us to change back to our former lives and, if I sign a major client within the next few days, then you make me a partner at SC Communications.'

'I really don't think—'

'I've crunched the numbers, Sean. If I bring in what I think I can bring in, I'll generate enough cash to keep you in business, and that, bro, is worth fifty per cent of the company.'

'Twenty-five per cent!'

'Sean, if I was asking for twenty-five per cent in a month's time, I'd be asking for twenty-five per cent of nothing. I'm going to save your arse.'

'I don't know, I—'

'Take it or leave it.'

'OK,' he says.

I'm so annoyed at myself, and so fearful of the decision I've just made, that I don't even say goodbye to Sean. I walk over to the boys, tell them I've got to go, get a couple of high fives and a small lump in my throat for my troubles, and watch them disappear into the next hall attentively marshalled by my guilty-looking brother.

And he's not the only one. I'm staggered that I've let the boys become tantamount to hostages, albeit it to a benign, temporary captor, and I'm terrified that I might lose Sara. I could have fought back, called his bluff, fudged some kind of lame explanation to the kids, but Sean appears to be on some crazy crusade.

I need to try to forget the tight knot of worry in my stomach. This morning I was trying to save my brother's company through sheer altruism. Now, well, my motives are a little different. They have a percentage sign after them and will be realised in solicitors' letters and contracts with red seals on them.

I haven't got time to hang about, I've got a deal to close.

22

Sean

I watch Tom leave the museum still not quite believing what has just occurred, or my part in it. As he passes the final exhibit I notice that he's lost his trademark lope, exiting the Victorian edifice like a man on a mission as opposed to his more typical man-on-his-way-to-Homebase gait. I wait a few minutes for the boys to tire of archeology before herding them into the car. I can barely direct my attention to their banter, let alone the unbroken dinosaur-related interrogation to which they subject me during the ride home.

'Dad, Dad, how many different dinosaurs were there?'

'Dad, do they really work out what dinosaurs ate by looking at their poo?'

'Dad, who's harder – a Giganotosaurus or a T Rex?'

You get the picture. Both of them appear to have inherited their mother's gift for cross-examination. It's partly my thin knowledge of history other than some misty recollection of the Romans and the Industrial Revolution, but mostly the shock of recent events that prevents me from making much of a contribution to the bracing debate in the back of the car.

As much as the deliberation regarding pterodactyls fighting land-based dinosaurs or otherwise is distracting, I am sunk in a pit of worry. One part of me recognises the arguments that I put forward are, on some vague level, justifiable. Yes, I am looking after the boys in a totally capable fashion; yes, our agreement runs to the following weekend, and yes, I can convince Sara that I'm Tom . . . All of these I stand by, pretty much. So what's turned my stomach into a churning pit of acid? Oh, well, maybe that would be the fact that I'm putting my brother's marriage and my own relationship with him and his family under unimaginable stress. Given the likelihood of my screwing things up with Maja, this would leave me with precisely zero meaningful relationships in my life. As much as I'd like to gain admission to the real intimacies of family life, my obligation to protecting Tom and my secret should supercede everything else.

And Tom is tougher than people give him credit for. Back in the days when all we cared about was music, our mates and a decent bag of grass, we'd been out to a party somewhere out in Docklands and were driving back with a couple of friends in Tom's decrepit old Fiesta XR2. The car's crapiness was no hindrance to Tom treating it like a Ferrari. He would take it down to the car wash that all the cabbies use in King's Cross, have it valeted, drop so much money on its mechanics annually that he could have afforded to buy a whole new ride. The sun was poking its head up and London was quiet and restful, the blues of the night now shaded with the pink of a bright June day. We were just passing round the last of the Thai grass that we'd scored especially for the gig, when Tom hit the brakes hard. We were all thrown forward in our seats, seatbelts snapped taut by the force, as the car skidded. There was a thump against the car before we screeched to a halt.

'What the fuck?' said Mickey in the back.

'I think I hit a cat,' said Tom grimly.

Mickey and Malik swivel round to look out of the back window. I open the door and take a look. About 100 yards back, a cat is lying on the ground. The four of us get out to take a look. As we approach it we can see that it's not dead. It yowls pathetically, trying to get up, a feat made impossible by the fact that its back legs are crushed. It's as good as dead.

'Oh shit,' says Mickey, crushing the spliff on the grey tarmac.

'It's a fucking mess,' says Malik.

'There's no way it's going to make it,' I add.

Tom walks off. I watch as he opens the boot of the car.

'Jesus. What do you reckon we should do?' I say. 'Can't we call a vet or something?' The weed is making me feel a little paranoid. The sight of the dying, yowling cat is not helping my party come-down. The cat makes a pathetic attempt to drag itself to the side of the road.

'Well, we can't just leave it here,' says Malik. 'I mean, look at it. It's a mess. Some poor kid's gonna be looking for his cat and he's gonna find it like this.'

'So, what are we going to do?' asks Mickey. 'Take it to hospital?'

'I dunno,' I say. 'It's going to die soon. Maybe we can just leave it.'

'You can't leave it like that,' says Malik. 'It's out of order.'

The stoner conference on the dying cat is interrupted by Tom's return. He lays an old rag over the cat before stepping back and hitting it precisely on the head with a jack. The yowling stops. Tom hits it again for good measure before turning round and heading back to the car, with the three of us watching, open-mouthed. He throws the jack back in the boot, before turning to us and saying, 'Come on then.'

I watch as Malik picks the cat up with the rag and slings it over the fence.

'We don't want some little kid to find it, do we?' he explains.

'How do you know that there's no little kid in there?' I say, gesturing to the fence over which he's slung the cat corpse.

'Good point,' he says, stoner paranoia in his voice. 'Shit.'

By the time Mickey, Malik and myself are back in the car, Tom is strapped in and ready to go. He puts his foot down, and we're off towards Highbury Corner. There's a heavy silence that lasts until Tom eventually speaks.

'It had to be done,' he says matter-of-factly. 'It was suffering. Sometimes you've got to be cruel to be kind.'

Despite my assurances to Tom, the responsibility of playing his role is not exactly a breeze. "Tom's" new-found domesticity has definitely raised the level of Sara's finely tuned wariness. Of course, I'm all bluster with Tom, but keeping up appearances is making me uneasy. On the occasions that Sara's around I tiptoe about the house avoiding her. I remember Tom telling me that if Sara has to leave the house early in the morning, he'd sleep in the spare room, as he needs to read to get himself to sleep, which would keep her up if she's in the bedroom. I employed this tactic last night, as Sara needed to leave the house at 6 a.m. this morning in order to get down to Winchester. It's convenient and practical, but I'm not sure that I'm going to be able to employ it for the rest of the week. Despite my expectations to the contrary, it seems that married couples might actually enjoy a sex life.

From her manner I can tell that Sara is disappointed that I've pulled this stunt. When I tell her that I feel like staying up to read after she's asked if I'm coming to bed, she says, 'Oh, OK then,' her voice laden with disillusionment. Once again, her husband has let her down. I smile and say something like, 'Sleep well' or 'See you tomorrow' in a way that a man might address his maiden aunt, not his wife who's in the mood for some hardcore, animalistic, no-holds-barred sex.

We get home from the museum and I prepare dinner while the boys kick a football around the garden. I keep it simple – pesto and pasta with a bag of M&S salad leaves, just the kind of meal that Tom might prepare. Sara comes home from work tired and grumpy. She disappears to shower away her shitty day and comes downstairs wearing a bathrobe. She opens a bottle of red and pours a large glass.

'You want one?' she asks, seemingly irritated by the fact that she has to ask.

'That would be great,' I reply while whipping up a salad dressing. She pulls a glass out of the cupboard while I rap on the window to let the boys know that it's time to eat.

'They must be starving,' I say.

'Paula called me today,' she says.

'Oh, how is she?' I ask brightly, pleased by the interaction. Maybe I met this woman at one of Tom and Sara's tedious parties.

'I don't know,' she says sniffily. 'I didn't really have time to chat. She wants to know if we want to have dinner with her and Sanjiv on Saturday.' I definitely remember Sanjiv. We shared a spliff together in the garden at one of the aforementioned drinks dos at which everyone talks about house prices and their kids' schools. He was a little too obsessed with weed, in an undergraduate kind of way (I think that I remember him joking that 'there is no hope without dope'), but this might have been because he hid the damn thing behind his back when his wife appeared at the window to check where he was.

'Sounds good,' I say, and in a moment of role-play excellence I walk over to the calendar and write the occasion in the box for next

Saturday, below the only other entry – the boys' football tournament.

I rap on the window again, drained pasta steaming in my face. The boys turn round and make 'L for Loser' signs at me.

Sara fills her glass for a second time, pouring a generous measure. 'Good day?' I ask.

She shrugs and takes another sip before standing up and walking to the back door.

'Come on, boys,' she calls, at which point Patrick and Michael trot compliantly towards the house.

We sit down and I serve up. Sara manages the feat of talking only to the boys throughout the meal. By the time we finish and Sara has taken them upstairs to oversee bath time, I am anticipating an uncomfortable night of silent treatment. This throws me somewhat, confirming something that has been lurking beneath the surface, namely that part of my motivation for sticking the swap out for these few extra days is to try and help Sara feel a little happier about her marriage. I want to know what it's like – however distantly – to live with someone for whom you've foregone all others.

I'm hoping that a bit of light entertainment TV coupled with Shiraz could be the solution. Instead, we sit and watch a documentary about orphans in post-Ceausescu Romania. Amazingly this doesn't lighten the mood. I notice that there are only a couple of inches left in the wine bottle and I've only quaffed a glass.

'So where are you sleeping tonight?' she asks suddenly, her eyes still fixed on the screen.

I grit my teeth. 'Well, seeing as you're getting up early tomorrow, I thought that I'd read in the spare room for a bit,' I say, doing my best to strike an 'I didn't realise that this was a leading question' tone.

Sara just nods, before going silent. As punchlines go, it's among the most devastating.

From the thunderous look on her face I am clearly not making her happier. If I'm reading the signs right, what she needs right now is a good session between the sheets. It's terrible to admit, but I'm dangerously close to allowing myself to be swayed. I need to decide whether to remove myself from this possible disaster or to allow the chips to fall where they may.

'This isn't working, is it?' She says it in a matter-of-fact way, as if she's so tired of thinking about the subject that she can barely bring herself to consider it further.

'We're both tired,' I say.

'I'm not talking about tonight, for God's sake.'

'No,' I say. This is getting worse by the minute.

'It's not like it's just since I've been back, either,' she says, draining the wine bottle. 'Everyone has blips. But I don't want to be in a relationship where we just drift apart and can't be bothered to do anything about it.'

This sounds ominous. I try to look engaged and concerned, ready to tackle life's challenges, while all I'm hoping is that the wine and the lateness of the hour will persuade her that now is not the right time. Tom is not going to be happy. When he left the marriage wasn't exactly blooming, but he's been away for a while and I've forgotten to water the plants.

'What do you think, Tom?'

'I don't know,' I say, pathetically. 'I think that we're going through a lot, but I don't think that it's much worse than what other couples go through with work and kids. I think that we've just got to keep working at it.'

Sara nods. And I wonder if I might actually have said the right thing. It *sounded* like the right thing, which is, let's face it, all men are ever trying to say when they get into this kind of discussion with their other halves. Oh, we might have opinions and feelings about a particular subject, but these are worthless when stacked against the desire to remove ourselves from an uncomfortable situation. All we really want is to be able to ask: 'What do you want to hear?' and then to be able to deliver verbatim whatever it is that we're told. This, of course, will have absolutely no bearing on our actions, rather it will simply buy us some breathing space until the next sticky conversation.

'What do *you* want?' asks Sara.

Easy.

'For this family to be happy and healthy,' I say.

Sara sighs. 'Look, this isn't fucking *Miss World*. I don't want to hear your a capella version of "Amazing Grace". I'm trying to talk with you, Tom. This is part of the problem. All you ever do is push me away.'

There's silence, during which I wish that I were anywhere but here. Seriously – Abu Ghraib, the most neglected parts of North Korea, in a tanning booth with Dale Winton – I just don't care. The silence moves with glacial slowness. I can feel its inertia. What's worse is that I know that it's me that's expected to fill it. Men have been padding these expectant silences for centuries in order, ironically, for a quiet life. And, to tell the truth, I'm not a bad pregnant silence filler. But this silence is the Royal Albert Hall of silences, and Sara is expecting me to fill it. With what? An explanation of Tom's low-grade depression, which, in clinical terms, is more the sniffles than the flu? With an invocation of undying love? Some opera? Clearly whatever I say is not going to be enough, or right or, most importantly, what Tom would say. There I was thinking that I was working diligently to save Tom and Sara's marriage, only to discover that I've blundered into my own marital Chernobyl.

'Look, I'll just go and put the kettle on,' I say breezily, with the suggestion that I'm really keen to get into all this over a nice cuppa.

'You will not go and put the fucking kettle on,' says Sara.

'Right you are then.'

'I'm serious, Tom. If you want silence then become a Trappist monk. You might as well be, all the action I'm seeing.'

'What are you talking about?'

'Can I make it any clearer? How about: I've got cobwebs growing . . . ' She searches for the appropriate word, before settling on 'down there' while gesturing at her crotch. 'How did that happen, Tom? How did making love to your wife become such a chore? Am I so repellent to you that you can't face having sex with me? Or are you just too damn lazy?'

I think about answering this one, but clearly it's a rhetorical question.

'I resent you making me feel like this, Tom. It's hurtful and it makes me wonder what the hell we're doing if this is any indication of our future.'

The Royal Albert Hall is looming again, so I step into the spotlight and decide to fill it.

'I do want to make love to you,' I say. This is possibly the most truthful thing I've said to her since she's returned.

'Then why don't you?' she says. My attempt to save the day is rapidly descending into disaster: her tone is invitational, not a question.

'There are reasons,' I say, reaching deep inside me to find what possible reasons there might be for my brother not to want to get jiggy with his beautiful, smart, sexy wife at every possible opportunity. An opportunity not unlike this. I look over at her intelligent eyes, and she's staring directly at me, waiting. And who would know? Seriously. Me. That's who. I'd know. Tom wouldn't. Sara wouldn't, unless I pulled some stunt that Tom has never tried that involved blancmange and ferrets . . .

'Tom. Are you having an affair?'

I take a moment to process this information. The suggestion is absurd, verging on barking mad. Ludicrous really. I stifle the early stages of a smirk that threatens to spread across my face. Hilarious. Tom? Have an affair? Oh, I dare say he's had the odd moment of flirtation with some of the mums from school, but really – Tom, have an affair?

But then it occurs to me; why the hell not? They've grown apart. He meets a lot of women through school and at the park. He's clearly tortured about something. And God knows he's got time on his hands. I'm outraged at the thought that he'd betray Sara . . . But this doesn't mean to say that I feel justified in giving it to her doggy style on Tom's sofa. (Although, truth is told, I'm a little tumescent at the thought of it.)

That's it. The excuse.

'I'm having a few problems,' I explain, laying it on thick. I might as well go for it. There's really very little to lose at this point.

'Downstairs, you mean?' says Sara, trying to coax the information out of me. I nod. 'Can't get it up?' she says, not offering the degree of linguistic sensitivity recommended by healthcare professionals.

'They call it erectile dysfunction these days,' I explain, with what I think is an appropriate level of defensiveness.

Sara slides up the sofa. 'Well, maybe I can help,' she says. Holy shit: she's offering to blow me . . . No, she's not. She's offering to blow her husband who, of course, does not have erectile dysfunction of any kind but who will find that when he returns home on Saturday his wife will be under the impression that he's unable to raise the flag, so to speak. That's a nice little landmine for him to step on. Mind you, if he plays his cards right he might get himself blown, which can't be a bad welcome-home present.

'It's complicated,' I say. 'I know that things have got a bit slow in the bedroom department, and I know that a lot of that is my fault. I'm going to go to the doctor's.'

'How long have you had it?' Sara asks.

'A couple of months,' I say vaguely, testing to see whether the timeframe is plausible.

'Well, you need to get it sorted,' says Sara, her tone a mixture of understanding and impatience. 'We're a married couple, you know. You've got to think about your health and how that impacts on the rest of the family.'

'Sorry.'

'Never mind sorry, you get yourself down the doctor's and sort it out, OK?'

'OK.'

'What is it with you? You could have a tumour the size of a pumpkin on your neck and you'd still be swallowing aspirin and hoping that it would clear up.'

'I hate going to the doctor.'

'Everyone hates going to the doctor, Tom. The rest of us are just a little more adult about it. Look, I don't mean to go off on you. It's just that I know that it's me that's got to make the running in these situations otherwise we'll end up as one of those couples who live like best friends.'

I nod, knowing that it's time that I said something. Thankfully this looks like it's wrapping up. Sara yawns.

'I'll get down the knob doctor first thing tomorrow then,' I say.

Sara rolls her eyes and stands up. 'Well, looks like all our problems are over then.'

'Yes,' I say, keen to draw a line under the conversation. I gather the wine glasses.

'You're not serious, are you?' she says emphatically.

'Of course not. I was being sarcastic.'

'Sometimes, Tom, you're just plain weird,' she says.

Sara doesn't even say goodnight. She just heads off upstairs, very slightly wobbly on her feet.

Well, I can honestly say that that was an unmitigated disaster. Not only did I succeed in further damaging Tom's clearly faltering marriage, I ended up by telling his wife that he's suffering from erectile dysfunction. What the fuck was I thinking? I was like a schoolboy in the headmaster's office. Just looking for excuses, I'm amazed that I didn't blurt out: 'The dog was sick on my homework!' Tonight I crossed a line that officially designates me as a potential danger to myself and Tom and Sara. I'm not sure that I should even be giving myself advice any more, let alone meddling in the lives of others.

Should I call Tom? Of course I bloody should. He needs to get back here and sort this out pronto. I need to warn him about his wife's state of mind. So much for my wondrous talent for communication and manipulation of image, all I've managed to communicate this evening is that Tom's got a limp dick. The thing is, though, I made such a fuss about seeing the life swap through to the end I really don't know if I can face calling him up and telling him that, um, actually he was right.

Sara leaves early the following morning. I know this because I'm lying awake in bed having spent much of the night grappling with the overwhelming responsibilities of my next few days: namely, don't screw up Tom's marriage (if possible, make it better) and find a way of communicating to Maja that I'm a warm, loving soul who is good boyfriend material. I don't think I've slept properly since Sara got back. I need to rest, but I'm too wired and my mind is tumbling ever further downhill.

When I hear the front door shut I get up, shower and burst into the boys' bedrooms in full-on Mr Motivator mode. Despite their foot dragging and whining, the boys get to school on time without significant injury. It seems like a good idea to prepare a meal that's a little out of the ordinary for Sara tonight, but first I need to get to the doctor's so I can reassure Sara I'm doing something about my 'condition'.

I'm told that there are no appointments but, if I'm willing to wait, someone will see me once all the asylum seekers have been helped. I hang out in the waiting room with the spluttering widows and long-suffering refugees until my name is called. I knock on the pistachio-coloured, institutional door and enter to see – blimey – the best-looking female doctor I've seen since, um, Maja. This is my first encounter with the NHS in a long while. My, how things have changed. Having said that, what I'd give right now for a middle-aged Indian man with cold hands.

'Hi.' I smile. I keep it low wattage.

'Take a seat, Tom,' she says, completing a piece of paperwork from the previous patient. I sit compliantly and listen to the scratching of her ink pen on the paper. She has an athletic build, with tanned legs pointed towards me. Her features are fine, with a slightly upturned nose and a thin, vulnerable mouth.

'What seems to be the problem?' she asks pleasantly, her task completed.

'Well,' I say, leaning forward, 'it's a little delicate.' Unconsciously, I've placed my hands over my gonads. She smiles encouragingly, knowing that she's in for *one of those* visits.

'What is?'

'Sorry?'

'What's delicate?'

'Oh, the thingy. The problem. I've been having a little trouble.'

She's beginning to tire of this. 'What kind of "trouble"?'

I think of Sara. I've got to show that I'm taking active steps to repair the relationship.

'Down here,' I say, pointing to my crotch.

'What kind of trouble exactly?' the doctor persists.

'Well, it's hard for me to, you know, raise a smile.'

'You're suffering from erectile dysfunction?'

I nod.

'OK,' she says, patiently. 'How old are you, Tom?'

'Thirty-nine.'

'And you're in good health, generally?'

'Yes.'

'Any changes you've noticed? Weight loss? Loss of appetite? Changes in your bowel movements? Sleeplessness?'

I shake my head. She continues her routine.

'Do you smoke? Drink? Are you on any medication?'

My aim here is twofold. Firstly, to convince her that the 'problem' is entirely down to stress, and secondly, to get her to prescribe Viagra. I have no interest in vacuum pumps, penile implants, intra-urethral pellet therapy. What I want from this doctor is oral, so to speak. Hard evidence, for Sara, that the problem is being addressed.

'Let's take your blood pressure,' the doctor says, wrapping a sleeve around my forearm and tightening it with a rubber pump. She examines the dial.

'It's slightly high, but nothing to worry about.'

I shouldn't do this, but . . . Jesus, I can't help myself.

'I've been under a lot of stress recently,' I blurt out.

'Really?'

'Yeah. A *lot* of stress.'

'And you think this might explain your problem?'

'Yeah, I do. I really do.'

'Why have you been under so much stress?'

'Work. I lost my job. And that's had a bit of a knock-on effect at home.' I try to look as sympathetic a figure as I can.

'I see,' she says, looking thoughtful. 'Have you talked to Sara about this?'

What? She knows Sara. *She knows Sara.*

'Yes, of course. She's been very supportive of course . . . ' Hang on a minute, I see an opportunity here . . . 'But it's affected our marriage.'

'I see. Well, I think that you might want to try some lifestyle changes. You need to exercise regularly, make sure that you get enough rest, eat properly. Try not to drink alcohol, avoid coffee and tea.'

'Is there anything I can take?' I ask speculatively.

'You can try St John's wort,' she suggests breezily. 'It's a herbal remedy that you can find at most good chemists. It really works for some people.'

'I was thinking of something a little stronger than that.'

'You mean medication?'

'Yes.'

'I think that we should try the lifestyle options first, and then we can move on to other approaches, if absolutely necessary.'

'Really?'

'Really.'

Play the female solidarity card.

'Because I feel that it would really help Sara and I if we could get, you know, a little help.'

'So you're talking on behalf of Sara as well?'

'I suppose so.'

She drums her fingers on her desk for a while.

'This isn't something you should do lightly, you know.'

'We've thought about that – but we feel it's for the best.'

'There are potential side effects.'

'We just need something to get us over the hump, you know, until the psychological stuff sorts itself out.'

The time-pressed GP looks at her watch, scrunches up her mouth as if she's tasted something bitter, turns back to her desk, picks up her fountain pen and begins to write.

The wonders of modern medicine will be borne out when Tom returns. I'll have to tell him to give Sara a right seeing to on Saturday night – that should sort the pair of them out. Maybe I should pop down to Starbucks and get them an album of 'latte friendly jazz' just to set the mood. Maybe not.

After visiting the doctor, once I've organised the food for tonight, put a couple of washes on and grabbed a bite to eat, it's time to head over to the park and for the penultimate training session before the football tournament. The weather's turning grim, it's a little too cold to stand outside for an hour watching young boys getting progressively muddier while chasing a football around a scrubby makeshift football pitch. I'm early, watching figures take shape as they appear out of the November gloom. I've got to make this time with Maja count. I've got to make the relationship work. She hasn't returned my calls for two days, which feels like an eternity. I'm feeling antsy, maybe even slightly desperate. She's wrapped up in a winter coat, a thick scarf twisted round her neck like a woolly python. We hug and she pecks me on the cheek before slipping her arm under mine. OK, we're off to a good start. Don't fuck this up, Sean.

'You look good,' I tell her. Her nose is a little red from the cold. I lean forward and kiss it. 'Hang on a second . . . ' I say. 'Are you taller than the last time I saw you?'

'New boots,' she explains, lifting her right foot. 'Top Shop. I love them so much that I'm even wearing them to the park. I don't think that I'm going to be able take them off until spring.' She admires them, turning her foot from side to side. 'It was love at first sight.'

'So how's everything?' I ask lamely. As much as I'm enjoying her holding my arm I'm aware that I need to make sure that neither Patrick nor Michael witness our canoodling. I can't shake her off though, in case I send out the wrong message.

'What, since three days ago?' she says sarcastically.

'I believe that's the last time I heard your news.'

'Sorry I haven't called you back, I was working like a donkey. But what would you know about that, Mr Man of Leisure?'

'Oh, more than you think.' I laugh. 'That toilet bowl doesn't clean itself, you know.'

'Work's OK,' she says. I pretend to search for something in my pocket in order to pull my arm away from her. Given my performance with Sara last night I can't afford to screw up anything else. She reaches into her pocket to pull out a tissue and blow her nose. 'The cold weather is a blessing, in one way. Stab wounds tend to be so much easier to treat.'

'How come?'

'People are wearing more clothes. I suppose that thicker jackets are tougher to cut through.'

'Good to know,' I say. 'I'll bear that in mind when it next goes off at closing time and I'm stabbing someone up.'

'I've got a lot more where that came from.'

'Well, maybe we should get together one evening,' I suggest. 'I'd love to know more.'

'How's Saturday?' she asks.

My first day back in my 'normal' life – perfect.

'I was going to do some knitting on Saturday, but if you insist.'

'I do.'

'Great. I'll bring a Kevlar vest so we can go through some of those stabbing motions.'

We stand and watch the boys who are red-faced and over-serious in their exertions. Despite the conditions, there's great comfort in simply standing in the middle of a muddy field (in her case in a brand-new pair of Top Shop boots) and being together. I can't remember feeling like this about, well, anyone really. All my relationships have been marked by the fact that they're largely based on talking. Whether it's at work, with girlfriends, friends and especially with Tom and Sara who like to fill silences with words. I decide not to say anything until Maja talks to me. It's something of a foolish exercise, making me self-conscious of the silence, rather than simply relishing it.

Maja is tougher than me – she has every reason to be, after living through years of warfare – and her toughness manifests itself in a spareness, an economic way with words and behaviour that communicates as much as chit-chat. She's happy to have a frivolous conversation, but she doesn't need to fill every waking moment with chatter and commentary. She knows that much of what happens to us on a daily basis isn't worth mentioning. I've not heard her complain about the congestion charge, or about missing a bus, or getting the wrong delivery from the Taj Mahal. She's learned that these small interruptions in one's grand strategy for happiness and well-being are insignificant, that if we load them with power and meaning then we do ourselves a disservice. We make our lives hard when really they're not.

I watch her following the action, her collar turned up against the cold.

'You know I really like you, don't you?' I say to her.

'Did you read that in a magazine, or something?' She laughs. 'You know, "Ten Ways To Press Her Love Button", maybe?'

Maybe it did sound a bit sappy . . .

'Have you got any champagne or chocolates in your pocket?' she continues. 'Diamonds would be nice as well.'

'You're brutal,' I say. Despite her piss-taking I'm glad I let her know, all the same. If there's to be any future for us, then she's going to have to hold on to this sentiment over the next few days as I offer her some explanation of how I've been passing the previous fortnight.

I need to get her to trust me, for her to know that, despite the weirdness, I only wish for good things to occur between us.

She smiles and I forget about Patrick and Michael and Matthew and I lean in and kiss her. And she kisses me back. The boys are all too occupied with their huffing and puffing to notice, and I take this as a sign: that the world keeps turning even if you do things that you're scared of, things that you can find plenty of reasons or excuses not to do. We part and carry on watching the game.

'What do you want?' I ask. It's literally what I want to know, but once I've uttered the words I wish that I hadn't worded it like that. She doesn't turn to look at me while she answers, keeping her eyes on the pitch.

'I want more life, fucker,' she says.

I turn to her. Not only do I not understand what she's said to me, it's the first time that I've heard her swear. She laughs at my surprise, covering her mouth with one hand and touching my forearm with the other.

'What?' I say, half amused, half baffled.

'It's from that movie,' she explains. '*Blade Runner*. Someone asks that robot thing, "What do you want?" and he says, "I want more life, fucker." My friends and I, we used to say it to each other when we were in Sarajevo and things were really bad: "I want more life, fucker." And, you know what? I thought that it was a bit of a crazy line, but it made sense in our situation, which was pretty bad. But, I've come here and I live in London and I still feel the same way. I think everybody does, whether you're driving a bus or you're a rock star: "I want more life, fucker."'

I laugh. 'That's excellent,' I say. 'I'm having that. You mind if I steal it?'

'Please do,' she says. 'Fucker.'

The boys finish practice and we wander over to the changing area. While they're inside, we make plans for Saturday night. I'm glad to have nailed down another date, but I know that I'm going to have to tell her things that may, rightly, cause her to either batter and fry my gonads, or batter and fry my gonads before throwing them to a pack of wild dogs. I feel a sense of loss, even at the moment that I'm contemplating this. I look out across the park trying to capture the moment when . . .

Dear God, I see Sara walking towards us.

My first response, incredibly, is to run, like some schoolboy who's been caught scrumping apples (I've no idea who scrumps apples, certainly I never have, and I imagine most schoolboys these days would throw bleach in your face rather than 'leg it'). I decide that my only course of action is to keep the meeting brief, with as little revelation of information as possible. Maja is turned away from us, momentarily on her mobile. I keep an eye on her while I offer Sara a rictus grin and a peck on the cheek.

'What a surprise,' I say.

'Got off early, so thought I'd come and see what all the fuss is about,' she says, smiling. I think that she might actually be here as part of an attempt to normalise our relationship, Sara's version of an olive branch.

'Well, I'm afraid that you've missed the action,' I explain. My mannerisms and way of speaking have become over-animated, a result of my trying to convince everyone (and myself) that everything is *absolutely fine*. I can tell that she's clocked Maja, but isn't quite sure whether the two of us have been chatting, or just happened to be standing in the same vicinity. The boys appear. Hallelujah! There's a problem though – they're with Matthew. No matter, I'll whisk them away and explain it all away to Maja later . . .

Everything is going to be all right. Then I hear something bad happening: Maja is finishing up her call. I quickly collect the boys, who are thrilled to see their mum. As the three of them chat I try to usher them away from Maja and Matthew . . .

'Tom?' It's Maja. The women look at each other, and there's a moment of confusion. I decide to try and 'manage' it.

'Um, Maja, this is Sara. Sara, Maja.' Despite my attempts to keep them apart the two women approach each other. Oh Lord.

'Nice to meet you, Sara,' says Maja. 'Your boys play as well?'

Sara looks at me momentarily, before saying, 'Yes,' with a slight laugh in her voice. 'These two here.'

'Oh,' says Maja. 'I'm sorry, I didn't realise.' I follow Maja's gaze, she's staring directly at Sara's wedding ring. I need to put an end to this.

'So, we'll see you guys at the final training session then,' I say breezily. 'Last one before the tournament.' I start walking towards the exit to the park.

I hear Maja say, 'Okay, see you.' I think that I might have got away with it. But, as Patrick and Michael trot ahead of us I feel Sara's arm snaking around my waist and, before I know it, she's pulled herself towards me and plants a kiss on my lips. To any witness, this is not the behaviour of a separated couple (some witnesses would have observed that this isn't the behaviour of a married couple either, but that's an entirely different discussion) and, to me, there's something odd about the kiss. Sara presses tightly sealed lips against mine, as if she's playing a role, not delivering a snog. We part and she does something that I can't ever remember her having done before: she winks at me. And, even as I'm wondering whether this is a wink that's sexy, or fun, or an accident I can't help turning round to see if Maja has noticed.

She has. Her head is turning away from me. I feel a split second of relief that I haven't had to look her in the eye, and some consolation that I haven't provoked another balls-up with Sara, but I'm crushed by the inevitable consequences of this. Sara pulls me tight towards her, her hip resting against mine and – forgive me – even as I mourn the loss of Maja I'm hoping that she might try and kiss me again.

23
Tom

I get up early to run in Holland Park. A Rocky-style uplifting bout of exercise will get me geed up for today's presentation. The air is thick but the sky is blue, with the sun burning off the mist that's hanging in the air. I try and work out if this offers any portents: my destiny has become inextricably bound with the day's events. Tragically, whenever any attractive female comes into range I speed up considerably and check my watch, as if I'm training for an athletic event and I need to ensure that my pace is on point. As soon as I'm past whichever oblivious girl I'm trying to impress I slow down, ever mindful that I've got to run home: there's nothing more shameful than being dressed like Steve Ovett only to slink past a bus queue doubled up with a stitch and coughing like an emphysemiac.

As I slather on Sean's grooming products I rehearse my presentation for the hundredth time. I hold my neck and back under the hot water in an effort to loosen them up, but then get paranoid that this will serve only to plump my skin like a hot dog and I'll be forced to attend the meeting looking like a cross between a boiled crustacean and Donatella Versace. The last occasion I presented anything was at a dreary conference down in Croydon where we were forced to 'bond' in a converted country house hotel that smelled of stale carpets and farts that had been trapped for years. Mealtimes saw each of us corporate hostages queuing for a buffet of pseudo-sophisticated food served up by surly Eastern European women irritated by the fact that they'd yet to encounter the Britain they'd been peddled by a human trafficker back in Tirana.

The meeting is at ten o'clock. I really don't feel like eating breakfast – I've felt sick pretty much constantly since capitulating to Sean at the Natural History Museum – but know that if I fail to put anything in my stomach I may well feel dizzy in a couple of hours and talk gibberish to the client. I eat a hurried bowl of cereal while listening to the *Today* programme on Radio 4, which I hope will arm me with a current affairs' anecdote with which to break the ice with the client and demonstrate how up-to-the-minute I am. 'Unless Ivory Coast's ruling FPI party stay as part of the transitional government and return to the negotiating table I can't see peace breaking out with the rebels in the north, can you, Andrea?'

Running out of the house I jump into a cab. I place my laptop on the seat next to me and give it a little pat: big day today, my little electronic friend.

I try to stay focused on the task in hand, and keep down my breakfast, as the driver works his way through the menacing London traffic with the skilled bravado of an end-of-the-pier impresario. Suddenly the driver slides back the plastic partition with a thunk of intent.

'See the game last night, then?'

'Yeah,' I say, giving him free rein.

'What you think, then?' Shit. The one taxi driver in London who wants to hear what his passenger has got to say.

'Well, I was sort of working,' I explain, feeling any claim I have to being a proper football supporter melting.

'Thought they got lucky meself.'

'Who?'

'Chelsea.'

'Yeah, you're probably right. It was never a penalty.' I run through the four main sections of my PowerPoint. Although I've got the digital dog and pony show memorised, I want to make it seem as natural as possible. I'm sure that's how Sean operates. It's feeling a little claustrophobic in the cab, so I open a window and allow some cold, dirty air to blow over me.

'Nah, never a penalty,' the driver says, shaking his head. I notice that he has a Millwall air freshener hanging from the rear-view mirror, which leads me to suspect that he might not be an entirely objective observer.

'They're lucky like that, though.' He says this with an air of resignation, as if it were a widely accepted fact. Now, usually I am the first person to enter into a conversation in which Chelsea are given a gratuitous and iniquitous shoeing, but this morning is not the morning. I pull out my mobile.

'Just got to check my messages,' I explain to the driver, and for some inexplicable reason I point to the phone. The driver puts on Radio London, discernibly turning up the volume when the traffic report comes on, the subtext of which appears to be: *Massive snarl-ups on pretty much every street in London this morning, Chris. Really not sure if it's worth going into work, as it looks like we're all fucked until lunchtime.* Traffic reports seem to me to be a huge waste of time. Anyone who's spent a morning in London knows *before they leave the house* that the roads are jam packed with enraged mums in 4X4s ferrying their little darlings the 500 crack-dealer-infested yards to their schools, builders trying to drink scalding tea in polystyrene cups while sexually harassing any woman who comes within yelling distance of their Transit vans, and Somali war criminals lying low from prosecutors in the Hague by ferrying mullered clubbers around Streatham. We pull up at a traffic light near Marble Arch, alongside what appears to be the last of these. I watch as my driver takes a good look at the beaten-up Nissan and its driver and begin to feel uneasy. My stomach, provoked by the movement of the cab, is bubbling away. The cereal and milk in my stomach feels like it's curdling. I wonder if I've got an ulcer, that the stress of the swap is beginning to have a physical effect.

'Look at that . . . ' he says. I feel a familiar sense of dread as I await the inevitable moment when the taxi driver turns into a candidate for the BNP. You know what it's like. You're coming back from the pub on a Friday night and you have a bit of a laugh with the driver who seems like a good bloke but, before you know it, he's used a term like 'jungle bunny' that you've not heard since primary school.

'*Just look at that* . . . ' I brace myself, and start dialling my own number, so that my mobile will ring and I'll have an excuse to avoid the impending diatribe on asylum seekers and the failings of goverment immigration policy.

'Those tyres are completely bald, and I think he might have a flat. See that?' He's pointing now, and the movement of his hand attracts the Nissan driver. The taxi driver pulls his window down and gestures at the tyre.

'Oi, mate, you need to get that sorted.'

The driver of the other car looks at him quizzically.

'Your. Front. Tyre,' says the cab driver in his best 'great-white-god-come-from-sky-in-iron-bird' tone.

The man in the other car gives him the thumbs-up and shouts, 'Thank you.' The taxi driver nods like the lawman who's just doled out a heapin' helpin' of justice. My relief is tempered by the fact that I am now calculating whether I can make it to the office without spilling my guts. My breakfast is planning a return. The physical effects of the swap are now as apparent as the psychological ones. My head swivels violently as I see a woman in the street who . . . No, no, it's not her. Jesus, for a moment I thought I saw Sara.

'Of course, it ain't that hard to win everything when you've got the money they have,' continues the driver.

'Who's got the money?' I say, trying to breathe deeply. I need to get oxygen into my system. My heart is beginning to race and I'm wondering if I'm suffering motion sickness or having a panic attack. A couple of weeks ago I would have been able to blame this on 'bad beer'. I need to get to the office . . .

'Chelsea. Chavski. Who do you support then?'

'Me? Oh, QPR.'

'So you must hate them even more than I do!' He's thrilled to finally get some information out of me. Yes, I do hate them. Probably more than him, but all I really want is to get out of this bloody cab. The presentation, the situation with Sean, the lies I'm telling Sara and the boys, it all seems to be closing in on me.

'Actually, the traffic gets pretty bad around here,' I say, looking for a way out. 'Just drop me here.'

'You sure?' he says, not even slowing down.

'Yeah,' I say weakly, pulling in deep lungfuls of icy air.

"Cos I've got a nice little shortcut around here, and we'll miss all the traffic.'

'I really . . . ' Despite the open window I now have beads of sweat the size of sweetcorn kernels bursting onto my forehead.

'Come on, let's give it a go.'

'No, please just pull over . . . ' There's a rush of thick, syrupy fluids into my mouth.

'It'll only take a few minutes—'

I manage to blurt out, 'STOP THIS FUCKING CAB NOW!' before I throw myself towards the window, my mouth plump with the contents of my stomach, and throw up all over the side of the cab. The vehicle thuds to the kerb and I stagger out and slam the door shut. The side of the car looks like it's been shat on by a giant seagull, although close inspection reveals the expensive non-carb-based granular clusters that I discovered in Sean's cupboard and feasted on only twenty minutes ago. The driver trundles around to inspect the scene.

'That's just cuntish,' he says, hands on his hips in a why-oh-why-oh-why stance. I have a suspicion that he's thrilled about this, as not only does it offer something that confirms the fact that the entire planet is conspiring against him, it also gives him a talking point to discuss with every customer for the next few months.

'Look,' I say, checking my shirt and jacket, 'there's no damage inside.' I pull out my wallet and hand him a twenty-pound note. 'Take it through the car wash on me,' I say. 'How much is on the meter?'

'You're out of order, son,' he says, jabbing a finger in my direction. 'Look at my fucking cab. You should have said something.'

'I asked you to stop,' I say.

'No, you didn't.'

'I did.'

'No, you fucking didn't.'

It's clear that Monsieur Cabby is happy to stand and argue the toss this morning. I dare say that arguing that grass is actually red and that lager is the sweat of Finnish elves that are kept in brutal underground conditions might be on the agenda. I have enough on my plate right now, the last thing I need is more grief. I peel off another twenty and thrust it at him like it's a weapon.

'Have it your way. Now take this and get on your fucking bike.'

With that, I turn on my heel and storm up the road in the direction of the office. I check my watch, I've still got a half-hour before the meeting begins and, other than the taste of sour milk and stomach bile in my mouth and a flop sweat that makes it look like I've just got out of the shower, I'm in great shape to seal a big-money deal. The taxi passes by me, offering an ironic and provocative toot of its horn, but I'm happy just to be on two feet. My stomach is settled for the moment, the suit is unharmed and . . . as I watch the cab disappear towards Gloucester Road, I realise that I've left my laptop with the only version of the pitch that I'm supposed to be presenting in twenty-nine minutes on the back seat.

'Morning, boss.' It's Denton, as irritatingly bright-eyed and bushy-tailed as the pair of Labradors that undoubtedly furnish his parents' pile in the Cotswolds. 'What's up?'

'What's up is that I've left my fucking laptop in the back of a cab,' I reply.

'Oh,' says Denton, and for the first time in the week that I've known him he stops smiling. Then, because he feels that he needs to add something: 'Bugger.'

'Bugger, indeed,' I say.

At that moment Ollie walks in. 'What?' he says, sensing that something bad has happened. 'They cancel us?'

'There's been a little diversion from the plan,' I say. Ollie raises his artfully stubbled chin. I imagine that the just-rolled-out-of-bed look he favours must have taken him a good couple of hours to master this morning.

'We're not going with the PowerPoint,' I say. Ollie rolls his eyes upwards as far as they'll go and holds them there as if he's considering the most absurd thing he's ever heard.

'Oooooo . . . Kkkkaaaaay . . . ' he says very slowly.

'These people have seen PowerPoint after PowerPoint,' I continue, hoping that something inspirational will come to me. 'We're not going to demonstrate that we're a different kind of agency, that we think originally, if we just give them another glorified slide show.'

'So,' says Ollie sarcastically, 'we're going to land this account by "kicking it old school".'

I look at the pair of them: Denton desperate for me to say something that he can agree with, Ollie eager to snipe at whatever I offer, and realise that I'm on my own. All semblance of teamwork has gone out of the window. This is why Sean rewards himself so handsomely I suppose, because when it comes down to it, it's him and a roomful of people he's trying to persuade to do something they don't really want to do. And clearly he's good at it, good enough to have Denton and Ollie on his team, knowing that it's always going to be him that has to step up and take the plunge.

'We're going to convince them, Ollie, not by using little product mock-ups, animated characters or pithy slogans that relate to their "brand experience", but by looking them in the eye and talking to them.' I pause for a moment, trying to figure out if they're coming with me. I get the feeling that all Denton needs is for me to point him in the right direction and he'll be off and running, but Ollie is more dubious.

'Call me crazy, fellas, but I get the feeling that the only way to convince these guys how passionately we feel about their product, and what inspired ideas we've come up with to communicate their brand message to their customer, is to get in their faces and tell them. No trickery, no gadgetry, no bullshit.'

Ollie sighs, although whether this is out of frustration or resignation I'm not sure.

'Ollie – everything OK?' I ask.

'Look, Sean, I don't know about this,' he says. 'I'm all for communicating directly, all for trying out new things, but this is messed up. We work in a visual medium, for God's sake.'

'Which is exactly the point,' I say with Eureka!-type animation. 'It is drastic. These people are sick of working with agencies that either patronise them or kiss their arses. We're going to offer them a different type of relationship, one that is rooted in honesty.'

'All right,' says Ollie. 'You're the boss. Just so I'm clear, you won't be needing any of the storyboards I've prepared then?'

'Don't be silly, Ollie,' I say. 'Course I fucking do.'

Ollie grins, ruffles his waxed Beckhamesque hairdo and trots back to his office to get the boards that he and his cocaineist art director have been working on. Denton offers me a huge grin before answering the ringing phone.

'They're here,' he says eagerly.

It's got to be said that the Deutsche Mobilen crew aren't exactly a laugh a minute, so it's times like this that I realise that the thousands of pounds that Denton's parents lavished on his posh education was money well spent, such is the ease and charm that he unleashes upon the client. I wonder if Denton took classes in mesmerising (and appearing to be mesmerised) when I was doing some waste-of-time nonsense like metalwork. I know that I can't rely on Ollie to open his mouth, which is fine. He can sit there being troubled and creative, as long at Rachel is on top of her game, which she is.

As much as I've witnessed her professionalism before, watching her in this meeting it's clear that she's hungry for success in a way that only someone who's in a hurry to prove themselves can be. I can tell that the clients – two rather stiff middle-aged women and a slightly younger, bookish man – are buying her. So much so that I almost drop the ball when she hands it to me. I fumble very slightly before hitting my stride, training them with my most sincere and direct manner, but I feel them drifting a little. I keep at it, but the more regular sips of water, crossing of legs and scratching of itches are the hallmarks of an indifferent audience. I think about the boys and Sara. I want to go home with some kind of achievement under my belt, something to show for the past couple of weeks, but I feel myself struggling to make headway. I'm becoming more aware of what I'm saying, conscious of the weaknesses of my own recommendations and, as always happens when I get nervous or have to deal with something vitally important, I begin to feel a crushing tiredness sweeping over me. Even Denton has stopped smiling. The tight knot of dread in my stomach tightens.

'To Sean's point . . . ' Thank God, Rachel has come to my aid to try to breathe a little oxygen into our visitors who are quite possibly entering the early stages of a coma – one of the women has even just glanced at her watch . . . It's all going wrong. And it can't go wrong. I won't allow it. This deal means too much to me. It can't not happen but, right now, I think that we might need a miracle . . .

There's a knock at the door and Aileen sticks her head in.

'Um, Sean, I'm very sorry to interrupt, but something urgent has come up.'

I look across the desk at the Deutsche Mobilen team and I can tell that this might be the final nail in the coffin.

'Aileen, we're right in the middle of this. Can't it wait?'

'I don't think so, Sean,' she replies. 'It won't take long. It's something that you need to attend to personally.'

I'm caught in two minds, but I'm so convinced that we've (or, more specifically, *I've*) blown the meeting that I decide to get up. At this stage, I can't see what harm it can do that I couldn't do myself by simply opening my mouth.

I hear Rachel and Denton covering for me as I leave the room to discover my taxi driver waiting in the hallway looking sweaty and a little stressed. Why the hell is he here? I look at Aileen for answers, but the driver pipes up.

'I thought you might want this.' I look at the object in his hand and it takes a few moments for me to realise that, at the end of his outstretched arm, he's holding my laptop case. Like Stanley stumbling across Dr Livingstone I feel light-headed with excitement. An unlikely hero has emerged, one who doesn't like to go south of the river after 8 p.m. unless he's on his way home, but one who may have rekindled the dying embers of my presentation, and with it the possibility of a coup that will save both my own and Sean's arses. I never believed in unicorns and fairy godmothers before, but I do now.

Before he can react, I reach forward and grasp the driver's face with both hands and pull him towards me. He leans forward compliantly, and I plant a kiss on his shaven, crimson dome. I release him, and he stares back at me, startled.

'I think you might just have saved my life,' I say. Seemingly in a daze, he passes the laptop to me, and I hug it to my chest as if it were life itself, which, in a way, it is.

'The address was on the case,' explains the cabbie, almost apologetically. 'Sean Cunningham.'

'That's me.' I smile. 'You are a knight in shining armour, sir, and deserving of a worthy reward. Aileen, please get the gentleman's details and sort out something appropriately lavish. Dinner with as many Michelin stars as you can handle – on me. Talk to Aileen, she'll take care of you.'

I return to the meeting room, where Rachel is boldly discussing SC Communications' ability to 'truly integrate into the customer mind-space'. Bless her, she's a creative, and she's talking like a suit. I unzip the bag, snap open the laptop, get it hooked up to an AV unit and unleash my bag of tricks. Explaining that I now feel that our ideas can be best communicated visually, I launch into my well-rehearsed shtick, with an almost electrical pulse running through me. It's quite amazing how quickly the client responds to the pretty pictures and graphics that I whizz through with dizzying energy and enthusiasm. And I can tell, I can just *tell*, from their faces and body language, that they're excited by and believe in what I'm telling them. I've morphed from apologist to evangelist, telling them exactly how to publicise and market their brand and, as they ask questions that (to me, at least) are sure-fire purchase indicators, I begin to realise that they're just like anyone else: they want solutions, they want answers, they want someone to help them through the slalom of life.

And I'm glad about that, I really am because, as I shake their hands and peck their glowing cheeks on their departure, I'm sure that I've given them what they wanted. And something else as well – I did the best I could.

I return to the conference room where Denton, Ollie and Rachel are clearing up and puffing out their cheeks in relief.

'What do you reckon then?' Rachel asks me.

'Let's go to the pub, shall we?' I reply.

We choose an undistinguished place just off the King's Road. Not so much a pub as a boozer. Despite its proximity to the office, none of us has been in here before. Denton, Ollie and Rachel are more likely to be seeking out cooler places than this bog-standard watering hole. No music, no cocktails, Sky Sports News on the telly, a detached landlord . . . Nice. While everyone piles around a small table stained deep with circular tidemarks left by glasses, I go and get a round in. I put my elbows on the bar towel and wait for the landlord to finish fixing a measure to a bottle of gin.

'I wouldn't lean on there,' he comments without looking up. At that moment I feel a cold sensation creeping up my elbows. 'Fella spilled a half earlier,' he continues, helpfully. I lift my arms off the soggy beer towel and examine the dark stains, like slate-coloured patches, on my suit. The publican looks over at the others, seemingly surprised to have an office group in the establishment so early. He casts his eyes around the room, perhaps worried that we're going to scare off his daytime drinking crowd who require peace and quiet in order to work on their crosswords.

He pours us four pints of Stella (or 'Wifebeater', as Denton inexplicably refers to it) and I carry them over to the others. As I turn from the bar I notice Rachel. She's just lit a cigarette and is exhaling the first lungful of smoke, her chin pointed upwards, her lips puckered, her cheekbones prominent. It feels like I'm looking at a girl I've never met before, a girl you might see in the pub and wonder what it would be like to go home with. As I approach the table, I can hear Denton and Ollie arguing about the merits of *Napoleon Dynamite*, Rachel looks at me with a *Jesus* look on her face and we share a fleeting moment of intimacy. The prospect of chatting with Denton and Ollie seems incredibly tiresome. After the presentation I don't have the energy to engage with their irrepressible male jousting. The three men all sit on stools around the table, with Rachel on the bench, her back to the wall.

'Cheers,' she says, raising her glass to me.

'Cheers,' I say, clinking glasses with her. The others join in and we all take our first sips of lager. All four glasses hit the table at the same time with a satisfying thud.

'This is pretty much your usual routine, isn't it, Denton?' jokes Rachel. 'You know, knocking off early and getting a few in before heading home to the Mrs.'

'Not really,' says Ollie. 'He's usually in here for breakfast.'

'Is that what I'm paying you for?' I joke.

'Well, you know,' says Denton, taking another sip of his pint. I notice that he's already nearly halfway through his drink. 'A high level of tolerance for alcohol comes in useful with clients. Take them out, get 'em all squiffy and then get them to sign on the dotted line. It's the oldest trick in the book.'

Rachel giggles.

'What's so funny?' I say, starting to laugh as well. Her laughter is contagious. Denton and Ollie look at her. Rachel is still sniggering. Eventually she manages to control herself long enough to explain.

'It's Denton,' she clarifies. 'Some of the words he uses. He said "squiffy". I mean, who says squiffy?'

'Well, I bloody do,' says Denton unapologetically, but with a self-deprecating smile on his face.

'Well, I don't,' says Ollie in his authentic mockney accent.

'Of course,' says Denton. 'You're a model of sobriety after all.'

Rachel picks up her pint and takes another sip. 'Well, I don't know about you lot,' she says, 'but I'm in the mood to get really squiffy.'

'Me too,' I say, positioning myself as Rachel's drinking partner. 'Wasted.'

'Paralytic,' says Rachel.

'Off one's tits,' I say.

'Shit-faced,' she offers.

'Kaylied.'

'I've not heard that one,' she sniffs.

'It's Scottish, I think.'

Ollie and Denton are sitting watching, wanting the competition to continue.

'Go on then,' encourages Denton.

Rachel takes a drag on her cigarette and considers her next move. 'Keved up,' she says eventually.

'Elephant's trunk.'

'Is rhyming slang allowed?' asks Denton. No one replies.

'Defcon one,' says Rachel. The tension is rising. I don't know where she pulled that one from.

'Wrecked,' I counter, with the assured coolness of a grandmaster.

'Blitzed.' Damn. She came back strong. I'm struggling here. Of course, an obvious one . . .

'Smashed.'

'Bollocks,' she says, betraying signs of nervousness. 'That wasn't my go, by the way . . . Let me see . . . How . . . about . . . fucked up.'

I could be in trouble here. Then it comes to me.

'Mullered.' I think that might be it. She's gone quiet and contemplative as Denton, Ollie and myself hang on her words.

'Ga ga on bitch piss,' she laughs.

'*What?*' I laugh.

'Ga ga on bitch piss.'

'*Ga ga on bitch piss?* What the hell is that?'

'It's a well-known phrase down my way . . . ' she says, trying to maintain a straight face.

'I'm sure that it's a well-known condition, but what the hell does it mean?'

'Well, you know what "bitch piss" is, right?'

'No.'

'It's those mixer drinks, you know, like Bacardi Breezers, that girls go out and get "kaylied" on.'

'So, "Ga ga on bitch piss" basically means pissed up on alcopops?'

'Precisely,' she says.

'Well, I don't know if I can compete with that,' I admit.

'Rachel wins!' declares Denton. 'Right, who wants a beer to celebrate?' Rachel and I put our hands up.

We order some lunch, have a couple more rounds and a session on the trivia machine and, before I know it, the afternoon has almost passed.

'I'm gonna jet,' says Ollie. 'Got to meet someone.' He stands up, tucking his Berry in the pocket of his army fatigue-style jacket. 'Keep it real, people.'

Excellent, one down. I've just got to outlast Denton and it's just me and Rachel. And then what? With all this beer I just don't know. I'll worry about that when I have to.

'He's probably just getting back for *Home and Away*,' says Rachel, nodding her head towards Ollie, who's passing by the window on the other side of the pub. Denton laughs and heads for the gents'.

I finish my pint.

'Sorry, unprofessional,' she says.

'No, no,' I say. She pulls another cigarette out of the packet, taps it on the table top and lights it.

'You won't be able to do that soon,' I say.

'We'll see,' she says. 'I bet loads of people are just going to ignore all that crap.'

I'm seeing a different side of her in the pub. The booze and not being in the office are making her looser, more comfortable in her own skin. So often at work she seems anxious, burdened by a need not to screw things up. I move around to sit on the stool that Ollie was occupying. I'm close enough to see that there's a little green in her blue eyes, and a thin, milky scar running down her chin. And I'm hoping, as the beers slip down easily and ever more quickly, that she's not suddenly going to declare what she's got to leave now, to go and meet friends, or go to dinner, or hook up with a boyfriend, somewhere else, somewhere I won't be invited.

'You want one?' she asks, holding up the cigarette packet. I hesitate for a moment. 'Go on,' she says. 'Soon you won't be able to have a smoke in a pub. How un-English is that? Not being able to smoke in a pub? Diabolical liberty, as my gran would say.'

I take one of the cigarettes. I haven't smoked for almost four years. I've made a rule of avoiding nicotine to the extent that I've stayed out of pubs I've found particularly smoky. Yes, I know, what a ponce, but what they say about ex-smokers is true – we're a zealous bunch. Either that or we're just weak . . .

'There you go,' says Rachel. 'How good does that feel?' And the nicotine in my system does feel good, sat in a pub in the late afternoon with nowhere to go with a pretty, lippy girl with time on her hands and a good line in boozy banter.

'So, how long ago did you stop smoking?' she asks.

'A long time,' I say. 'A long time. I missed it though. Missed it every time someone lit up and got that look on their face.'

'I know that look.' She nods.

'Oh, you know that look, do you?'

'I do, I do.'

'What is it then?' I ask.

We're hunched close to each other now. The tip of my index finger is only an inch from her hand, which is resting on the pub table.

'It's a sort of sex look,' she continues, exhaling smoke.

'A sort of sex look?'

'Yeah, you know . . . relief. Satisfaction.'

'You've obviously been sleeping with the right people,' I say, aware that I have crossed a boundary into fully-fledged worker–employee sexual harassment lawsuit territory. Never mind, Sean can afford it.

'Or smoking the right cigarettes,' she adds. 'You know, for me,' she says, 'working your way through a packet of cigarettes on a night out in the pub is a bit like going on holiday with a new boyfriend.'

She pauses, waiting for encouragement.

'How?'

'Well, the first cigarette is like the first night of sex after a day getting sunburned and drinking sangria; you know, it's just what you need, like a reward. The next two or three are good but, after that, you just sort of stop noticing you're doing it and by the end you just wish you'd never started in the first place.'

'Which is why you should never go on holiday with a boyfriend,' I say. 'Impetuous, meaningless sex with anonymous Euros of indeterminate nationality is never in the brochures, is it? But, frankly, it's the only reason to leave the country.'

'Here, here,' she says, banging her pint glass against mine. 'And talking about meaningless Euros of indeterminate sexuality, here comes Denton.'

'What, you think he's . . . ?' I snigger. It's such a seemingly absurd thought that I can't help but laugh.

'You know what they say about rugger buggers,' she whispers through the smoke.

The level of our flirting is now so extreme that I can't imagine talking like this can lead us anywhere but bed. I'm enjoying myself so much that I wonder whether I should just relax and submit to the inevitable. How much harm could it really do? And think of the benefit – I'll have got it all out of my system, cleared the decks to start anew with Sara.

Denton sits down, politely oblivious, and immediately notices me smoking.

'Might as well join the club,' he says, picking up Rachel's cigarettes. 'So, what are you up to later?'

I wait to see what Rachel says.

'What's on offer?' she asks non-committally. 'What day is it? Tuesday? Nothing on the telly tonight, and my flat mate is away . . . '

I don't hear the rest of the sentence. All I hear is 'my flat mate is away . . . '

I don't really have to tell you what's going through my head, do I?

Normally I pull back from this kind of conversation, but I'm drunk and having a good time and feeling a little bit reckless, and can't help basking in the proximity and heat from a girl whom I normally wouldn't even know how to talk to. I just can't help myself. I look at her legs. Her skirt has ridden up above her knee and I can make out the shape of the muscles in her upper legs. I want to lean over and squeeze them to test their elasticity.

'Just spoke to Aileen, she said it was quiet in the office today,' says Denton. He looks up, hoping that he's sparked conversation. Rachel is shredding a beer mat.

'Normally it's so quiet in your office that you can actually hear yourself scratching your own arse.' says Rachel.

'I have people to do that for me,' says Denton. 'What do you think assistants are for?'

'You probably need a couple of assistants, the size of your arse,' I say. Both Denton and Rachel laugh, but I'm not sure I should have made the joke. I think it might have overstepped the mark, what with my boss status. Rachel seems to have picked up on my concern.

'Can you imagine the amount of bollocks it's possible to talk if you're in the pub every night?' she asks. 'Just the sheer amount of utter nonsense that comes pouring out of people's mouths when they're recovering from work with the aid of alcohol? I reckon if someone filmed our entire evening out and played it back to us in real time that would be enough to stop us drinking for life.'

'But that's the point, isn't it?' I chip in. 'That's the whole point of pubs – they're places you can say stuff that you might not at work, or at home.'

'Like "mine's a Stella",' says Denton, prodding his empty glass to bring it to Rachel's attention.

'I'll get them,' I say.

'Oh, no, no, no,' says Rachel, reaching for her purse. 'We're not at work now. I don't want to be accused of not getting my round in.' She produces a twenty-pound note, which she hands to Denton. 'Be a love, Denton,' she says, staring him in the eye, 'could you go to the bar for me?'

'Of course,' says Denton. 'Three more Wifebeaters?'

We nod. Rachel lights another cigarette and turns her legs towards me so they're running parallel with the bench. And we have another pint, and another, and the beer barely tastes of alcohol now. And before I know it Denton has gone, and the two of us are sitting next to each other on the bench and, although the pub is pretty full, no one asks to use the other half of our table – it's as if we've built ourselves a little sex fortress. I look up at the clock and discover that we've been in the pub for five hours. I stand up to go to the toilet and find that I'm not too steady on my feet.

'We need to eat,' I say to Rachel, who laughs like this is the funniest thing she's ever heard. By the time I get back there's a fresh pint waiting on the table for me.

'One for the road,' says Rachel, banging my glass and slopping beer over the edge. And I know that I should be leaving, and I know that I should really be thinking of this last pint as my absolute, definite last drink of the evening, and I know that I shouldn't be wondering what colour knickers Rachel is wearing, but I'm thinking and not thinking all these things because I've had a few drinks and I'm wondering whether, maybe, just maybe, I won't end up going back to my wife and kids once Sean and I have stopped messing around. After all, I'm very sure that things would be great with Rachel. She's young and ambitious, got the world at her feet. It's this kind of energy and spirit I should be exposing myself to. Maybe I don't just need two weeks as Sean, maybe I need an entire lifestyle makeover.

'I'm starving,' I say.

'It's fun doing this,' she says.

'How do you mean?'

'Well, stop me if I'm talking out of turn, but coming to the pub, getting "kaylied", it's not really the kind of thing we normally do, is it?'

'I suppose not,' I say. 'I'm glad we did it tonight though.' I become aware at this point, that we're actually leaning on each other for support, and the realisation is both horrific – dangerous intimacy alert! – and a huge turn-on. I haven't been this close to a woman other than Sara for a decade. Actually, I have; but my senile nan can't count.

'How come you didn't come to my thirtieth party?' she asks.

'I can't remember,' I say. I consider concocting a feeble excuse, but decide that it's not worth it. 'Where was it again?'

'Just at my flat,' she explains. 'It was a laugh. I know that it's hard being the boss and everything, but you should have come.'

'Where do you live?'

'Just off Fulham Road.' She stand up, pulls on her coat, slings her bag over her shoulder. 'Come on,' she instructs me. 'Let's go.' She leans over the table to take another gulp of beer. And before I know it we're pushing through the muggy pub, with its stale smells and body heat, and out in the street. The wind stings my cheeks, but clears my head a little. I stand in the street looking at Rachel, not sure what to say. I don't want this evening to end, but I really, really have to go . . .

'Come on,' she says, grabbing my arm and leading me up the street. I feel powerless, like I've no say in the matter, such is her determination. And she doesn't have to say it, but I know that we're going back to her flat, which seems like the best idea I've ever heard, but also the worst.

'My flat mate, Claire, she's a chef,' she explains. 'She went away today, but I know she worked the lunchtime shift. She usually leaves tons of stuff in the fridge. They chuck it away otherwise.'

So that's the excuse. Back in my day it was a not so subtle invitation in for a coffee. These days you get a full-on meal. That's progress.

We reach her flat in a tidy early-Victorian street. What the hell am I doing? I need to think of an excuse. I really shouldn't step through the door. This is suicide. I'm going to end up sleeping with one of Sean's employees who thinks that I'm Sean himself. Worst of all, I think that I might have fallen for this girl. Can I give up my family for the promise of carefree living and semi-regular nookie? Don't go in, man . . .

The common area is none too promising. Piles of bills for former tenants, a semi-institutional carpet, paintings you'd be too embarrassed to give to a charity shop. But once we get inside the flat I'm glad to discover that it's spacious and in good nick. Upstairs is a large kitchen and living area. I see a staircase leading downstairs which, I suppose, is where the, um, bedrooms are. Rachel roots around in the fridge, pulling out plastic containers and dumping them noisily on the kitchen table. I take off my coat and survey the photos on the mantelpiece. They're the same photos Sara and I had on display ten years ago – smiling boozed-up twentysomethings on holiday, at parties, in love.

'Come on, then,' she says. I turn to see that she's sat at the kitchen table and is already eating. I walk over and sit down.

'It's a bit of a mess,' she says, 'but it all tastes good.' She points out the contents of each container and foil package. 'We've got some string beans done with garlic, some black rice – I think that it's got coconut milk in it, there's some sort of roast pork in there and, oh, this is good . . . ' She puts a large of slice of something that looks like a Spanish omelette on my plate.

'Oh, I almost forgot . . . ' She gets up and fetches a couple of beers from the fridge, roots around in a drawer for an opener. I notice that she's taken off her shoes and the cardigan she'd been wearing earlier. This seems like a gesture of intimacy. Or drunkenness. I need to get out of here, not have another beer. But I'm in such a beer groove that it's hard to tear myself away, and the food is delicious and the shape of Rachel's legs is so nice in her tights. This will be my last beer. One more, and I'm getting out of here.

We finish our food and sit talking about TV for a while. The night is unwinding. Rachel slinks off to the sofa. I go to sit in the armchair next to her, but she pats the sofa. I sit at the other end of the sofa but, discouraged, she continues to talk while rearranging herself on the sofa so that, oh my God, her head is in my lap. She's making this seem like the most normal thing she's ever done while my head spins from booze and confusion. I should go.

No. I should fuck her.

No. I need to leave.

Screw her.

Get the hell out.

Get jiggy.

Flee.

Then, suddenly, I feel a new sensation below my waist. A vibration. I pull the Berry out of my trouser pocket and answer it. This action alone is enough to drag me back into the real world.

'Uncle Sean?'

Jesus, it's Paddy.

'Hey, mate. What are you doing up so late?'

'I had a bad dream. Dad said I could call you.'

Hearing Paddy's voice with Rachel's head on my lap is without question the most irreconcilable moment of my life.

'Well, I'm glad you called.'

'Have you been practising your chess?'

'What do you think I'm doing right now?'

Rachel gives me a look, unsure who I'm talking to. She sits up, suddenly self-conscious.

'Practising chess?' he says hopefully.

'That's right.' Great, another lie. Actually, son, I was drunkenly sizing up whether I should have sex with one of your uncle's employees.

'So we'll play at the weekend, OK?' I say. And we will, Paddy, I swear we will.

'OK. Night.'

'Sleep well.'

I look down at Rachel. Whatever was going on between us has altered. She gets up and walks into the kitchen and puts the kettle on.

'I should go,' I say, apologetically.

'Yeah, yeah,' she says, feigning enthusiasm, like everything is fine and there is no awkwardness between us. Temporary sobriety has put the skids on what was about to occur.

I close the door behind me. And, yes, I was relieved not to have crossed a line, committed an act of treachery that can never be undone, but also I'm disappointed in myself. I feel like this might be another thing to add to my list of failures, a never-to-be-repeated opportunity scorned. Hearing Paddy's voice touched something within me, but Rachel had illuminated something entirely different, something that can't be replaced. I turn my collar up against the wind and am just about to strike out for the Fulham Road when I hear the front door open behind me. I turn and look up at the silhouette in the doorway behind me. It's Rachel. She smiles flirtatiously.

'Hi,' I say.

'Hi,' she says.

'I didn't forget anything, did I?'

'Well, in a manner of speaking you did.'

'Um, do you know where I can get a taxi round here?' I enquire diplomatically.

'Shut up, and come back inside.'

24
Sean

A couple of weeks ago it was as likely that I'd arrive on a hot date wearing vegan shoes as I would brood about women. Today I can't get Sara or Maja out of my fevered head. I'm so aware that I could destroy Tom's marriage that I'm terrified to be around Sara. As for Maja, I have no idea how I'm going to explain Sara's snake arm after soccer practice. Not even sure what I'm going to say, I try calling her, but I'm catching blanks. She's not picking up her mobile. I kid myself that she's not picking up because she's working, when I remember that she's not even at the hospital – she's on nights for the next few days. That's sorted then: I'll wait until the afternoon, when I'll corner her at the final football practice and I'll make the pitch of my life. I'll speak as I've never done before – straight from the heart.

I distract myself, wander around the house pottering at various jobs for an hour before I recheck the mobile to see if Maja called. No messages. I prod the thing, trying to summon it to life. It's then that I find myself putting on my coat, getting in the Volvo and driving over to her house. On the way I run through various possibilities, ways of convincing her that I'm neither a psycho nor just plain old certifiable. I turn up nothing. She lives over in Kensal Green on a street where, in the seventies, homeowners were inspired by Ted Moult to rip out creaky old casement windows and replace then with sturdy aluminium. Thirty years later, the process is being reversed as the middle classes squeeze out the ageing Jamaicans, Guyanese and Indians. I park outside the house and wait. The street is still. Sitting there in the big estate car, I feel calm in a way that's become alien to me over the past few days. I'm absolutely exhausted. Cream crackered. The 'experts' they trot out on TV always go on about stress tiring you out. There's no question that they're right. (And let's not forget it causes erectile dysfunction as well.) My state of exhaustion is compounded by my having been up half the night, my mind churning, searching for the right words to say to Maja. I'm feeling a little, shall we say, low energy today. A little pick-me-up, some bathroom refreshment, would be just the thing . . .

But I'm not going to succumb. I'm sure that turning up on Maja's doorstep jabbering nonsense won't help my cause to any degree. I've just got to focus for a couple more days, that's all. God, this car is comfortable. An old man shuffles past on the way to the boozer or the bookies. I rouse myself to go and ring Maja's doorbell.

It's a typical three-bedroom, turn-of-the-century Edwardian brick house with a tiny, tidy front garden and red-tiled garden path. I ring the doorbell and see a figure moving inside. My mouth is dry. I give my face a little slap to try to wake myself. I can see a body looming on the other side of the door, and even before it opens I know that it's not Maja. It must be Matthew's dad, the doctor. I find myself facing a man roughly my age. He's a little bigger than me, with a crew cut, and is handsome in a tough sort of way. I clock him as that rare breed – a middle-class bloke who might have a go back if a van load of scaffolders has a pop. He doesn't say anything, just nods impatiently at me.

'Um, is Maja in?' I ask.

He looks at me suspiciously and disappears inside the house, leaving the door open a crack. I don't know why he's giving me dirty looks.

The door swings open again, and I'm just about to greet Maja, when I see that the bloke is back.

'What's your name?' he asks hurriedly, as if he's got a lot better things to be doing than dealing with me, which is probably the case.

'Um, Tom,' I say. He looks right through me, seeing my black heart. 'I'm a friend from Matthew's after-school football.'

He nods at me and disappears inside again. I remain on the doorstep feeling a little lost.

'Look, she's not in,' says the man on his return.

I look at him as if I might have something to tell him, but fail to open my mouth.

'Sorry about that,' he says, closing the door on me. I see the shadow of his body moving towards the back of the house and hear him talking to someone. I ring the bell. The shadow looms at the door again.

'Look, she's not here, OK?' he says emphatically.

'You did tell her it was Tom, right?'

'How can I do that when she's not here?' he asks. I want to say: *Actually, you don't need to because she can hear everything from her hiding place behind the kitchen door.* But I don't, I say: 'All right.'

He goes to close the door and I irritate him further by saying, 'Can I leave a message?'

He rolls his eyes theatrically, which is when two words go through my mind: *knob jockey.* How can Maja be staying with a twat like this? I pretend to consider my message for a few moments, during which he drums his meaty fingers on the doorframe. The suggestion is that, should he put his mind to it, he could probably rip it off and snap in over my head. In my current state of exhaustion, I might not even notice. 'Hmmm,' I say, dragging it out. 'Can, you, um, tell . . . Maja that, um . . . ' I pause a few moments. 'Can you tell her that Tom called? If she could bell me, that would be great.'

'That's all?' he asks, mock helpfully.

'Ye—' I start to reply, but the door is already closed.

I get back in the car, unsure exactly what I've just witnessed. My mind races through the possibilities. Can I have lost her this quickly? We barely got to know each other. I can't believe I fucked this up. I need to think about how I can get through to her, win her heart. I sit back in the leather seat and . . . *I should give my eyes a little rest . . .* Maybe, it's nothing . . . *I should just take five minutes . . .* Maybe she just needs some time *Unwind a little, after all, I've been under a lot of stress . . .* He didn't seem like Maja's type anyway . . . *ZZZzzzzzzzzzzz . . .*

BANG! BANG! BANG!

The sharp rapping of knuckle on glass wakes me. I open my eyes to

269

see a policeman gesturing for me to get out of the car. I wind down the window. The policeman is wearing one of those stab-proof Fifty Cent-style Kevlar jackets. My eyes are heavy, my mind blurred, but I try and summon the tax-paying, non-criminal Sean, the Sean who only usually has contact with the police when he's the one pointing out the pikeys who keyed his car or had his mobile off an alfresco table.

'Morning, officer,' I say, still feeling shaky from the sleep.

'Can you get out of the car, please, sir?' he says. I'm not sure that I like the tone of his voice. I open the door and follow him around onto the pavement. I certainly don't like the way his partner, a plump Asian woman, is muttering into her radio. It's the usual 'alpha, tango, Charlie' guff, but she's keeping a watchful eye on proceedings. Gradually it occurs to me that this isn't just some motoring offence. Maybe they think that I'm someone else, or that I'm casing one of these houses.

'Can you tell me what you're doing here, sir?' he asks. He's a wiry ginger with a nose that's been shifted sideways after impacting with something immovable, looks like he can hold his own at kicking-out time on Kilburn High Road. His lips are barely there though. What exists of them is a purplish colour, as if he's been eating blueberries. The strangeness is enhanced by his eyes, which are brilliant blue, but laced with thin red capillaries.

'I was sleeping,' I explain. 'I fell asleep.' That should do it. Then I think back to my delivery – I have no idea why I repeated myself; it simply adds to a growing atmosphere of guilt.

Ginger Bollocks gives me a meaningful look and sighs.

'Sir, do you know a Ms . . . ?' he checks his notebook here, before saying, 'Maja Petrovic.' He pronounces her first name with a hard 'J'.

'Yes,' I reply. 'She lives right here. I popped round to have a quick word with her.'

'What's your name and address, sir?'

Oh, God. I knew that there would be a moment of reckoning; but this . . . This is not the way that I could ever have imagined it. Now is the time to tell the truth. But maybe not.

'Tom Cunningham. Twenty-three Park Drive.'

The policeman looks over at his Oompa Loompa sidekick who I

notice, to my alarm, has her hand on her belt near where she keeps her truncheon, her pepper spray . . . her cuffs. The business end of her profession. She nods solemnly.

'Can I see your driving licence please?' the cop continues.

'Um, I don't have it with me,' I explain.

'I need a form of identification. Do you have a wallet?'

I pull Tom's wallet from my back pocket and hand it to him with a growing sense of doom. I am now fully awake for the first time in three days; my alertness balanced by the tight knot of nausea in my stomach. He picks his way through it slowly, examining the cards, as if he's looking to check my credit rating, not introduce me to the Met's modern methods of suspect interrogation. Standing there with a little moisture on my face from the drool that escaped the corner of my mouth while I was sleeping, I think to myself: Hang on – I've done nothing wrong, yet I'm allowing Starsky and Hutch here to put me on the back foot. I decide to try another tack: the outraged middle-class burgher.

'Officer, really, I don't know what's going on here . . . ' I say in my best I've-been-compliant-but-my-patience-is-running-out-so-you-better-have-a-bloody-good-excuse-for-wasting-my-time-or-I'll-be-on-the-blower-to-your-superiors type of thing. He gives me a look. And guess what happens next? You'll like this: he spins me round, and before I know it I've been cuffed by his pal. And all I can think about is how the caution sounds *exactly* like it does when you hear it on the telly, and how I have absolutely no idea how I'm going to get out of this one.

At the station the desk sergeant who books me in has a mantra, every line of which ends 'do you understand?'. I nod my head and murmur 'yes' but, frankly, I don't understand. I mean, I understand that I've been charged under the Protection from Harassment Act, 1997, which I was thrilled to learn, translates as stalking. All I am told, before I am slung in a cell, is that 'there has been a complaint'. The specifics of this are, I'm told, currently under investigation. Now, I'm no Sherlock Holmes, but even an educationally subnormal lamp-post might take a wild guess that the unspecific 'complaint' may well have come from Maja.

'Got a lawyer, have you?' the desk sergeant asks.

'Um, yes,' I answer, thinking this will show them that they're messing with the wrong guy, 'my wife.'

'Oh dear.' The sergeant sniggers quietly to himself while never taking his eyes off the paperwork on the desk in front of him.

I sit in a cell plastered with illiterate graffiti and illustrations of both male and female genitalia (clearly drawn by an equal-opportunities artist, both are identically bad), with a triple-headed problem of not insignificant proportions. Firstly, explaining to Sara exactly what I've been doing hanging around outside another woman's house (I can't tell her that, in the words of the cliché, it isn't what it looks like because it's *far* weirder than that). Secondly, working out why the woman in question might want to accuse me of stalking when I think I might be in love with her. Thirdly, convincing a woman who has just had me arrested and charged with stalking and thinks that I am still married to someone else that she might be the solution to my commitment phobia.

I'm killing time, frustrated that we're missing Michael and Paddy's final football practice before the tournament, when the cell door opens and I'm ushered back upstairs into the waiting area where I'm brusquely told that, after completion of the 'investigation', I am not to be charged. There is no apology, no explanation, I am simply asked to sign for my belongings and told that I'll be taken back to my car if I care to wait for a few minutes. Having dismissed me, the desk sergeant, still staring at his ledger, says with a sigh, 'Your lawyer didn't sound too happy though.' I leave the police station and search out a mini cab.

'So, let me get this straight,' says Sara. She's standing in the kitchen in her black work clothes, which, depending on her mood, make her look either like a hot, bereaved woman or an undertaker. No prizes for guessing this evening's disposition. 'You're arrested, they bang you up, and then they release you without charge?'

'Yes,' I say. I've decided that the simplest way to avoid getting myself in deeper shit than I'm already in is to offer as little precise information as I can.

'Unbelievable,' she says. 'Unbelievable.' She paces the kitchen for a few seconds, her hands clasped.

'Where were you when they picked you up?'

'Marquess Drive,' I say, hoping that there won't be a follow-up question, although I should know by now that, with Sara, there's always a follow-up question.

'What were you doing over there?'

'I, um, was dropping something off.'

'To whom?'

'A parent of one of the boys at football.'

I can see that I've interrupted her train of thought with this new information. She's interested in what I've just revealed.

'What were you returning?'

'Oh, you know, some football kit. It was in the car.'

I can see her lawyer's juices flowing now.

'What football kit?'

'A shirt . . . shorts . . . socks.'

'And why was it in the car?'

'Patrick picked it up in the changing room. He wanted to take it over to the boy's house that night, but we were late, so we came home. I was passing today, so I thought I'd drop it off.'

'How do you know where he lives?'

Jesus. She's digging deep.

'Well, we dropped him home once. It was pouring with rain, so we gave him a lift.'

I've been truthful. Sort of. There was no football kit. The boy was not alone.

'And why couldn't you have waited until this afternoon's football practice to give him his stuff back?'

'I dunno,' I say. 'I suppose I could have waited, but it was an impulse thing – I was passing. Anyway, you know how much those things start to stink if you leave them lying around.'

She smiles in recognition. I take this to mean that she hasn't found any holes in my story.

But then her face hardens. She's no longer in the family home, she's working.

'Did you tell them your name and address when asked?'

'Yes.'

'Did you resist arrest?'

'No.'

'Did you give them any reason to believe that you were committing any kind of public order offence?'

'What do you mean?'

'Were you pissed?'

'Of course not.'

She's quiet for a moment, the gears turning in her head.

'I am not happy about this,' she says. 'Not one little bit.' Oh. Shit. I scramble to think which part of my story is leaking water. I need to get out of the kitchen. I need to leave the house. I'm drowning in lies and half-truths, weaving my webs only to have them picked apart and exposed. I'm not up to this – and why should I be? This isn't the life I chose. It's not fair on me, it's not fair on Sara and the boys, and it's not fair on Tom. I resolve to get the hell out of here . . .

'You have been treated appallingly, both by the police and by whichever busybody made those awful allegations against you.'

I look up at her and see the outrage in her eye, and it's clear that – God bless her – Sara has got my back.

'I'm going to make some calls and—'

'Please don't,' I say, maybe a little too quickly.

'Tom, this is simply not acceptable.'

'I just want to forget it,' I say. 'It was a mistake. It's all over.'

'But, Tom, this could have taken a serious turn.'

'It didn't, Sara.' I try to say this as nicely and firmly as I can. 'I really appreciate your getting involved – and, of course, you're right – but I just want to draw a line under it.'

'You're sure?'

'Yes.'

'Because if everyone acts like this, Tom, abuses of power and procedures that propagate wrongful arrest will continue to flourish.'

I shrug my shoulders.

'OK,' she says. I can tell that she's a little disappointed, but I'm encouraged that my situation brought out the warmth in her, put us back on the same side again.

'Guess what?' she says rhetorically. She pours herself a glass of water while I ponder the imponderable.

'What?' I say eventually.

'After last night I thought that we should go out for dinner.'

'Great,' I say. 'I'll get the boys ready—'

'No, Tom,' she interrupts. 'Just you and me.'

She takes a sip of water before uttering the most terrifying words a man can hear.

'We need to talk.'

I've had enough, can't take any more. I need to bail out. I try calling Tom to put a stop to all this, but he's not picking up. In the car on the way to the restaurant – a new French–Vietnamese place in West-bourne Park – I chatter away like a commentator at the Grand National. My blabbering is constant, a wall of white noise built to prevent her from beginning a conversation that might drag us from the shallows of domestic trivia to the deeper waters of adult complexity. Some of the areas that I touch upon include whether it's too early to be putting nuts in the bird feeder, whether we should invest in one multi-functional remote for our audio-visual needs instead of relying on the four that are currently in use, and whether the sea is nicer in the western or eastern Mediterranean. As Sara is driving, she's distracted, in particular when she's trying to find a parking space and manoeuvre the car before the patience of the driver behind evaporates. But once we start walking towards the restaurant she's fully aware of the fact that my mouth hasn't stopped working since we left home.

Where the fuck is Tom?

'Are you OK?' she asks.

'Yes, why?'

'Well, you're going on a bit.'

'Am I?'

'Yes, you are.'

'Oh.'

'It's not that I'm not interested in what you've got to say,' she explains, 'I'm just not very interested in what you're saying right now.'

I laugh. 'Well, I suppose I'm not even very interested in what I'm saying most of the time.'

'Don't be so hard on yourself,' she says. 'I don't want you slipping back into that hole of self-pity.'

'Thanks for the pep talk,' I say, a little more meanly than I meant.

We stop outside the restaurant. I've been here before, of course. It's good, lively and informal. That's the upside. What I can't forget is that there's nowhere to hide tonight – it's just Sara and me. My understanding of an unannounced evening in the world of married people is that it offers one of two possibilities: a romantic evening out that's destined to end in Olympic-standard sex, or a lot of hand-wringing analysis of 'where the relationship is at'. I'm going to be honest here – neither of these scenarios is attractive in any way.

What I would give now for Tom to answer the phone. Why couldn't Sara have waited just a day or two for a heart-to-heart? Tom and I are due to switch back at the end of the week. What makes things even worse is that there is something about Sara's manner, an executioner's calmness, that makes me suspect something's up. There is small talk before we order, handleable chit-chat before we turn our attention to the menu. She goes with the healthy female medley of fish and vegetables and I, because I've been exemplary in my appetite since arriving chez Sara, order crab cakes followed by a beef salad.

'The beef is just seared, sir. Is that all right?' asks the waitress.

'Fine,' I say. 'Walk it over here for all I care. Black and blue, that's how I like it.'

The waitress smiles, but shoots a look at Sara, sympathising perhaps with a woman who is subjected regularly to such bravado. I run a quick calculation: if the kitchen is quick, we can be out of here and in bed in an hour and a half, tops. This sounds fine until the word 'bed' reverberates around my head. I'm just concocting an excuse to sneak off and call Tom again when Sara smiles sweetly and asks: 'Are you having some kind of crisis?' Talk about direct. I take a sip of wine, buying some time.

'How do you mean?' I say, brilliantly avoiding answering her question.

'I just don't understand it,' she says. 'Over the past few days you've been cooking, cleaning, organising the boys, and you've never, ever ordered meat rare before.'

'I'm fine,' I say, smiling amiably as couples that have been married for a while but are still head over heels in love with each other are supposed to do when they get a night away from the kids.

'Well, guess what?' she says. 'I'm not fine with it.'

'But . . . Hang on a minute . . . '

She raises her hands in a gesture for me to continue. She waits to see what card I'm going to play.

'I . . . I . . . I thought you liked the fact that I'm making more effort around the house.'

'You're not listening to what I'm really saying. I appreciate the effort, but I don't understand your transformation into Mrs Doubtfire. I feel like I'm living with a middle-aged sexually repressed maiden aunt.'

'You mean, it's like you're being pussy whipped?'

'Whatever . . . The male version of that. Dick whipped.'

'Dick whip,' I say. 'Sounds like the worst dessert ever made.'

I know she thinks this is funny as she pauses for a moment. But she doesn't take the bait. She wants to continue the tenor of our conversation.

'Look, I've been thinking . . . '

I take a big breath as it approaches like a looming typhoon. Why the hell isn't my brother picking up the phone? I'm well and truly fucked. Maybe we both are.

'I've been working too much recently. I think that it's affecting the boys. I mean, turning up for the football the other afternoon and missing the whole thing . . . Well, I felt like the worst mum in the world, especially with that other woman there.'

'Who?' I say, unconvincingly.

'You know exactly who I'm talking about. The pretty one.'

'Oh, Maja,' I say, as if the penny has just dropped.

'Yes, Maja. I don't think that it's fair on the boys. It's not fair on me, and it's not fair on you. After you lost your job there was a lot of pressure on you to keep the household together. For a while you were drowning – I'm sure that you'd admit it. And now you're bloody Jamie Oliver in the kitchen and taking over the house with your tidying and organising. I came back the other day and the place was immaculate, there were fresh flowers in the living room, the smell of something baking ... I thought we'd been broken into by gay burglars.'

I raise my eyebrows. 'You can't have it both ways, Sara. I'm either a total waste of space or interfering. Which is it?'

'I don't want either,' she says. 'I don't believe that I've got to choose between the guy who's totally tuned out or the one who's freaking out because the broccoli's overcooked.'

'But there's nothing worse than soggy broccoli.'

'Actually, there is. Look, what I wanted to tell you is that I've got a sabbatical owed to me next year and, well, I think that I'm going to take it. I don't want to wake up tired and old in a few years to discover that I don't know the boys and that you've got another family with the girl from the chippy.'

I look at her. It's not what I was expecting. I'm now failing Tom, the kids and Sara as well. Tom needs to hear this – I'm convinced that his complaining would dissolve if only he could hear Sara talking this way. And he's not the only one to benefit from her words: Sara has made me realize that – if our relationship isn't to be stillborn – I need to communicate properly with Maja. Then her face changes – she fixes me with a look that can only mean trouble.

'Anyway, that's quite enough of that. Let's talk about Sean for a while, shall we?'

And then it occurs to me. She hasn't called me 'Tom' all evening. Does she know? Am I busted? An alarm like the shrieking ones they have on submarines just before they dive deep under the ocean goes off in my head. Sean the slick, cold-hearted charmer is no more. I realise that I have a potential disaster on my hands.

This is Big Stuff. I'm not equipped for this. I've got no place being here. I knock back a mouthful of wine.

'How is he then?'

'Um, he's fine, I think,' I say.

'Really?' There's an inquisitive smile on her face. Is my discomfort amusing her?

'Yeah.'

'It's just that he hasn't been round recently and I wondered whether everything was OK, because—'

'I need to go to the bathroom.'

I don't hear what she says next. I just get up and leave. I walk to the front of the restaurant and disappear.

That's enough for me. The life swap is over.

25
Tom

It's hard to know if you'd recognise your own penis if you were shown a picture of it. Imagine a body part ID parade. You'd pretty much be able to pick out your own hands, or limbs. Definitely your own torso. But your dong? Now there's a challenge. First and foremost I almost never look at it from that angle, only ever from above. Secondly, how distinctive are they? Aside from size and the presence or absence of a foreskin, you've got precious few clues to work with.

This is what I'm thinking as I'm standing on Sean's heated bathroom tiles staring at my not-quite-young-but-not-quite-old body. I am naked, a state that is habitually only a fleeting moment between removal of a towel and hastily pulling on my underpants. But the quietness of Sean's house and the luxury of time offer the occasion to absorb the unvarnished facts of my physical state. I turn to the side and examine my profile. Evidence of a slight belly is easily eradicated with a little attention to my posture and some tensing of my stomach muscles. The musculature of my chest, arms and back is all visible. It's a little odd this self-examination, the stark unfamiliarity with my own physique makes me wonder quite why I do it so rarely, although the evidence in the mirror provides an explanation of sorts.

Yet my physique is not my primary concern. I've had a headache for two days now, a dull, obstinate ache towards the front of my skull under my hairline. I'm exhausted from telling myself that everything is OK, that things are going to work out fine. Jesus, I'm doing a terrible job of convincing even myself. The throbbing continues, morning, noon and night. I tell myself that it would be a lot worse if I'd ended up sleeping with Rachel (although an indistinct sobriety intervened in the end, it was undeniably a close-run thing) but it makes no difference: the potentially disastrous conclusion of the next twenty-four hours is amplifying a gnawing anxiety.

I stare into the mirror, attempting to make a face that's as honest as I can imagine.

'Sara,' I start again. Still not right. Too whiny.

'Sara.' Wrong again. Too sombre.

'I've got something that I need to tell you . . . ' It's a bit portentous, but it sets the tone all right. I come in close to the mirror so that my nose is virtually pressing against it. Is my contrition plausible? Am I to be believed? Or will Sara see just crocodile tears, a desperate man motivated more by self-preservation than by remorse?

Aside from my family fiasco I'm aware that I should have heard back from Deutsche Mobilen by now. No news can't be good news given the time pressure of their launch schedule. There's no way I can face going into the office any more, not after the Rachel thing, so I'm hiding out at Sean's, alone and fretful, counting the seconds until Sean and I can reclaim our former lives, or what's left of them. I mope around the house searching for ways to kill time and to distract myself from the racking headache and misgivings swarming my mind. To relieve the tension and kill some time I take a bath.

I'm lying in Sean's truck-sized tub when the phone goes. I check the number and it's Andrea from Deutsche Mobilen. I let it ring, composing myself. I've been waiting for this call, but now it's here I can barely face picking the handset up.

I stand bolt upright, water cascading from me.

'Hello?'

'Hi, Sean, it's Andrea. How are you?'

Actually I'm naked, depressed and covered in bubble bath.

'I'm great, Andrea. Are you back in Dusseldorf?'

'Yes, we got back last night.'

'Well, let me tell you that it was great meeting with you all when you were in London, and if you need anything further please feel free to—'

'Sean,' she interrupts. 'I'm calling to let you know . . . ' my buttocks clench so tightly they could crack a walnut, 'that we don't have a decision yet.'

No decision. No fucking decision? The most important professional moment of my life and she doesn't have an answer? What are they waiting on? The second bloody coming?

'I totally understand,' I say to her, as smoothly as I can muster.

'I just wanted to let you know that we're working on it, and that I'm hoping to be able to have a more constructive conversation imminently, in all likelihood later today.'

'Well, I appreciate you letting me know,' I say.

I turn the phone off and flop back in the bath. All that work, all that industry and hope, and I'm still waiting for some cubicle jockey to juggle budgets. The call causes me to revisit the starkness of the situation. I've passed up an opportunity for my brother to pocket ten million quid by refusing to sell a company that is on the brink of extinction. Why on earth didn't I at least call Sean and ask him? How on earth am I going to tell him that I decided that it was in his best interests not to pursue the offer? Who the hell did I think I was trying to engineer a company-saving deal? And how can we even have a semblance of a normal relationship after I've masterminded a calamity like this? On top of that, I've misjudged my family life in a quite catastrophic way. Who was I kidding that Sean and I would get away with this? With my marriage in an already fragile state I decide that Sara and I are best served by my *leaving home to re-experience life as a bachelor*? Lunacy. Utter lunacy.

I've proved an abject failure at being Sean. I've botched the thing in a way that even the worst cowboy builder would find an embarrassment. I lie back in the bath and think about just sliding underneath the water and not surfacing. I've spent nearly a fortnight as Sean, I've managed to ruin his business and fuck up my marriage, and I've not even managed to get laid to relieve the pain. On Saturday we swap back and I don't even know what I'm going back to. I watch the clock crawl forward with tedious slowness and even reuniting with my family begins to feel like an invitation for disaster rather than a happy return.

The afternoon passes painfully slowly before melting into evening. I'm killing time, trying to find something to hold my attention when all I can feel is disappointment and gloom. There has been no call from Deutsche Mobilen and I can't help thinking that, if Andrea was going to sign off on the deal, it would have happened by now. I'm picking at a Chinese take-away – chicken and cashew nuts with special fried rice – wondering whether I can look Sara in the eye without her immediately detecting my betrayal, when I hear a faint ringing. I get up and fish the mobile out of my bag, noting that I've got three missed messages – all of them from Sean. He's probably calling to work out how we're going to swap back. How the hell am I going to tell him about what I've done to his company? I press the Berry to my ear, eyes closed like I'm just about to leap from a cliff.

'All right, Sean?'

'Tom, you've got to get down here right now.' He speaks so quickly that each of the words runs in to the other.

'Hold up, hold up . . . What's the matter?'

'I can't handle this any longer, Tom,' he says. His voice is urgent and edgy, but there is still conviction there. 'You've got to hear her, Tom. She's talking and talking. She's talking about you and her. You need to be here. This is all wrong. You're the one she wants, not me.'

I'm terrified – how to step seamlessly back into my real life as if nothing unusual has occurred in the past two weeks? – but also suddenly overcome by a need to see my family. I need to put an end to this.

'Where are you?'

'Koi. In the toilets. Move your arse.'

I close the phone, pick up the car keys and leave the house, not even bothering to lock the door behind me.

My prayers are answered. I'm outside the restaurant in five minutes and – sweet Jesus! – there's a parking space right outside. I scope out the restaurant to see if Sara is at one of the tables in the front. The place is heaving. I scan each of the diners and conclude that she and Sean must be seated in the back section behind the kitchen. I walk in and, thankfully, the floor and waiting staff are all overwhelmed, so there's no one around to ask time-consuming questions. The place is low-lit, virtually dark, so it takes me a couple of moments to remember that the men's toilet is down a staircase to my right.

I crash down the stairs and open the door to see my brother arranging his hair in the mirror.

'Hanging around the toilets *again*?' I say to him. It's amazing how flippant you can be even when it feels like your world is ungovernable.

'Thank fuck,' he says.

'Where is she?'

'In the back.'

'And why . . . ?'

'She's come here for a reason, Tom. It's something major. I don't belong at the table any more. It's stuff you should hear, not me . . . '

'I know,' I agree. 'It's time.'

'She loves you, you know.'

'Is everything all right?'

'I think so . . . ' He doesn't sound too sure. He looks shaken, like he's witnessed something he's taking time to digest.

I reach for the door handle.

'You forgotten something?' he asks.

I realise that we need to change clothes again.

'Tell you what, no underpants though this time, OK?' he says with a wink. 'I bought you some new ones just the same as mine. My treat.'

We're undressing when the door to the toilet opens and a waiter sticks his head round the corner. I see his face go from the workaday to startled.

'Oh, sorry, sirs,' he says as he darts his head back and slams the door. Sean and I look at each other and there's a moment's pause before we start laughing and Sean says: *Oh, sorry, sirs*, in a foppish voice. The laughter continues as we change clothes, disappearing before rising again, acting as a bridge between us, some relief from the current tension.

Once changed, I give myself a quick check in the mirror. It feels dramatic in a different way to the initial swap. This time my clothes might have changed but I feel composed. I feel like myself. Then I remember that I've got to go upstairs and face Sara, that the stakes are as high as they could possibly be and I'm filled with a grim determination. I turn to my brother.

He comes towards me and we man-hug awkwardly.

'I've got to go,' I say. 'She must be wondering what the hell is going on.'

Sean nods.

'Look, she was saying earlier that she wants things to work between the two of you. I don't know if I've been any help, but I know that she's ready to work it through. She wants to give you a chance, Tom.'

Suddenly he doesn't appear so sure of himself. 'I think,' he adds. 'Now don't fuck it up.'

'Thanks for the inspirational pep talk,' I say. As I disappear onto the other side of the door I hear him exhale loudly, as if trying to cast out the burden of our plight.

I walk through the humming restaurant; waiting staff expertly moving about me, looking for my wife. I walk through the entire place, wondering if I might have missed her. After I've done a second circuit of the place I stop a waiter and describe Sara to him.

'You were sitting there, weren't you?' the waiter asks, indicating a table that a couple of bus boys are clearing. 'The lady just paid and left.' I rush outside the restaurant but can't see Sara. I run back in and bump into Sean, who's in the doorway.

'Where did you park?' I ask him.

'A couple of streets over there,' he says, gesturing. 'Why?'

'Sara's gone.'

'Shit,' says Sean.

'Quick, let's take your car.'

We drive round to where Sean and Sara left the Volvo and find an empty parking space. I wonder what on earth is going on in her mind and whether I might be losing mine.

'Sean, get me home as quick as you can.'

Sean steps on the accelerator and we power violently up the road. Just then, his phone goes. He fishes inside his jacket pocket.

'Do you *have* to get that?' I protest, but I can tell that he's already back in his old life again.

'Hi, Andrea,' he says.

Jesus, it's Andrea Schnell. Sean looks over at me suspiciously. I watch his face brighten.

'Wow, that's great news,' he says. He sticks the phone under his chin and thumps me on the arm in celebration. 'We're very excited. Let's touch base tomorrow.'

He looks over at me.

'You crafty sod.' He laughs. 'You did it.'

I want to smile, but I'm too preoccupied. I just nod knowingly.

'Bloody hell,' he says. 'That is amazing. *Amazing.*'

'Thanks.' It's the best I can muster as various disaster scenarios involving Sara and the boys whizz around my head like mini explosives. We ride in silence until we get near home.

'Just here,' I say firmly, as we near the end of our street. I want to walk the rest of the way to organise my thoughts.

'You should be really proud of yourself,' he says as he pulls over. I jump out of the car, and as I slam the door I hear him say, 'Welcome aboard, partner.'

I return, as I left, on a still night, with nothing moving on the street. As I approach the house, the quiet is broken by the sound of a window sliding open. I look up to see Sara disappearing back into the room before returning with – hang on – the contents of my underwear drawer and throwing them out of the window. I watch as my socks and pants fall among the rotting leaves and gravel of the front yard. What on earth is she . . . ? Next thing I know, half a dozen shirts land on me, followed by three pairs of jeans.

'Sara!' I call to her. I try and soften my voice so as not to shout and alert the entire street.

Sara peers out. 'Oh, there you are,' she says. 'I suppose you'll be needing this.' She slings a holdall down to me.

'What are you doing?' I ask. A stupid question really. What I want to know is why. Have the few days she spent with Sean proved completely intolerable, or is it something she's been meaning to do for a long time? Is this it? Is this how my marriage ends, with my socks and vests hanging from the branches of the silver birch in the garden?

'Hang on a minute,' she says. 'I'll just go and fetch your toothbrush.'

'Sara, please,' I appeal. I look up at the bedroom window. There doesn't appear to be anything else heading my way.

The front door opens and suddenly Sara is there. I survey her face: astute, protective, tough, all the things that I liked about her that first night at the Fridge, the qualities that have bound our marriage together when it might have been easier to kick me out and call it a day a long time ago.

'You better come in,' she says.

I step into the warm familiarity of the house and it smells and feels like nowhere else. I can't believe that I've managed to fuck this up. It really is quite an achievement to have had it so good and to have allowed it all to go to waste. I follow her through to the kitchen. She leans against the countertop, her arms folded in front of her.

'So?' she asks.

'I need to talk to you.'

'Did you go to the doctor today?' she says abruptly.

'What?'

'You know, your little problem.'

'I really—' She cuts me off, and standing in the silent kitchen I wonder if I've made a fatal mistake.

'Don't worry,' says Sara. She smiles, nods her head and laughs to herself.

It's at that moment that I finally decide that I have no choice but to tell her what has happened over the previous two weeks. The least I owe her is honesty, whatever the consequences.

'Sara, I've done something very bad, something you might not be able to forgive me for.'

She fixes her gaze on me. I am aware that she's taking calm, even breaths.

'Sean and I swapped lives,' I say as dispassionately as I can manage. 'He's been living in our house for two weeks. I've been at his place and checking up to make sure that the boys are OK. We intended to do it while you were away but, obviously, you came back before we managed to swap back. We just did it – just now. That's why it was so long when I – or rather Sean – went to the toilet.'

I can barely look at her.

'I want you to know that the boys didn't notice a thing. I was around a lot of the time except the last three days when things went, um, a bit pear-shaped. Sean and I had an agreement that he would always sleep in another room from you.'

Silence. This is hard to read. The upside is that she's allowing me to explain without interruption. The downside is that I might just hang myself. She stares back at me, stony-eyed.

'It's insane, I know, but we felt we wanted to know what it was like to be in each other's skin. I remember you saying to me that I should reach out and help Sean. In a way, this was my attempt to do that. We both went into it with the best intentions, as hard as that might be to believe. It was a stupid experiment that got a bit out of hand when you came back early from Liverpool . . . '

She stands rigidly, seemingly nonplussed and I wonder which of Sean's spare rooms I'm going to sleep in tonight. I think about my boys and how long it's going to be until I see them again.

'Good,' says Sara eventually, as if she's passing judgement on a piece of work. I remain silent and then it hits me . . . *she already knew*.

'You, um, worked it out?' I ask.

'Do you think I'm an *idiot*, Tom?' she asks in her best I'm-ten-moves-ahead-of-you barrister voice.

'You must have noticed by now that one of the many great things about being a woman,' she says, 'is that if we can't get what we want by using our intelligence, we can get what we want by pretending to be oblivious.'

I reach for the kitchen counter, knocked off-balance by this new disclosure.

'I decided to flush Sean out this evening for a number of reasons. Firstly, I was getting bored with the whole bloody performance. I'm sure that the pair of you were fully aware that the fiasco was wearing a bit thin. Secondly, I realised that, more than anything else, I wanted to know if you had any respect for me. By coming clean about your "experiment", as you call it, I have an answer of sorts.'

I have absolutely no idea what to say to her. I know that words are essential but, paralysed by an overwhelming requirement to gauge exactly the right sentiment, I remain silent.

'I think I fingered the pair of you a couple of hours after I got back from Liverpool,' continues Sara, her tone a little more breezy now.

'Sean really is a terrible show off, and his mannerisms are different to yours. It wasn't that hard. And then there was his whole "I'm sleeping in the spare room" shtick. I mean *pleeaaaase*.'

She walks over to the wine rack and examines a bottle.

'Still, we had some fun with that.'

Finally, I recover the facility of speech.

'Look, I know that it was an absolutely insane idea—' I start. She cuts me off almost immediately.

'Insane. No, not insane. Misguided, yes. Naive, definitely. At first I was a little freaked out by the sheer nerve of the pair of you. Then I thought that it was pretty funny, like you were ten years old again and trying to get one over on a teacher or something. So I decided to get into the whole thing, to see how it worked out, to mess with Sean a little. Poor thing, I hope that I didn't upset him too much.'

'Oh, no,' I smile, 'I think that it was probably, you know, character building for him.'

'Well, we'll make a man of him yet,' she says. She reaches up into the cupboard and pulls out a couple of wine glasses. I almost want to collapse with relief, realising that I'm going to be sleeping in my own bed tonight.

'So, here's what I'd like you to take away from this, Tom. Listen well: tonight, if you hadn't told me about this weirdness, I would have informed you that I was divorcing you.' She offers a little laugh; I feel a deep black pit in my stomach.

'But you did tell me. So we can move forward. But just remember this: mistakes I can handle; deceit I cannot.'

She uncorks a bottle of red wine and pours two glasses, handing me one. We knock them together and drink.

'You might want to go and collect your clothes from the front garden though,' she laughs. 'I thought that it would be good for you to really know what it would be like to have no family home to go to. It was my own little "experiment". We'll consider ourselves equal, shall we?'

I nod, vaguely humiliated, but also elated. Because I've told her the truth and can breathe easy again, and because I'm going to see my boys tomorrow morning. But also because the woman I love was smart enough not to need any grovelling because she's already turned the tables on me. And although I should feel strange that my wife has knowingly lived with my brother, it's actually a relief to find myself outsmarted.

'I've missed you, Sara,' I say, and it's true, I have missed her. 'I know that I've been acting a little odd over the past few months, and I'm sorry. I know that it's been rough for you. But I want you to know that I'm back.'

I walk over to her, put my arms around her waist and kiss her. She kisses me back, tasting of red wine.

'Look, I know that it's been rough for you,' she says. 'And maybe you feel like I take you for granted sometimes, but it really isn't like that. When you lost your job I had to come up with the goods. I had to do it for my family. And I know that, maybe to you, it must seem like I'm putting my career before my family, and especially before our marriage. But even when I'm in court, in the middle of a deposition or whatever, I never stop thinking about you all.

'Tom, you're a great dad. I think that you know that, but I want you to know that I think that too. The boys certainly think that. They worship you.'

I smile to myself. Of course deep down I know it, but I've never actually thought it before, lost in the day-to-day of finding the right coats and shoes and getting to and from places where there are urgent appointments to be kept, I never allow myself to really be aware of it.

'I've got something else to tell you,' I say.

'You're not pregnant are you?' she asks.

'It's too hard to tell,' I say patting my stomach.

'So what's the big announcement?'

'I've got a job.'

I have to say that the incredulous look on her face isn't maybe what I was hoping for (she would have perhaps been less surprised if I'd announced that I actually was pregnant) but, under the circumstances, it's understandable.

'What?' She grips my hand. 'That's fantastic news! What is it? Tell me, tell me.'

'It's a long story,' I say, 'but Sean asked me to work on a project, so I've been doing this thing for him, you know, and, well, it worked out and he offered me a job today.'

She puts her arms around me and gives me a hug.

'I'm very proud of you,' she says in a tone that she only usually reserves for the boys. 'But I want you to know that I was proud of you before as well.'

'When I was a deadbeat loser?'

'Tom, why do you think I married you, eh?' she asks. 'I've got a thing for deadbeat losers.'

The phone rings and Sara picks it up. I'm ecstatic to be home. The past two weeks have been so unsettling and tense I feel like flopping down on the sofa next to Sara and the boys and not moving for six months. I look up and Sara is handing me the phone. She rolls her eyes. 'It's Sean,' she says. 'Tell him that I'll deal with him later.'

'All right, Sean?' I say self-consciously. I am aware that Sara is sipping wine only yards away from me. I listen for a few moments before putting the handset down, approaching my wife and taking her hands. I look at her and pray that I'm not pushing her beyond the point of no return.

'Please don't kill me,' I say to her, 'but I've got to go.'

26
Sean

So, here I am. Back in my big, valuable house, alone again. The place feels a little cooler than I remember, and quiet. Quieter than I've noticed before. Compared to Tom and Sara's place, it's like *nothing* happens here. I shuffle inside and try and summon relief and enthusiasm to be 'home'. I should be happy; it's been featured in *Wallpaper*; for God's sake, a friend once described it as a 'drop your knickers' house, but I stand there in the hallway on my non-triumphant return, looking up the sweeping, ornate staircase wondering what the hell I need all this space for. As I walk into the kitchen to turn the heating up I scan the floor for stray pieces of plastic – soldiers, robots, weapons – to avoid. This, of course, is not necessary.

Nursing a large vodka I survey my custom-built cabinets and state-of-the-art appliances. I've got to try and be positive. Tom, unbelievably, has saved my business. I have somewhere to go during daylight hours, a reason to get out of bed. I pull the drawing that Patrick gave me out of my pocket, flatten it on the work surface and examine it for the umpteenth time. Tom must have been eating dinner when I called from the restaurant. There are remnants of a Chinese: chicken with cashew nuts and special fried rice by the looks of it. I wish he'd ordered spare ribs. God, I love spare ribs. The food has gone cold, and I've lost my appetite anyway. I throw the dirty dishes in the sink and spend at least a minute wondering what day of the week it is. I lean over and hit the 'play' button on the answer machine.

'You have no messages,' comes the patronising electronic voice. Talk about Billy no-mates. I get my, Berry out and have a flick around, the buttons are silky and easy-to-the touch after Tom's Sputnik-era brick. There are over three hundred entries in my address book. I flick through a familiar catalogue of drinking buddies, party animals and sex partners. I don't want to talk to any of them. I spin the device on the kitchen counter, wondering what to do next. I stare at the phone, knowing that there's only one number that I want to call, and it's a number that belongs to someone who recently tried to have me arrested. Talk about star-crossed lovers – she's more likely to serve me with an ASBO than send a love letter.

The doorbell rings. I catch myself flinching before I remember that there are no kids asleep upstairs to worry about. I go to the door and see Ellie leaning against one of the pillars. I'm spellbound by her unexpected beauty. She's got a scarf tied around her neck and a body warmer, giving her an athletic look that promises active, dynamic lovemaking. But somehow all that doesn't seem like enough any more.

'Hi,' I say grimly, opening the door.

'Well, thanks for the warm welcome,' she says. She examines me closely. 'Everything OK?'

I nod unconvincingly. I can't summon the upbeat, I-can-walk-on-water Sean. We stand uncomfortably in the hallway.

'You on your way out?' she asks.

'No,' I say, confused by her question. Then I look down and realise she's talking about my coat. I've not taken it off in the hour that I've been back. 'Oh, no, just came in.'

'So . . .' she says.

'I'm sorry,' I apologise. 'Please – come in.'

I usher her into the house. 'This is yours,' she says, handing me a book she's been clutching to her chest.

'Oh, right,' I say.

'Don't you remember?' she asks. 'A couple of weeks ago.'

'Yeah,' I say. I wonder how Tom got on. Of course, it would be unethical and immoral for him to have taken advantage of the lovely Ellie. Why wouldn't he have screwed her? I mean just look at her – she's been created in God's workshop of magnificence.

But I know that he didn't lay a finger on her. Not because he didn't want to – my God, he'd be insane not to *want* to – but because he's got standards. Not just standards that are judged by others, but stuff that only he will know about, the stuff that all of us have inside us that provides the credit and debit, the ledger of information relating to how we think about ourselves, our strengths, our weaknesses. The lifetime of give and take, ups and downs, triumphs and disasters that comprise each and every one of us. In Tom's case, I'm fairly sure that the aggregate of that will allow him to go home to his family knowing that he might not be perfect, but when he was tested, he reached deep within himself and wasn't found wanting.

'Drink?' I ask.

She takes off her scarf and body warmer. This is the point at which my instincts normally take over. But tonight . . . nothing. Not a flicker. I just feel the dead weight of my Maja failure hanging over me.

I fetch her customary glass of white wine.

'How's your week been?' she asks, hitching her heavenly backside up onto a kitchen stool.

I laugh.

'What's so funny?' she says with a suspicious smile.

It's the first time I've broken out of a grimace since she arrived.

'Let's just say I had an interesting week,' I say, rattling ice cubes in my glass of vodka. She takes a sip of wine.

'That's nice,' she says, looking at the glass dreamily before returning her focus to me. 'There's a rumour going round that you landed the Deutsche Mobilen contract,' she says elliptically, waiting for me to fill in the blanks. I'm not exactly sure, but I think that she actually licks her lips at the thought of this.

'I couldn't possibly comment,' I say, raising my glass to her.

'Well . . . If you need to bring anyone in to work on the creative . . . '
She drums her fingers on her chin in mock contemplation.

'Got anyone in mind?' I ask.

She reaches over the counter and strokes my face.

'Just a friend,' she says, flirtatiously.

There's a pause before I say to her, 'You didn't call.'

She pulls her hand back slowly.

'Did I need to?' She's frowning slightly.

'Well, there are rules,' I say. I'm trying to keep it light, but I want her to know that we're not ending up in the sack tonight. I know my romance with Maja is over, and it wasn't exactly Barbara Cartland territory, but I need to retain a degree of decorum in the way I handle myself. I can't turn into Wile E. Coyote, standing there holding the sticks of ACME Co. dynamite while Road Runner makes a mug of him time and time again.

And maybe this is where Tom has something to offer. He would have worked out by now that I shouldn't even be sitting here. Yes, Ellie is gorgeous and we have a great time together, but I can't be with her. Not right now. Not ever. As teenage as it sounds, I just want Maja. I want the one I can't have.

'I'm sorry, Ellie,' I say, 'but I've got to make a call.' I'm sort of apologising, but I'm not really.

'Oh,' she says. Then she nods, understanding. This kind of move isn't usually part of our foreplay.

'To be honest, maybe this evening isn't going to be the best for us to, you know . . . '

'I know.' She scratches at something on the countertop with her nail.

'Look, I'm . . . ' I raise my hands in regret.

She gathers her things and moves towards the door.

'There's no need to apologise,' she says. 'Really. We've always said no strings and, well, if you've got other fish to fry I won't outstay my welcome.'

'It's really not like that,' I say.

She gives me the look of a woman who knows that she's being lied to. I nod the nod of the busted, and show her the door.

Then I dial Tom's number.

Fifteen minutes later Tom pulls up outside the house. As wretched and tense as I feel, I smile when I see him.

'So everything's OK?' I ask. 'You and Sara?'

'Sean,' he says, biting his lip. His face is a muddle of sadness and desperation. 'She's kicking me out,' he says. He looks at the floor and all hope drains out of me. Between the two of us we've managed to destroy a family and a budding romance. Then Tom looks up and smiles a roguish smile.

'You bastard,' I say. 'You had me going there.'

'She guessed, you know.'

'And she's all right about it?'

'Well, I don't know if she's all right about it, but I think that in a strange way it's cleared the air between us. We're going to make a go of it.'

There's definite hope here.

'I'm pleased for you, mate,' I say. 'I'll come over and see her soon. Talk it over, you know. That is, if you want me to. And, look, I want to say that I'm sorry about some of the stuff that happened. When you wanted to call it quits, I didn't behave very well.'

Tom nods. 'There's some stuff I've got to tell you about the company as well,' he says gravely.

'What?'

'It's all fine now, I'll tell you another time,' he says, taking a deep breath. 'Look, let's get on with this. I want to get home.'

It sounds good him saying that.

'Oh, one thing,' he says, with a perplexed look, 'Sara asked me if I'd been to the doctor earlier.' He seems slightly muddled. 'Very odd. What's going on?'

'Long story.'

'Right, let's get on with it.'

'I need you to do exactly what I say,' I explain.

'Oh, no, we've just—'

'Tom, have we or have we not undergone a life-transforming experience over the past two weeks?'

'You're beginning to sound like a televangelist.'

'Hear me out, bro,' I interrupt. 'Has this change largely occurred because of the new levels of trust that exist between us?'

'Well, the Natural History Museum was hardly a high point, was it?'

'Are you willing to help me take control of my destiny?'

'You're scaring me, Sean.'

'Go with it, Tom.'

'I would, if I had any idea what you're talking about.'

'Help me out, Tom.'

'*How?*'

'Please.'

'*How?*'

'Hit me on the head with this.' I pull a cast-iron sauté pan from the kitchen counter. He shakes his head – not to reject my suggestion, but to clear his mind.

'You want me to hit you over the head with a frying pan,' he says clearly, as if to ensure that there hasn't been a misunderstanding and we're actually embarking on a fry-up.

'Yes.'

'Why?'

'Love,' I say, because this is the only word I can think of that communicates my motivation.

'OK,' he says, scratching his head. 'I'm going to need a little more than that . . . '

'I need to see Maja,' I explain. 'I'm not going to let her walk away. She won't answer my phone calls, won't let me near her house, she thinks that I might be in love with an estranged wife who hasn't even ever been my wife—'

'Why would she think that?' Tom interrupts.

'It's complicated. Here's the thing though: she's at the hospital right now. In A&E. I need an injury, something that will force her to have to see me. I can't just walk in there with stomach pains or a headache or something – I need drama. I was thinking about it . . . Tom, do you know the two parts of the male body that bleed most profusely?'

Tom shakes his head.

'The head and the penis,' I say, pointing, respectively, at both parts of my anatomy. 'And given that I have no intention of injuring my knob, I have elected to sustain a head wound. Nothing too serious, you understand, just a bang that's forceful enough to open a wound. I'm going to need a few stitches.'

'You are absolutely off your rocker,' he says. Nevertheless, he picks up the pan and gauges it, as if he were trying to estimate its weight. Then he makes a couple of tennis-style motions.

'New balls please,' he says in his best tennis umpire's voice.

'Nothing below the waist, Tom. Let's keep it strictly cranial.'

'So, whereabouts do you want me to hit you?'

I motion to a spot halfway between the middle of my forehead and my ear. I figure that blood flowing down the face and into my eyes will generate an acceptable level of spectacle.

'What's that?' asks Tom. I turn to see what he's pointing at before hearing a hollow, metallic thud and everything turns black.

'Sean. *Sean.*'

I'm aware of the voice, but I'm not sure how it relates to me. I can hear it, but don't understand that it needs acknowledgement. There is a warmth to my face. Someone is lifting my shoulders, trying to wake me . . . I open my eyes and see my brother. He looks concerned, but I can tell that he's also amused.

'Think I might have overdone it a little there,' he chuckles.

I take a couple of deep breaths.

'Jesus,' I say. 'What the fuck?'

'Didn't want you to see it coming,' he explains. 'I thought that it would be easier that way.'

I sit up and, perversely, am relieved to see that there is blood all over my shirt. Tom helps me get to my feet. I feel a little unsteady.

'You wanted some claret,' says Tom. 'Well, you got it. Here,' he passes me a tea towel. 'Press it against the cut. It looks bad enough.'

'Thanks,' I say.

'A pleasure,' Tom says with a grin. 'Let's get you to the hospital.'

A&E at Central Middlesex Hospital. Nice. I walk in looking like any other pisshead who's ended up on the wrong side of a bottle of Stella after a heated exchange in a pub car park. Maybe my balance is a little off, but getting assaulted with a frying pan almost proves to be a waste of time as, on my way to register, I skid in an errant mound of vomit that a porter hasn't had a chance to clear up. I breathe deeply and think of Maja. I need to figure out where she is and insist that she treats me. My head is beginning to ache. I need to focus. I can't fuck this up.

The digital clock on the wall tells us that the waiting time for the drunks, elderly and dangerous teens who are the constituency of this scuffed room with chairs ominously bolted to the floor is two hours. I'm wondering which optimist is in charge of this. The last time I was here (ruptured Achilles during Sunday league) I waited, in agony, for four hours. It was right after carnival and the place looked like a post-battlefield hospital. Tonight, except for some kid in a Burberry baseball cap who keeps making unspecific threats towards the two burly and indifferent Nigerian security guards watching over the group, the place is quiet, each patient resigned to his or her mishap or folly.

'So, what are we going to do?' asks Tom.

'I'm thinking,' I say. I pull the tea towel away from my head. The heavy bleeding has stopped. I poke gingerly at my wound. The cut isn't painful, but the bruising is beginning to make my head swell to elephantine proportions. I better get to Maja soon before I turn into John Merrick.

'Maja is the senior on duty though,' I say, 'so she might just be in the back there dealing with patients.'

'I'm going to have a quick scout around,' says Tom, standing up. 'I can tell you where she is then you can swoop in and do your thing.'

He walks off purposefully. 'Tom!' I beckon him back. He returns. 'Just one thing: you don't know what she looks like.'

'Good thinking, Batman.'

'Late thirties, long black hair, which she usually wears pulled back. Olive skin. Looks Italian. About Sara's height. If it helps, think of it like this: Sara dressed in scrubs.'

'I'd prefer it if she was wearing a nurse's uniform,' Tom says with a wink.

'Here's the thing: shut up,' I say, aware now that my head is beginning to throb. 'Go and find her.'

'Right you are,' says Tom. 'Shame about the suit though, eh?' He nods at my shirt and suit, which are stained with semi-dried blood. I can feel where the liquid has formed a thick crust on the side of my face below where my hair is matted.

I watch as Tom waits for the receptionist to be distracted before disappearing to the treatment area. The kid with the baseball cap is back with a skinny white girlfriend, her hair pulled up agonisingly on the top of her head, giving her the full Croydon face-lift. They are having a rambling, semi-coherent argument, trying to establish who is responsible for losing their lighter. I tune out this twaddle and compose myself. I need to make sure that, when I eventually see Maja, I'm going to make a degree of sense. I need to tell her the truth, to unload some of the bizarre complications of my life. Given that she's already cast me into the wilderness, I'm pretty sure that it's a largely futile exercise, but I need to clear my head and let her know who I am, even though this inevitably means telling her about the previous fortnight. The irony, of course, is that I've probably been as honest with her as I've been with anyone. Given that I've been pretending to be someone else for the last two weeks, this doesn't speak well of my dependability.

All this is about to change when I notice a flurry of activity over by the front desk. I look up to see the receptionist talking urgently to one of the security guards who nods gravely before passing into the treatment area. Moments later I see him frog-marching Tom out of the door. Wisely, Tom doesn't look in my direction. I sink lower into my seat, hoping that no one has noticed that the two of us have arrived together. Maja must have spotted him snooping around and, thinking it was me, called security. She's serious. It's looking hopeless – this deluded exercise is a total waste of time – Maja wants no part of me.

Desperate times call for desperate measures. Seizing the moment, I lurch out of my seat and stumble along the wall of the waiting area. The others are either too tired or too intoxicated to notice my Frankenstein-like stagger, but those who do see me look horrified by my state. Miraculously, the receptionist is hunting for some paper-work in a filing cabinet as I pass her. I find myself in the treatment area with a white board on the wall displaying information about each of the patients. Corresponding doctors' names are listed, including Maja Petrovic. I feel nauseous at the sight of her name, just wishing that this was over, that we were together. Nurses pass by, with no one paying any particular attention to me. They duck in and out of curtained-off areas where patients are being treated. Each of the areas corresponds to a number on the board. There are no feet visible under the curtains in one particular area, so I grab the pen and quickly write a fictional name in the appropriate space and Maja's name as the designated doctor before slipping inside and sitting on the edge of the bed.

After a few moments I hear feet approaching. I stick my head between the curtains and see a nurse.

'Excuse me,' I say, 'but I was told that Dr Petrovic was on her way to see me.'

'She's very busy,' said the nurse in a singsong Welsh accent. 'We've had a couple of traffic accidents come in about half an hour ago. She'll get to you as soon as she can.'

'OK,' I say.

'Has a nurse seen you?'

'Briefly,' I reply. 'She told me that Dr Petrovic would definitely want to see me though.'

'I'll get someone to come and clean you up in the meantime.'

This is not something I want to hear. The whole point of the head wound is the dramatic potential of it. If Maja sees me in this state surely she wouldn't be able to leave me like this. Hasn't she signed a Hippocratic oath or something like that?

'You know, if you lot are busy,' I say, 'I don't want to get in the way. Just as long as the doctor sees me I'll be fine.'

'All right,' says the nurse. 'They'll just want to check you out, make sure there's no concussion, anything like that. Fight was it?'

'Oh no,' I say, embarrassed, 'I, um, tripped. Banged my head.'

'Yeah, and my arse plays the banjo,' says the nurse with a laugh before disappearing onto the other side of the curtain.

I sit listening to the ebb and flow of casualty, and it occurs to me that it would be even more dramatic to be slumped on the bed when Maja enters. I lie back on the sheet of paper that covers the bench and wonder what unspeakable things have happened in this small space, what unpleasantness has leaked onto the vinyl beneath me. Suddenly the curtain is pulled back and she's standing there, a white coat over her everyday clothes, a stethoscope spilling out of her pocket beneath a laminated badge identifying her as a bona fide employee of the hospital. It takes a second for her to recognise me before a cross look passes over her face.

'Bloody hell, Tom, what happened?' she exclaims. *Jesus. I'm still Tom.* Where the hell do I start? There's surprise in her voice, but no alarm. As much as I'm trying to focus on what I've got to say to her I love seeing her like this – at work, in charge, absolutely confident.

'I asked them to throw you out, not beat you up,' she says.

Oh well, it's a start.

She approaches me and I notice that there's a male nurse, a young Asian guy, next to her, looking mildly confused. Maja senses this.

'We know each other,' she says matter-of-factly, as if she could be describing the bloke who works the night shift at the Esso garage who she sees when she pops in for twenty Bensons in the small hours. 'Look, Sunil, I've got this one. Can you take care of Mrs Bernstein in seven? It's just a twisted ankle. Put a bandage on her and she can see her GP tomorrow.'

So then, it's just her and me.

'Look . . . ' I say, the well-drilled words that I've ordered so clearly in my mind evaporate when I need to use them.

'The cut's not too bad, but it's going to need stitches,' she says, pawing my head with her surgically sheathed gloves. Her upper body is pressed close to me, her breasts at the same height as my face.

'Maja, I really—'

'Did you lose consciousness?'

'What?' I am so completely focused on winning her over and the magnitude of what I'm doing that I wonder momentarily what she's talking about.

'Oh, I don't think so. Or not for long anyway.'

'Any vomiting?'

'No.'

'Dizziness?'

'No.'

'Blurred vision?'

'No.'

'Just some confusion,' I say, trying to be conciliatory. She doesn't bite.

'Right, I'll get one of the nurses to stitch you up,' she says, snapping off her gloves and throwing them in the bin next to the bed.

'Maja, please, I need to talk to you . . . '

'I've already had you slung out of here once,' she says. 'Don't make me do it again. So, what happened to you?'

'I walked into a lamp-post,' I explain, lamely.

'At one in the morning when you're not even drunk?'

'Who says I'm not drunk?'

'Well, you'd be the only person in here who isn't,' she says.

'Including you?' I ask.

She rolls her eyes.

'Look,' she says, 'I had you slung out of here earlier because, well, I saw you creeping about and . . . I've got stuff I need to tell you, but this isn't the right place.'

'You could have called me.'

She shrugs.

'I see,' I say. 'I've got stuff I need to tell you, too. Things I've been meaning to tell you for a while now, but, frankly, I haven't had the balls.'

'I know what you've got to tell me, Tom, it's hardly rocket science.'

'I know what you're thinking, and you're completely wrong,' I say emphatically. She raises her eyebrows.

'So, you're going to surprise me, are you?'

'And how,' I say.

'Well, I think you might have met your match,' she says enigmatically, opening the curtain to leave. 'I've got a break in an hour. Meet me in the canteen for bad coffee and digestives.'

She's right. The coffee, despite being promoted as 'cappuccino', is the same institutional brew that makes you long for a sharp object with which to scrape the inside of your mouth clean. There's an acridity to the flavour that makes me wonder whether I should be cleaning the bath with it or drinking it. Both Maja and I pretend to take a sip of our drinks while the momentous silence between us swells.

'So, who's going to go first?' she asks eventually.

'I'm happy to start,' I say. 'But I'd like us to have a rule: we both hear the other out. No matter what.'

'That sounds ominous,' she says.

'I just think that it's fair,' I say. 'On both parts.'

'All right – but let's decide who starts by tossing a coin.'

I nod. I like the Cup Final flavour of this. She pulls a nugget out of her pocket and flips it in the air. Impulsively I reach out and catch it. I can't wait. I want to tell her.

'I'll start,' I say.

So I tell her. I tell her about the swap. I tell her that the kids aren't mine. I tell her that my name isn't Tom. And I tell her that I never once wanted anything other than to be honest with her and to pull myself out of this teenager's bedroom of a mess. And I tell her that if

303

she can see past all that then she's probably a better person than I am. Which, of course, she is. Our agreement notwithstanding, I expect her to stand up and walk away after instructing the security guards to throw my deceitful arse out into the two-hour-limit car park. I expect to come unstuck.

She looks at me blankly, although a slight movement in her jaw reveals that there's something going on that I can't know, and maybe won't ever.

And then she starts.

'Matthew is not my friends' child – he's my son,' she says purposefully. 'The man you met when you came to the house is Matthew's dad. I'm staying there for the time being. He wants me to come back and live with him – that's why he called the police.'

'*He* called the police?' I say, surprised. I perk up a little.

'I'm sorry about that, Tom.'

'Sean.'

'Whoever you are. No, Seb is a little stressed out right now.'

Seb? *Seb*? I knew he was a twat. His 'stress', however, explains his failure to roll out the red carpet on my recent visit.

'What does he do if he's really pissed off? Plant landmines under the garden path? Unleash pitbulls? Hire assassination squads?'

'All right, Sean.'

'I'm all for home security, but it looks like I've got nothing on your proto warlord.' I pause. Shut up, Sean. Maja actually knows a thing or two about warlords. 'I'm sorry,' I say.

'He sees you as a threat, Sean.'

Instead of hearing what she has just said to me and processing its significance, I barrel on: 'Oh yeah, I can see that knocking on your door and—'

'For Christ's sake, Sean!' She speaks quietly but fiercely. 'Will you get off your fucking high horse for a moment?' She takes a sip of her coffee. 'I thought that we were going to hear each other out.'

I nod in agreement and keep my big gob shut. No more interruptions.

'We met at college,' she continues. 'We were both at UCH. It was easy to get a visa back then. I went back and forth to Sarajevo and everything was fine. Then two things happened: the war started and I got pregnant. I had Matthew in London, but I had to go back to Bosnia to help my family.'

She pauses for a moment and takes a sip of coffee. She's concentrating now because, although she must have told this story dozens of times, it's still painful for her.

'It was hard. There were such terrible things going on and Matthew was so young and needed me. But I couldn't leave: there were visa problems; I was working night and day at the hospital and for a long time it was impossible to leave. It was just too dangerous. We were getting shelled. There was no electricity. There were snipers shooting at us on the way to work.'

She's staring into her coffee cup now, repeating a story she's recounted many times, although maybe not out loud. She talks quickly, as if the rhythm and speed will prevent the words from gaining traction and harming her.

'So Seb and his mum ended up looking after Matthew, pretty much until he was four.' She pauses for a moment and looks up at me. 'Terrible really, isn't it?'

'You couldn't help it though.'

'No. Not really, although a mum excusing herself by saying "I couldn't help it" is pretty lame, don't you think? There were times, I suppose, when I could have maybe got out, made it to Western Europe. But what then? I had no visa, Seb and I have never got married, and he wasn't exactly going to bring Matthew to live in a war zone.'

'He could have married you in Bosnia,' I suggest, engrossed in her story, searching for resolution. 'He could have made it there by—'

She waves her hand to cut me off.

'No. I didn't want that: if Seb had been killed then Matthew could have ended up an orphan. Anyway, I decided that I didn't want to marry Seb then.'

I wait for her to speak, but she falls silent, lost in thought.

'And now?' I prompt her. 'What about you and Seb? You and Matthew?'

'It's complicated.' She shakes her head and lets out a little laugh. 'I seem to say that all the time, don't I? "It's complicated." I wish things were a little simpler, but there you have it. I told you that Matthew wasn't mine because I couldn't face going into the whole thing. Matthew is still a little sensitive about calling me "Mum". It's beginning to get better, though. I've got indefinite leave to stay here, but I don't want to marry Seb.'

Result! I try not to jump out of my chair as if I've just scored the winning goal in the World Cup final in the last minute against Brazil. Instead, I twizzle my plastic stirrer around my plastic coffee cup.

'We had our time,' she continues. 'And it was great when we were together. But it's over for us. We need to move on. Both of us. I've applied for joint custody of Matthew, and we're working that out. The problem is that Seb doesn't want us to split up, and it's more disruption for Matthew . . . I know that he knows that both of us love him, but it's hard, after all he's been through.'

'Look,' I say, 'I don't know anything about raising kids. All I know is that you're doing everything you can to bring him up the right way. He's a good kid and he's old enough to know that sometimes adults screw things up, even though most of the time they're just trying to work things out for the best.'

Her eyes are red and pregnant with tears, but she doesn't cry. I imagine that she's done enough of that over the years. I lean across the sticky table and take her hand.

'Don't be too hard on yourself,' I say. She looks at me and smiles an unconvinced diagonal smile. 'Seriously,' I add.

We sit there in the hospital canteen in the middle of the night. Me glazed with blood, sporting eight stitches in my head, not really knowing whether I've blown the best chance I'm ever going to have for something real in my life; Maja dazed by the decisions she has to make and burdened by historical misfortune. I want her so badly but I say nothing; we just sit quietly, listening to the scraping of the chairs the caretaker shifts while he's cleaning.

'I've got to go,' she says. 'How's the head?'

'Bit sore,' I lie. It's bloody killing me. I should really see if I can hit her up for some opiates. Maybe not. It won't set the best tone.

She stands, leans forward and kisses me, ever so gently, as if she's just trying to roll the skin of her lips momentarily against mine. It passes in a fraction of a second, but I hoard the instant and remember it as if it had lasted for hours. She runs her hand through my hair, puts both of her hands in the pockets of her white coat and starts to walk off towards A&E with a tight little smile on her face.

'Want to hear a hospital joke?' I ask. My voice echoes in the empty room. I'm speaking a little too loudly. She nods.

'A bloke is out on the golf course and he gets a message on his mobile that his wife has been taken seriously ill and is in hospital. The doctor says that he has to come immediately. The bloke thinks: Bollocks to that, I want to finish my game. So he carries on playing. He finishes all eighteen holes and then drives over to the hospital. He finds the doctor, who asks him where the hell he's been. The man tells the doctor that he's been playing golf. "Well, there's no more golf for you," the doctor says. "No chance – your wife is very seriously ill. To all intents and purposes, she's a vegetable: you're going to be pushing her around in a wheelchair and changing her nappies, not playing eighteen holes." "Oh my God," the man says, shocked. "Only joking!" the doctor laughs. "She died two hours ago."'

I have no idea why I thought that telling her this might be a good idea, but Maja bursts out laughing. It's a loud, quickly repressed whoop, but there's no doubt that the joke hit the mark. I watch as she walks to the exit, shaking her head gently from side to side.

Epilogue
Tom

'Look at the state of you!' laughs Sara.

I have just stepped out of a steam room, my head whirling, my face plum-coloured and my body drenched with sweat. A less alluring sight, it's hard to imagine. Sara is not exactly a picture of demureness. She's been lounging in a hot tub for the best part of twenty minutes, avoiding playing footsie with a couple of Korean businessmen who keep getting out to theatrically perform sets of press-ups.

'Got any water?' I gasp. I need to sit down and rehydrate.

'Over there,' she says, pointing to a bottle of mineral water that sits next to a pile of towels. I walk over and start downing the thing, desperate to get fluids back in my body.

'Hey!' One of the Koreans is gesturing that I'm drinking his bottle. I look over at Sara, who is hooting with laughter. She walks over to a small fridge, wiping a tear from her eye, and retrieves a bottle of Evian for me. Her flip-flops drag along the floor.

'Very funny,' I say as she hands me the bottle.

'Anything to keep you amused,' she says, pecking me on the cheek.

'You sure that you don't want to stay in the hot tub with your mates?'

'Not likely,' she says. 'Those bloody things are lousy with bacteria and accountants.'

We're away for the weekend in Barcelona, doing the things we used to do before kids and work and debts got in the way. We can afford the odd luxury now and again, even if it means giving the credit cards a little bit of a pounding. It's not like I'm getting rich from SC

Communications, but Sean and I are managing to maintain the clients we have while picking up the odd new one. And now that Maja's on the scene, we can leave the kids with him, safe in the knowledge that the Playboy Channel won't be the primary source of entertainment in the household.

We leave the hotel for a stroll and a boozy seafood lunch. Sara holds my arm and pulls herself tight to me when we walk through the sleepy streets. It's like we're in our early twenties again and can't get enough of each other. She's managed to address her 'life-work balance', to make sure she's at home more, and it hasn't affected her work a single bit, her career is going from strength to strength. She's lost the guilt she used to carry with her, and doesn't feel solely responsible for the financial health of the family.

Having her around more has been good for all of us, especially the boys. As ever, it's the small things, the odd comment, the silly joke that's the stuff of family life and this was what I was missing back when I was mired in the dumps. I think to myself at these moments, as I do the times when I simply want to walk out the door, *I can do this.* And, amazingly, that's all it takes.

We slowly wind our way back to the hotel and make love before falling asleep in our shuttered room. Nothing moves in the street below. We wake, groggy from sleep – and lovemaking – at an unaccustomed hour. Sara suggests a swim, so we head back down to the pool. I complete a couple of lengths before squatting in the shallow end to cool off. A waitress, all bronzed Mediterranean skin, haughty cheekbones and bee-sting lips, walks along the side of the pool. I can't resist swivelling to see what happens when she bends over to deliver her tray of sweating glasses.

Before I know it, my back is pressed against the pool wall and Sara has hooked herself around me. Her hair is swept back from the weight of the water. A couple of drops have gathered at the end of her nose.

'Enjoying the sights of Barcelona?' she asks, rubbing her nose against mine.

'I love Gaudi,' I say.

'I'm so glad to hear that.'

She continues to hang on me. I want to ask her to get off, but as she's just caught me checking out a waitress's backside, it's probably best to grin and bear it.

'I was just wondering what those cocktails are,' I say, nodding towards the drinks that she's just delivered.

'Really,' says Sara in a tone that demonstrates, beyond all doubt, that I'm an idiot. I try offering her a sheepish grin.

'You know how much I love you, don't you?' says Sara sweetly. This is nice. She's being magnanimous and—

Hold on a minute, she's just slipped her hand inside my trunks. Her fingers are warm as they clutch my balls. What on earth is—

'And do you know how you can make me love you even more than I do?' she asks. Her voice has taken an almost girly turn, and I wonder if she's up for a little hanky panky in the shallow end when—

OUCH!!!!!

She twists my balls like she's wringing out a dishcloth. It's all I can do not to yelp.

'*What did you* . . . ?' I say pathetically.

'Shhhhhhh . . . ' she says, putting her index finger to my lips. 'So, Tom, do you understand what would make me love you even more?'

'Yes,' I whimper, amused by her cheek.

'That and a nice foot massage when I get home.'

'OK.'

'Every day.'

'OK.'

'I love Barcelona,' she says, and pushes herself backwards into the cool, clear water beyond me.